THE OUROBOROS CYCLE, BOOK THREE

A LONG-AWAITED TREACHERY

A LONG-AWAITED TREACHERY

G.D. FALKSEN

WILDSIDE PRESS

To Jay Lake.

THE OUROBOROS CYCLE, BOOK 3

Published by Wildside Press LLC.
www.wildsidebooks.com

Ebooks available at wildsidepress.com

CHAPTER ONE

Mid-Summer, 1893
Svaneti, Georgia

Summer had come to the Shashavani valley, casting away the winter snows and supplanting them with golden sunlight that warmed the fields, the forests, the running river, and the countless flocks of sheep. The villagers had taken to the fields once more, some tending farms and flocks, others cutting timber from the deep forests or sifting gold from the rivers. It was a quiet ritual of awakening that had been carried out year after year, generation upon generation, for as long as anyone could remember.

At the castle of the Shashavani, situated in the heart of the valley, life continued almost undisturbed by the passage of the seasons. Only the lengthening of daylight brought any real change to the habits of the Shashavani scholars who walked the castle's halls, seeking refuge in the candle-lit libraries and avoiding windows that had been left open for stargazing that the servants had forgotten to close before daybreak. For just as the sun brought vigor to the villagers who languished in the Shadow of Death, its light brought pain to those blessed with eternal life.

And so it was that noontime found Doctor Varanus Shashavani huddled in the corner of her study, hiding in the shadows as sunlight slowly crept across the chamber, let in through a pair of windows she had forgotten to shutter until the onset of day made it impossible for her to close the curtains. But Varanus thought little about the light, only noticing it when it drew close enough that she began to feel the pain; and even then, she merely drew back a little further into the corner, amid the nest of books and scrolls and her own rapidly growing pile of handwritten notes.

"Eventually, *liebchen*, there will be no more room for your papers."

Varanus smiled a little and looked up to see Korbinian, her long-departed lover, lounging in one of the armchairs across the room. He grinned at her, a lock of dark hair falling across his eyes in a most charming manner. Death had been kind to him: even after thirty years, he was still the same beautiful youth he had been the night of his murder.

"I will place them into stacks," Varanus replied, returning to her work.

"But the sunlight is spreading, *liebchen*," Korbinian said. "Look, it has already consumed Aisha of Damascus."

"What?"

Alarmed, Varanus reached for a large, leather-bound manuscript that sat just beyond the creeping edge of sunlight. She grabbed it with one hand and pulled it back into the shadows with ease despite its considerable weight. Her skin prickled where it had been touched by the light, but the exposure had been little enough that there was no harm.

Setting the manuscript down amid her other books, Varanus smiled at Korbinian and said:

"It would seem your concern was unnecessary."

"And Soslan the Alan's *Third Treatise*..." Korbinian answered.

Varanus swore and reached into the sunlight again, grabbing for a collection of scrolls bound together in a roll of leather. Again her flesh tingled at the touch of the sun; and as she was forced to crawl forward a few paces to reach the treatise, this time the exposure was long enough to make a dull ache form in her bones, which lingered for a few minutes as she withdrew into the shadows again.

"No harm done," she said.

Korbinian grinned with delight and clapped his hands.

"Marvelous, *liebchen!* Marvelous! But eventually you will have no more space left in the shadows. Perhaps it would be better if you closed the curtains."

"And subject myself to a faceful of morning sunlight?" Varanus asked, returning to her books. "My skin is one thing, but I have need of my eyes. And besides, I would have to stop reading, and I am in no mood for that sort of nonsense."

She pulled the manuscript of Aisha's *Compendium* onto her lap and began comparing certain passages to her pile of handwritten notes.

"If you are so concerned, perhaps you should close them for me," she added.

"You know I cannot do that, *liebchen*," Korbinian replied, approaching her. "Besides which, I have much more important things to do."

"Such as...?"

Korbinian knelt before Varanus and gently pressed his lips to her cheek. "Such as kissing you, my darling."

Varanus smiled softly and looked at him out of the corner of her eye. Such an incorrigible fellow. He knew she had work to do, but always he insisted upon interrupting her.

"You're something of a distraction," she said, as she gave Korbinian a gentle kiss in return.

"I have been told that it is one of my finer qualities," Korbinian answered.

Varanus looked into his eyes in silence, gently stroking his cheek with her fingertips. His skin was smooth and warm beneath her touch, just as when he had been alive.

"*Liebchen*," Korbinian said.

"Yes?" Varanus asked.

"Your friend has returned."

"What?"

Across the room, the door to the hallway opened with a click and an almost imperceptible creak. Startled, Varanus's eyes darted toward the door. When she looked back at Korbinian, he had vanished.

"I have returned!" announced Varanus's dear friend Ekaterine, as she swept into the room and removed her shawl. "The family is doing wonderfully and—" Taking in the sunlight from the open window, she gasped in alarm and cried, "Oh good God!"

Ekaterine ran to the window and pulled the shutters closed before frantically yanking the heavy curtains into place. She turned to Varanus and gave her a stern smile, her dark eyes still wide with alarm.

"I know, I know," Varanus said, looking up from her reading and sighing.

"Doctor, the sun!"

"I know!" Varanus repeated. With the threat of the sun now removed, she stood and shook the wrinkles out of her skirt. "I was reading last night by moonlight and lost all sense of time. The first I noticed the sun, it had already boxed me into the corner."

Ekaterine smiled and took Varanus by the hand. "Well no harm done. But you must be more careful, Doctor. Even with Lord Iosef's regimen, you won't be able to withstand the sunlight for many years to come."

"Yes," Varanus agreed, "about three hundred to be precise."

She allowed Ekaterine to lead her to the sofa, where they sat.

"Ah, so your research has made progress while I have been away," Ekaterine said.

"Some," Varanus said. "Not as much as I would like, but some." She motioned to a tea service that sat on a nearby table. "Something to drink?"

"Tea? I would love some." Ekaterine reached for the pot. "Allow me."

Varanus smiled slightly at the sight of her friend behaving so domestically. The tea would be old and rather cold—it had been brewed the afternoon before—but it was still better than nothing and much better than waiting for a fresh pot.

"And what have you discovered during my absence?" Ekaterine asked as she poured. "I see a copy of Aisha of Damascus's *Compendium* over there.... Do I take it that you've finished with the Konstantine?"

Aisha of Damascus had been one of the Shashavani's foremost scholars of medicine. By the time Konstantine Shashavani had departed on his great sojourn after the Mongol Invasion, Aisha had already taken over as the resident expert on the Shashavani condition, before she herself had departed into the wilderness sometime in the sixteenth century.

"More or less," Varanus answered, sipping her tea. Even hours old, it was rather refreshing. "I have examined all that the librarians could find...and would allow me to depart with."

She frowned at this. It was a damned nuisance not being allowed to remove original texts from the Shashavani libraries. She understood the principle of preservation so dear to the archivists, but she much preferred to conduct her studies in her own rooms or in her workshop. And a copy, no matter how well transcribed, was still a copy. It could be fallible.

"You could read in the library," Ekaterine ventured, though her mirthful tone made it clear she knew what Varanus's answer to that would be.

"Rubbish," Varanus said. "The library is far too loud. All those people...reading."

"A cacophony of books," Ekaterine agreed. She took a sip of her tea and said, "Three hundred years? I suppose I've never asked."

"Between three and five hundred years, depending on the amount of exposure to sunlight during that time," Varanus said. "Konstantine, Aisha, and Soslan all agree on that point. The ranges differ depending on the accounts, but I have extrapolated."

Ekaterine grinned. "How delightfully clever of you. And to think, my dearest friend will be the next Konstantine. It's quite exciting."

"I think perhaps Brother Magnus will have something to say about that," Varanus remarked.

Magnus the Dane was another scholar of the Shashavani condition, although his work was far too esoteric for Varanus's taste. Magnus was a natural philosopher rather than a proper scientist. However brilliant, he was a man of mysticism, not medicine. But alas, their work overlapped enough to make him a constant nuisance where the availability of texts was concerned.

"Oh pish," Ekaterine scoffed. "Magnus can keep to his alchemy. You'll see: by the twenty-first century, they'll be calling you the 'foremost scholar of medicine among the Shashavani.'"

Varanus laughed at this and said, "The twenty-first century? I am having enough difficulty thinking about the twentieth as it hurtles rapidly toward us. I can scarcely comprehend a hundred years from now."

"One becomes accustomed to it," Ekaterine assured her.

The way she said it made Varanus shiver a little.

"I'm not certain if I wish to become accustomed to it," she said. Changing the subject, she asked, "Now then, how is your family?"

"They're well," Ekaterine replied. "Everyone hale and healthy. Although," she added, smirking at the thought of gossip, "it seems my granddaughter has fallen for a Circassian boy. It's caused something of a scandal in the village."

"So I would imagine," Varanus said.

Some thirty years ago, fleeing massacre at the hands of the Russians, several Circassian families had been granted leave to settle in the valley and form their own communities along the river. By the laws of the Shashavani, the Muslim Circassians were free to practice their customs and faith, but from time to time tensions arose between them and the Christians of the valley.

"By all accounts he's a very charming boy," Ekaterine said, sounding proud of her granddaughter's selection. "And more than a little bit handsome."

Varanus smiled. "So the Circassian beauties are not only the womenfolk?"

"Not according to my granddaughter," Ekaterine replied. "And she seems very happy, so I wish both of them the best good fortune."

Varanus raised her teacup. "Good fortune to them." She took a drink and looked at Ekaterine, shaking her head. "I can scarcely believe that you have children, Ekaterine, much less grown grandchildren."

Ekaterine smiled and stroked her cheeks with her fingertips. Though several decades Varanus's senior, she looked only a few years older, not even into her thirties. Like all those Shashavani who still walked in the Shadow of Death, Ekaterine's aging had slowed tremendously. But unlike the Living, it had not stopped, and that was something that troubled Varanus. Being immortal, she knew that one day she would outlive Ekaterine, and that was a loneliness she dearly wished to avoid.

"I take great pains to preserve my youthful appearance," Ekaterine said, pretending to be haughty but unable to hide a giggle at the nonsense of it. "I milk bathe."

Varanus shuddered, suddenly remembering certain horrors from their visit to London five years ago.

"No talk of wellness, Ekaterine," she said. "Wellness reminds me of London, and London reminds me of my son."

"And he never writes," Ekaterine said.

"And he never writes," Varanus agreed. "Though I wish he would. I am becoming rather concerned about him. I fear his aunt's death might weigh upon him."

Ekaterine looked skeptical. "From what I remember of her, I would think his aunt's death would do the opposite." She shrugged. "But no matter. I have returned and I am eager to get back to work!"

Suddenly, a sharp clattering noise sounded from outside the window. It was faint, muffled by distance and the curtains, but it was loud enough to make Ekaterine jump.

"My goodness, what is that?" she asked, looking toward the window.

"Luka is demonstrating the new Maxim guns I bought him," Varanus answered mulling over her tea. "He's been doing it all morning. It's quite annoying, to be honest."

"As annoying as the library's cacophony of books?" Ekaterine asked.

"Almost," Varanus said, eyeing her nest of papers and scrolls. "Almost, but not quite."

CHAPTER TWO

Luka sat beneath the shade of an overhanging canopy, smoking a pipe and watching silently as his newest acquisition—the Maxim gun—filled the air with the clatter of automatic gunfire and the lawn with shell casings.

The Maxim gun had been set up in one of the outer courtyards, away from the main library in the hope that the noise would not disturb the scholars at their studies. Bales of hay had been placed as targets to demonstrate accuracy at various distances, and now a Shashavani soldier—a young Circassian woman named Seteney—sat at the machine gun, firing round after round into one of them. Other soldiers stood around watching the display, the older ones with amusement, the younger ones with astonishment. Most of them had never seen such a weapon before: it was a dramatic improvement on the volley guns and hand-cranked revolving cannon in the armory.

Luka turned slightly and looked at the woman who sat beside him, smoking her own pipe and watching Seteney's demonstration. She was Lady Zawditu, the Marshal and Strategos of the Shashavani. Like Luka and the other soldiers under her command, she wore a chokha coat and trousers and a sword and a brace of pistols on her belt. Though of advancing years, she was still robust and strong. Her graying hair was long and tightly braided, woven through with golden thread. She had lived hundreds of years, but though her dark skin showed lines of age, she gave no indication of weariness.

"A most impressive display, Luka," Zawditu said. "Most impressive indeed."

"Thank you, Strategos," Luka replied, bowing his head. "I endeavor to give satisfaction."

Zawditu chuckled softly. "And this time you have succeeded. This new machine of yours shows great promise. Much better than the mitrailleuse."

"Much better than the mitrailleuse," agreed Mata Kaur, Zawditu's aide-de-camp, who sat on the other side of her, watching the demonstration through a pair of field glasses.

A Sikh of the Punjab, Mata Kaur had spent her early life as a warlord defending her people against the persecution of the Mughals. Now she was Zawditu's closest officer, and Luka suspected that Zawditu was grooming her for command in a few centuries' time.

"However," Mata Kaur continued, "I have misgivings regarding the use of water to cool the weapon. I do not like the prospect of the added weight. Surely this 'Maxim gun' is already too heavy."

"The weapon heats very quickly, My Lady," Luka answered. "Water—or perhaps some heat-absorbent chemical—is the only solution known at present."

Zawditu exhaled a long plume of smoke before she said:

"Surely this weapon is to be used for defense. We shall have them mounted over the passes of the valley and the gates of the castle. Let the enemy come to us and be destroyed."

"It is the conventional wisdom," Luka noted. "And it has proven very effective."

"Perhaps," Mata Kaur said, "but it is my habit to mistrust any weapon that cannot be used on the offense. It would seem to be only half effective."

She smirked a little as she said this and Zawditu and Luka both laughed.

"I will speak to Boris and the engineers," Luka told them, after the laughter had died down. "Perhaps they can devise some solution to the issue of weight."

"Very good, Luka," Zawditu said. "Very good."

At that moment, Luka heard shouting from the gate, accompanied by the pounding of horses' hooves. All three of them turned in the direction of the noise, as did several of the soldiers. Soon enough, a horse charged into the courtyard, ridden by a young Svan named Koba—a distant cousin of Luka's, which showed in the shade of his dark brown hair and in the style of moustache he was trying to grow. Koba rode with one hand, using his other to help secure a man who rode behind him. Koba's passenger was bloody, exhausted, and he looked nearly dead. He all but fell from the horse as the soldiers hurried to help him down.

Luka was on his feet instantly and ran to join them, with Zawditu and Mata Kaur close behind him. He grabbed Koba's passenger and kept the poor fellow steady on his feet. The man babbled almost incoherently in Circassian, in which Luka had very little fluency. All he could make out was something about an attack, which was plain enough to see from the man's battered condition.

"What is the meaning of this?" Zawditu demanded. "Koba, what has happened to this man?" She quickly pointed at one of the soldiers standing nearby and shouted, "Bring me a doctor!"

Koba swung down from the saddle and bowed to Zawditu.

"I do not know, Strategos," he replied, his face pale with worry. "I came upon him while on patrol. He was running from someone or something. I thought it best to bring him here."

"You did well, my boy," Zawditu said, patting Koba on the shoulder. She turned to the Circassian man and said to him, as precisely as she could manage, "What happened to you?"

By then, Seteney had joined them in the company of the remaining troops. As she came close enough to recognize the man, she ran the remaining distance and grabbed him by the arms. The man gasped at the sight of her and almost began to weep.

"Seteney, you know this man?" Zawditu asked.

"He is my uncle," Seteney said. She began speaking to the man rapidly in their native tongue. As their conversation progressed, her face contorted into a scowl and one hand gripped the hilt of her sword. Finally, she turned to Zawditu and Luka and spoke:

"He says that our village has been attacked by armed men. He does not know who they are. They've burned houses, attacked people in the streets.... He tried to ride for help, but they shot his horse and it died on the way."

A muscle in Zawditu's cheek twitched as she clenched her jaw.

"Luka," she said, without looking at him, "take a party of soldiers and investigate what has happened. Mata Kaur, have the castle secured and signal the guard posts for reports."

"Yes, Strategos," Luka and Mata Kaur both said in unison.

Luka studied the soldiers for a moment and selected his party, addressing each in turn:

"Seteney, Koba, Movses, Anuka, with me."

* * * *

They rode out into the countryside, Luka at the head of the party with Seteney as his guide riding alongside. Seteney's village was located along the river to the north of the valley, at the edge of one of the deep forests that girded the fields and pastures. Like the other settlements in the valley, it was a town of towers, of brick and stone, strongly built and easily defensible. But the roofs were wooden, and several of these had been set on fire, as had a number of sheds, barns, and various outbuildings. Had Seteney's uncle not reached them, the smoke from the fires would have alerted the Shashavani before long.

There were bodies in the streets, cut down with swords or stabbed through with crude spears. Luka grimaced at the sight of the violence and held his carbine rifle ready, but he saw no sign of the attackers. Whether they had finished their business or fled at the sound of horses, they were gone now.

"My God!" Movses exclaimed at the sight. There were children and elderly among the men and women. "Who would do this?"

"It cannot be anyone from the valley," Koba said. "Bandits perhaps?"

Anuka, her carbine braced against her shoulder, glanced toward them and asked, "How did they breach the pass without someone raising the alarm?"

Luka wondered the same thing. The passes into the valley were all well guarded, and while bandits sometimes managed to break through, it was a rare occurrence. Inevitably, the trespassers were sighted and caught by one of the patrols before they could cause trouble. What had happened to the village was a horrible anomaly of which Luka could make no sense.

"You there!" someone shouted in Circassian. "Who are you?"

Luka looked up and saw men standing on the balconies of several of the towers above them. Their clothes were bloody, and they all carried muskets, which they aimed at Luka and the other soldiers.

"I am Luka of the Shashavani!" Luka replied, his Circassian broken but intelligible. "We have come to help. Is there one among you who speaks Svanish?"

As the native people of the Shashavani valley were Svans, Svanish was the *lingua franca* of the Shashavani, though nearly matched in prevalence by its cousin tongue, Georgian.

"I do," answered one of the Circassians, a young man with a bloody wound across his temple.

"What happened here?" Luka asked him.

"We were attacked," the young man replied, his tone a mixture of anger, fear, and confusion. "The men came upon us from the forest with swords and spears."

"Were they mounted or on foot?"

"On foot, though they were so swift in their attack they may as well have been on horseback. We did not know what was happening until they began to...to kill."

Luka's mouth contorted in a scowl. How was that possible? Men on horses might have ridden through a poorly guarded pass without being captured, but on foot they would surely have been shot, unless bandits had found some new entry point into the valley, which was even more troubling.

"Who were these men?" he asked.

"They were like you," the Circassian said. "Svans."

"And why did they attack you? For treasure? Or to take captives?"

The young Circassian did not answer for a moment, but his expression spoke of hatred and betrayal. Finally, he answered:

"They came to kill us. To kill us because we submit to Allah."

Luka exchanged looks with the rest of his party, reading confusion on their faces. The very thought of killing over a question of faith was alien to the valley people. Even Luka, who had traveled among the ignorant in the outside world, still could not understand such foolishness. And for such evil to have been brought there, into a land ruled by wisdom and by the Law of Shashava....

Beside him, Seteney's hand clenched upon the hilt of her sword and her body shook with fury, but her face was calm and she was silent. Still, Luka could not blame her for her rage, and he admired her restraint in the face of such evil done to her people.

"We were promised," the Circassian man said, drawing Luka's attention back to him. His voice quivered, as if uncertain whether to shout in anger or weep with despair. "After what the Russians did to us, we were promised that it would never happen again. We were told that in this place such things do not happen!"

"Such things are forbidden here," Luka answered, bitterly acknowledging that what was law could still be violated in practice. "And I give you my word that the men who did this to you will pay for their crimes with their lives."

"You are a Svan," the Circassian said. "And a Christian. Like the men who sought to murder us! How can we trust that there will be justice? There was no justice when the Russians came!"

"I am not the Russians," Luka answered. "I am Luka Davitdze Shashavani, and I will uphold the Law of Shashava, for it is the highest law in Heaven or upon the Earth. This I swear to you."

"You may trust in him," Seteney said, nodding to Luka. "He shall uphold his oath, as shall I. By God, these men shall be punished."

The Circassian nodded slowly and relayed this news to his fellows. Many of the other men looked skeptical, but relief showed on the faces of some. One old man began to weep and quietly withdrew into the building.

"More soldiers are coming to tend to your wounded and help put out the fires," Luka said. "But we must pursue your attackers before they can make their escape. What direction did they go?"

The young Circassian pointed toward the forest and said, "That way, into the woods. Only a few minutes ago. They fled when we escaped inside, and they realized they could not breach our houses. We wounded some. There will be blood."

"Good," Luka said. It would make them easier to track. And it was heartening to be reminded that, though they lived lives of peace, the valley people could defend themselves in the event of war. "How many?"

"Uh...." The Circassian spoke to his fellows quickly before answering, "Some twenty or so. We did not have time to count them."

Luka nodded. "We will find them." He turned his horse toward the forest and motioned to his troops. "Come."

"Twenty men?" Koba asked aloud, sounding skeptical. "We are only five. It would not seem a fair fight."

"No," Anuka said, patting Koba on the shoulder, "but these men have done nothing to deserve the privilege of favorable odds."

* * * *

The trail left by the attackers was easy enough to follow. The men had rushed headlong through the brush in their flight, snapping branches and tearing the leaves from bushes in their passing. Footprints were plentiful where the ground was soft enough to leave them, and here and there were marks of blood—left either from the men's own injuries or from the weapons they had bloodied during the massacre.

It was difficult riding through the dense forest. They sometimes had to take a more circuitous route around the thick undergrowth, where the horses could not pass. And more than once, Luka was obliged to dismount to pick up the details of the trail where they could not be easily seen from the higher vantage point. But he preferred not to leave the horses behind. So long as the forest pathways permitted it, their greater speed was an advantage he wished to exploit; and being outnumbered, the advantage of height would be a welcome benefit if it came to violence.

Presently, Luka heard voices speaking through the brush ahead of them. Readying his carbine, he motioned for the others to fan out and approach in a crescent, to hopefully catch their quarry at rest and cut off their escape. He advanced into a clearing and saw some two-dozen men sitting and standing about the place, tending to the wounds they had suffered. They had weapons with them: some swords and spears, but also improvised agricultural tools. These men were not bandits at all.

"We should not have run," one of the men said angrily. "We should have stayed and killed more of the heathens!"

"And what good would that have done?" another demanded. "They fled into their towers! They had muskets! We would have been shot if we had remained."

"God would have protected us," a third man countered. "We were given a sign. And now, instead of doing God's work, we have run from our holy task. We shall surely be punished for that—"

They stopped talking as Luka advanced into the clearing. The men on the ground leapt to their feet. Some grabbed for their weapons, while others started to run—only to be stopped as Seteney, Koba, Movses, and Anuka entered the clearing and surrounded them. Seteney in particular looked ready to start shooting at the first provocation, and Luka could not blame her for it.

"Who are you?" one of the men demanded of Luka, pointing a sword at him.

"I am Luka," Luka replied. "We are Shashavani."

Several of the men swore. Some looked afraid, others suddenly hopeful.

"We're in for it now," someone said.

"No, no, they will understand," said another. "They are men of God."

"Good Lord," Koba whispered, aghast. "They're valley folk...."

Luka held up a hand for silence.

"You have committed violence against your neighbors," he said, "which is in violation of every just law known to man. What do you have to say for yourselves?"

One of the men—the one who had argued that they should have stayed and continued their attack—advanced on Luka. He held his head high and addressed him proudly:

"We have made war upon the infidel. It is as God intends. He shall be pleased with us, as should you."

"Blasphemer!" Seteney snapped at him. "Murderer! I should cut your head from your body!"

"Steady," Luka told her. "All in due time." He looked back at the ringleader. "There are no infidels in this valley. All who obey the Law of Shashava are welcome here, and none shall do them harm. You have violated our most basic principles! And for what? A difference of faith?"

"You do not understand!" the ringleader answered. "How can you not understand? Are you not Christian? Those people were Mohammedans! It is our sacred duty to destroy them that the world may be made pure!"

Luka felt himself shiver with disgust.

"Who has taught you these lies?" he demanded. "What priest has confounded your reason with such falsehood?"

"No priest," came the reply, "for in this land all that is taught is heresy! But God spoke to us through the Blessed Virgin, who came to me...came to all of us to show us God's will."

There were murmurs of assent from the other men.

"The Virgin Mary appeared to you?" Luka asked, his tone thick with skepticism. "To *you?* And she instructed you to murder innocent people?"

"Not innocent! Infidels!"

The ringleader approached Luka further until he stood right beside Luka's horse. The poor creature whinnied softly at the stench of blood and the movements of the stranger, but Luka merely patted its flanks to steady it.

"She appeared to us and instructed us to find all the infidels in the valley and to put them to the sword," the man continued. "For soon the time is coming when the Lord shall return to us to reign in glory and to judge the living and the dead! And we have been chosen to clear a path for His righteousness! So the Blessed Virgin told us!"

Luka exhaled, trying to measure the anger he felt at such blasphemy. To think that a man could be so depraved as to justify barbarism as the "will of God"!

"I hardly think," he said slowly, "that the Blessed Virgin, the mother of our Lord, would instruct you to murder *children!* Nor that God, who is the creator of us all, would *ever* desire the death of any of His children, whatever their faith. For as Shashava said, 'we have all been granted a portion of wisdom, each in our own way and in our own tongue, and so together we shall find Truth'."

"Blasphemy!" someone shouted. "Heresy!"

"God commanded their deaths!" came another cry.

"No God who is God could desire such a thing!" Luka shouted. "It is man who desires the death of man, not God! And the Law of Shashava forbids it! All who are obedient to Shashava's commandments may reside in peace and harmony among us. This has been our way for a thousand years, and you shall not change it with your fanciful stories of visions."

"The Blessed Virgin said that also," answered the ringleader, holding his spear to Luka's throat. "When she revealed herself to me, she said that the Shashavani are apostates who have turned from God, for they follow the teachings of Shashava when they ought to follow Christ!"

Nearby, Seteney looked at Luka and asked, "May we please just kill them, Sir?"

"In a moment," Luka replied. "I am being unreasonably patient." He grabbed the spear that had been thrust at him and shoved it to one side. Snarling, he addressed the mob: "The Law of Shashava is Wisdom and Justice. No God who is God would issue commandments that contradict Wisdom and Justice. Therefore, if the dictates of your faith contradict the dictates of Shashava, then your faith has been misunderstood and you must reexamine it."

"Blasphemer!"

"I will give you one chance," Luka said, "and one only. Throw down your weapons and surrender to me, and you shall be tried fairly. Otherwise, I will kill you for what you have done."

"You? Kill us?" The ringleader scoffed. He tried to pull his spear away from Luka, but Luka held his grip below the spear point and the man simply struggled in frustration. "Infidels and apostates cannot defeat the army of God! We have been chosen! We are protected! It is you who shall die!"

Finally, he yanked his spear away from Luka's grasp and raised it, preparing to strike Luka full in the chest. The other men raised their own arms and took up their leader's cry as he shouted:

"Kill them!"

CHAPTER THREE

"Apparently, it was a massacre."

"Indeed," Iosef mused, as he walked down the corridor alongside the blond and bearded Magnus the Dane. "I am surprised that Luka showed so much restraint. He has never had much patience for brutality meted out against the innocent."

"Perhaps he is mellowing in his old age," Magnus said. It was a joke, of course: Magnus himself was more than a century Iosef and Luka's senior, and he certainly did not regard himself as "old".

"I think not," Iosef said. "The day Luka's temper 'mellows' is the day that Christ returns, and we are all granted the Kingdom of Heaven."

Magnus laughed loudly at this. "And I suppose, even on that day, Luka will berate the Lord for not keeping His followers better behaved." Then he added, "The Lutheran faith excepted, of course: we are above reproach."

"Quite," Iosef said. The corner of his mouth turned up slightly in a smirk, however.

Magnus was prideful and arrogant, but at least he was quick to mock his own excesses. Of course, recognizing the folly of one's own pride did not equal humility. Magnus often bragged about a duel he had once fought with the scholar Tycho Brahe over a disagreement regarding a certain alchemical principle that both men later swore never to divulge. Iosef was willing to accept the story, though Magnus's claims that he had also been Brahe's lover, Iosef took with rather more skepticism.

"How many survived to be interrogated?" Iosef asked.

"Four," Magnus answered. "And I imagine they will all be swiftly beheaded once the matter has been fully investigated. The Law of Shashava must be enforced lest we fall prey to our darker impulses."

"Mmm." Iosef nodded slightly. "What a strange contradiction it is: the Law of Shashava would make for a better world, but the only way to enforce it is through violence and death."

"Every law is enforced through violence," Magnus said. "At least this one is worth the sacrifice."

"So I fervently hope," Iosef agreed.

Ahead of them, the corridor ended in a set of great double doors made of silver-inlaid wood. Guards in armor stood at either side, and they bowed to Iosef and Magnus at their approach.

"This is where I leave you," Magnus said. "I wish you well with your report. I must away to my business."

"My thanks for your company Magnus," Iosef said. "Where are you bound? Your laboratory?"

Magnus shook his head. "Something far more important than my studies."

"Ah, dueling."

Iosef nodded to Magnus and the two exchanged bows of farewell. The guards quickly opened the doors for Iosef and welcomed him into the Council chamber, which had stood as the place of leadership for the Shashavani for centuries, since the days when Shashava still walked among them.

The room was large and round in shape, with a towering ceiling that rose high above its occupants. The walls were decorated with paintings, mosaics, and other adornments, all bringing glory and beauty to the room and its proceedings; but the single most important feature of the chamber was a simple stone table, made in the shape of a wide crescent, almost forming a circle. The center was hollowed out so that speakers could easily address the entire Council, and it was to this center point that Iosef walked.

In the early days, the Council had been composed entirely of Shashava's Companions, the ten great thinkers who had first been inducted into the Shashavani Order, all seated to either side of Shashava's chair. Now they had all vanished into the wilderness—or into death, like Basileios, the bloodthirsty general who had driven the Shashavani into civil war after Shashava's disappearance many centuries ago. The new Council was far younger than the first, but perhaps no less wise; most of them had held their positions for almost five hundred years.

Iosef knelt upon the polished marble floor and bowed his head to Lady Sophio, who sat in Shashava's chair. She was the eldest among them, the Vicar of Shashava, one of the last who remained that had known Shashava personally. It was only fitting that she reigned until their founder finally returned.

"Eristavi," Iosef said softly, bowing his head to her and addressing her by her formal title.

He looked up and caught her eyes, which smiled at him even as her mouth was still. To his relief, he saw that she was in one of her more lucid moments, free from the chaos of memory that sometimes took her.

She had lived more than a thousand years, and there were days when it wore upon her terribly. But today was not such a day. And that was good.

"Iosef," Sophio said. "My husband. Stand."

Iosef rose to his feet and bowed again, a movement that he then made to the elders at either side of the table.

"I have come as I have been bidden," he said. "I am here to answer whatever questions you may put to me."

"And we are pleased by it," Sophio replied. "You are familiar with the recent violation of the Law that was committed two days ago in the Shadow of Death?"

The Shadow of Death was the Shashavani term for mortals and the mortal realm, where death and disease still held sway.

"I am," Iosef answered. "I was told of an attack upon one of the Circassian villages by persons unknown. The attackers fled into the forest and were hunted down by my sworn brother, Luka. That is all I know of it."

One of the Council members, a Scottish philosopher of politics named Margaret the Hebridean, looked at Iosef with a grave expression and said:

"There is more, Brother Iosef, which you ought to know. The men who attacked the Circassians were not strangers to this land. They came from other villages, seeking to sow strife within our sanctuary."

What? Iosef thought. Was such a thing possible?

"I do not understand," he replied. "I thought that all who resided here were sworn to obey the Law of Shashava?"

"Sworn, yes," Sophio said. "Though it seems that some of them have been drawn from the path of wisdom into ignorance and hatred. The villagers of this land have always been wayward followers of Shashava, but it seems that these brigands have forsaken wisdom altogether."

"What was the motivation for their crimes?" Iosef asked. "If I may be permitted to inquire."

It was Reza of Samarkand, the great Persian engineer, who answered, his voice tinged with anger:

"They sought to murder the Circassians for being Muslim. It was a clear violation of Shashava's laws."

"How is this possible? Surely they were raised to believe in the path of wisdom, even if they were not strong enough to follow it always."

"They were misled," Sophio replied. "They each claim to have been visited by a vision of the Virgin Mary who instructed them to arm themselves for war, to ready themselves to slaughter the infidels and the heretics."

"Heretics?" Iosef asked.

"Us," said Iese of Kartli, a learned scribe formerly of the Georgian court. He stroked his bearded chin for a moment, troubled by the knowledge. "Apparently, we are all heretics and nonbelievers for placing the Law of Shashava above the Law of God."

The other members of the Council shook their heads at such foolishness.

"Surely the Virgin Mary did not actually appear to these men," Iosef protested. He still was not certain why he had been summoned. There was clearly a purpose for it, but it had not yet been revealed to him.

"Certainly not," said Margaret, almost scoffing at the idea—as much as any elder of the Shashavani could be said to "scoff", for by that age their emotions had become so dulled and subtle that it was often difficult to discern them at all.

"But," Sophio said, "it is possible that *someone* did appear to them, someone who wished to turn the weak-minded and the ignorant against us. And we may know who."

"Who?"

"Iosef, you recently returned from investigating the actions of a Basilisk, is that correct?" It was Margaret who asked.

Basilisks were rogue Shashavani who had succumbed to corruption and the temptation of their great physical prowess. They sought mastery over mankind rather than the quiet pursuit of knowledge. Basileios had been the most heinous of them, but there had been Basilisks before and after him. It was necessary to maintain vigilance against them, lest their brutality draw the attention of the mortal world.

Iosef nodded. "That is correct. I was dispatched at this council's request, you will remember."

He waited for the Council members to dig up the details of their instructions from within their memories. Certainly, it must have been so insignificant a matter at the time that they only half recalled it now. At their age, to remember all things clearly could only lead to madness. Only by compartmentalizing memories and ideas could they carry on with their centuries-long work without forgetting anything important.

"We so recall, husband," Sophio said, nodding. "And we are pleased by your diligence."

"I am here to serve," Iosef answered. "I tracked the Basilisk to Paris initially, where I encountered the remnants of her activities in the catacombs there. I followed her to London, and again I arrived too late. By the time I discovered her lair, she had moved on."

"And then you followed her to America?" asked Philippa of Nicaea. "To Boston?"

It did not surprise Iosef that Philippa recalled the details of his report better than the others: a Greek nun, she had operated a monastic spy ring during the dark days of the Latin Empire. She had always been the most attentive to news of the outside world.

"That is correct, My Lady," Iosef said.

"And in Boston you encountered the Basilisk?"

"Briefly," Iosef answered, "but yes. I found her lair in a network of tunnels beneath the city, as I had in London and in Paris before that. We spied one another at a distance. It seems she considered me little enough of a threat to let me live, and I am thankful for it."

Margaret leaned forward over the table and looked at Iosef with a grave expression.

"This is very important, Iosef," she said. "The Basilisk.... Was she Edith the Saxon?"

Iosef frowned at the mention of the name. In truth, he had gone to observe, not to deduce, and the matter of the Basilisk's identity was something he had intentionally kept from his mind. But as he considered the question, he felt a sense of dread at the realization that it could easily have been so. Certain things he had seen in Paris, London, and Boston did indeed correspond with the *artistic* nature of Edith's known atrocities.

"It may have been Edith," Iosef replied. "I cannot say for certain. I cannot even be certain that it was a woman. I only viewed her at a distance and her face was concealed. She wore a dress and her hair was long, but I never saw her features."

"What was her purpose?" asked Lakshmi of Bengal, a natural philosopher and astronomer from the Indies. "What was she doing in these secret places?"

Iosef was silent for a moment, recalling the sights with perfect clarity. It was enough to make one shudder, even one of the Living for whom the heart beat slowly and fear seldom was felt.

"She was...conjoining bodies," he said.

"*Conjoining?*" Philippa demanded.

"In Paris I found skeletons that had been constructed from the remains of many different bodies. They were...statues...adornments. Skulls with laurels made of hands, or torsos with many arms. It was very artistic even as it was profane."

"She has done such things before," Margaret said. She frowned and a shadow fell across her pale countenance. "It has been observed."

"In London," Iosef continued, "I found whole bodies not yet succumbed to rot arranged in just such a way. But as their flesh was still on them, they had been sewn together to make grotesque forms: centaurs and serpent-men and other such things. Some of them were altogether abstract, forming shapes and images rather than identifiable creatures."

He looked at Sophio, but she merely stared silently at him, listening and contemplating as was so often her way.

"And these things were kept secret?" asked Margaret. "In previous cases, she has put her creations on display to torment those who walk in the Shadow of Death."

"I believe they were experiments," Iosef answered. "She was testing different ways to combine the human form, however crudely it proved to be."

"To what purpose?"

Iosef hesitated to reply:

"The creation of living statuary."

"What?" Reza asked.

"In Boston, I discovered her lair soon enough after her departure that her work was still fresh," Iosef explained. "I found there the fruits of her labors. She had taken...pieces of yet-living men and women and...grafted them onto one another so that a man might have four arms and no legs, but still be capable of some manner of movement. Or that she might have a candelabrum that could speak and observe."

He shuddered, the memory of the sight quickening his pulse so much that he almost felt it.

"I merely give examples. In truth, there were so many and of such varied nature that I do not know if I could describe them all. But they were clearly decorations that were alive."

"How long did they remain so?" Sophio asked, her expression never changing. Her voice was emotionless, but Iosef sensed unease in her.

"Not long," Iosef said. "Many had died before my arrival. The rest expired shortly thereafter. But I am certain that the making of such living statuary was her purpose. And what troubles me most is the suspicion that Boston was not the finished result, but merely another test along the way. The Basilisk has not revealed these things to the world because they are not ready to be revealed. They are not finished. But once she has perfected the technique, I am certain that she will reveal them, and I dread to imagine the result."

"Panic and chaos," Philippa said, scowling. "Truly it must be Edith. This speaks of her madness in volumes."

"It is likely," Sophio agreed, speaking softly. She blinked a few times, seeming to come back to herself. "But the more pressing question is, was Edith the Saxon the same 'Blessed Virgin' who appeared to our prisoners?"

"The sowing of chaos and horror where there is peace?" Margaret asked rhetorically. "That has always been her purpose. She has done so in the outer world; why should she not do so here?" Margaret motioned to Iosef. "Especially if she is concerned that she has been discovered."

"It would not be unlike her to spread discord among us so that we would be unable to disturb her real work," Philippa said, "though it troubles me to think that she may have violated the sanctity of the valley. How could she gain entry?"

"It is not impossible," Sophio said. "The Living find it simple to come and go as they please. We all know this." The other members of the Council nodded to the truth of her statement. "But until now, the fear of discovery and of our retribution has been sufficient to keep the Basilisks away in the outer world."

There was a long silence as the rest of the Council considered the implications of such a development. Finally, Margaret spoke to Sophio: "Did you sense her?"

Sophio considered this for a time, frowning. At length, she answered: "I...do not know if I sensed her or not."

Suddenly, Sophio seemed confused. The analytical certainty that had been there a moment before was gone, replaced by doubt. She looked at Iosef, and she almost seemed afraid—afraid that her memory had failed her or that her mind had slipped, mistaking the events of one century for the events of another. It had occurred before so many times, but suddenly Sophio was aware of it while it was happening.

"So you may have sensed her?" Margaret asked insistently. "She *may* have been here?"

"I..." Sophio stammered, struggling to sort one memory from another, no doubt searching for an event she could not remember but that should have dominated her recollection.

Iosef would have rushed to her had he been able, but among the Council such a display of affection would be impossible. Instead, he looked into Sophio's eyes and silently bid her to focus her thoughts on him, on what was certain, and to draw herself back into a state of calm. He did not know if it worked, but the momentary panic seemed to fade.

"It is possible," Sophio said to Margaret, her tone calm again and her resolve returned to her. "I may well have sensed her. Indeed, we all ought to have sensed her, for we are old enough to do so, even those on this council who never met her."

Margaret nodded, her face betraying a look of shame. "We ought to have noticed when she came among us," she said. "The safekeeping of the valley is as much our responsibility as it is yours."

"It is more our responsibility," Iese interjected angrily. He looked around at the rest of the Council before turning back to Sophio. "We are your advisors, Eristavi. It is our duty to aid you in safeguarding the valley, and in that, we have failed. We have allowed a serpent to slither into the garden and threaten the tree of knowledge."

The other Council members looked at one another, slowly nodding in agreement and murmuring their apologies for the lapse in their duty. In the end, only Philippa remained silent, her brow furrowed in thought, her eyes darting from one member of the Council to the next.

"Our duty aside," she said, "I must question whether it is even possible for a Basilisk to gain entry to the valley without our notice. Must we seek phantoms in the shadows when a simpler answer may be before us?"

"Meaning?" Reza asked.

"We have as yet no proof that *anyone* appeared to these men," Philippa said, speaking to Sophio. "We give the valley people great autonomy so long as they obey certain principles of the law. Is it so impossible that there were men among them who by their very nature hated and distrusted those whose customs are different? One man claims a visitation from the Virgin Mary and suddenly they all claim it. Such things have happened in the outer world. They could happen here. Why must we seek conspiracies when there may be a simpler answer?"

Reza rose from his chair and addressed Philippa:

"Why are you so quick to dismiss such a possibility, Sister? Are you truly so afraid of the possibility that a Basilisk may have violated our sanctuary?"

"No," Philippa protested, "it is merely that I—"

Suddenly, Sophio rose to her feet, silencing the room. She studied her advisors without a word as if examining and admonishing each of them for some uncertain sin. Then she turned her gaze toward Iosef.

"Husband," she said, "we thank you for this intelligence. You may depart with our blessing. And our gratitude."

This last statement was said with a flicker of uncommon warmth. Iosef knew how close Sophio had come to losing sense of herself, and she was grateful for his presence.

"It is my pleasure to serve, Eristavi," Iosef answered. "I shall take my leave."

He bowed to Sophio, never taking his eyes from hers. He inclined his head to both sides of the Council and withdrew from the chamber.

In the corridor, Iosef took a deep breath to steady himself. Sophio's madness was growing. She often forgot her time and her place, but the incidents were becoming more and more common, and more and more unsettling. And the fact that Sophio had become so confused was a new development. Normally, when the madness took her, she was confident and certain, recalling information that was true but which had no bearing on the moment. To have forgotten something so serious as sensing the presence of a Basilisk....

Something would have to be done. It was the same thing he had been telling himself since he had first noticed the fits of madness a hundred years ago, but now he would have to act before his beloved wife was lost...and the House of Shashava with her.

CHAPTER FOUR

That evening, Varanus made her way to the portico above the dueling salon in the north wing of the castle. Left open to the outside on three sides, it was favored by many of the more physically active Shashavani for sparring and exercise on moonlit nights—or in the light of day by those Shashavani old enough not to fear the sun.

Tonight, the moon was full and the sky was cloudless, leaving the portico painted silver against the night. Torches and lanterns offered their light as well, but Varanus had little need of them, nor did either of the men she saw exchanging thrusts and parries upon the dueling floor.

The braggart Magnus Eriksen stood nearest to the door, and in true form, he was regaling his opponent with tales of his exploits in his mortal life and during his travels in the outer world. Varanus shook her head at him, but she watched the display all the same as Magnus and his opponent danced back and forth with a flickering of steel. Both men fought bare-chested, and in the moonlight Varanus found herself admiring the sight. Magnus might be insufferably arrogant, but Varanus could not deny that he possessed a certain elegant masculinity that was at least aesthetically pleasing.

"Oh *liebchen*," Korbinian murmured in her ear, "you will make me jealous if you stare at him so."

"Oh, hush," Varanus replied softly, and the two of them shared a knowing smirk. No man, however handsome, could ever take the place of Korbinian. He was her all, now and forever.

Magnus's dueling partner paused a moment after deflecting a blow and gave Varanus a subtle nod of greeting. The duelist was a big man, older than was common among most of the Living—for he had come to them later in life. Indeed, with the gray streaks in his beard, he almost reminded Varanus of her late grandfather, such was his appearance, character, and bearing.

"Vaclav," Magnus said, rebounding from his failed strike and repositioning himself for the next attack, "have I ever told you of the duel I fought with Tycho Brahe at the University of Rostock?"

"*Ad nauseam*," replied Vaclav the Moravian—often called "Vaclav the Hussite", for he had been a follower of the great Czech reformer Jan Hus before joining the Shashavani.

"We quarreled, he and I, over a question of alchemical secrets," Magnus continued, tapping his blade against Vaclav's. "And to my great shame, I was over-exuberant and cut his nose from his face!"

Varanus approached the dueling ground and said, "I thought it was Brahe's cousin who cut off his nose."

"Huh?" Startled, Magnus turned in place to look at Varanus. "Doctor Varanus? I did not hear you—"

Grinning at Varanus, Vaclav bounded forward and thrust his rapier at Magnus's throat. Magnus remembered himself and drew his sword up, deflecting the blow at the last moment. Wheeling about, he gave his sword a flourish and glared first at Vaclav, then at Varanus.

"Unsporting!" he roared, though his angry tone could not disguise the amusement in his voice. "Uncouth! Craven and cowardly! The both of you!"

"Easy now, Magnus," Vaclav said, advancing on the Dane and trading a few cautious thrusts. "It is hardly Doctor Varanus's fault if a young pup like you cannot stay aware of his surroundings."

"Ha!" Magnus laughed, deflecting Vaclav's next thrust and answering with his own. "At least I am not a doddering old relic!"

As he and Vaclav began to circle one another, he said to Varanus, "Tycho's cousin, my foot! That was merely a story we concocted to preserve my reputation!"

"Mmm-hmm," Varanus answered.

Beside her, Korbinian laughed. Turning to face her, he walked backward out onto the dueling floor, somehow managing to step in between the two fighters, weaving ever so slightly so that their rapier thrusts passed around him, always threatening to strike him but never landing.

"I don't believe a word of it," he said. "Mind you, I'm not about to argue the point with a man holding a sword."

Varanus shook her head at him and mouthed the words, "How pragmatic of you."

Naturally, neither Magnus nor Vaclav took any notice of Korbinian.

"And what can we do for you, Doctor?" Magnus asked Varanus. "Have you finally come to return the copy of Soslan's *Third Treatise* that you so disgracefully absconded with?"

"Certainly not," Varanus replied, holding her chin high and folding her arms. "Which is to say, I'm certain I don't know what you mean by that. Surely the *Third Treatise* is in the archives. Perhaps you should search with greater diligence next time."

"Ha, ha!" Magnus scoffed, though his mirth was sincere. "You're a regular wit, Doctor Varanus."

"And you, Doctor Eriksen."

Magnus traded a few more blows with Vaclav before attempting a singularly ambitious thrust when it seemed the other man was not paying attention. Older and more seasoned by almost two centuries, Vaclav reacted instantly, deflecting the thrust with only a moment's uncertainty. The two men grinned at one another and drew back, resuming their dance, swords at the ready.

"Ah, the duel," Korbinian said, still standing invisibly in the middle of the match. He leaned backward quickly to avoid being skewered by Vaclav's blade, which made Varanus gasp instinctively. She knew that he could not be harmed, not now that he was dead, but it was still a frightening thing. "This brings back memories, you know."

"Don't be horrid," Varanus whispered.

It was a duel that had taken Korbinian's life, and the very mention of it brought Varanus back to that terrible Christmas Eve night. She clenched her eyes shut and willed herself to forget again.

"Oh, *liebchen*," Korbinian said, touching Varanus's cheek.

Startled, Varanus opened her eyes and saw him standing directly before her, looking at her with sad and apologetic eyes.

"I did not mean to upset you," he added. "I would never wish to do that. But the past is the past; we cannot change it. We can only go forward, together."

"Together," Varanus murmured in agreement, smiling and taking Korbinian's hand in hers. She gently pressed his palm to her lips and kissed it, her movements as subtle as she could manage so that the others would not notice anything peculiar.

"Did I ever tell you about the summer I spent in Potsdam with Voltaire and Frederick the Great, Vaclav?" Magnus asked.

"Many times," Vaclav answered.

"Hmph." Undeterred, Magnus glanced toward Varanus. "You, Doctor? Have I told you?"

"1751, was it?" Varanus asked.

"Ah, such happy days." Magnus sighed.

However poignant his remembrances—if they were even true—they did not distract him from the duel, for he deflected a pair of sharp thrusts by Vaclav and replied in kind with his own.

"Of course," he continued, "it could not last. They quarreled, you know."

"So History tells us," Varanus noted dryly.

"It was over me," Magnus said, smirking. "They simply couldn't share me."

"I shall take your word for it," Varanus replied, her tone indicating that his word was, she believed, the sole evidence for the claim.

Magnus grinned and turned back to Vaclav, who had been waiting, poised to strike but holding back his attack until his partner was ready again. When Magnus looked at him, Vaclav lunged, and Magnus all but fell backward to evade the blow. Magnus hit the ground, rolled, and came up in a crouch, thrusting his rapier into Vaclav's stomach.

Everything was still and silent for a moment as they stood there: Vaclav with his sword raised, his expression confused; Magnus on the ground, straining at the furthest reach of his arm to make the strike. Slowly, Magnus withdrew his sword. Vaclav lowered his own blade and touched his belly. He pulled his hand away and found it covered with blood.

For a moment, Varanus found the portico and the duelists fading away, fading into that horrible Christmas Eve night thirty years ago, as Korbinian stood before her, his fallen enemy's sword thrust through his chest. Varanus shuddered and closed her eyes tightly against the image.

When she opened them again, the vision was gone, and Vaclav was helping Magnus to his feet. The wound in his belly was already beginning to close. The two men laughed at one another and patted each other on the back.

"Well done, Magnus," Vaclav said. "Your reach is improving."

"I am full of surprises, my dear Vaclav," Magnus replied. He turned to Varanus. "And what can I do for you, Doctor? If you haven't come to return Soslan's *Treatise*...."

"I have come to speak to Father Vaclav, actually," Varanus said.

"What?" Magnus asked, sounding surprised.

Vaclav laughed loudly and slapped Magnus on the shoulder.

"Well, it seems that some people still have time for a doddering old relic," he said. He handed his sword to an attendant and retrieved a long silken tunic in exchange, which he pulled on over his head once his wound had stopped bleeding. Approaching Varanus, he asked, "How may I be of service, Doctor?"

"It is a matter of some complexity, Father Vaclav," Varanus replied. "Are you certain you have the time? I would hate to interrupt your sparring...or Doctor Eriksen's fond recollections of Potsdam."

At this, Magnus scoffed and waved Varanus away with his sword.

Vaclav grinned and said, "Oh, believe me, Doctor, over the years dear Magnus has regaled me with his stories so many times, I daresay I recall that summer better than Voltaire himself did."

"Or at all," Varanus mused, which only set Vaclav laughing again.

* * * *

"So you see," Varanus told Vaclav, as they walked through one of the upper corridors of the castle, "it is really the whole nature of being that concerns me. What it is to be Shashavani. Each point, each quality, is individually fascinating, but the whole interconnected state is really what I must decipher."

Vaclav chuckled a little and shook his head.

"Your enthusiasm is inspiring, Doctor Varanus," he said, "but I would advise temperance in the matter. This is a question that has puzzled many of us for centuries. If we have not answered it in a thousand years, it seems unlikely that we shall do so in the next hundred. Even with so keen a mind as yours devoted to the question," he added with a sincere smile.

"Oh, I do not expect to find all the answers tonight," Varanus replied, "nor even in the next century, but eventually I will unlock the secret."

"But you have reached an impasse?" Vaclav asked.

"Indeed, yes," Varanus said. "You see, I have studied all the texts that I can find on the matter. Well, all of the major ones at least."

In truth, there were so many books and scrolls and manuscripts in the Shashavani libraries that she suspected even the librarians themselves did not have a full count of them. Every few years, lost texts were discovered; and every few years, more texts were forgotten, waiting to be discovered anew in some future century. Varanus had encountered many cases where a writer had referenced an earlier Shashavani text that was known to be somewhere in the archives, yet could not be found, and so the writer's own commentary was used to discern the content of the earlier work until it resurfaced.

"Well," Vaclav said, chuckling, "I am a scholar of religion, philosophy, and the arts of war, none of which pertain to your question. What service may I be to you, other than as a friendly ear?"

"You were close with Soslan the Alan before he departed on his last sojourn, is that correct?" Varanus asked.

Vaclav sighed wistfully and nodded.

"Yes," he said, "Soslan and I were dear friends while he was still among us. I often miss his company."

The poignancy of Vaclav's tone gave Varanus a touch of sadness. She could well understand such a feeling of loss. She dreaded to think how lonely life would be if she were ever to lose Ekaterine. At least she would always have Korbinian, but then it was not the same; nor would

Ekaterine be a substitute for Korbinian if he ever left her for good. And Vaclav had no Korbinian, at least as far as Varanus knew.

"Did he ever speak to you regarding his work?" Varanus asked. "Any...any theories he had not yet written down or formulae that he left out of his *Treatise?* Research that he had conducted but not shared?"

"I fear not," Vaclav replied. "Soslan was always eager to discuss his work when it was finished, but seldom before. It was a matter of pride, I think. He did not want to share something that might prove to be a failure. But he did mention that there was something *different* about the blood...our blood. What, he did not expound upon."

"Oh, that much is certainly true," Varanus agreed. "I have already conducted an extensive examination of my own blood, along with blood from those still walking in the Shadow of Death. We are *changed* somehow, that much I can discern. But *how* we are changed, *why* we are changed, that I cannot make out. I have examined countless samples beneath a microscope, but still the secret eludes me. The device is simply not powerful enough for my purposes."

Vaclav spread his hands and said, "I fear that there is little I can do to aid you, my good Doctor." He paused and held up a finger as a thought came to him. "All I can suggest is this. When I was a young man still in my mortality, I followed the examples of Wycliffe and Hus in criticizing the corruption of the Church. And whenever we preached reform, we always asked one simple question: 'Is there a scriptural basis for this principle of Canon law or religious custom?' And from that we would determine whether something was truly the will of God or rather the invention of man."

He chuckled a little and added, "I see now that such a rule is too simple. The Bible is but one scripture among many scriptures, each with its own part of wisdom. But the principle remains. Find the source, Doctor Varanus. Always find the source. Read your Konstantine and Aisha and Soslan, your Symeon and Padmavati. But do not merely trust their words. Rather learn their methods and recreate their results."

"Of course," Varanus said, betraying more of her frustration than she intended. Vaclav's words were good advice, but they were redundant. "I am a scientist, Father Vaclav, not a philosopher. The first thing I tried to do was recreate the experiments of those who came before me, but still the truth eludes me as it eluded them."

She expected Vaclav to take offense at her dismissal of his advice, but he simply smiled and put a hand on her shoulder, looking rather pleased by her independence of thought.

"Build a better microscope?" he offered, perhaps in jest.

But that suggestion, quite unexpectedly, set off a chain of thoughts in Varanus's mind. She shivered at the experience as a cascade of half-memories and unformed ideas flooded her mind. She found herself re-considering her earlier experiments, which had been done to mimic the work of Konstantine and the others. But Konstantine had not enjoyed modern equipment or modern knowledge. Surely there was a better way for each of those experiments to be conducted!

And then Vaclav's words reverberated in Varanus's ears, bringing forth an idea that should have been her first course of action.

Find the source.

"Father Vaclav, thank you!" Varanus exclaimed, embracing him tightly. "You have been immeasurably helpful!"

"I...you are welcome?" Vaclav stammered, bewildered.

Varanus turned and hurried down the corridor back toward her rooms.

"Doctor Varanus, where are you going?" Vaclav called after her.

Varanus looked over her shoulder and replied:

"To build a better microscope!"

And to find a better sample to study with it, she thought.

CHAPTER FIVE

Varanus left Vaclav and went directly to her rooms, her sudden revelation burning in her mind. Vaclav could not have intended it, but his words had reminded her of the one resource that she had not examined. She had studied blood samples, she had tested the nature of her undying body, and she had painstakingly replicated the experiments of those who had come before her, but she had never once thought to go to their source.

She found Ekaterine in her study, lounging on a sofa while she read from Aisha's *Compendium*. Without looking up, she raised one hand to wave at Varanus and asked:

"Do you think, perhaps, that we ought to begin returning some of these books?"

"Absolutely not," Varanus replied, crossing to her and leaning against the armrest. "If people started returning books to libraries, who knows what trouble might result."

"Well, books might become available for other people to read," Ekaterine said.

"Oh yes. And then someone else might take them, and suddenly they wouldn't be available for me to read, quite possibly at some critical juncture." Varanus shook her head at the thought. "No, no, far more sensible to amass them here where I know they'll be safe."

"How utterly practical of you," Ekaterine told her.

"Come," Varanus said, closing the book in Ekaterine's lap. "I need your help with something."

Ekaterine sighed loudly, but it was in jest. She smiled, looking only slightly exasperated at the demand, and set the book aside.

"Very well, if you insist."

"I do, most emphatically," Varanus answered.

She took Ekaterine by the hand and pulled her along to the door, moving so quickly that Ekaterine almost tripped getting up from the sofa.

"Oh my goodness!" Ekaterine exclaimed. "What are you so excited about?"

"A solution, Ekaterine," Varanus said, retrieving the Gladstone bag she used as a samples case. "Possibly *the* solution."

"To what?"

"To everything."

* * * *

Varanus led Ekaterine down into the deepest parts of the castle, through basements and sub-basements, past secret archives and forgotten crypts, into corridors that had seldom been used in centuries. This was the old part of the castle, a chthonic fortress used by Shashava and his followers during their earliest days, until the prosperity of the Order and the swelling of its ranks had made possible the construction of the grand structure that it now inhabited.

There were some soldiers stationed on guard in these lower places, but they were few, and their purpose was more the protection of ancient relics than proper security. There was no known entry to so deep a place save through the castle itself, and any interloper would surely be caught before reaching the forgotten halls. Indeed, aside from historical interest, there was but one reason why the Shashavani returned to those deep places time and time again. Varanus and Ekaterine had each visited it once before in their lives, and though it had been many years ago, Varanus still remembered the way.

They finally arrived in an empty chamber lit only by the flickering lantern that Ekaterine carried. It was bleak and barren, its sole adornment a large block of stone that sat in the very center. Varanus knelt by the stone and ran her fingertips along it, feeling the delicate curves of writing that had been chiseled into its surface. Put simply, it was a warning, a prohibition against the foolishness and arrogance of man, and a reminder that only the virtuous and the wise could hope to attain the undying light of wisdom unscathed.

Pretty poetry, Varanus thought, *but poetry nonetheless.*

Ekaterine stood beside her, her expression one of concern.

"I know this place..." she said softly.

Varanus nodded but did not reply. Placing her shoulder against the stone, she braced her feet and began pushing. The block was heavier than she had expected, and for a time she grimaced and grunted, unable to make it budge. She had seen Lord Iosef push it open during her first visit to the chamber, and though he had struggled at it, she had always assumed that it would be more or less a simple matter. But the stone was heavy, and it almost seemed to fight against her, pushing back through some unseen force.

"Doctor..." Ekaterine continued, sounding apprehensive and more than a little afraid, "you cannot be intending what I think you're intending...."

"I am," Varanus replied.

"We shouldn't be here," Ekaterine said. "This place is sacred."

"It's not sacred," Varanus said. "There is nothing supernatural about this place. It's entirely material."

"But we don't have the right—" Ekaterine protested.

Varanus took a deep breath and sat up, looking at her friend.

"Ekaterine," she said, taking the woman's hand, "there is a scientific principle to our nature. It has eluded the greatest minds of our order for centuries, and while I have tried everything in my power to crack its secret, it has eluded me as well. The answer is down there, in our source, and the reason why no one has been able to discover it yet is that we have all refused to examine that which made us what we are. I am not going to make that mistake. The answers to our origin, to our very nature, are down there, and I am going to find them."

She looked into Ekaterine's eyes and added, "I will not force you to join me, but even if you refuse, I will go alone. I must do this. I will never rest until I know the truth."

Ekaterine looked away and sighed. Her mouth twisted into a frown, and she started to say something, but it seemed she thought better of it and was silent for a time. Presently, she looked back at Varanus and shook her head.

"Well it's foolish of you," she said, "and you'll surely be caught if you don't have someone sensible helping, so move over and start pushing."

Varanus grinned at her, deeply relieved. She and Ekaterine set their shoulders against the block and began pushing. Under their combined strength, the block slid back, revealing steps that led even deeper into the earth.

Taking her Gladstone bag in one hand and Ekaterine's arm in the other, Varanus led the way into the passage at the bottom of the steps. The passage was long and sloping, its walls adorned with paintings and mosaics of mythic scenes and great figures in the history of the Shashavani. During her first visit, Varanus had marveled at them, but she had never examined them properly. Now, with the light of Ekaterine's lantern, she did so and was amazed at the state of preservation, for the images were centuries old, and yet they were almost fresh in appearance.

"I'm rather surprised there aren't any guards placed down here," she mused.

"That's because none but the Living have the strength to move the stone," Ekaterine answered. "And the Living would never think to do such a thing." There was an appropriate pause. "Most of the Living."

"You can always go back," Varanus reminded her. "I can make it on my own from here."

"Nonsense," Ekaterine said.

They continued on in the darkness a little while longer, to where the murals showed images of Shashava and the Companions. All were depicted in the manner of icons, their faces more stylized than real. Their hair was long, their features smooth and angelic. Their clothes and adornments gave indication of their proclivities—priests or scholars or kings—but in truth there was little else to clearly distinguish them from one another. And such was the androgyny of the images that it could not be clearly reckoned who was a man and who was a woman, which was fitting Varanus realized, for there were few among the elder Shashavani whose sex was actually recorded in the histories, and none of them save Sophio were present to clarify the matter.

The first image was of Shashava, the ancient scholar who predated Christ and whose expression of serenity calmed Varanus by the very sight of it. Next came The Three—Konstantine, Valdemar, and Marduk—who were the first of the Companions to answer Shashava's call, and following them, Basileios the Accursed, the Byzantine general whose corruption had nearly destroyed the Shashavani in civil war. Tradition held that the four of them had joined Shashava in the city of Constantinople, founding the Shashavani Order. After them came the other six Companions, of later date but of no lesser standing: Sarah the Khazar, Nino of Imereti, Ruben the Armenian, Mazyar of Bukhara, Zoe the Ascetic, and Fatimah of Baghdad.

"I've often wondered if this is what the Companions truly looked like," Varanus said to Ekaterine, her tone light and teasing.

Naturally, aside from the symbols of their station, they all looked more or less the same, all save for Basileios, whose painted eyes held a malice that should not have been so easily conveyed by the simplistic medium.

"Of course not," Ekaterine answered with a laugh, sounding relieved to be thinking about something other than their act of trespass. "These were all painted after Shashava and the Companions had left on their great sojourns. I doubt that the painters had even met them. There are few enough still with us who ever did so."

"And those that do remain have poor recollections," Varanus noted. As a scientist fixated upon details, she was constantly troubled by the ambiguity with which the Shashavani regarded matters such as the appearance, origins, or even the sex of their founders.

"Not poor recollections," Ekaterine said, scolding. "Selective ones." She patted Varanus's hand. "Once you reach a certain age, you will understand, I have no doubt. You may remember everything, but you may only *recall* some things with clarity. Selective forgetfulness staves off madness. And tell me, what is more important: to remember someone's face or to remember their wisdom?"

Varanus shook her head, still annoyed at it all.

"Yes, yes, the point is taken," she said. "Still, a point of reference would be nice. Half the time I don't know if I am reading a man or a woman."

"Would it make any difference?" Ekaterine asked, as they turned and continued down the passage.

"I suppose not," Varanus said. "But for whatever reason, a part of me would prefer to know. It changes nothing, but it does gnaw on me sometimes. Especially since you all insist on using your Georgian pronoun even when speaking *French*."

One of the greatest points of frustration Varanus had encountered among the Shashavani was on the matter of language. As Georgian had only one pronoun for both men and women, the Shashavani used it almost exclusively, even when speaking in a foreign tongue. And whenever the language in question demanded the gendering of words, they would switch between the two with little reverence for accurate context, sometimes in the midst of a sentence. At least they had the sense not to do so in the outer world, but for Varanus, used to her *ils* and *elles*, it was a great irritation.

"Oh that's just mortal parochialism speaking," Ekaterine said. "After a century or two, you'll soon get used to it."

"I don't want to get used to it!" Varanus protested. "I demand rigidly certain trivialities! It makes it much easier to be comfortable with science, which is never trivial and seldom certain."

Ekaterine laughed and teased, "Well, you can take solace in the knowledge that Sarah the Khazar was *probably* a woman; not because of her name—because names are meaningless—but because we are told that she joined Shashava in part because she was prohibited from becoming a rabbi like her father because of her sex."

"Thank God!" Varanus cried, pretending great relief. "Certainty at last! I believe Sarah the Khazar shall be my new favorite Companion."

"*And* evil Basileios," Ekaterine continued. "Horrible as he was, we at least know he was a man. He was a Roman general, which was something they didn't often allow women to do." She snapped her fingers as a thought came to her. "Oh! And Valdemar, for the same reason. He was a Rus warlord. I don't imagine there were many women commanding Northman armies in those days."

"Nor today either," Varanus noted.

"But you see, the point is that we don't know," Ekaterine said. "Androgyny, ambiguity, it prevents assumptions. The flesh is only the flesh, but the mind is what truly matters. All the Shashavani, from the old to the young, are judged and valued by the contents of their minds, not the shape of their bodies. Really, it's the only sensible way to go about things."

"Such a pity it's a view not shared by the mortal world," Varanus said.

"Well, mortals are stupid," Ekaterine replied with a shrug. A moment later she looked embarrassed and put a hand over her mouth. "I suppose I shouldn't have said that. It was unkind of me."

"Quite right, Ekaterine, and shame on you," Varanus told her. "Mortals can't help being stupid."

To which Ekaterine simply laughed.

They continued on down the corridor as it twisted around in a spiral until at last the stonework and murals gave way to the natural walls of a cave that predated even the oldest parts of the castle. They were deep in the earth now, and Varanus could not help feeling a weight upon her shoulders. Such vast depths were oppressive to both body and soul, and yet there was a familiarity to it as well. There was something almost calming about it, though she could not place why.

The passage finally ended in a large grotto lit by an eerie blue glow that issued from thick veins of fungus clustered along the walls, interconnecting and covering the place like iridescent cobwebs. The very sight of them had sickened Varanus during her first visit; now, they fascinated her, and she found herself walking toward one cluster with her fingers outstretched to touch it.

"Doctor?" Ekaterine asked.

Varanus quickly turned away and gave her friend a smile of reassurance. Hefting her Gladstone bag, she walked to the far end of the grotto where rested a pool of water that shone with the same unnatural light as the walls. It was shallow at first but quickly sloped away, descending into darkness and into flooded caverns that might have no ending.

"Are you sure about this, Doctor?" Ekaterine asked nervously. "It's not too late to go back. No one need ever know."

"No one *will* know, Ekaterine," Varanus replied as she knelt, "unless you tell them." Ekaterine would never do such a thing, Varanus knew that. "But I can do this on my own. If you don't wish to be a party to this work, I won't think ill of you for it. You can take the lantern and go back. I can manage on my own."

"And leave you in the dark?" Ekaterine asked, trying to hide her misgivings beneath a tone of humor. "Nonsense. You'd surely lose your way, and then I'd never have anyone to talk to."

Varanus smiled at this and said, "Thank you."

She turned back toward the pool and began removing glass vials from the Gladstone bag. She took one of them, removed the stopper, and lowered it toward the water to take a sample.

These were the waters of life that made the Shashavani immortal. To some they gave inhuman prowess and eternal life; to some they gave merely longevity and health; and to some they brought only death. They were the key to unlocking the Shashavani condition, and by God she would have her answers.

As she filled the first vial and set it back in the case, she saw Korbinian standing on the water a few paces away from her, looking down with his hands on his hips.

"Are you certain about this, *liebchen?*" he asked. "You may be caught. And if you are caught, what will be the punishment?"

"I don't know," she whispered back, continuing with her work. "To my knowledge, no one has ever done this before."

"The punishment might be death," Korbinian reminded her.

"Then I must make sure I'm not caught, mustn't I?"

Korbinian knelt before her and smiled, a trickle of blood creeping from the corner of his eye. One droplet slid down his cheek and onto the water where it vanished without so much as a splash.

"Good," he said, touching her chin with his fingertips and raising her head to look at him. "After all, if we're both dead, who will I have to talk to?"

CHAPTER SIX

Autumn

"Damn and blast!" Varanus swore, looking away from her microscope and striking the top of her worktable with the palm of her hand.

Across the room, Ekaterine looked up from her reading and asked, "Something amiss?"

"No," Varanus said. Then she quickly corrected herself: "Yes. I'm not sure. Something is amiss here, but no matter what I try, I cannot work out what it is."

Ekaterine set her book aside and joined Varanus at the table. Leaning down, she put her eye to the microscope and inspected the sample.

"I see water," she announced. Looking at Varanus, she added, "Quite unexpectedly."

"Oh, hush," Varanus chided. "There's more to it than just water, but the secret of it eludes me."

The samples she had taken from the underground pool had proven largely uninformative, and even after months of study, she was still little closer to unlocking the question of their nature and origins.

"It seems abnormally clear," Ekaterine said, after giving the microscope a second look. "Very few microorganisms or impurities. Though not surprising for a subterranean spring, I suppose." She paused. "Oh! And it's glowing!"

"Yes, I noticed that as well," Varanus said.

It had taken her a few times to realize it, but the water held small flecks of iridescence that flitted around with no clear direction or purpose. She had tried to observe them under the strongest lens she had, but even that gave no proper indication of their nature. And to the naked eye, they were completely invisible.

"I don't remember seeing these before," Ekaterine added. "Which sample is this?"

"The ones we took yesterday," Varanus replied. She changed the slide under the microscope to an older sample. "And this one is from the batch we took during the summer."

"Ah!" Ekaterine gasped. "No light. No light at all!"

"It's why we didn't notice it the first time," Varanus explained. "I had thought I saw light in the samples we took in late August, but when I examined them a week later, it was gone."

"Meaning...that whatever causes the light dies out after time," Ekaterine exclaimed, suddenly excited. "What do you suppose it is?"

Varanus folded her arms and considered the question.

"It could be an organism," she said. "I would *like* it to be an organism. The possibilities there are endless. Of course, it could be some manner of chemical residue or impurity in the water itself that simply disintegrates. It might not even be related to the secret of the water at all, but at least it is interesting."

"Quite interesting," Ekaterine agreed.

Varanus pushed the microscope aside and stood, stretching her arms over her head. She had been seated at the desk for so long that she had lost track of the hours.

"How are the mice?" she asked.

Ekaterine made a face. "Dead."

"Again?" Varanus mused on this for a moment. "Very interesting."

"Interesting perhaps, but I shan't be doing it a fourth time," Ekaterine said firmly. "I don't think it's at all fair for one thing. And waters of life are clearly not intended for those of the rodent persuasion."

"Quite right," Varanus agreed. The mice had been something of a failure, though their autopsies had been equally intriguing. Most had died from apparent nervous shock, but a few had displayed the disintegration of their internal structures. "Perhaps a dog next time."

"No," Ekaterine said.

"No?"

"No," Ekaterine repeated. "Doctor, I'm not superstitious, but I do believe that the waters of life are special. There is a reason why only humans are able to ingest them and live, and I think that is ample reason to leave them be where test subjects are concerned. Inspect the water under a microscope all you like, but by God please stop administering it to living creatures just to see the results."

Varanus was only half listening, and she said aloud, "I wonder if it is related to body mass. What about a horse—"

"*Doctor!*" Ekaterine cried.

"Yes, yes, all right," Varanus said quickly. "No more test subjects, word of honor. It really is a shame, though. I would very much like to study a body continuously from the moment the water is administered until it either wakes up immortal or dies in its sleep. I wonder if anyone has ever done that before."

Ekaterine sighed loudly and shook her head.

"If anyone has, it will have been Konstantine. But I should hope not. This is water that grants immortality. There should be a reverence surrounding it. That is to say, I certainly don't believe that we're chosen by God to become immortal, long-lived, or to die, but there is *something* going on. Some manner of test, surely."

"Ekaterine," Varanus said, taking Ekaterine's hand and looking at her very seriously, "I simply cannot accept that. We are not *judged* when we drink that water. Our worthiness is not weighed by it. If that were the case, it would be a most unreliable judge of character. Consider the Basilisks, who are surely among the most unworthy, and yet they did not die when they were being tested."

"I suppose—"

"And you, my dear Ekaterine, are without a doubt the most worthy of all the Shashavani," Varanus said, making Ekaterine giggle a little, embarrassed and amused at the compliment. "And yet, you still walk in the Shadow of Death. If this water is a judge of us, it is a most unreliable one."

"Flattery," Ekaterine protested.

"No," Varanus insisted. "This water, however spectacular, interacts with the body in a purely physical manner and produces a quantifiable result, and I am going to discern how and why it does it."

Ekaterine put her hands on her hips and frowned at Varanus for a few moments, trying not to smile. Presently, she said:

"Well, if anyone has written down observations on those sleeping from the water, it will be in the archives, and it will likely have been Konstantine. More than that will require the assistance of a librarian."

Varanus sighed and said, "Back to the cacophony of books, I suppose."

She put on her coat—the better to hide newly borrowed reading material—and made for the door.

"Oh, and Ekaterine," she said, "there are some skin samples on the desk ready to be exposed to the sun. I have numbered them and noted the length of exposure of each. Do be a dear and take notes on them while I'm out."

"Skin samples?" Ekaterine asked. She shuffled some papers around until she found the case that held them, and she gasped at the quantity. "Whose skin?" she demanded, sounding more than a little horrified.

"Mine, of course," Varanus answered.

* * * *

It was late afternoon. Varanus did not even realize what time it was until she reached one of the outer corridors and saw the orange glow of dusk filtering in past the curtains. While the entire castle was sealed against the light during daytime, the exterior halls were never as secure as the private rooms. There were enough paths that were wholly sheltered from the light that the young could get about without much danger, and the old enjoyed a touch of sunlight from time to time. Varanus enjoyed the light as well; she simply could not allow it to touch her, so she walked along the wall away from the windows, skirting the rays of the dying sun that crept in through the cracks.

In a broad, high-ceiling hall where several corridors converged, she encountered Lord Iosef approaching from an adjoining passage. He was simply dressed as was his custom, and the somberness of his black chokha made Varanus's rather plain European dress seem extravagant by comparison.

Iosef nodded at her and gave the barest hint of a smile.

"Good evening Varanus," he said. "It has been some days since last we spoke. How have you been keeping?"

Varanus almost laughed. "Some days." It had been nearly two weeks by her count since their paths had crossed. But for a Shashavani who counted life in centuries, not decades, that was perhaps akin to a handful of hours.

"Indeed, My Lord," Varanus replied. "I am well. And yourself?"

"My studies have kept me busy," Iosef answered, "with long hours and little rest, which is to say that I am very well and quite pleased by it."

Varanus shook her head at him, though it was subtle so as not to be rude. There was that slight smile of his. She could not tell if he was making a joke or being quite serious, and in all honesty, either was possible.

"Where are you bound?" Iosef asked.

"To the library," Varanus said, motioning toward the corridor in question.

"Ah, returning books I presume," Iosef said.

"Certainly not, My Lord," Varanus replied. "To be honest, I can't imagine why people keep asking me that."

"Why indeed." Iosef folded his hands. "I have been searching for an original copy of Soslan's *Third Treatise*. You wouldn't perchance know where I could find one, would you?"

Varanus felt her mouth tighten at this, but she kept smiling pleasantly. He was teasing, surely, but with such seriousness that it almost seemed an innocent question.

"If I find one, you shall be the first to know," she told him.

As they conversed, Varanus saw a man enter the hall from the direction of one of the gates. He was short and willowy, with dark hair and a thick beard, and his chokha and boots were severely worn. He must have been a traveler just returned from some great sojourn; the Shashavani who did so often forgot to tend to the upkeep of their clothes, since their bodies were all but immune to the elements.

Iosef raised a hand to greet the man and called to him:

"Good day to you, Brother Teimuraz. Finally returned to us?"

"Hail and well met, Iosef," Teimuraz answered, bowing his head to him.

He nodded politely to Varanus but otherwise paid her no mind, which caused Varanus to bristle slightly. She knew that it was not an intended slight—being so young, she was simply dismissed as a novice, a situation that was not likely to change until she had lived past her first century—but she found it quite irritating.

"What news from Turkestan?" Iosef asked.

"Mmm," Teimuraz answered. "Developments. Many developments. But before I make my report, I must speak to Lady Sophio and the Council."

"Is something amiss?" Though his tone was level, there was something in Iosef's countenance that suggested concern.

"Not amiss, no," Teimuraz said. He paused and then spoke softly, as if concerned that they might be overheard—though whether it was meant to include or exclude Varanus, she could not tell. "I have found the tomb of Arslan Khan."

Iosef was silent for a moment. His eyes widened ever so slightly as to suggest astonishment, but his expression remained placid.

"You are certain of this?" he asked.

"As certain as one can be," Teimuraz said. "On my journey home, I passed a tomb built of stones and earth upon the shores of the Aral Sea, isolated and unmolested, and the tomb untouched by robbers. It was a place that was shunned. Even the birds would not fly above it."

"That is as the legends state," Iosef agreed. "Did you enter it?"

For a moment a shadow fell over Teimuraz's countenance and he answered, "No, no I did not. I felt...a presence. I did not feel it safe to tarry."

"A presence?" Iosef asked. As Teimuraz began to draw away, Iosef caught his arm. "What do you mean by that?"

"As I say, I must report to the Council."

He and Iosef fell silent as a newcomer—one of the elders named Iese of Kartli—approached them from the opposite end of the hall. Varanus did not know the man personally, but she was aware that he was counted among Sophio's advisors.

"Did I hear mention of the Council?" he asked.

"My Lord," Iosef said, bowing his head to Iese. Varanus quickly did the same.

"Iosef." Iese turned to Teimuraz and nodded to him in greeting. "Welcome back, Brother Teimuraz. We were unsure when you would rejoin us. How is the outer world?"

"Turkestan," Varanus added helpfully.

Iese and Teimuraz both glanced at her with what might have been irritation—it was so damned difficult to read emotion on the faces of the Shashavani—but Varanus swore that she saw the corner of Iosef's mouth turn up into a smile at her words.

"Thank you," Iese said.

"The outer world is the outer world," Teimuraz said. "It will not improve itself merely for our convenience. And I daresay that it will be a bitter winter, but at least there should be a warm spring to follow."

"Amen to that," Iese said. "But you spoke of the Council?"

"I must speak to the Eristavi at once," Teimuraz answered. "I have—" again he lowered his voice "—discovered the tomb of Arslan Khan."

Iese was momentarily silent.

"A development indeed," he finally said. "Come, I will have someone bring you fresh clothes and...a bath. And I will ask that the Council be called to order that you may make your report."

Teimuraz seemed puzzled, clearly no longer recognizing the smell of the road that hung about him.

"Why would I need a bath?"

Iosef cleared his throat softly and said, "We shall leave you to your business, My Lords."

Taking Varanus by the arm, he led her in the direction of the library. Varanus went without complaint, and she was silent until they had departed the hall.

"Who is Arslan Khan?" she asked.

Iosef chuckled and replied, "He is the man who very nearly conquered the world."

"Ah, I take it he was French then," Varanus quipped.

"No," Iosef said.

"English?"

Iosef gave another one of his slight smiles.

"Tell me Varanus, are you familiar with the Kara Keçi? The so-called Black Goat Turks?"

"I am not," Varanus said. "Am I to presume from the name that they raised black goats?"

"A logical enough guess, but no," Iosef answered. "The Black Goat Turks were a steppe tribe that more or less dominated the lower Volga during the Middle Ages, terrorizing their sedentary neighbors and exacting tribute from the other nomadic tribes that occupied the region.

According to the Arab scholar Ibn Fadlan, they took their name from a demonic figure called the Black Goat, which they worshipped as a god. Ibn Fadlan tells us that the Volga Bulgars—who were his primary source of information on the subject—lived in terror of the Kara Keçi, who would raid them mercilessly in order to take captives for sacrifice to the Black Goat."

"Chilling," Varanus said. "It's like something from one of Ekaterine's Gothic novels."

"That is certainly true," Iosef agreed. "We have similar accounts from the Rus, the Khazars, the Bulgarians, even the Byzantines and the Persians, all of whom suffered Kara Keçi raids at one point or another. We are told that the captives would be taken out to some desolate place on the steppe—a place 'shunned by all living things' if one believes such a tale. The Bulgars claimed that the victims were then washed in ashes and sacrificed like cattle to the head of a goat that was freshly cut off and placed upon an altar. And then, it is said, the Black Goat itself would appear to them and speak to them through the head. And through the head, the Black Goat would give them commands and signs of its favor."

Varanus paused and blinked at this. After a moment she said:

"I take it back. It's not a novel at all. It's a farce."

"Absurd, yes," Iosef agreed. "Certainly we can assume that the Black Goat did not actually appear to them, and the head did not actually speak. But such beliefs were a matter of great seriousness to them, and their countless victims were all too real."

"Of course," Varanus said.

"There are certain similarities between the Black Goat faith and the Cult of the so-called Dark Faun that was so powerful during the decadence of Imperial Rome," Iosef continued, "but I find the parallel unlikely at best."

"Why is that?"

"Simply put, the Kara Keçi were reported to be practicing their faith well before Ibn Fadlan arrived among the Bulgars in the early tenth century, but they did not begin raiding the Balkans or Byzantium—the furthest points north and east that the Roman cult is known to have spread—until a century later. So I maintain that the one could not have informed the other. It is perhaps the only great matter on which Sophio and I vehemently disagree."

"Sophio?" Varanus asked. "Why would she care about such a thing, My Lord?"

Iosef seemed momentarily surprised by the question.

"Why, because Sophio is one of our foremost experts on the Cults of the Black Goat, as she puts it, though I disagree with her use of the plural. Like me, she is profoundly curious about the question of mythology made manifest: how mundane events lead to the invention of gods."

"Ah, of course," Varanus said.

She had always assumed that Sophio was too blinded by madness and politics to care about real studies, but perhaps that had been a foolish conclusion. After all, even lunatics and government ministers needed hobbies.

"Sophio studied the Kara Keçi quite extensively in her younger days," Iosef continued. He frowned slightly. "She recalls only certain details clearly now, but her writings on the subject are in the archives... somewhere."

"I am certain they make for a fascinating read," Varanus said, her tone more dry than intended.

"I would not know," Iosef replied. "Most of them were lost before my time. But I have supplemented what remain with Sophio's current recollection and with the other accounts that we have until such time as her memory becomes...clearer."

Iosef's expression clouded slightly at the acknowledgement of Sophio's madness. Varanus was troubled at so rare a display of distress in her mentor, and she quickly prompted him with another question.

"What were they like, these Turks of the Black Goat?" she asked.

"Aptly named," Iosef replied. "It seems that the Kara Keçi took great pains to emulate their 'goat god'. We are told, mostly by Russian sources, that they wore headpieces with horns and goatskin trousers, leather coats trimmed with black fur, and even boots shod with iron in such a way that they resembled hooves. And the men wore their beards long and narrow, like a goat's. The monk Kyrill of Ryazan claims that they rode under the standard of a goat's head placed upon a spear and describes them appearing from all directions in packs like wolves. The few Shashavani accounts that we have do seem to confirm this, though certain observations are...inconsistent. And the Kara Keçi appear to have had an unusually egalitarian society for the time and place: it seems that women held positions of authority and raided in almost equal numbers to men."

"Very sensible of them, but I wonder why that is," Varanus mused.

"Perhaps because any who may serve the Black Goat, must serve," Iosef suggested. Though spoken humorlessly, the statement was clearly a joke.

"It's gone back to being a Gothic novel all of a sudden," Varanus said. She quickly returned to the original subject: "And who is Arslan Khan? One of these Black Goat Turks, I assume."

"Indeed," Iosef answered. "At the beginning of the thirteenth century, the Kara Keçi had spread throughout the steppe, apparently intermingling with the Cumans and Kipchaks who dominated the grasslands north of the Black Sea. We are told by Persian sources that a great warrior named Arslan Khan arose on the steppe between the Black and Aral Seas and that he issued a call to the other Black Goat Turks, summoning them to him. How the message could have reached them so quickly and why they would have obeyed him, the sources do not say, but they are confident that it happened.

"The Kara Keçi came together from the four corners of the steppe and united into a great host. Sophio herself confirms as much: she was studying them firsthand at the time, attempting to record parallels between the Black Goat and the Antlered Maiden of Yugra. By about 1215 the Kara Keçi had carved out a vast territory for themselves. They had pushed the Cuman-Kipchaks westward at least as far as the Volga, possibly to the Don; they had reduced the Khitans to a virtual tributary state; and they were raiding along the Silk Road with impunity."

"You say that he 'very nearly conquered the world'?" Varanus asked.

They turned into a portrait-lined gallery as they continued on their way. For a moment, Varanus felt like they were being watched from the shadows, which of course was silly. It was just her mind playing tricks on her while she was being told stories of ghosts and phantasms.

"Surely you are familiar with Temüjin and what he was doing at about this same time," Iosef said.

"Genghis Khan," Varanus replied. "And he was uniting the tribes of Mongolia."

"When the Kara Keçi subjugated the Khitans," Iosef explained, "the Khitan throne had just been usurped by Kuchlug, a prince of the Naimans who had fled to the Khitan court after his people were defeated by Temüjin. The Kara Keçi invasion was very swift, we are told, and it seems that the Khitan armies were largely spared destruction. Their forces were shattered and encircled, causing them to surrender with minimal loss of life, and it seems Arslan Khan was content to leave the Khitans powerful enough to secure his eastern border while he raided the rich lands of Persia to the south.

"But Kuchlug, still hateful toward Temüjin and perhaps made overconfident by the power of his newfound overlord, attacked the Karluks, a vassal tribe to the Mongols. Temüjin sent an army under one of his greatest generals, Jebe, to deal with the challenge to his authority, and in due course Kuchlug was defeated, captured, and died. The Mongols went on to capture the whole of the Khitan territory, which was a clear affront to the Kara Keçi."

"So many invasions," Varanus mused. "I sometimes wonder if the world wouldn't be a much better place if people simply took up gardening more often."

"Very droll, Varanus," Iosef said. "Naturally, Arslan Khan called the Kara Keçi forces back from their raiding and rode to do battle with Jebe. And even though all the mortal accounts we have of the engagement were written by scholars favorable to the Mongols, it is clear that for possibly the only time during their period of expansionism, the Mongols were outmatched. They had the advantage of numbers and they had Jebe, who was one of the finest military minds in history, but time and time again, we are told, the Kara Keçi outmaneuvered them, ambushed them, and raided their camps and supply lines—'as far east as Mongolia', Juvayni claims, which is clearly an exaggeration.

"Fanciful stories are told to explain why a small tribe of pagans could have inflicted such injuries against an empire that would go on to conquer most of the known world. It is claimed that they had the power to vanish from sight or to travel vast distances by the light of the moon or that they were impervious to steel."

Varanus laughed at this. "Ah, historians." She raised a hand. "But tell me, if they were so successful, why wasn't it Arslan Khan who conquered the world?"

There was surely an exciting tale to be told there.

"Because he died," Iosef answered, rather flatly.

"Oh," Varanus said, disappointed. "It seems we've returned to farce."

"I should clarify," Iosef said, "for had he lived, he would surely have subjugated the Mongol tribes and driven them to conquer the wider world, just as Genghis Khan would do. You see, the turning point came during the third major engagement between Jebe and Arslan Khan, one which, we are told, would have resulted in the destruction of Jebe's army had it been lost by the Mongols. While leading his troops, Arslan Khan was struck by an arrow—Sophio believes it was shot by Jebe—and he died shortly thereafter. And for whatever reason, upon his death the Kara Keçi all but crumbled. They surrendered *en masse* while Arslan Khan's bodyguard fled the field with his corpse."

"Which they brought to his tomb, no doubt," Varanus said, pleased at having connected the tangled thread of the narrative.

"Indeed," Iosef replied. "Eager to find Arslan Khan's body to make an example of it, the Mongols interrogated the Kara Keçi, in particular the bodyguards, who were captured on the steppe after laying their leader to rest. There are lurid stories of torture, some of which may even be true, and when it became clear they would not divulge what they knew, they were executed. But, the legends say, the men who carried out the interrogations all died within a few hours of one another, under the darkness of the new moon, seemingly each by his own hand."

"It's become a Gothic novel again."

"But the stoicism of the Kara Keçi was all for naught. Hamadani relates that a Kipchak herder passing through the region discovered the tomb and reported it to the Mongols, hoping to gain a reward."

"Farce," Varanus declared.

The corner of Iosef's mouth turned up into a thin smile.

"In the end, the Mongols located the tomb, built of earth and stone upon the shores of the Aral Sea, in a place of desolation—"

"Shunned even by the birds," Varanus finished for him, remembering Teimuraz's statement.

"Just so. Several soldiers examined the tomb but could find no way to enter it. The entrance was blocked by a single slab of stone too heavy for even a group of men to lift. And it is said to have borne the symbol of a goat's head painted on it in blood, and all around the tomb were said to be the heads and skulls of other creatures. After several hours they left empty-handed, though Juvayni claims that these men also died by their own hands, or possibly by wild animals, on the night of the new moon within a few hours of each other."

"Juvayni has a fanciful imagination," Varanus noted.

"Sometimes he does," Iosef agreed.

"Forgive my curiosity, My Lord, but if Sophio was present at Arslan Khan's death, how is the location of the tomb any great mystery?"

"Once it became clear that the Mongols had supplanted the Kara Keçi as the dominant power on the steppe, she returned home to give a report of everything she had seen," Iosef explained. "Many of the Shashavani in the region did the same. It was only afterward that she learned of Arslan Khan's tomb from mortal sources, and by then its location had been lost."

"And what happened to the Kara Keçi?" Varanus asked. "Slaughtered?"

"Surprisingly, no. It seems the Mongols were so impressed by their ferocity and skill at arms that the Kara Keçi were simply integrated into the Horde. There are even stories from the Persians and the Rus of 'black goat demons' leading the vanguards of the Mongol armies. But alas, beyond such accounts, we have no knowledge of them. Eventually, the Black Goat Turks simply faded away from history."

Varanus felt a shiver run down her spine, which was absurd, and she folded her arms angrily. Imagine, being unnerved by such an exaggerated tale. She suspected it had something to do with her failure to rest properly for the past week. It was a dreadful habit of hers and it often put her on edge.

"You ought to tell the tale to Ekaterine," she said. "I am certain she would enjoy every lurid moment of it."

CHAPTER SEVEN

Late that evening, Iosef returned to the set of rooms he and Sophio shared as husband and wife. The main chamber was vast: two floors high and equally as wide, with walls the color of alabaster and a domed ceiling painted with the constellations. At the far end of the room, a great set of arches led out onto a balcony. There were countless books and bookshelves along the sides of the room, representing a private collection of knowledge that rivaled even some of the smaller libraries elsewhere in the castle. The chamber was draped in silk, and it smelled pleasantly of roses and frankincense from the burning braziers that formed a circle at the very center.

Iosef walked to the balcony and stood there for a time, breathing the cold mountain air and watching the stars. A breeze flowing off the mountains passed him, ruffling his hair and making his chokha ripple against his body. There was a weight in the air that troubled him. He had sensed it all evening, ever since his meeting with Teimuraz. Something was amiss. One did not demand a meeting with the Council upon first returning from a sojourn unless the news was urgent, and for those gifted with immortality, urgency soon became an unfamiliar concept.

He did not hear Sophio enter the chamber, but at the sound of the door closing, he turned in place and saw her walking toward him. Sophio's white gown flowed like water in the breeze against her body. Her ebony tresses writhed like serpents, sliding off her shoulders and floating behind her as if possessed of life. That moment, indeed every moment he looked upon her, was like the night of their first meeting. She was beautiful and terrible and majestic.

Iosef withdrew from the balcony and approached her, his hands outstretched for hers. Gently they met, touching palm-to-palm, and entwined their fingers as they silently studied one another.

"Good evening, husband," Sophio said. Though she spoke softly, her voice resounded with authority, something that would never—and should never—be stifled.

"My love," Iosef replied. He gently raised the back of her hand to his lips and kissed it, lingering there for a moment to smell the fragrances of jasmine and spice that hung about her. "How was Council?" he finally asked.

Sophio was silent for a time, perhaps considering the best response. It was a habit common to all the elder Shashavani and one to which he had become accustomed. It spoke not of hesitation or duplicity but of an intrinsic wish to make a statement that was at once the most accurate and the most clear.

"It proceeded well," Sophio replied. "We discussed the matter of the harvest and other such concerns. And Brother Teimuraz furnished us with a report of his sojourn in the outer world, which is why you have asked."

Iosef smiled at her observation.

"Indeed, my love, that is why I asked."

Sophio nodded, possibly in agreement or possibly at the confirmation that her deduction had been correct. Iosef had dwelt with her for more than a century and a half, but there were still some qualities of her mood that he could not discern. In time, he knew, it would all become clear. He would understand her as she understood him: completely and with even greater affection for it.

"Has he discovered the tomb of Arslan Khan?"

"Possibly," Sophio replied. "Teimuraz at least seems certain of his discovery. We will not know until it has been verified." She looked away, a hint of uncertainty in her eyes. "I certainly...would like for it to be correct. I witnessed Arslan Khan's rise and fall with my own eyes; the study of his tomb would so comfortably conclude that chapter of my studies." She looked back at him. "But it would be foolish to assume."

"But not to hope, surely," Iosef ventured.

"Perhaps not," Sophio said, looking into his eyes. "Hope is significant in its own way." She dropped her hands and turned half away from Iosef, gazing into one of the braziers. "But I am troubled by it as much as I am hopeful."

"Why, my love?" Iosef asked.

"Teimuraz spoke of a...presence," Sophio said softly. "A presence that he sensed within the tomb, which compelled him not to enter. That is why I am troubled."

Iosef frowned slightly and said, "Teimuraz has always been esoteric in his beliefs. He may believe that the tomb is haunted or afflicted by the occult, but surely you do not."

"I believe only what the evidence proves to me," Sophio replied. Suddenly she turned back to Iosef, startling him with the abruptness of her action. "But I am not troubled by the thought of ghosts or demons, my dearest. He may not know it, but I believe Teimuraz truly did sense something...something very real and very material. He is of the age for such an awakening."

Iosef nodded slowly.

"A Basilisk," he said.

"Yes," Sophio answered. She reached up with one hand and placed it against Iosef's cheek, gazing into his eyes with a look that might have been adoration of innocence or sympathy for it. "You are too young to fully understand, but as we age, we begin to *sense* each other even over great distances. To...*know* one another. It is fleeting and inconsistent, coming and going as it will, but the old know the old even a world apart. And what Teimuraz says, I know to be true."

Iosef felt a shudder at this revelation. He had assumed Teimuraz's story to be all talk, but talk alone was not enough to so unsettle Sophio. And the fact that she was unsettled unsettled him as well.

"Do you sense someone there now?" he asked, gently placing a hand on Sophio's arm.

Sophio looked down at the hand, then up at him.

"I sense someone to the east," she answered, "and to the north and to the west and to the south. I *always* sense *someone*, my love. Always. They are seldom the same for long, but they are always there."

"That is why you were disturbed that you had not noticed when a Basilisk stole into the valley and drove those men to madness," Iosef said, speaking the question as an observation.

Sophio was not given to displays of emotion— none of the old were—but there was a hint of distress and anger that furrowed her brow ever so slightly and brought a tightness to her mouth.

"I should have sensed it," she replied. "Someone so close, I should have sensed it and known who it was in an instant, but I did not. I sensed nothing. I sensed no one. And my failure led to the death of innocents and to chaos within the lands of Shashava."

Iosef took her face in his hands, gently caressing her cheeks and brushing the hair back from her temples. Looking into her eyes, he said:

"My love, you have guided and ruled in Shashava's stead for five hundred years. Despite treason and corruption, the rise of the Turks and the conquests of the Russians, the House of Shashava remains safe and peaceful thanks to you. You cannot know all things at all times, that is for your advisors to aid you with. We were *all* deceived, my love, but despite that, we are safe."

Sophio took Iosef's hands in hers and rested her forehead against his shoulder. Iosef tilted his head so that his cheek brushed Sophio's hair and he kissed her softly.

"I am the only one left who knew Shashava," Sophio whispered. "I am the last. The others have gone, and I must keep Shashava's house safe until they return. And I fear that I am failing them. Every day when I rise from contemplation, I fear that it will be the day that I fail them."

Iosef held her tightly and ran his fingers through her hair. It was so unusual for Sophio to reveal such vulnerability; she rarely did it with him and never in front of others.

"You have not failed them," he assured her, "and you will not fail them. You are the greatest and wisest among us. And you are my love, now and forever."

Sophio looked up into his eyes and said, "I do not know which I fear more, Iosef: failing to protect the House of Shashava or failing to protect you."

"You will fail at neither, my love," Iosef said, kissing her softly on the cheek.

He pulled Sophio into his arms and lifted her from the ground. Sophio laughed softly at the motion and threw her head back, the tails of her long braids flowing across the stone floor. She looked at him with her dark eyes and said:

"You presume to carry the Vicar of Shashava? Your elders would not dare do such a thing, husband."

"I do it because it makes you smile, my love," Iosef said, touching the tip of his nose to hers and looking deep into her eyes. "I would risk anything to make you smile."

Sophio touched Iosef's face with her fingers and ran the tips of her long nails down his cheek, tickling the flesh but not cutting it.

"I would gladly slaughter the world just to know that you were safe," she said, her eyes aflame. "If I cannot protect you, my love, what is there to protect? But how can I know that you are safe with such corruption in this world?"

"We shall protect one another, my love," Iosef told her. "And together, we shall protect the House of Shashava. Together, we can accomplish anything."

Sophio sighed and closed her eyes. Even draped in Iosef's arms, she looked regal and exalted, every inch a queen and as close to divinity as Iosef had ever seen.

"How strange," she said, "that you have only been in my life these few decades, and yet I cannot imagine it without you."

"Nor I, you," Iosef agreed. He smiled and kissed her forehead. "But, thank God, such a thing will never come to pass. We have eternity before us. Together."

"Together," Sophio murmured, bringing her lips to his.

Iosef awoke to sunlight. A glance at the glow around the shuttered windows told him that it was noon at least. He had not slept, of course, for the Living had no need of it, but he had allowed his body to lie dormant while his mind reflected upon greater matters. And in the depths of his meditation, he had not noticed when Sophio arose from the bed. Now he found himself alone.

Of course, it was her business to come and go as she pleased, but it did surprise Iosef that she had not roused him. Rising from the nest of scented pillows and silken sheets, Iosef returned to the main chamber, and there he saw Sophio bathed in the sunlight that shone in through the arched doorways. She was seated in a chair, staring ahead silently.

Iosef approached her slowly and pulled the curtains closed, plunging the chamber into darkness again. Still Sophio looked ahead, unmoving.

"My love?" Iosef asked, carefully touching Sophio's shoulder.

Sophio did not move at his touch, but she seemed to become aware of him. She blinked twice, very slowly, and asked him:

"Am I mad, husband?"

"Mad, my love?" Iosef asked in reply. He placed both hands on Sophio's shoulders. "What troubles you that you ask such a question?"

"Yesterday, I spoke at length with Queen Tamar," Sophio said. "We discussed many things, including the situation of the Georgian monasteries in the Holy Land and the question of when certain texts they possessed would be given into the hands of the Shashavani for safekeeping. It was a pleasant conversation."

"My love," Iosef said, hesitantly, "Queen Tamar died almost eight hundred years ago."

There was a long silence.

"I know that," Sophio finally said. "What I do not know is whether I imagined the conversation so clearly that it appeared to be real...or whether I remembered a true conversation from long ago and could not tell that it had happened in the past, not the present."

Iosef frowned and closed his eyes. It was not the first time that such a thing had happened. Over the course of two hundred years, he had seen countless times when Sophio confused the memory of a past event with the reality of the present. It was common among the elder Shashavani, whose countless lifetimes of memories so often compounded upon one another to confuse present and past.

One could stave off madness by compartmentalizing thoughts, by selectively forgetting memories until they became useful, and such was a common practice. But stress and exhaustion were like hammers striking at the cracks in such resolve, and Sophio, as the Vicar of Shashava, carried an immeasurable weight upon her mind. Iosef counted it a miracle that her moments of confusion were not even more frequent and more disruptive.

"It occurs, my love," he murmured to her. "We all suffer the madness of memory, even I, and I am yet young."

Sophio shook her head and said, "Oh, Iosef, you cannot imagine it. It is everything and nothing at once. It is a thousand voices crying out and each of them demanding an answer." She clenched her eyes shut and continued, "There was a time when I could still silence it all, so long ago. I knew a memory for what it was and it did not mislead me. But now...."

"My love," Iosef said softly, kissing her temple and whispering in her ear, "you have occupied Shashava's throne for five hundred years, as long a time as Shashava. No one but you could have withstood the weight of such responsibility for such endless time. Anyone else would have shattered long before now."

"You do not understand," Sophio replied. "It is my responsibility to maintain the House of Shashava until Shashava or the Companions return. I must keep it safe in their stead. And if I am losing myself, how can I carry out that task?"

"You need rest, my love," Iosef said. "We all need rest, and you have had so little of it."

"How can I rest when I must be ever vigilant against corruption? If I am not the Vicar of Shashava, who can be trusted to carry out that duty? When The Three left, it was chaos...." Sophio shuddered at the memory. "Those who would take power are so easily corrupted by it. There is no successor I could appoint, Iosef. Any who would accept the task could not be trusted with it."

Iosef sighed. It was the same reply he had received for decades, repeated each time he urged Sophio to contemplate relinquishing the throne.

"But surely, the Council could rule—" he began.

"No," Sophio said sharply. Then, more softly, she explained, "When The Three first left in search of Shashava, there was a council put in place to rule. They became greedy and corrupt, they formed pacts and alliances in search of power, and they killed one another, each claiming the right to be Vicar of Shashava. I cannot allow that to happen again."

"I know, my love, I know," Iosef replied. Silently, his mind turned, struggling to find some solution that she would accept. "But perhaps... perhaps a sojourn in the outer world. Just you and I."

Sophio shook her head and said, "I cannot leave the House unattended."

"Not for long, my love," Iosef insisted. "A few months, perhaps a year. Too little time for evil to take root, but time enough for your mind to rest. The Council can be trusted to manage affairs for so short a time, surely."

There was silence as Sophio considered the suggestion. Iosef had little hope for it, however. He had suggested sojourns before, and she had not accepted them.

But slowly, Sophio nodded.

"I suppose that it is...necessary," she said. "And a year is too short a time for the Council to fall to corruption." There was another long silence. "Very well, husband, you and I will sojourn in the world. I only hope that it is time enough for healing."

"I am certain of it," Iosef replied, holding her in his arms and silently praying that it would be so.

CHAPTER EIGHT

A few days later, Sophio called a meeting of the Council to outline her plans to them. Iosef went with her, though he remained standing behind her chair throughout the proceedings, watching and observing silently. However unique and privileged his station as Sophio's only student, he was not a member of Council, and it was not his place to speak unless addressed by one of them.

After attending to a few matters of infrastructure in anticipation of the approaching winter, Sophio rose from her chair and addressed her advisors.

"Sisters and Brothers," she said, "I have an announcement. I intend, in two weeks' time, to depart on a sojourn in the world. My husband, Iosef Vardanishvili, will accompany me. In my absence, I expect this council to maintain order and to govern in my stead."

There were a few murmurs among the Council, and most of the members looked at her in astonishment. In particular, Philippa frowned openly at the news.

"Eristavi, is that wise?" she asked. "You are the Vicar of Shashava. We are merely your advisors. It is your prerogative to rule, not ours."

"And as such, it is my prerogative to delegate authority within the House of Shashava as I deem appropriate," Sophio replied. "And I exercise that authority now." She paused for a time, considering her next statement with her usual care. "I have dwelt too long within this haven of wisdom and contemplation. I fear that I have forgotten the world. I look inward when my eye should turn outward as well. Do not forget that Shashava went on many a sojourn before the final departure, as did The Three and the rest of Shashava's Companions. I have come to realize that it is wise to do so."

There was a long silence. While Sophio spoke the truth, she had never departed for the world since ascending the throne. It must have seemed to the Council that such a thing would never—perhaps could never—come to pass.

"How long do you intend to leave us?" asked Marie of Toulouse, who in her mortality had been a preacher of the Cathar faith until her views on voluntary poverty and the equality of women had proven too radical even for that reform-minded sect. "I think there is little question that we *can* govern in your stead, but I believe what troubles us is the question of how long we must bear this responsibility."

There were nods among the others and quiet statements of agreement.

"We are yet young, Eristavi," said Reza of Samarkand. "Even together, we do not have your wisdom or your insight. And what if there were to be division?"

"I trust in your ability to come to consensus," Sophio replied, looking around the room. "You are, all of you, wise. I was not much older than most of you when I ascended Shashava's throne. You have experience enough for this task, and I trust in your judgment. I shall be gone for only a few months. Iosef and I will return in time for Easter, for the villagers delight in such festivals, and we would not miss their happiness for the world."

There was silence again. At length, Margaret the Hebridean spoke:

"I, for one, trust your judgment, Eristavi, and your decision. I am daunted by the task, certainly, but if you have faith in us, then I shall have faith as well."

"And I," said Iese of Kartli, nodding his head firmly, though there was a hint of hesitation in his voice.

"I am certain that we all share the Eristavi's faith in us," said Thoros of Yerevan, whose powerful build made him the largest member of the Council. It had served him well in his mortality as an aristocrat-warrior and military theorist. "Our misgivings merely show our ignorance. If we are wise enough to give council, surely we are wise enough to administrate a regency."

Philippa shook her head and said, "Eristavi, I do not mean to question you, but I have grave misgivings about this so soon after the attack in the valley. What if there were to be another incident?"

"Then I would trust you to attend to it justly and forthrightly," Sophio replied. She spoke with confidence, but there was a hint of hesitation in her voice. Iosef knew why: the question provoked Sophio's own guilt at having allowed such a transgression to occur in the first place.

"And we shall," Iese said, "if such a thing even occurs. I suspect that we shall enjoy a long and quiet winter. And of course, though it may be a bitter one, a warm spring shall follow when our Eristavi returns to us."

"Poetically said," Margaret told him dryly. She turned to Sophio and asked, "Where do you and young Iosef intend to wander, Eristavi? Have you decided?"

There was another pause and then Sophio said:

"Yes. I intend to visit the tomb of Arslan Khan. I wish to verify Teimuraz's report, and assuming that he is correct in his assessment, I wish to put to rest certain questions regarding Arslan Khan and his resting place. It will be a...pleasant diversion."

She spoke as if she was unsure about the use of the word "pleasant", unsure that it was the most accurate way of describing the satisfaction she would feel at putting those questions to rest. It was such a delightful, peculiar thing to hear Sophio speak, Iosef thought. He found beauty in her overly precise choice of words as he did in so many things about her.

"And what if Teimuraz's other statement is correct as well?" asked Philippa. "What if his 'dark presence' is real? What if—as I suspect we all fear—it proves to be a Basilisk?"

"Yes," Margaret agreed, "what if it proves to be Edith the Saxon? She may have fled there after her attack on the valley."

"Why assume that it is her?" asked Reza. "It could be any Basilisk and, of course, it could be none at all."

"It is a logical assumption," Iese said. "So soon after Edith's violation of our peace, word comes that there may be a Basilisk lurking nearby in Turkestan? I can easily believe that she fled there after her work here was done, to plot and scheme and plan further outrages."

"If it is Edith the Saxon, that is troubling," Marie replied. "She is old...older than us. It is said that Basileios himself—cursed be his name—found her in Constantinople after her family had been cast into exile by the Normans...."

"And that he tutored her to be his bloodthirsty protégée," Thoros finished. "We all know the stories."

"Edith was tainted with malice before Basileios brought her to us," Sophio said, her voice calm and her words frank. "She was tainted even before William the Bastard stripped her family of their lands and cast her into exile. But I knew her, for I was old when she was young."

Sophio placed her hands on the table and leaned forward, studying her advisors with fire in her eyes. One-by-one, they all drew back and looked down, unable to meet her gaze.

"If this *is* Edith the Saxon," Sophio continued, "then I shall deal with her just as I would deal with any other Basilisk. I will destroy her utterly as punishment for her crimes both here and in the mortal world."

CHAPTER NINE

Late Autumn

Varanus looked up from her notes and turned to Ekaterine, who sat on the floor in a pile of skirts and embroidered lace, examining samples of sun-charred flesh and bone.

"Ekaterine, is there something terribly important that I'm forgetting?" she asked.

"Umm..." Ekaterine replied, tapping her lips with her fingertip. "Lord Iosef and Lady Sophio are leaving on their sojourn in three days."

"No, it wasn't that." Varanus frowned. "Lady Sophio is actually leaving the house?"

"Yes."

"Truly?"

"Truly," Ekaterine said. "It's quite exciting, really. They say she's never left since she assumed the throne. I wonder if they're planning a festival of some sort." She made a face. "They probably are. I shall be very cross if I'm not invited."

"Sophio doesn't quite seem like the festive sort," Varanus noted. "I imagine she'll simply slip away under the cover of daylight."

What a pity she's planning to return. Varanus had suffered from an antagonistic relationship with Lady Sophio ever since she had been inducted into the Order. And it was hardly her fault: perhaps she was a little dismissive of certain outdated protocols, and yes she made a habit of borrowing books and not returning them, but that was no reason for Sophio to suspect her of impudence and duplicity!

But of course, Sophio was completely mad, so there was no point in trying to make sense of her. A pity she couldn't be locked away in the attic or some other sensible course of action. Leaving the valley was the first reasonable thing she'd done since Varanus had known her. If only she'd go away altogether and leave saner minds in charge. Not that the Council was exactly what Varanus would call "sane" nor were any of the elder Shashavani, come to think of it. Iosef insisted it was a more lucid and enlightened frame of mind that one simply had to grow into, but Varanus had her doubts.

"We've run out of water again," Ekaterine offered, slightly abashed. She was so very uncomfortable with the whole project, and Varanus simply couldn't imagine why.

"That's it!" Varanus exclaimed, snapping her fingers. "We need more water. Come along to the grotto."

Excited at the prospect of fresh samples and her mind whirling over new tests to conduct, Varanus grabbed her Gladstone bag and walked across the room to Ekaterine.

"Come along," she repeated, tapping Ekaterine on the shoulder. "Time is wasting, and there is science to be done."

"I don't think you're using that word correctly," Ekaterine said.

" 'Done'?" Varanus asked.

Ekaterine merely looked at her for a few moments. Then she said:

"I don't think we should do this."

"Discuss science?"

"Take the water," Ekaterine answered. "We should not have done it the first time, or the second time, and certainly not the third time. And we should not do it now."

Varanus took Ekaterine by the arm and hauled her to her feet.

"Oh, tush," she said. "In the past few months, we have discovered more about the nature of that water—indeed, of the Shashavani condition—than the rest of the Order has managed in a thousand years!"

"A slight exaggeration," Ekaterine said. "We have discovered that we know very little and that modern science is desperately in need of a more advanced microscope, but otherwise we have glowing spots in water that disappear after a few days, and we don't know what they are or what they do."

"We know that the body burns in sunlight from the inside out," Varanus reminded her. "More or less."

To Varanus's surprise, her tests had revealed that, while the surface of the skin showed the first signs of burning at the touch of sunlight, prolonged exposure caused the bones themselves to heat and decay, consuming the flesh from within. It was quite illogical, and she could not imagine why this might be, but there it was.

"You did not need the water to discern that," Ekaterine said.

"True," Varanus agreed, "but I do wonder what would happen if we exposed the water to sunlight. It might catch on fire!"

"It might..." Ekaterine replied, "or it might prove to be water."

Varanus folded her arms and said, "You have no sense of wonder."

"We should not be taking the water," Ekaterine insisted. "It is *wrong*, and clearly whatever secrets it has, we do not possess the means to uncover them."

"You don't have to accompany me," Varanus reminded her. "I can do it myself."

Ekaterine stood and shook her head. Taking Varanus by the arms, she said:

"Don't be silly. I wouldn't dream of letting you do something so foolish on your own! I only wish that you wouldn't do it at all!"

"It will be the last time," Varanus said. "I promise you, the last time." *Until the New Year*, she thought.

Ekaterine would come round to it eventually. It was just a matter of time. And if Varanus could find some way to make this next batch produce more conclusive results, Ekaterine might begin to see the benefit in what they were doing. The stumbling block was clearly a lack of progress; once that was removed, Ekaterine would surely support the endeavor wholeheartedly.

* * * *

They went to the lower corridors as surreptitiously as possible. In the upper halls no one would think twice at seeing them out, but in the catacombs it would be a different matter. Few people went into those deep places except on special business. There was nothing there for most of the Shashavani; only rarely did one find cause to visit the crumbling old chambers, whether for nostalgia or in search of knowledge forgotten over the centuries. There was no protocol against visiting them, of course, but if they were seen, they would be noted and remembered, and that might bring up awkward questions.

As they neared the grotto, Varanus heard the sound of voices speaking quietly in an adjoining room. She motioned Ekaterine to silence and together they crept forward to get a look. Around a corner and through an old brick archway, Varanus saw a small chapel, long abandoned but still with its own manner of beauty. The flickering lamplight illuminated the painted walls, the bare altar, and two figures that stood inside the doorway: one was dressed in simple robes, the other in an embroidered chokha and bearing the arms of a warrior.

After a few moments, Varanus recognized them as the Greek nun Philippa and Zawditu, the marshal of the Shashavani.

"You do realize what you are asking, don't you?" asked Zawditu.

"It is a small thing," Philippa insisted. "Simply...rearrange the duties of the castle guards once the Eristavi departs. I do not ask you to limit their numbers, merely to change where they are placed."

"That is no small thing," Zawditu said. "And it will be noticed."

"You are the Strategos," Philippa replied. "It is within your authority. No one will question it."

"And you ask that the guards assigned to the Council chamber—"

"Answer to me, yes," Philippa said. "And I ask that you ensure the loyalty of the guards assigned to the armories. It is simply...pragmatic."

Zawditu frowned and turned to look at one of the painted walls, the lamplight casting a brooding shadow over her face.

"It is conspiracy," she said.

"It is necessary," Philippa countered.

"You realize what will happen if we are found out. It *is* conspiracy and conspiracy is treason."

"No one would believe it," Philippa said. "You the Strategos, I a member of Council. We are above reproach, thank God."

Zawditu considered this and nodded slightly.

"How do you plan to explain yourself to Lady Sophio when she returns?" she asked.

"There is no guarantee that she will return," Philippa replied. "She is departing on her first sojourn in five hundred years. She claims that she will return by Easter, but I know the lure of a lengthy wander. It may be years before we see her again, and in that time order must be maintained."

Zawditu looked back at Philippa and said, firmly, "I will maintain order...*and* security. Neither you nor any other member of the Council need worry about such a thing."

Philippa quickly raised her hands, conceding the point to Zawditu.

"That is all I ask."

"Good," Zawditu said. She took a step toward Philippa and said to her, very directly, "We will speak no more of this. It is not safe, not even here."

"Agreed," Philippa replied.

Zawditu made for the door, and Varanus and Ekaterine quickly ducked back into the darkness of an adjoining cellar to avoid detection. A short while later, Philippa followed, leaving them alone again.

"What do you make of that?" Ekaterine asked as they resumed their journey.

"Politics," Varanus said, unable to keep the distain from her voice. "I have no time for it."

"Don't you think we should tell someone?"

"As she said, who would believe us?" Varanus replied. "After we are finished here, we will tell Lord Iosef and see what he has to say about it. I suspect he will say we should not worry about such things."

"*And* he will ask what we were doing down here," Ekaterine added, sighing.

That gave Varanus pause. It would be terribly awkward to explain how they came to overhear the conversation in the first place. And after all, Iosef had always advised her to avoid embroiling herself in Sha-shavani intrigues. Perhaps it would be best to say nothing and leave the matter to older heads with far less important things to do.

"On second thought, let's not mention it," Varanus said.

Ekaterine looked conflicted about the matter, but she nodded.

They made their way to the grotto entrance, and together they pushed the altar away from the passage. They had become quite used to the effort over the past three attempts, and now it was almost easy.

The rest of the activity had become equally routine. They descended into the tunnel and walked in silence to the grotto. Varanus glanced at the murals watching her from the walls. For some reason, she could not shake the irrational feeling that they were looking at her and that they were very displeased. Such nonsense! It was clearly Ekaterine's nay-saying getting to her. If Shashava and the Companions had known what she was doing, surely they would have applauded it! The others might talk about the "sacred nature" of the water and the ritual surrounding it, but Varanus felt certain that had Konstantine enjoyed access to a modern microscope, he would have used it to examine the water just as she was doing.

Varanus collected her samples as quickly as she was able, though she made sure to fill each bottle to the absolute top. This would be her last trip there for a while—until Ekaterine saw sense and accepted that it was a good idea—and Varanus would have to make do with whatever she brought back this time.

Stoppering the last bottle, she placed it into the Gladstone bag and hefted the collection. It was not heavy—well, not for her in her current state—but it was certainly cumbersome. She and Ekaterine returned through the passage again in silence. Varanus glanced at Ekaterine and Ekaterine glanced back, but neither seemed sure of what to say.

But, as she climbed the steps, Varanus felt quite cheerful. They had done it! Another collection successfully made; another batch of samples to examine. And now, Varanus had a much better sense of what tests to perform. She *would* unlock the mystery of the Shashavani. It only required time.

At the top of the steps, she froze. In the doorway to the chamber, she saw Philippa the nun waiting for her, arms folded patiently, her expression curious and more than a little angry.

Ekaterine gasped and quickly covered her mouth with a hand.

"Oh dear," she murmured.

"I thought so," Philippa said, slowly approaching them. "Doctor Varanus, Sister Ekaterine.... What precisely are you doing here?"

CHAPTER TEN

"What were you thinking, Varanus?" Iosef demanded, as he closed the door to Varanus's cell.

The news of Varanus's transgression had taken him completely by surprise, and he was still unsure of how to react: whether he should be furious at her for violating such a sacred trust or impressed at her audacity.

Varanus was seated on a simple wooden divan at the far end of the cell. She looked up at Iosef, her expression conveying nothing so much as irritation at the whole situation.

"Why am I here?" Varanus asked.

"You know the answer to that," Iosef replied, slowly approaching her.

"I know that I was taken here and imprisoned against my will for having been in the catacombs," Varanus said, "which I had always been told was a place open to all of us...however uncommon it is to visit them."

Iosef sighed inwardly. Varanus was being stubborn, as was her custom. It was one of the many qualities he admired in her, but this was one of the times that an admirable quality displayed its downside.

"You entered the grotto without permission and stole the waters of life," Iosef told her. "Until now, that was almost inconceivable. And it is treason."

Varanus stared at him with absolute astonishment.

"*Treason!*" she exclaimed. "Why would it be treason?"

"Varanus, do you not understand the implications of your actions?" Iosef could scarcely imagine her ignorance on the matter. "The waters of life are our most carefully guarded secret. It is our duty to protect them from the corruption of the outside world. If the unenlightened were to obtain them—"

"What does any of that have to do with me?" Varanus asked, rising to her feet. Her face still held its look of irritation, but now it was tempered with a growing pallor of concern; she was beginning to understand the full implications of her situation. "I took the water for experiments! I am trying to discern its nature!"

"Why?"

"*Why? Why not?*" Varanus replied. "That water is the key to our nature. My Lord, I have been trying to unravel the secrets of the Shashavani condition for almost two decades, and before me the Order has wrestled with the question for centuries. And all for nothing!"

"Hardly for nothing," Iosef said. "We have learned much about the capabilities and limitations of our bodies. We know how much time is required to harden ourselves against the touch of the sun. We can predict the longevity of those of us who still walk in the Shadow of Death. We understand the development of our physical capabilities such that we can, through selective training, speed their progress fully within just a few years. We know much, Varanus."

"But we do not know the cause!" Varanus protested. "The water is the source, but we do not know why! *That* was the purpose of my experiments! And I am so very close, I know it! The answers are just within my grasp!"

Iosef shook his head. Varanus was so consumed by her curiosity that she put aside all concerns of personal safety and of protocol. It was a common affliction among the Shashavani, but in most cases such transgressions ended in minor injuries and arguments, not in something so profane.

"It was not your place to do so," Iosef said. He kept his voice soft, but the fervor was there, lurking behind it. "Why did you not ask permission first?"

"I..." Varanus stammered. She quickly fell silent, unwilling to answer.

Iosef knew why. She had not asked because she knew the request would have been refused.

Varanus folded her arms in anger and looked away.

"I planned to make a full report once I had conclusive results. I was trying to benefit all of us, My Lord. But I do not make a habit of divulging my experiments until they have borne fruit."

"You cannot expect Sophio and the Council to accept such an explanation," Iosef said. "You do understand what they believe was your intent, don't you?"

Varanus was silent for a few moments. Presently, she said, "No, I do not."

"It is believed that you may have intended to use the water to give the gift of the Shashavani to the uninitiated," Iosef replied.

He did not believe it, of course. Such a thing would have been unlike Varanus. But the others thought it, and that was a problem.

"No!" Varanus exclaimed, aghast. She understood the implications of such a thing. "No, I swear it!"

Iosef nodded. "It may be difficult to convince the Council of that, but I will do everything I can to clarify your actions to them."

"I thank you for that," Varanus said. She still sounded torn between apprehension and anger.

"And regarding Ekaterine—" Iosef began.

"Where is she?" Varanus demanded. It sounded as though she had been harboring the question for some time, but was afraid to ask because it might have put Ekaterine in danger to mention her.

"In a cell of her own," Iosef replied. "She has already been questioned regarding your actions. Now she will be left to wait in solitude that she may better reflect upon her transgression until such time as her fate has been decided."

Varanus sighed with relief.

"She had nothing to do with it, you know," she told Iosef.

"I find that unlikely," Iosef replied.

"It is the truth," Varanus insisted. "She did not even know what I was doing. She...she followed me into the catacombs and...and she tried to stop me. She argued that what I was doing was wrong, and truly I ought to have listened. But as she was attempting to convince me to return the water and never venture there again, Sister Philippa came upon us, and she clearly did not take the time necessary to realize Ekaterine's innocence."

Iosef was silent for a time, and he felt a small smile creep across his lips.

"What is so amusing?" Varanus demanded.

"Ekaterine said almost the same thing about you," Iosef replied. "She insisted that it had all been her idea. You had protested, but in the end she convinced you to do it with assurances that it was a right and fitting course of action."

"It is a lie!" Varanus protested. "It was all my idea!"

"Yes, I know that," Iosef said. "Ekaterine would not have committed such a transgression. But similarly, she *ought to have* restrained your impulses more effectively. She has her own culpability."

"She is not my keeper."

"No," Iosef agreed, "she is your friend. And as your friend, I would have expected her to give you better council before you did something as foolish as this."

"I already told you, My Lord, she did not know," Varanus said.

"Of course." Iosef sighed and folded his hands. "Varanus, listen to me very carefully. Soon you will be brought before the Council to account for your actions. When you do, you must be as polite and respectful as you are able. You may not agree that you have done wrong, but you have, and that is how they see it. They will expect arrogance. You must show them contrition."

"I understand," Varanus said after a lengthy pause. "I will be...contrite."

"Good," Iosef said.

His nodded to Varanus in a manner that he hoped might be reassuring but which probably was not. Turning, he made for the door. After a few paces, he heard Varanus call to him:

"My Lord, there is another matter you should know of."

Iosef looked back and asked, "What is that, Varanus?"

"The woman who found me in the catacombs...Sister Philippa," Varanus said. "There is a reason why she was down there to catch me about my business."

"Oh?"

"She and Lady Zawditu were meeting in secret there," Varanus explained. "They were discussing certain actions to be carried out once you and Lady Sophio departed for Asia."

Iosef cocked his head and studied Varanus carefully.

"What sort of...actions?" he asked.

"From what I overheard I cannot be certain," Varanus said, "but there was talk of changing guard assignments in the castle. Philippa wanted assurances that the soldiers in the Council chamber would be loyal to her. I cannot say for what purpose, but I do think it warrants investigating...as much as my little *transgression*."

"Did Ekaterine overhear any of this?" Iosef asked.

Varanus hesitated before replying, "Possibly. I cannot say. You will remember, she followed me into the catacombs. She did not accompany me. I cannot say what she may have overheard."

Iosef narrowed his eyes and frowned. Conspiracy? And to what purpose? Philippa had been a loyal member of the Council ever since Sophio had first assumed the throne, and as Strategos, Zawditu was equally above reproach. And, of course, no one would believe such a claim, certainly not one made by someone so young who awaited trial for treason. They would say that Varanus was merely trying to turn the attentions of the Order away from her and onto others. And perhaps she was....

But I do not think so, Iosef told himself.

And, of course, Varanus may have misunderstood what she overheard. It may have been perfectly innocent. Then again....

"Thank you for this information, Varanus," he said, turning again to depart. "I will investigate accordingly."

The timing of it was so utterly impossible, Iosef knew. Only a few days before he and Sophio intended to depart.... He could not bring these concerns to her directly. If Sophio feared conspiracy, she was likely to cancel the sojourn that her mind so desperately needed. And she might not entertain the possibility again for centuries. Her sanity would not bear the strain of it all for even another hundred years.

"My Lord," Varanus called to him as he reached the door.

"Yes, Varanus?"

"Am I.... Am I going to die?"

Iosef looked into Varanus's eyes clearly and directly. He waited a moment for the connection to be made and understood.

"No, Varanus," he said firmly. "Not if it is within my power to stop it."

* * * *

Varanus's talk of conspiracy and secret meetings troubled Iosef, and he went in search of Lady Zawditu. He found her in the main armory, overseeing a complement of soldiers as they took inventory of the weaponry. Swords and pistols, bows and rifles were laid out on tables, waiting to be checked, oiled, listed, and restocked.

Zawditu turned at Iosef's approach and nodded to him.

"Iosef," she said.

"Strategos," Iosef answered in greeting. "May we speak?"

Zawditu looked at him curiously. "Koba," she said, passing her pen to the soldier next to her, "finish cataloguing the needle rifles, then ask Boris if the mitrailleuses have been cleaned and oiled."

"Yes, Strategos," Koba said, bowing his head.

Zawditu approached Iosef and said, "We may speak. What do you seek?"

Iosef was silent for a moment, carefully considering his words. While he did not doubt the truth of Varanus's story, neither did he doubt Zawditu's loyalty. He needed to get to the heart of the matter without his questions being mistaken for accusations.

"I do not mean to trouble you, My Lady," he said, his voice low so as not to be overheard, "but it has come to my attention that you recently met in secret with Sister Philippa in the catacombs and that certain matters of a...questionable nature were discussed."

Zawditu's eyes narrowed ever so slightly at Iosef's words, but her face was emotionless and inscrutable.

"From whom do you receive this information?" she asked.

"You already know that," Iosef answered.

"You are right, I do," Zawditu said.

Given the timing of the meeting coupled with Varanus's arrest, there could be little doubt about that. Of course, for Zawditu to acknowledge as much was as good as admitting that she had been there, but why should she hide it? She was above reproach.

"Was there such a meeting?" Iosef asked.

"You realize that you have no authority to question me," Zawditu said.

"Of course," Iosef replied, bowing his head to show that he did not mean to challenge her. "You are Strategos. You answer only to Sophio and to the Council."

"And still you ask?"

"I do not accuse you of conspiracy," Iosef said.

"But you accuse Sister Philippa?" Zawditu asked, the hint of a laugh in her voice.

Iosef hesitated. Accusing an elder of the Order, especially a member of the Council, was dangerous. He enjoyed a privileged position as Sophio's only student, but that would not protect him if Philippa took offense at his unproven insinuations.

"I am curious as to what passed between you," Iosef answered. "What she said to you. Whether I *should* suspect her of something."

"Why?"

"Because I want to protect my wife," Iosef said. "And that means I want to know whether a member of the Council is plotting against her."

Zawditu was quiet for a time, mulling over Iosef's words. Presently she smiled at him.

"Philippa came to me concerned, she said, about the possibility of unrest in Sophio's absence. Not at first, of course, but within a few years."

"A few years?" Iosef asked, astonished. "We shall return by Easter."

"You *may* return by Easter," Zawditu said. "May. But you know the lure of the sojourn, Iosef. I knew it myself in my younger days. You will leave intending to return within a few months, but while you walk about in the world, you will lose track of your time and your place. You have experienced this yourself, Iosef. You know how simple it is to forget."

Iosef felt himself frown despite his best efforts. It was true, what Zawditu said. Time passed so quickly for the Shashavani, especially for the Living, who could not even mark the passage of time with their own bodies. It was a simple thing to lose track of time.

"And if we do not return?" Iosef asked. "If we mistakenly wander for years rather than months?"

"You must remember, Iosef, that Philippa is old. She remembers the dark time, the killing time, when The Three left us in search of Shashava and the Order devolved into chaos and bloodshed. She told me that she fears what may happen if Sophio does not return. There may be power struggles and factions again."

"And what did she ask of you if that happened?"

"Philippa asked me to ensure the loyalty of the soldiers stationed in the castle, especially those guarding key positions," Zawditu said. "The Council room, the armories, the gates. She wants them to be loyal to her rather than to someone else who might seek to usurp Shashava's throne."

"And to whom are they loyal?"

Zawditu smiled. "To me, of course. And so they will remain."

"Is that why you are ordering an inventory?" Iosef asked.

"Inventory is inventory, Iosef," Zawditu replied. "Weapons must be aired and oiled from time to time in case they should need to be used." She patted Iosef on the shoulder. "Go and wander the world with your wife, Iosef. I will keep her kingdom safe until her return."

* * * *

The following day, Iosef went to the Council room with a deep sense of apprehension. He suspected that Varanus had been antagonistic when questioned, and that would not make things go well for her. Sophio and the Council were already suspicious of Varanus for her stubbornness and her unconventional methods, and the nature of her crime was so extraordinary that there was no clear precedent. Iosef feared that they might kill her out of hand, simply for the sake of expediency.

Iosef entered and took a place at the end of the table where he could be seen and could address the Council. He bowed to them all and exchanged a long, meaningful look with Sophio.

Presently, the doors opened again, and Varanus was brought in by a pair of soldiers. Varanus was not restrained, but only because there was no need. Any attempt to escape her fate would be seen as an admission of guilt, and the soldiers—Shashavani who still walked in the Shadow of Death—would not hesitate to carry out an appropriate sentence.

Fortunately, Varanus seemed to appreciate her situation. She eyed the soldiers and the Council members warily and muttered to herself. Iosef did not hear what words of self-assurance she uttered, and he did not think it appropriate to listen. Perhaps she was praying, though that seemed unlikely.

"Doctor Varanus Shashavani," Sophio said, her voice soft but somehow managing to reverberate around the chamber, "you have committed trespass against the House of Shashava. You were discovered having entered the secret places beneath this fortress and taking without approval the waters of life for purposes unknown. All that remains is to determine your punishment."

Varanus's eyes flashed with anger and she opened her mouth to protest, but something interrupted her and she seemed to think better of it. Instead, she looked to her left, her mouth twisting in anger. She muttered something under her breath.

She was, no doubt, used to the idea of trial proceedings where evidence would be given and she would be asked for her plea. But such things were unknown among the Shashavani. The Council had already heard all the evidence there was to hear, and now they would advise Sophio before she, with her centuries of wisdom, decided Varanus's fate.

"This is a grave transgression, Eristavi," said Marie of Toulouse. "We must consider it with all due seriousness. But we must also remember that she is young, not even past her first century. If her actions were motivated by ignorance, her age may warrant consideration."

"She claims ignorance," Iosef said. It was not properly his place to speak, but Sophio would indulge him—and therefore, so would the Council. "She told me, as she no doubt told you, that she took the water for the purpose of studying it, to discern its nature...to discern *our* nature. A worthy goal, though her methods cannot be condoned, and of course must be punished."

He saw Varanus's eyes flash again; again she opened her mouth to speak, and again she thought better of it and merely muttered under her breath, looking away.

"Above all, I would beg clemency, Eristavi," he said directly to Sophio. "This transgression was committed by my student, one who is still young. As such, the responsibility falls on me as well."

"This is true," agreed Reza of Samarkand. "You were responsible for her, Iosef. She is in your charge."

"It is not the first transgression," added Caroline the Burgundian, the historian of European court intrigues, who, it was whispered, had engineered the alliance between England and Burgundy during the Hundred Years' War. "You have been over-indulgent with her. She was permitted to enter the world before the end of her first century and to visit the home of her birth on the occasion of her grandfather's death. Normally that would not be permitted, and yet at your request it was granted."

It was an exceptional thing to have done, Iosef knew. Normally newly initiated members of the Order were not permitted to leave the valley until they had lived a hundred years so that there was time for their friends, relations—indeed anyone they ever knew in their mortality—to die. It was a principle of security that no one who knew them could see them and realize that they had not aged. But in truth, Iosef was skeptical about it. With discretion and care, one could travel freely without such concerns; Iosef himself had traveled the world while still shy of his century, though he had been much closer to it than Varanus.

"I know this," he said. "I understand my mistake, but I still believe that Varanus has not acted with treachery, only well-intended ignorance."

"She may claim that she wished to study the water to better understand our nature," interrupted Iese of Kartli, "but we cannot believe this. In my estimation, the only true reason to steal the water would be to bring the gift of life to the uninitiated. And that crime," he added, leaning forward and slamming his fist against the table, "is treason of the highest order. It must be punished by death."

There were a few soft words of agreement from some of the other members of the Council. Indeed, it troubled Iosef to see how many seemed to agree with the suggestion.

He turned to Sophio and addressed her directly:

"Eristavi, I beg your mercy for my student. She did not act out of greed or malice or corruption. She acted in search of knowledge, which is the ultimate purpose of our order. How can we condemn her for that? No harm was done in the act. The water was not given to the uninitiated. She knows now that she was mistaken in her actions. She is contrite." He looked at Varanus. "Aren't you?"

Varanus opened her mouth in anger, but again she had the sense to restrain herself. She looked away for a few moments and then looked at Sophio. She bowed her head and said simply, "It is true. I understand my...error. And I beg forgiveness for it."

"In light of this," Iosef continued, "I believe that the best course of action would be to place her in confinement, where she may think upon her crime and reflect on how she shall conduct herself in the future."

"Foolishness!" Iese snapped. "This crime is treason. And to have committed it on the eve of your departure, Eristavi.... The initiate's arrogance is boundless. Let her head be cloven off, and her body burned to ashes *tonight* that you, my Prince, may depart on your sojourn without such concerns to trouble you."

"This is sensible," agreed Thoros of Yerevan. "The punishment is suitable to the crime, and this act of trespass should not be allowed to disrupt our work. For that reason alone, death is fitting."

"My Lords, My Ladies, Eristavi," Iosef cried, "let us not be rash. We do not lightly take the Living and return them to death and darkness. We have forgiven greater transgressions than this. Was not clemency given to many of those who aided Basileios in the civil war? Those whose crimes were few and light and who acted out of fear or were misled?"

This did win him a few nods of agreement. Even Philippa seemed to agree, though it was very difficult to discern her thoughts on the matter.

"Eristavi," Iosef said to Sophio, "*I beseech you*, grant my student clemency. Place her in a cell for the duration of our sojourn, where in solitude and silence she may think on her mistakes and come to better understand our ways and their wisdom. When we return at Easter, then let her be released and examined again so that she may prove her contrition."

Iosef looked directly into Sophio's eyes, pleading with her in silence. But Sophio's expression remained emotionless.

"There is wisdom in this, I think," Margaret the Hebridean said after a lengthy reflection. "Much wisdom."

"What?" demanded Iese, staring at her. "You cannot mean that, Sister."

Margaret considered the matter again and replied, "No, Brother Iosef is correct. We should not act rashly. Sister Varanus has acted rashly. She has allowed her arrogance and her lust for knowledge to blind her. *She*, in her youthful folly, has acted without thinking. We must not follow her mistake, Brother Iese. It would be wrong to shed the blood of the Living before the Eristavi departs on her sojourn." She looked around the Council room at the other elders, and her eyes rested upon Caroline the Burgundian. "You agree with me, do you not, Sister Caroline?"

Caroline seemed surprised at the question but she simply nodded.

"I do."

"The suggestion is a reasonable one," said Xasan of Mogadishu, the Somali chemist and philosopher of society. He had long been the voice of moderation during the Council's more extreme disagreements. "It is unseemly to shed the blood of the Living without fitting cause. And while this transgression is great, she is yet young. I agree with Sister Margaret and Brother Iosef. Let her be confined and reflect. She may learn from that. She will not learn from death."

There was a long silence and then Sophio slowly nodded.

"I have considered the words of my councilors and I agree. Though her crime is great, Varanus has acted in ignorance." She looked at Iosef, and her expression made clear that her next words were for him alone: "She will be given a chance to learn from this mistake. If she does, she will be spared. But if she continues in her error after this, she will die."

Iosef glanced at Varanus, expecting—indeed fearing—how she might react to such words. If she openly took to anger at what Sophio said, she might be killed outright. But she did not. Instead, her eyes were downcast, and she said nothing but a few quiet words to herself.

"I thank you for your wisdom and your mercy, Eristavi," Iosef said to Sophio. "And my student thanks you for them as well."

CHAPTER ELEVEN

On the next day, Iosef and Sophio departed on their sojourn, clad in simple woolen robes and thick-soled traveling boots and carrying long wooden staves to aid them on their journey. Sophio walked with her cowl down so that her hair might flow wildly in the frigid winter breeze, but as they departed in daytime, Iosef had no choice but to wear his up to shield his flesh from the sun. He also covered his eyes with dark glasses, and his face with a mask for the same purpose. He was yet young: the touch of the sun could kill him.

Almost half the Order turned out to see them, which was incredible. Most Shashavani were so engrossed in their studies that the passage of time had no proper meaning. Save for those involved in the politics or the administration of the House of Shashava, it was likely that most of them would not realize that Sophio had departed until after she had returned.

They descended from the Caucasus into the lowlands of Imereti and Kartli, through snow-covered forests and fields, and they followed the great Mtkvari River until it emptied into the Caspian Sea. There they turned south and walked along the frigid shore for days and days, making their way through northern Persia and toward the great wastes of the Karakum Desert.

They went on foot, walking with a measured but swift pace. There had been no question of bringing horses, for in the dead of winter and with the absence of provisions, the animals would not have lasted long on the journey. But with their inhuman stamina, Iosef and Sophio had no difficulty walking for the better part of twenty hours a day, resting only occasionally to meditate, to speak quietly in one another's arms, and to reflect upon their journey.

There was no need for provisions, which allowed them to travel unhindered by baggage. Sophio was old enough that she had no need of sustenance, and Iosef, though still young, had almost reached his second century; he could subsist on nothing but water, if only for a few months' time. It would be hard going, but perseverance was good for the soul.

A few weeks into the journey, they stopped to watch the sun set over the sea. Iosef held Sophio in his arms, wrapping his cloak around her as if to warm her against the snow-flecked wind. It was unnecessary, of course—neither of them even felt the cold, save as a dull ache that had followed them since their departure—but it was a gesture, and gestures mattered even among the Living.

"How are you, husband?" Sophio asked, gazing off across the dark, ice-rimmed water. She stroked Iosef's cheek with her fingertips. "You are as cold as death."

Iosef chuckled. "As are you, my love. It is winter and we are wearing sackcloth."

"It is good Svanetian wool," Sophio replied, smiling slightly. "Warm and strong. I daresay it will weather the journey better than we."

"Perhaps," Iosef said. "Certainly better than I will." He gently kissed Sophio's cheek. "But I would walk these wastes naked so long as I could walk them with you."

"Mmm," Sophio murmured. She leaned her head back and rested it against Iosef's shoulder. "Unseemly, but I do not think I would mind that. Perhaps we should make the rest of the journey in the nude, you and I."

"How very ascetic," Iosef replied.

He kissed Sophio's soft lips and held her there for a time, savoring the taste and feel of her, holding her against him until they were like two pillars of ice slowly merging into one whole. After a time, he released her and spoke again:

"Perhaps we should remain here in the world and become stylites."

Sophio laughed, her voice light and gentle. Already the weight of the centuries seemed to have lifted from her. She was still stoic with age, but somehow the warmth of youth had returned to her. It was the side of her that she allowed only Iosef to see; but removed from all others, she showed it now almost constantly, rather than in moments of solitude.

"We should spend our lives seated atop pillars?" she asked, amused at the suggestion.

"As husband and wife, we are one flesh," Iosef said, running his fingertips along the back of Sophio's hand, along her arm, and up the back of her neck. "So we would require only one pillar."

Sophio laughed again and smiled at him.

"You and I together in the world," she said. "This is paradise." She looked off toward the sun as it finally died beneath the horizon of water, leaving the world in a growing snow-swept darkness. "I could not have imagined how free so short a sojourn would make me feel. It is as though a chain has been taken from around my throat. I can breath again. I can feel again. It is...wonderful, my love."

"I am glad of it," Iosef told her, holding her close. "You are my whole world, Sophio. It was agony seeing you in pain, my love. But now it brings me such joy to see you free of it."

Sophio nodded slowly and said, "I think I did not realize how much my mind had been clouded until now."

"That is all past," Iosef said. "We are in the world, and the House will keep until your return. Here there are no worries, only solitude and silence."

Sophio studied the darkness of the sea for a while.

"I should not have resisted the world for so long," she said. "I see that now. I had forgotten the relief of it. Even Shashava and the Companions sojourned at times while they ruled. Even Shashava could not withstand the weight of rulership without escape. What arrogance to think that I could."

"Not arrogance, my love," Iosef told her, kissing her temple. "Courage. That very courage that I admire and adore above all things."

Sophio turned in his arms and knelt before him, her eyes shining in the darkness like those of an animal. Her lips parted in a smile that was both beautiful and terrible to behold.

"There is a part of me that wishes simply to leave," she said. "To take you and walk the world forever. To leave the House of Shashava as Shashava has left it."

"We can," Iosef told her, stroking her cheek. "If you wish it, it shall be so."

Sophio pushed back Iosef's cowl and ran her fingers through his hair as she looked into his eyes.

"How ever did I live without you, my love?" she asked. "How did I survive almost a thousand years before I found you?"

"Because you are the greatest of us, my dearest Sophio," Iosef replied. "Strong as iron, wiser than time, beautiful like the dawn. You are all and everything."

"We are all," Sophio corrected. "You and I. For we are one flesh."

She pressed her lips to his and pushed him back into the snow as her dark hair fell about them like smoke and concealed from them the light of the moon and stars.

* * * *

They did not sleep but still Iosef woke at the approach of dawn. As the first rays of the rising sun prickled his flesh in anticipation of the burning to come, he opened his eyes and quickly pulled his cowl up over his face. He reached for Sophio but found that she was no longer beside him. Frowning, he sat up and put on his sunglasses before looking about for her.

After a moment's searching, he saw Sophio some distance away, seated cross-legged in the snow with her open palms outstretched to greet the dawn. The wind was blowing hard off the sea, and Sophio's hair wove a wreath around her face like a creature possessed of life.

Iosef turned his face away from the sun and walked to her side. He knelt and placed a hand on Sophio's shoulder. Her eyes were closed and she did not look at him, but still she smiled.

"You are awake," she said. "I had wondered if you would miss the dawn."

"I did not intend to rest so long," Iosef replied, gently pushing aside her hair and kissing her ear. "Perhaps my body was weary from the road."

"You are hungry," Sophio corrected. "It has been weeks since last you enjoyed proper sustenance. You are not used to such deprivations, my love. It must be hard on you."

"I shall manage," Iosef said with a slight grin. "After all, I am now a stylite. I shall subsist on nothing but my prayers and morning dew."

"There is no morning dew," Sophio said to him, her smile growing broader. "It has all frozen like the land."

"Snowflakes then," Iosef told her.

He reached out with one fingertip and touched a snowflake that had stuck against Sophio's eyelashes. With great care, he drew it away and studied it. Sophio opened the eye in question and looked toward him, her smile growing so broad that she showed her ivory teeth. Having drawn her attention, Iosef placed the snowflake on the tip of his tongue and consumed it.

"See?" he asked.

Sophio closed her eye again and said, "I suspect that a single snowflake will not sustain you. Perhaps we should find you some cattle to devour. It would make a most pleasurable diversion."

"Nonsense," Iosef replied.

"Man does not live by snowflakes alone," Sophio reminded him.

"Is that not bread?" Iosef asked.

"Bread is more substantial than snowflakes."

"This is true." A thought occurred to Iosef, and jokingly he said, "What a pity that I cannot simply drink your blood, my love. I am certain that it is sweeter than ambrosia."

At this, Sophio's eyes opened in alarm, and she slowly turned her head to look at him.

"Do not say such things, Iosef," she told him. "Our blood is poison to the Living as surely as to those in the Shadow of Death. If I could, I would feed you with every part of myself so that you would not have to suffer hunger upon this journey...but it cannot be so."

"I know, my love," Iosef reassured her. "I spoke in jest, nothing more."

Sophio smiled quickly and nodded. Closing her eyes, she turned her face toward the sun again.

"I could not bear to lose you, Iosef," she said. "And if I were somehow the cause, the pain of it would be so much worse."

"Do not fear, my love," Iosef answered, stroking Sophio's hair. "I have no intention of dying, not now that I have found you to make my eternity whole."

He sat beside Sophio and watched her as the sun shone against her pale face, making her glow like the snow that surrounded them. She was so very beautiful, the most beautiful woman Iosef had ever known. And, Iosef realized, with giddy excitement, the cloud of madness that had weighed upon her in the valley was already lifting. She was more alive, more coherent, and since their leaving, she had never once mistaken a moment of the past for the present. It might still happen—indeed, he feared that it would at least once before their journey was out—but it would do no harm. The journey was what Iosef had hoped it would be: Sophio's salvation.

"A stranger approaches," Sophio suddenly said, drawing Iosef from his contemplation.

"Where?" Iosef asked, quickly standing and looking around as best he was able. When he turned toward the sun, the light stung his face and he was obliged to look away again. But no matter where he looked, he saw nothing but rock and snow.

"At a distance," Sophio replied, "but approaching. You will see. From the southeast."

Iosef looked to where Sophio had said and waited patiently, the rough sea wind blowing hard against his back. Presently, he saw a figure appear in the distance, crossing the vast expanse of rock and frost that led to where they waited on the shore. The figure approached slowly, seemingly without haste, but eventually Iosef saw that it was a woman. She was tall—as tall as Iosef, as he gauged at the distance—fair of complexion but rosy-cheeked. Her hair was flaxen in color and long, streaming out behind her in the wind, some of it braided, other strands left free. She was dressed in a long damask robe of what might have been blue and gold silk, but it had been so worn by wind and sun and dirt that the colors were drab and the patterns upon it were almost unrecognizable.

The woman leaned on a staff of polished ebony as she walked, though Iosef suspected she had no true need of it. The woman was clearly among the Living, for she crossed the frozen landscape bareheaded but with no sign of cold. As she drew near, Iosef studied her carefully. The meeting might only have been chance, but it was very strange. The odds of encountering another Shashavani in such a barren place were slight indeed, and Iosef could not help but fear some untoward purpose behind the stranger's arrival.

And as he looked upon her countenance, Iosef found himself thinking back to his encounter with Edith the Saxon in the tunnels beneath Boston. He had not seen her face then, but truly her hair had been long and fair, and she had been of a certain height; and this stranger could be one of the English Saxons.

As the stranger neared them, Sophio finished her meditation and stood. She turned and nodded to the newcomer, studying her intently. The stranger approached and did the same, no doubt recognizing Sophio as the elder of the two, and therefore, both the wiser and the more dangerous.

"I *know* you," Sophio said, narrowing her eyes, not so much with suspicion as with the struggle to remember.

"And I know you, Sister Sophio," the stranger said.

"But I know not from where or when," Sophio added, frowning slightly. "I see you clearly in my mind's eye but not what is around you or what passed between us. That is all fog and shadow."

"It was a long time ago," the stranger replied, smiling. "You will recall in time."

"How shall I call you?" Sophio asked.

Again the stranger smiled and she answered, "Olga shall suffice for now."

"Olga," Sophio repeated. She tilted her head and continued to study the stranger. "I know you Olga."

"Indeed you do," Olga agreed, her tone pleasant and friendly, which only made Iosef all the more suspicious. "You will recall in time; I do not doubt it."

"Of course," Sophio said.

Olga looked at Iosef. "I *do not* know you."

"I am Iosef, son of Bagrat," Iosef told her, bowing his head.

Now it was Olga who narrowed her eyes, studying Iosef very intently until Iosef was forced to look away from her gaze.

"Perhaps I *do* know you," Olga said, her tone tinged with the hint of suspicion. "Only now it is I who cannot recall when or where." A lock of her hair blew across her face, and she gently tucked it back behind her ear. "Perhaps we have met already...or perhaps I merely heard tell of you from another. I too shall recall in time."

"Of course," Iosef said, bristling.

He kept his eyes downcast, considering his thoughts. It would be easy to assume that the woman was Edith, remembering him from their encounter in America; and it was dangerous to make assumptions. Then again, it was equally dangerous to dismiss such possibilities out of hand.

"Where are you bound?" Sophio asked Olga.

"To the Aral Sea," Olga replied. "I sensed a presence there resting upon the northern shore. And so, I have gone in search of this old friend to see who it may be. Just as you are doing, I expect."

Sophio nodded. "This is so. It seems we have a common purpose."

"What chance you crossed our path," Iosef said, endeavoring to keep his tone sincere and innocent. He doubted that he was successful.

"Not chance at all," Olga said. She addressed Sophio, "I sensed you at a distance as you no doubt sensed me, and I came in search of you. It is lonesome walking the world by oneself. My curiosity overcame me."

Sophio considered this and nodded again.

"Will you join us?" she asked.

"Of course," Olga told her. "It will be good to travel among"—she looked from Sophio to Iosef before she finished—"familiar faces."

Sophio smiled and motioned toward the empty shore ahead of them.

"We must retrieve our walking sticks," she said. "You go ahead and we shall catch up with you shortly."

Olga nodded and said, "Of course." She turned and continued walking northward with her long, easy gait.

When Olga had moved out of earshot, Sophio said softly, "I *know* her, but I cannot recall the memory of her. I know with certainty that I should recall it, but I cannot."

Iosef gently stroked her hair to sooth her frustration.

"It will come to you in time, my love. It will come soon enough." He paused and then asked, "Is she...Edith the Saxon?"

Sophio's mouth tightened and she replied:

"I cannot remember. And that is what troubles me."

CHAPTER TWELVE

Midwinter

Varanus lay on her bed and stared at the ceiling of her cell. The ceiling was decorated with a mosaic in a spiral pattern that always made Varanus dizzy when she looked at it. It was supposed to help with meditation, or so Iosef had told her. She did not believe a word of it.

The cell was as comfortable as a cell could be. It was bare and austere, but at least it was meant to inspire solitude and introspection rather than punishment. She did not know what to make of that, but an ascetic's cave was better than a rat-infested oubliette.

"How are you, *liebchen?*" asked Korbinian, as he gently stroked her hair.

Varanus looked up at him, her face conveying clearly the irritation she felt.

"I am bored," she replied.

"Bored?" Korbinian pretended to be aghast. "But there is so much here to entertain you! The solitude, the introspection, the...patterns on the ceiling."

"Enthralling," Varanus said. She groaned and covered her face with her hands. "Aagh! I feel like I am going mad! I must have activity! Books! But there is nothing! Nothing but silence!"

"And also me," Korbinian murmured, kissing her.

Varanus sighed. "I think without you I would have lost my mind these past weeks. And to think that there are Shashavani who do this voluntarily."

"Well, they say that reflection is good for the soul, don't they?" Korbinian mused.

"*They* are idiots."

"Mmm." Korbinian leaned back against the wall and folded his arms. "Come now, *liebchen*, be of good cheer, for soon it shall be Christmas."

Varanus growled at the mention of the holiday and glared at Korbinian. She watched him gently wipe away a droplet of blood that trickled from his eye.

"It is *not* nearing Christmas," Varanus said. "Not here. They still follow the Julian calendar here, so Christmas will not be celebrated for another two weeks."

"But we do not use the Julian calendar," Korbinian reminded her, again wiping blood from his pallid face. "We use the Gregorian. And the Gregorian calendar says that Christmas is in two days."

Varanus sighed. Sitting up, she kissed Korbinian softly on the lips and brushed away the blood that had begun to trickle from the corners of his mouth.

"You know that I cannot bear that day," she said.

Kobrinian looked at her sadly and said, "I know, *liebchen*, I know. But it is only a little while longer, and then it will have passed."

"True," Varanus agreed, "but then I will still be confined to this cell until Easter."

"Hmm," Korbinian mused. "This is also true." He shrugged sadly and looked up at the ceiling. "I suppose...we could always count the tiles in the mosaic...."

"That is a dreadful idea," Varanus replied. She paused. Then, with reluctance, she sighed and began, "One...two...three...four...."

* * * *

Ekaterine set down another armload of books with a dejected sigh and ran her fingers through her hair. It had been decades since she had last been confined to the archives, and she did not enjoy a return to that ignominious work. This was her penance for her complicity in Varanus's crime, but at least it was better than Varanus's forced seclusion.

Ekaterine had spent time as an archivist when she had first taken the cup, but then it had been appropriate. When one was young, one had to begin with lowly work, but she had long since advanced to greater independence and greater authority. To be back in the archives was shameful, which, she realized, made it a fitting punishment for her crime of arrogance.

Not that she disliked the archives; they were beautiful and deep, with countless shelves of books and scrolls housed safely underground. The libraries in the castle were bountiful in their literature, but even they only represented a fraction of the knowledge that the Shashavani possessed. They held only the most commonly needed texts and those that did not have to be kept under lock and key. For more esoteric material, the Shashavani went to the archives, and it fell to the archivists to locate the texts that they needed.

Ekaterine sighed and began returning the books and scrolls that she carried to their place on the shelves. She had been demoted to being an archivist. It was her duty to catalogue, to retrieve, and to shelve. Some of the Shashavani enjoyed the work and the solitude, and she wished them well for it. But an archivist simply tended the archives. They did not study the texts or conduct research—that was the work of the scholars— nor did they assess the content of the books and determine how they should be classified—that was the work of the librarians. They simply tended the archives. And Ekaterine hated every moment of it. She loved reading books; being surrounded by them but denied that particular plea- sure was agony.

"Excuse me, young lady," a man's voice addressed her from further along the shelves, "but can you perhaps direct me to a copy of Soslan's *Third Treatise*."

Ekaterine turned and saw Vaclav the Moravian striding down the corridor toward her. She smiled brightly at him, delighted at the prospect of the distraction.

"Father Vaclav!" she exclaimed. "What brings you to this solemn estate?"

"I am searching for a book," Vaclav said, returning the smile. "So- slan's *Third Treatise* to be precise. I understand that a missing copy has recently been found."

He meant the copy that had been borrowed by Varanus and not re- turned. When the Shashavani had searched Varanus's rooms, they had discovered her stockpile of texts and promptly returned them to the ar- chives. But though Vaclav's tone was teasing, it was not malicious.

"I *may* know where it is, Father Vaclav," Ekaterine said. She mo- tioned to him to follow her. "Assuming it has been returned to where it was the last time. But surely, this is not the work of a scholar. Tell me which texts you require, and I shall find them for you."

Vaclav laughed and replied, "Nonsense, this is a good place. A place of knowledge." He looked at one of the bookshelves and placed his hand against the wood. "It may be dark, it may be cramped, it may be lone- some...but it is important. And important things are to be respected."

Ekaterine fluttered her eyelashes and asked innocently, "Do you wish to become an archivist, Father Vaclav? We could exchange duties, you and I."

"I enjoy being a scholar," Vaclav said, though he seemed amused at the suggestion. "Though I have always felt that one may be a scholar and an archivist both."

"I will be certain to share your views with some of the scholars when they come asking for texts," Ekaterine replied.

"They will be well received, I have no doubt," Vaclav told her.

Ekaterine motioned for him to follow her.

"This way," she said.

She led him down the rows of shelves in search of the missing book.

"How is Varanus?" she asked hesitantly.

Of course, she had not been permitted to see her. She did not know if anyone else had either, but Vaclav was of middle years and well respected. He might have knowledge she did not.

"Alas, I do not know," Vaclav replied, his tone sympathetic. "But I have heard no ill news regarding her, and I often am privy to such things." He smiled at Ekaterine and placed a hand on her shoulder. "Do not fear," he said. "Her confinement is only a few months. She will be released very soon, very soon by our reckoning, and I have every confidence that when the Eristavi returns, Varanus will be released from her penance."

"I do hope so," Ekaterine said. She sighed. "I cannot imagine the House without her."

"You need not," Vaclav assured her. "All will be well, I am certain of it. And soon it will be Christmas. And that will be joyful."

"True," Ekaterine told him. "Christmas is Christmas, but I tell you truly, Father Vaclav, I shall not rest soundly until Easter."

* * * *

That evening, Luka sat on the northern terrace with Lady Zawditu, smoking a pipe and watching the coming of night as the sun descended into darkness.

"A very fine mixture, Luka," Zawditu said, exhaling a few smoke rings toward the dark red sky.

"I am glad that it pleases you, Strategos," Luka replied. "I live to serve, in smoking as in war."

Zawditu scoffed at this, but she chuckled. She took another puff of smoke and said, "I like you, Luka. You are loyal, brave, ruthless. And you are very capable. I think I shall make something of you one day."

"One day," Luka agreed, humorously but not disrespectfully. "Two hundred years is not a very long time."

Zawditu looked at him, amused but admonishing.

"No," she agreed, "it is not. But...you have grown from that young vagabond who brought a pack of Russians to our doorstep."

"I do apologize for that," Luka told her. "They were led by a man from Kartli. I was feeling generous."

Zawditu laughed. "He only spoke like he was from Kartli."

"Near enough, surely."

"You did not only bring Russians, you brought Brother Iosef," Zawditu continued. "And Iosef has made Sophio very happy. He has been the light of the sun in her darkness, and this pleases me. It is good for her and good for the House."

Luka exhaled his own series of smoke rings and smiled.

"I...know my duty, Strategos," he said, "and I do it well."

"Modesty is still not one of your virtues," Zawditu noted.

"In time, I will surely develop it," Luka replied.

"No, you will not," Zawditu answered frankly. She looked toward the sky again. "You remind me of myself, Luka. Modesty is not in your nature."

"As you say, Strategos."

They smoked in silence for a little while. Presently, Zawditu spoke again:

"Luka, I have been asked to make a report on the House's state of readiness before the Council in a few days' time. It will be very routine: lists of armaments, the number of troops, things of that sort."

"Of course," Luka said.

"I would like you to join me," Zawditu continued, exhaling a puff of smoke. "There will be nothing for you to do, of course, but it will be good for you to see how it is done."

Luka considered this for a moment, puzzled.

"Are you...grooming me, Strategos?" he asked.

"Grooming involves combs, Luka," Zawditu said. "I am teaching you to make you ready for command. I will not be Strategos forever, and Mata Kaur will need an aide of her own one day."

"I am...honored, Strategos," Luka said, stunned by the announcement.

Zawditu scoffed but then she smiled.

"Do not get ahead of yourself, Luka," she replied. "I said that I am training you not that you had been selected. That will fall to Mata Kaur when I retire...in a few centuries' time."

"Of course, Strategos."

"First," Zawditu continued, "let us see if you can stand in a room with politicians, listen to what they have to say, and keep your mouth shut."

CHAPTER THIRTEEN

Christmas Morning (Gregorian calendar)

On the appointed night, Luka went to the Council chamber as he had been instructed. At Zawditu's request, he brought Seteney and Movses with him, so they might "better appreciate the tedium of soldiering". He noticed different guards in place outside the door, though when they had been changed, he did not know. The last time he had been anywhere near the Council chamber was when he gave his report on the fanatics in the woods, and before then it had been years since he had even walked past the doors.

Inside, he saw fresh faces among the soldiers there as well, standing against the back wall of the room. That surprised him, but when he exchanged looks with Zawditu—who waited patiently inside the door—she conveyed no concern about the fact. To be expected, he realized: the soldiers could not have had their positions changed without Zawditu's authorization.

Luka and his troops settled in at the back of the room and watched the proceedings. Zawditu had been right to call him to observe the meeting. Standing through the talk and discussions and itemized lists of unimportant minutia required more fortitude than marching over rough ground with only two hours of sleep and a bullet in his chest. He glanced at Zawditu and saw her watching the meeting not with disinterested perseverance but with genuine attention to detail. Luka sighed inwardly. He did not relish the thought of command authority if it came with such bureaucracy.

After waiting through the ordinary business of the evening—the availability of supplies in winter, how the villagers fared during the season, the sudden influx of returned books that had slightly overwhelmed the archivists—Zawditu was called forward by Sister Margaret, the de facto head of the Council in Sophio's absence.

"Thank you for coming, Strategos," Margaret said. "I understand that you have been conducting a full inventory of troops and resources for our benefit, and this council is pleased to hear of your progress."

Across the table, Marie of Toulouse took another look around the chamber and asked, "Have the guards been changed? So many new faces, I am certain I do not recognize them."

"That was my doing," Zawditu answered. She respectfully did not comment on when it had taken place or the fact that most of the Council seemed not to have noticed.

"For what purpose?" asked Xasan of Mogadishu.

"It is my policy to do so regularly, you will recall," Zawditu said, "so that more of them can have experience with such important duties."

"Ah," Xasan replied, sounding only partly convinced. "Of course."

"And as Strategos, it is entirely within your authority to do so," Margaret said pleasantly. She laughed softly. "I had *thought* they looked different. So many things of which to keep track."

"Indeed," said Sister Philippa. "Thankfully we have you to manage such concerns for us, Strategos."

"Simply my duty," Zawditu answered.

"Now then," said Margaret, "let us be to business. A full accounting of our readiness, Lady Zawditu, if you please."

"Of course," Zawditu replied.

She moved to the center of the room and nodded to either side of the table in turn. Having offered her respects to the Council, she began a lengthy and detailed outline of the readiness of the valley in the event of war: the status of supplies, the availability of foodstuffs, armaments, ammunition, and horses.

Midway through, Margaret raised a hand to halt Zawditu and asked, "Who is the quartermaster at present?"

"Boris the Muscovite," Zawditu replied.

Margaret considered this and nodded.

"A very good choice, I think," she said.

"A very good choice," agreed Iese of Kartli.

Luka was inclined to agree. In his mortality, Boris had been an architect and military engineer at the court of Ivan Grozny. Luka had served with Boris several times—for they both still walked in the Shadow of Death—and he had found Boris to be a capable organizer and a fine companion in battle.

"Please continue, Strategos," Margaret told Zawditu.

Zawditu nodded and returned to her accounting. Luka listened patiently, acknowledging the importance of it all while at the same time gaining a greater appreciation for the tedium of command. He had never seriously considered a position of leadership, but now the idea had drawn even further from his thinking. A captaincy might do: he certainly enjoyed authority in the field, and he did believe that he exercised it well.

But he had come to realize that the exalted position of Strategos carried with it a number of distasteful duties of a bureaucratic nature.

When Zawditu had finished, Margaret stood and nodded to her.

"Thank you, Strategos," Margaret said.

"Of course, Sister Margaret," Zawditu replied, and she withdrew a few paces.

Margaret looked from her left to her right in a long arc that encompassed the entire Council.

"Well," she said, "the business of the evening would seem to be concluded. But there remains one final matter to be addressed."

As if by some secret signal, Thoros, Caroline, and Iese all stood as one, causing the other Council members to turn and look at them in surprise.

"Sophio is gone," Margaret continued, "and it is likely that she will never return. In the absence of a clear succession, we must now make preparations for the future."

"What is this?" demanded Xasan of Mogadishu. "To talk of succession! We have the Council, and the Council shall suffice until Sophio returns."

"Sophio will not return," Margaret said. "She is in the world after five hundred years. She has vanished from us like Shashava, and like Shashava, she will never rejoin us." She spread her arms toward the Council and spoke cheerfully, her tone conveying the thought of joyous news. "But let us not dwell upon what is past. I welcome you all to pledge your oath of loyalty to me and to follow me into a glorious future."

"You would proclaim yourself Vicar of Shashava?" exclaimed Marie of Toulouse.

"No," Margaret replied coldly. "Not Vicar. I am the Eristavi and the Eristavi alone. Shashava is gone and will not return to us. Why should we bow to the memory of a king that none of us ever knew? I proclaim myself the sole Prince of our order, both Caesar and Pope, until such time as one greater than I arrives to receive the mantle of authority from my hands."

She closed her hands into fists and spoke like a demagogue addressing the mob:

"Let us be of good cheer, friends. For too long we have hidden in the shadow of ourselves, bowing to foolish laws that restrain our greatness and our glory. Let us cast the memory of Shashava aside and walk proudly into a new dawn. I declare that we are Shashavani no longer, for Shashava has no power here. We are *Basilisks*, all of us, and proudly so!"

And with a baleful gaze, she looked at each seated member of the Council in turn, her voice now transformed into a growl that threatened retribution as much as it promised reward:

"Throw off the shackles of Shashava's laws and swear your loyalty to me as your comrades have already done. Convert...or die."

Silence fell over the chamber as the soldiers and the Council members alike stared at her in astonishment. The very though of claiming Shashava's throne was outrageous enough, but the command to abandon Shashava's laws was simply unthinkable. Luka was stunned into silence as surely as the Council, but he knew what was to come. He placed his hand on the hilt of his sword and looked at Zawditu. He saw that she had done the same.

Slowly, Sister Philippa rose to her feet and addressed Margaret with a tone of outrage and contempt.

"What folly is this?" she demanded. "You have the arrogance to claim Shashava's chair, and worse, the *madness* to demand that we reject the very principles that have guided and kept safe our order for *eleven centuries?* You have lost your mind, Sister Margaret, and I fear that you shall never find it again."

"I will take that as a refusal of my offer, Philippa," Margaret said, the corner of her mouth twisting into a smile. "Alas, you are lost. Fortunately for the rest of you, I address you all individually, not as one."

"How could such a brilliant mind be so stupid?" Philippa asked, almost conveying pity despite the anger in her voice. "You are outnumbered, Margaret. This council of the Living is divided, six over four. By that count alone, you will lose. And what is more, we have the loyalty of the Strategos and of the Army."

Philippa extended her hand toward Zawditu to indicate her. After a moment's silence, she looked toward Zawditu and asked, with only a slight measure of hesitation:

"We do, do we not?"

Zawditu smiled a little and said, "I am loyal to the Vicar of Shashava, whose throne you seek to usurp, Margaret."

At her words, clearly indicating where the Army's loyalty lay, the guards in the chamber drew their swords and held them out toward the four conspirators. Luka did the same, and his movements were copied by Movses and Seteney.

"It would seem that you are quite outnumbered, Sister Margaret," Philippa observed.

"Perhaps..." Margaret replied.

Her apparent lack of concern made Luka shiver. If it was mere bravado, it was convincingly done.

"Margaret of the Hebrides," Zawditu said, walking forward, "Thoros of Yerevan, Caroline of Burgundy, Iese of Kartli...as Marshal and Strategos of the House of Shashava, I arrest you on the charges of conspiracy, treason, and the attempted usurpation—"

She was interrupted by a loud knocking on the Council chamber doors.

"Just in time," Margaret said, smiling.

"Luka, secure the door," Zawditu instructed, without looking away from Margaret.

Luka snapped his fingers. "Mosves, Seteney, quickly!"

His two soldiers ran for the doors and made to bar them, but it was too late. With a tremendous crash, the doors were flung open, and a party of soldiers forced their way inside. They were fitted with armor of plate and chain, and they carried swords, axes, and muskets, which they pointed toward Luka and the guards. The loyalists, though outnumbered, addressed the newcomers with their own weapons, and an uneasy stand-off began.

As the soldiers parted to secure the room, their leader entered and advanced toward Zawditu. Luka recognized him immediately as Boris the Muscovite. He carried one of the Winchester shotguns Luka had brought back from America, which had been kept under lock and key in the main armory.

"Boris..." Luka began, suddenly hot with anger.

"Easy, Luka," Boris replied, keeping his weapon pointed toward Zawditu. "You will see: this is the right decision. You will be with us soon enough."

"This is *treason*," Luka snarled.

"I like you, Luka," Boris said. "Don't make me shoot you."

Across the room, Margaret smiled and addressed Zawditu and the guards:

"Brethren, as you can see, many of your comrades have already seen wisdom and come to our side. They know what is best for them. They realize what the future holds for us...and what it holds for our enemies."

"Lower your weapon, Boris," Zawditu said, glaring at him.

"My humblest apologies, Strategos, but no," Boris replied. "Not until you have sworn allegiance and proven your loyalty. You are too wily a fox."

"I must confess that I was concerned by the change of guard," Margaret said. "You certainly caught me by surprise with that, Lady Zawditu. But fortunately, I managed all the same."

Rusudan of Tbilisi, the Georgian linguist and geometrist, scoffed at Margaret.

"Your reinforcements still are few, Margaret," she said, "and they all walk in the Shadow of Death. You remain outnumbered by the Living."

"And the Living are more important than the dying?" Margaret mused, almost laughing. Her eyes narrowed. "How many of you have kept up your vigor, I wonder? How many have taken the time to build your strength? None, I suspect." She motioned to her allies with a single sweep of her hand. "While *we* have kept ourselves in readiness for this very moment for over five hundred years. So, I ask again, who among you will swear loyalty to me and receive salvation?"

Zawditu looked to Luka and an unspoken agreement passed between the two of them.

"None of us," she said.

At the look, Boris glanced momentarily in Luka's direction, perhaps on instinct, or perhaps anticipating an attempt to flank him. The moment that his eyes looked away from Zawditu, she grabbed the barrel of his shotgun with her free hand and thrust it upward, ducking down and leaning away as she did. Boris's eyes snapped back toward her and he fired, but it was too late: the shot went off into the ceiling.

And then chaos fell upon the room.

The guardsmen and Boris's soldiers fell upon one another, steel striking against steel in a flurry of sword blows. Stunned by violence they had not known in centuries, the Council sat in confusion, staring at the melee surrounding them with a stunned horror that should have been unknown to ones so powerful. Even the conspirators were slow to act, though this seemed more from complicity than shock.

Only Margaret and Philippa reacted accordingly, each leaping up almost in a mirror of the other. Philippa bounded to her feet as one of the soldiers lunged for her. She struck him twice in the face and tore the sword from his grasp. Across the room, Margaret similarly countered the first strike of a loyal guard who came at her, shattering the woman's sword arm and flinging her into the wall.

As Margaret retrieved her own assailant's blade, Philippa bounded onto the table and leapt for her. As Philippa hurtled across the chamber toward her, sword upraised, Margaret turned and in one motion flung her blade. The weapon caught Philippa in the chest at the top of her arc, penetrating almost to the hilt somewhere around her heart. Philippa jerked violently and blood spurted from her, watering the table and floor like rain. Philippa tumbled to the floor and lay there, twitching slightly as the paralysis of blood loss took her.

Having missed his first shot, Boris drew back a pace from Zawditu and pulled on the lever of his shotgun to chamber a new shell. Zawditu advanced on him, lunging with her blade in a series of strikes that were both furious and coldly precise. Boris did his best to deflect her sword with his shotgun, using it like a staff, but Zawditu had only a little difficulty in scoring cuts across Boris's face, arms, and legs—his throat and torso too well protected by his steel cuirass and gorget.

Snarling, Boris struck at Zawditu with the stock of his weapon, managing a hard blow to her chest that momentarily halted Zawditu's attack and forced her back, gasping for breath. Seizing his opening, Boris shouldered his shotgun and aimed it at Zawditu. A moment later, he fired.

Luka saw the attack even before Boris had lined up his shot. He dove forward to intercept, praying he would be in time, but knowing that he was too slow, too far away. For a moment, all he could see was Zawditu's proud and noble countenance, the beautiful face that Luka had adored from afar as a youth of the valley.

He did not see Movses—the Armenian boy from Ararat that had been recruited into the Order only ten years before—racing to intercept Boris from the opposite direction. A moment later, Boris pulled the trigger just as Movses threw himself in front of Zawditu. The cloud of buckshot hit Movses in the chest and head, and the boy fell, dead or soon to be.

"No!" Luka shouted. "No!"

He tried to leap upon Boris, bringing his sword down at the Muscovite's head, but Boris easily deflected so clumsy a blow. Two of his soldiers rushed to their commander's aid and drove Luka away with frantic thrusts and stabs that he was obliged to deflect and evade.

Saved from Luka's onslaught, Boris fired his shotgun once more, this time into the back of a hapless guardsman, and then drew his sword.

"I am sorry for the loss," he said to Zawditu. "He was a good boy."

Zawditu kept her sword pointed at Boris and made a few thrusts, testing him.

"He was," she agreed. "And you killed him."

Boris swung at Zawditu from the side and their swords clashed.

"I was aiming for you," he said.

"I had noticed that," Zawditu replied.

"Surrender and convert," Boris said, trying another cut from above. "No one else needs to die."

"I am quite pleased by my faith, thank you," said Zawditu, deflecting again and lunging at Boris.

Nearby, Luka managed to force one of his opponents away. Focusing on the other, he kicked the man's leg out from under him. As the soldier fell, Luka raised his sword and thrust it point down into his throat where it was exposed at the top of his gorget.

He struggled to remove the sword, but the dead soldier's body slumped to the ground, almost pulling him along with it. His remaining opponent took advantage of the opening and came at him, a sword in one hand, an axe in the other. Luka sidestepped the first swing and was about to drop his sword and try his luck bare-handed when Seteney pushed her way in between them and parried the next attack.

"Pistol!" Seteney shouted, drawing a revolver from a holster beneath her chokha and passing it blindly to Luka.

Luka almost swore at having forgotten to bring his own backup weapon, but he was grateful for Seteney's foresight.

"Clever girl," he said, taking the revolver.

"Learned from the best, Sir," Seteney answered, driving her opponent back and freeing Luka to move on to another target.

A glance toward the table told Luka that the Council's earlier hesitation at violence was ebbing. The Council members were now on their feet, struggling with one another, striking with the clumsy blows of untrained combatants that still managed, due to their inhuman prowess, to shatter bones and rend flesh. And while Caroline and Iese did not show the same level of martial skill as Margaret and Thoros, they were still clearly advantaged over the five loyalists who remained standing.

"Luka!" Zawditu shouted. "Get the Council to safety!"

"Yes, Strategos!" Luka replied, without really knowing how he was going to do so.

Another of Boris's soldiers came at him, and Luka shot her through the forehead. Grabbing her sword as she fell, he fought through the melee to the table and the Council. He saw Iese of Kartli holding down Reza of Samarkand by the throat, punching him soundly in the chest, clearly intending to carry on until Reza's ribs finally shattered.

Considering such behavior very bad form, Luka shot Iese five times in the face. For good measure, he struck Iese in the head with the empty revolver and shoved his limp body to the floor. Grabbing Reza by the arm, he helped the elder to stand.

"My Lord, can you run?" Luka asked.

Reza wheezed from the chest trauma, but he replied "yes" with a firm voice.

"*Then run,*" Luka told him.

As Luka turned to aid the next Council member—Lakshmi of Bengal—a blow struck him on the side of the head, sending him reeling to the floor. It felt like he had been kicked by a horse, an unpleasant experience he hoped never to repeat. Looking up, he saw Thoros standing over him. Thoros held the limp body of Rusudan of Tbilisi in one hand; his other hand flexed in and out of the fist that had just hit Luka.

Luka grabbed for his sword, but Thoros simply took a step forward and pinned the blade with his foot. Smiling at Luka, he threw Rusudan's body to the side, where it hit the wall and slid onto the ground next to Xasan, who was struggling violently with Caroline.

"You should have converted," Thoros said, reaching for Luka.

A few feet away, Zawditu had acquired two more soldiers, who had rudely imposed themselves upon her duel with Boris. As she deflected a series of swings from all directions, she had occasion to look back and saw Luka. Luka tried to look impressive for her, but since he lay sprawled on the floor, it likely did not work.

Zawditu gave him an irritated look, as if to say "Why aren't you doing what I told you to do?"

She stepped backward, away from another set of uncoordinated strikes, and spun in place. She lunged, extending her leg and arm to their fullest reach, and drove the blade of her sword through the side of Thoros's throat, severing the artery; a moment later, she spun back, just in time to parry another set of blows and stab one of her assailants in the unarmored place just under his arm. Her sword, now tipped with Thoros's Living blood, caused her target's wound to boil with the toxin.

Thoros grabbed at his throat as more blood spurted out. The Living were far more resilient than mortals, but their bodies were still human in structure, and those unused to severe physical trauma commonly reacted to it just as a mortal would. Thoros collapsed to his knees and clutched at his throat in an effort to stanch the flow of blood long enough for his flesh to heal.

Luka started to get up, but he was still dizzy from the blow and he slipped in Iese's blood—well *someone's* blood—and fell again. He was thankful that the flesh of his body had not been cut in the fighting, or the coating of blood would have proved painful and dangerous. As it was, the abrasion on his temple where Thoros had punched him stung from what little exposure it had suffered.

He looked up in time to see Zawditu dart back toward him a second time and slice Thoros's throat cleanly open, removing any real hope of his taking further part in the fight.

"Get up," Zawditu ordered, grabbing Luka by the arm and pulling him to his feet.

"Yes, Strategos," Luka answered, managing to stand with Zawditu's aid. He almost slipped again when she released him and returned to her fight with Boris.

"Now get the Council members away from here!"

Luka nodded, shook his head to clear it, and grabbed his sword.

"Seteney!" he shouted, looking around for her. Spotting her, he motioned toward Rusudan, Lakshmi, and Xasan. "Get them away from here! If they can't walk, carry them!"

Sliding over the table, he reached the body of Philippa, who lay where she had fallen, alive but immobile. The blood from Thoros and Iese pooled about her and hissed where it mixed with her own, but none of it seemed to have entered her wound. Luka pulled the sword out of her so that her heart might begin to heal and heaved her over his shoulder. He turned toward the door and saw Margaret standing before him, her face inches from his. Luka almost cried out at the sudden sight of her and he drew up his sword.

Margaret grabbed the weapon by the blade and pulled it from Luka's hand.

"You should run," she said.

Luka turned as Margaret circled him, but she did not attack. Instead, she walked to Shashava's chair and gracefully sat, folding her hands before her.

"Boris!" Margaret called. "Let them go."

Boris looked up, surprised, and slowly backed away from Zawditu. He looked around at the carnage surrounding him, and for the first time since the battle had begun, Luka did as well. Of the soldiers that Boris had brought with him, only two remained, as did one of the guardsmen. The fighting had been a slaughter, and Margaret's forces had not escaped it either. Across the room, Xasan limped away from Caroline, aided by Seteney and Lakshmi, while Marie of Toulouse dragged the body of Rusudan toward the door. Caroline—almost as bruised and bloody as her victims—did not have the vigor to follow.

"Let them go," Margaret repeated, smiling. She had still triumphed, and she knew it.

"We have more soldiers throughout the castle!" Boris protested.

"Yes," Margaret agreed, "and no way to call them. They shall do as they have been instructed, I have no doubt." She looked at Zawditu and her face grew cruel. "This is a reprieve, Strategos, nothing more. Time enough for you to reconsider your choice of allegiance."

Zawditu looked at the dead bodies of her troops—loyalist and traitor alike—and her mouth twisted into a snarl.

"Conspiracy, treason, and usurpation," she said. "And now, murder. Mark me, Margaret of the Hebrides, I will water the Caucasus with your ashes when this is done."

Margaret waved at her dismissively and said, "Go now, before I reconsider my generosity. It pleases me to know that you can no longer trust your soldiers."

"Some of them, no," Zawditu agreed, glancing at Boris. Then she looked at Luka. "Others, yes."

"Mmm," Margaret hummed, as she ran her blood-soaked fingers through her hair. "This will be an enjoyable game, I think. Just the diversion I require to pass the time." She looked away from Zawditu, evidently done with the loyalists. Snapping her fingers, she addressed her fellow conspirators, "Caroline, come here. There were only the three of them. You must try harder next time. And as for you, Thoros, do get up. It is so unseemly lying about on the floor."

She looked back at Luka and Zawditu and smiled wickedly.

"You have five minutes. You should be running."

CHAPTER FOURTEEN

Deep in the archives, Ekaterine and her fellows had no indication of the events transpiring above them. As chaos began to spread throughout the castle, the number of visitors to both the archives and the library above it slowed and finally stopped, but the librarians and the archivists carried on with their work in ignorance, merely pleased that they were no longer being bothered by scholars convinced that the lost manuscript *they* were seeking was of greater importance than all the others for which the archivists were searching.

But presently it occurred to Ekaterine to wonder at how quiet things had become. "I haven't seen any of the librarians in the past hour," she remarked to Alda, the archivist shelving texts alongside her. "Have you?"

"No," the girl replied, smiling at the realization. "It's marvelous." She spoke as if agreeing with Ekaterine.

"That's not quite what I meant," Ekaterine said. She frowned for a moment, torn between being pleased at the break in work and finding it intensely boring. "Would you finish shelving these books for me?" she asked Alda. "I'm just going to go upstairs and see if everyone has vanished into the woodwork suddenly."

"Brother Petre will be furious if he finds out," Alda cautioned her, looking uneasy at the idea of such behavior. "The librarians come to us, not the other way."

Ekaterine leaned out into the nearby corridor of shelves and looked to where Petre—an aging Shashavani of the Shadow with a thick beard and spectacles—sat at a work table, retouching the lettering in one of the many ancient tomes in his charge. It was tedious work, but the old archivist seemed to find great satisfaction in it.

"Brother Petre will not notice that I am gone," Ekaterine said. "I'm merely going for a breath of air."

"You're going to *read*," Alda replied. "We don't read books here: we preserve them."

Ekaterine grinned. "Which is why I am going upstairs to do it."

Before Alda could protest further, Ekaterine hurried up the stairs that led into the library above them. But as she reached the main floor,

Ekaterine saw that something was amiss. The chamber should have been filled with scholars engrossed in reading and with librarians busy keeping the texts in order, but instead it was eerily still.

But it was not silent. Instead of the dreaded "cacophony of books" that Varanus so hated, Ekaterine heard the sounds of low voices speaking and heavy boots tramping up and down the wooden walkways that circled and crisscrossed the library's upper levels. An instinct of caution took her, and Ekaterine ducked behind the nearest shelf to conceal herself before she crept forward to investigate.

She saw that the library's occupants had all been herded together into a clump at the center of the room, as far from any hiding places or cover as could be managed. Surrounding them were about two-dozen armed men and women, clad in plated mail and armed with swords and muskets. Most were Shashavani of the Shadow, as near as Ekaterine could tell—members of the Army, no doubt—but they included the Living among their number as well.

What was happening, Ekaterine wondered. These were Shashavani! The Order's own soldiers, each one sworn to protect their brethren and to uphold the Law of Shashava! But here they were, threatening their friends and comrades and holding them at gunpoint.

As Ekaterine watched, she saw a dozen more scholars marched down from the walkways by five more soldiers led by Jan the Hollander, formerly an adventurer of the Dutch East India Company and a man that Ekaterine had always counted as a friend. The sight of him shoving the captured scholars ahead of him like they were only so many cattle made Ekaterine's stomach turn.

As these last prisoners were made to join their fellows, Jan approached the leader of the soldiers, a woman with short-cut chestnut hair who held a Swiss halberd that rested against her shoulder. It took Ekaterine a few moments to place the woman, but she almost gasped at the realization that it was Lady Jane Fairfax, exiled Royalist, now Master-At-Arms for the Shashavani Order.

Jan bowed to Fairfax and the woman replied with a nod.

"Are these the last of them?"

"Yes, Lady Fairfax," Jan replied. "We have scoured the library, into each and every corner. These are the last."

"Good. And the upper levels?"

"Secured," Jan said, "and the doors all barred. There shall be neither entry nor escape except by this floor."

Fairfax nodded her approval. "Good." She turned to the crowd of prisoners and asked, "Are there those among you who can tell me to whom you owe allegiance? Come forward and be recognized."

There was a pause as most of the prisoners looked at one another in confusion, but presently almost a quarter of their number pushed past the rest and stood before Fairfax. Ekaterine narrowed her eyes as she watched. The question had meant nothing to her, but it had clearly been not only significant but also anticipated by those few who understood it.

"We serve the Winter King," came the reply, spoken almost in unison.

Fairfax studied the group for a moment before she nodded.

"Arm them," she said to Jan.

The remaining prisoners stared in shock and murmured to one another as the dozen or so turncoats accepted weapons from the soldiers and joined their ranks. Finally, one of the senior librarians, Demir of Ankara, pushed his way forward and approached Fairfax, his face contorted in anger. The two soldiers flanking Fairfax crossed their swords to bar Demir's way, but Fairfax raised a hand to call them off.

"What is the meaning of this...this outrage?" Demir shouted. "How *dare* you treat us in such a way! You will be punished for this!"

In the face of Demir's anger, Fairfax merely smiled and placed a friendly hand on his shoulder. At her touch, Demir drew away, but this subtle acknowledgement of Fairfax's power seemed to take some of the fire out of him.

"Brother Demir, be at peace," Fairfax said. "All will be explained soon. There is a change taking place in the House of Shashava, and it is for the better, I assure you."

"What change?" Demir demanded. "Why have you taken us captive in our own home? You do not have the authority—"

"I bear the authority of our Queen," Fairfax answered, interrupting Demir. "Our new Eristavi."

"New?"

Rather than speak to Demir directly, Fairfax held out her hand to the prisoners and addressed all of them:

"Brothers and sisters, Shashava is gone. Sophio is gone. We have been abandoned in an unkind world to the whims of politicians and their incompetent Council. It is time now not for a Vicar waiting for a homecoming that will never take place, but for a Prince to rule us with wisdom and with strength. For too long we have cowered in the shadows like monks, scribbling upon parchment by candlelight. Let us walk into the light and be known as kings."

"Blasphemy!" shouted Demir. "Heresy! You speak in violation of all of Shashava's laws!"

This cry was taken up by many among the prisoners, albeit only in murmurs and whispers. They were afraid, and unlike Demir, their anger had not overcome that fear.

"Heresy?" Fairfax asked, sounding amused. "Shashava is gone. The Law of Shashava no longer has meaning. Why enforce a flawed doctrine?"

"Do not speak so about the Law of Shashava!" Demir snapped. "The Law of Shashava is Wisdom and—"

Demir took a step toward Fairfax again, seething with anger. This time Fairfax halted him with the flat side of her halberd, which she pressed against his shoulder. She shook her head at him.

"You are trying my patience, Brother Demir," she said. "Pray be silent."

Demir looked at the halberd and scoffed.

"I am Living," he said. "You still walk in the Shadow. You cannot threaten me." He looked at the other prisoners. "We outnumber you four to one, Apostate. And we count more Living among our number." He turned back to Fairfax and snarled at her. "Release us or you will die."

Fairfax shook her head, almost sadly.

"I had hoped to find more wisdom in you, Brother Demir," she said. "And above all, a greater understanding of things. What good will the strength of ten men do you, Brother, if you never lift anything heavier than a book?"

With that, Fairfax spun the halberd in her hands and plunged its spear point into Demir's stomach. Demir screamed in pain, and his screams only intensified as Fairfax twisted her weapon in a circle to increase the trauma of the wound. As she pulled the spear out, Demir collapsed to his knees.

From her place of hiding, Ekaterine covered her mouth with her hands to keep from crying out. She had seen horrible violence in her lifetime—even done horrible violence, mostly in France and England during her travels with Varanus—but nothing to compare to this and never done by a Shashavani against a Shashavani.

Amid cries of shock and horror from the prisoners, Fairfax placed her boot against Demir's shoulder and pushed him until he fell back onto the ground. Demir shouted in anger and began to rise again; even in the face of such pain and trauma, the resilience of the Living was inhuman. But Fairfax was not finished. She plunged the spear into Demir again, pinning him against the floor.

"Will you yield, Brother Demir?" Fairfax asked. "Renounce the Law of Shashava and beg my mercy, and you shall have it...for I am under orders to dispense it in favor of death."

"I will do neither," Demir answered. "Kill me, if you will, but I will die with my honor intact."

Fairfax smiled. "As you wish, Brother Demir."

She pulled her halberd free of Demir's chest and took a step back. Realizing what was to come, some of the prisoners began to make movements to intervene, though Ekaterine could not imagine what they thought they could accomplish against armed men. And it made little difference, for Fairfax's soldiers kept their swords pointed at the prisoners and held them back. As scholars no longer used to violence, if it had ever been familiar to them, the prisoners lost their fire and drew back.

Fairfax raised her halberd and brought it down on Demir's neck, severing his head in a single, brutal blow. Ekaterine clenched her eyes shut at the sight, and she heard the cries of the scholars before either discipline or fear silenced them.

"Now," Fairfax said, reaching down and picking up Demir's head with her free hand, "all of you look and mark this well." She held the head out to them. "This is the price of disloyalty. Shashava is gone, the Companions are gone, and now Sophio, the eldest who remains, has left us as well. None will return to us. Now we owe our lives and allegiance to the Winter King. We owe our lives and allegiance to the new Eristavi. All who pledge their loyalty will live. Those who refuse will die like Brother Demir. Mark it well," she repeated.

Dear God, what is happening? Ekaterine thought.

"Orders, My Lady?" Jan asked Fairfax.

"Bring the prisoners to the Great Hall," Fairfax said. "If they go willingly, leave them unharmed, for they are our brothers and our sisters. Any who refuse...kill."

Jan bowed his head. "As you command." He paused and looked toward Ekaterine and the stairs. Ekaterine quickly drew back just in case, but Jan did not seem to have seen her. "What about the archives?"

"Those bookworms will remain in their caves until Judgment Day," Fairfax answered. "Place some soldiers on guard here. We will scour the archives once we return from escorting the prisoners."

"Yes, My Lady."

As Fairfax's soldiers marched the prisoners out of the library, Ekaterine withdrew to the stairs and rushed back into the archives. She had to warn the others. She did not know what was happening, but it was something and it was monstrous.

* * * *

"What you are talking about is madness!" cried Brother Petre, glaring at Ekaterine.

"If you don't believe me, walk up those stairs and look," Ekaterine replied, pointing toward the entrance. "Though you'll want to be subtle about it. They have soldiers on guard in the library."

"I don't believe a word of this," said one of the other archivists. "It's a trick. She's playing a joke on us."

Alda shook her head and stood firmly at Ekaterine's side.

"No, I believe her," she said. "Sister Ekaterine does not make up stories." She glanced at Ekaterine and amended, "Well, not stories like this."

"Your confidence is overwhelming," Ekaterine said, but it did give her the glimmer of a smile. That smile quickly faded. "Once they have taken their prisoners to the Great Hall, they will return, and they will take us as well. We must flee at once while there is still time."

"And where shall we flee to?" demanded another archivist. "If Ekaterine speaks true, the library is a trap!"

"There are other ways," Alda said. As the others looked at her curiously, she quickly added, "Other libraries that the archives connect to."

"They will be watched as well," said Petre. He seemed to slowly be coming to accept that Ekaterine may have been telling the truth. "If there is even any danger."

"They may not be," Ekaterine said. "And still, we must try. We have to escape if we can."

The archivists looked at one another, most of them still astonished at Ekaterine's story.

"What is happening?" asked Petre.

"I do not know," Ekaterine said, "but there are soldiers taking the scholars and librarians prisoner. And until we know what is happening, I would rather be out of the castle and safely in the countryside where we can hide. Wouldn't you?"

"This is all unthinkable!" Petre insisted.

"Unthinkable does not mean impossible," Ekaterine reminded him. "I know what I saw and I am leaving. And I hope that you will all have the sense to follow."

There was a lengthy silence as the archivists exchanged looks with one another.

"Which library should we use?" asked a third archivist, his voice betraying the growing panic that all of them seemed to feel.

"Not the main one, clearly," Ekaterine said, perhaps more flippantly than she ought. More gravely, she said, "I think perhaps we should split up. We'll go in groups, each one to a different exit. If we find one way barred, we'll try another, but that will give each group a chance to escape."

There was another pause. Finally Petre sighed and shook his head. "Sister Ekaterine, if this is some elaborate trick...."

"It's not, I promise you," she said.

Petre nodded. Presently, he replied, "Then I will take one group myself, and I pray to God that you and yours are delivered into safety."

* * * *

In the end, some of the archivists refused to leave, insisting that the texts could not be abandoned. Ekaterine tried to explain otherwise: the traitors, whoever they were, remained Shashavani. They would respect the sanctity of the texts even if they had no regard for the lives of those who tended them. But there were many among the archivists who simply could not imagine abandoning the books to other hands.

Ekaterine chose to depart through the cartographic library, reasoning that as it was relatively unused—expect at times of war or when a historian was curious as to a question of geography—it would be one of the last places Fairfax's soldiers would search. To her great relief, the room was empty, save for a few cartographers who quickly joined the band when alerted to the danger.

Uncertain of the extent of the threat and understanding that her followers were largely incapable of combat, Ekaterine led them away from the main rooms in the castle. She could not risk taking them through the surface gates or even the usual escape passages. Those would be known to the conspirators, and there was every possibility that they would be watched.

Instead, Ekaterine led her people downward, into the lower levels and toward the cisterns that kept the castle watered even in times of drought. There was a hidden spring there, kept safe in case of siege—though thankfully no enemy had ever breached the sanctity of the valley. As Ekaterine led her party toward one of the lesser staircases, she heard the sounds of heavy footsteps behind her. She quickened her pace until a voice called out to her:

"Sister Ekaterine! Stop!"

Ekaterine halted and looked back. She saw Jan the Hollander and a small party of soldiers hurrying in her direction. Ekaterine's followers outnumbered them, but Jan's people we armed and Ekaterine's were not.

"Brother Jan!" Ekaterine exclaimed, trying as hard as she could to sound pleased. "What are you doing here?"

Jan's hand was on his sword. Ekaterine took note of that. And his three soldiers carried muskets.

"Sister Ekaterine," Jan said to her, "I must ask you: whom do you serve?"

Oh!" Ekaterine exclaimed. She looked at Jan very seriously and repeated the words she had heard in the library: "I serve the Winter King."

At this, Jan relaxed and he smiled in surprised delight. The sight of it turned Ekaterine's stomach.

"I did not realize that you were one of us," Jan exclaimed. "This is good news." He pointed to the archivists. "And them? Shall we relieve you of their burden?"

"No!" Ekaterine exclaimed. She quickly amended, "They are with us, Brother. I have explained to them the wisdom of our cause, and they have sworn their loyalty."

Jan's eyes narrowed in disbelief. "Truly?"

"I have not explained everything, of course," Ekaterine said. "They will learn that in the Great Hall when the time comes. But they have seen wisdom in obedience, and I have found a use for them."

"Oh?"

"We go to root out anyone who may be hiding in the catacombs," Ekaterine explained.

"But you are unarmed," Jan said, frowning.

"We certainly don't plan to attack them down there," Ekaterine said quickly. "We will lure them to the main floor and let your soldiers capture them. But they will be more inclined to trust us if we approach them without weapons."

"Ah, sensible." Jan nodded.

Ekaterine motioned for Alda and the other archivists to continue onward, desperate to get them away from Jan and the soldiers without arising suspicions. But as she turned to join them, Jan caught her by the arm.

"Who authorized you to do this?" Jan asked. "By whose authority?"

Ekaterine thought for a moment, searching for someone she could name. Lady Fairfax was known to Jan, and he would doubtless know everyone who served her directly. And then Ekaterine thought of the secret meeting she had witnessed between Philippa and Zawditu. There had been evidence of conspiracy. It was the most logical thing she could put her mind to.

"We are acting under the orders of Sister Philippa," she replied.

Jan's face fell, and in that instant Ekaterine knew that she had spoken wrongly.

"Sister Philippa is not one of us," Jan said.

And Ekaterine knew that all pretense had ended.

"Run!" she shouted to Alda and the archivists.

"Stop them!" Jan ordered his soldiers.

Unable to pull away from Jan's grasp, Ekaterine grabbed the knife at Jan's belt and thrust it into his side. Jan grunted in pain and his grip slackened, but he did not let go. As Ekaterine struggled to break away, she twisted the knife and drove it in deeper. Snarling with anger, Jan struck his forehead against Ekaterine's, and Ekaterine's vision exploded into white light.

She came to moments later as she lay on the ground, dazed from the blow. Jan was next to her, bleeding as he struggled to draw the knife from his side. Dizzy, Ekaterine sat up as Jan's soldiers ran past her, shouldering their muskets. She grabbed for Jan's knife and yanked it out of him. Jan reached for her arm to stop her, but Ekaterine shoved him away and drew the weapon. Rolling over, she drove the knife into the leg of one of the soldiers as he ran past her. The man cried out and stumbled, and Ekaterine dragged him to the floor.

What followed was confusion. Amid screams and gunfire, Ekaterine stumbled to her feet and ran for the nearest soldier. She drove her knife into the woman's throat and tore the musket from her hands. Turning in place, Ekaterine shot the remaining soldier through the chest.

Breathing heavily, Ekaterine watched as the archivists fled for the nearest staircase, following the route she had laid out for them. Some part of her said that she should run to join them, but the confusion of the moment kept her in place, unable to move.

"Ekaterine!" Alda shouted, waving toward her. "Hurry!"

Shaking herself, Ekaterine broke through the confusion that clouded her mind. She had to keep moving. Jan and his soldiers were wounded, but they were not finished. And as a sudden reminder of this, Ekaterine heard a gunshot and felt warm pain in her side. She looked down and saw blood beginning to stain her dress. Stunned, Ekaterine looked back and saw Jan holding a revolver in one hand as he clutched his side.

He had shot her!

Suddenly more furious than pained, Ekaterine threw the empty musket at Jan, striking him in the head with it. Then, her good sense returning to her, she ran for the stairs and prayed silently that she would not be shot a second time.

CHAPTER FIFTEEN

In her cell, Varnaus gazed at the ceiling and sighed, feeling her will to live slipping away a fragment at a time. She had never before known such utter boredom. Even the social engagements that she had been forced to endure in her youth and during her recent visit to England had been positively fascinating by comparison.

"Do not be sad, *liebchen*," Korbinian murmured to her, stroking her hair with gentle fingers. "Only a few more months and you shall be free again."

"I am not sad," Varanus corrected. "I am despondent from inactivity."

"Oh, *liebchen*, it is agony to see you in such a state."

Varanus frowned at Korbinian sympathetically. "You could close your eyes, my love. Then you would not have to witness my pain."

"Nonsense," Korbinian said, kissing her gently. "What man could ever turn his gaze away from you?"

"Mmm." Varanus sighed again and touched Korbinian's face with her fingertips. "I sometimes think you are the only thing keeping me sane, my darling. What am I to do with such *inactivity*? They could have at least given me some books!"

"I could read to you from Shelley," Korbinian offered, producing a small book from somewhere.

"My darling Korbinian," Varanus said, staring at the ceiling again, "I think that in these past weeks you have read to me every last word that Shelley has ever written."

"Goethe, then?" Korbinian dabbed at his lips with a handkerchief to wipe away the blood that trickled from the corner of his mouth. "I do so enjoy Goethe."

"Or a pen and some paper," Varanus mused, returning to the matter of her boredom. "Imagine how much work I could be doing if they had only left me with some paper."

"My kingdom for some paper?" Korbinian asked.

"You haven't got a kingdom," Varanus reminded him. "And what's more—"

Korbinian suddenly held a finger to his lips to silence her.

"Do you hear something, *liebchen?*"

Varanus tilted her head and listened carefully. The cell walls were thick and solid, as much to keep out noise as to keep the penitents in. After all, the Shashavani so confined were there for "meditation" and "quiet introspection", Iosef had insisted, not for penal incarceration; though in truth, Varanus found the one to be much the same as the other. But despite the thickness of the walls and the door, she did seem to hear the very faint sounds of voices speaking and footfalls approaching her cell.

A moment later she heard a muffled scream from the corridor before it was almost as quickly silenced. This made her sit up in alarm, and Korbinian placed a hand on her shoulder to comfort her—though in truth, as blood trickled from the corners of his eyes and mouth, he was perhaps less comforting than he intended.

"What is going on?" Varanus wondered aloud.

"Who can say?" Korbinian replied. "But if I were to place a wager, I would say we are about to have company." He quickly wiped the blood from his face to make himself more presentable.

"That is not at all reassuring," Varanus told him.

"I am doing my best, *liebchen*, under rather trying circumstances."

"Of course."

Varanus crossed the room and place her ear against the door in the hopes of hearing what was happening.

"Listening at keyholes are we?" Korbinian asked from the opposite corner. Varanus had not seen him cross the room, but such a thing was hardly unusual for him.

"Hush."

At first Varanus could hear nothing. It seemed that the earlier commotion had ended, but this only made Varanus nervous. Screams followed by silence were never a good thing. But a few moments later, she heard the footsteps again, this time approaching her cell. And she also heard two voices speaking:

"—convert this one as well?" asked the first voice, which was gravelly and rough.

"I think not," replied a second. After a few moments, Varanus recognized it as belonging to Brother Teimuraz, lately returned from his sojourn in Turkestan. "She is a child, not even past her century. She is not worth the trouble."

Varanus froze as the voices reached her cell, and she heard the bolt being turned back.

"Besides, she is of Iosef and Iosef is of Sophio. We can neither use her nor trust her. Better to dispose of the unwanted now when it will be easier to manage."

Varanus looked at Korbinian, her eyes wide, her hands shaking. They were going to murder her! She had spent weeks in isolation, starved of both food and books, and now she was going to be murdered before she was given a reprieve of either!

"I think perhaps you should kill them, *liebchen*," Korbinian said to her, leaning against the wall and folding his arms. "Indeed, I am certain of it."

The door opened and Teimuraz rushed into the room, followed by a large man clad in mail. Both men had swords drawn. They advanced a few paces into the cell before realizing that the bed was empty. Before they could turn, Varanus struck.

There was no point in fleeing, she knew: they were far taller and would simply run her down in the hallway. Instead, she advanced on them and lashed out at Teimuraz's companion, reckoning him—as the larger of the two—to be the greater threat. Before either man had time to react, Varanus drove her foot against the big fellow's knee with enough force to break the joint. Caught by surprise, the man made a noise and fell to the ground.

Of course, he was not out of the fight, not by any measure. He was among the Living, and his leg would be whole again before long. But capitalizing on her moment of surprise, Varanus stomped on the man's hand with as much force as she could manage and then tore the sword from his grasp.

Though startled by the ambush, Teimuraz recovered quickly and lunged at Varanus. Varanus parried his blows as best she could manage, but despite surprise and overconfidence, Teimuraz still knew his business. As Varanus fell back under the blows, she felt her enemy's sword score cuts upon her face, arms, and even her sides. But the pain only served to fuel Varanus's fervor until whiteness rimmed her vision, and she could see little but the flashing swords, the blood, and Teimuraz's face.

Unable to match the speed of Teimuraz's sword-thrusts, it occurred to Varanus not to try. Instead, as Teimuraz lunged at her again, Varanus stepped forward onto the point of his sword, plunging it into her belly. The pain made her shudder, and she saw Korbinian standing behind Teimuraz, his face and clothes stained with blood.

"Oh *liebchen*," Korbinian said sadly, "how we suffer to survive."

Teimuraz snarled at Varanus, shouting obscenities as he struggled to pull his weapon free from her, but Varanus did not give him the opportunity. She twisted from side to side to break her enemy's hold on the sword as she stabbed him again and again with her own weapon. Finally,

Teimuraz let go and struck Varanus on the side of the head, pitching her into the wall.

Stunned for a moment, Varanus still managed to keep her feet. Teimuraz evidently did not expect her to recover from her injuries, and he turned to help his injured comrade.

"Now, *liebchen!*" Korbinian shouted. "Now!"

He was right. Varanus saw her opportunity and took it. She stumbled forward and stabbed the man on the floor through his throat to properly immobilize him. Teimuraz dropped his comrade's arm and stared dumbstruck at Varanus. He had evidently underestimated how much trauma could be withstood by one still within her century.

Varanus did not give him time to recover his wits. She grabbed Teimuraz by the collar and drove the point of her sword up through his chin and into his skull. Teimuraz gurgled something incoherent and shook, his body uncertain of how to respond to the confusion in his traumatized brain. Varanus let him fall to the ground before she too collapsed.

She was not certain when she regained her senses, but it could not have been long. Her body ached from the sword, but her other wounds were slowly closing. Very slowly, however: starvation was a cruel mistress to the healing process.

Teimuraz and the other man were still on the floor, but Varanus could not tell if they were alive or dead: the damage might have been enough, or they might recover. Only a proper beheading would make their deaths certain.

Korbinian knelt before her and smiled. He was still covered in blood, but under the circumstances Varanus could not fault him for it. Korbinian took her hands and placed them on the hilt of the sword.

"Let us attend to this," he said, "before it becomes any worse."

"This will hurt," Varanus replied, grimacing.

"More than it does already?"

Varanus gritted her teeth and closed her eyes. She took a breath, which hurt tremendously, and drew the sword from her body.

It was horribly painful and her head swam but somehow she managed it. When the sword had been removed, Varanus fell back against the wall and gasped for air. She didn't need it, of course, but somehow breathing seemed to make her feel better.

Presently, her body had mended itself well enough for her to rise again. Teimuraz was still on the ground, but the other man was beginning to move and groan, his throat almost intact. Varanus decided it was prudent to attend to both of them just in case.

When she had beheaded them, Varanus took up one of the swords and stumbled out into the hallway. The passage was empty, though there was blood on the stone floor. Several of the cells were open, and a look confirmed that they were empty. The other prisoners—"penitents"—had been taken somewhere, while Varanus alone had been selected for death.

She wasn't sure whether to be flattered or offended. Probably offended. Teimuraz had spoken of her youth so derisively, after all.

"What is going on?" she asked aloud.

"I cannot say, *liebchen*," Korbinian answered from behind her. "But I will tell you this: I would feel much more comfortable with a shotgun. Or possibly an elephant gun."

Varanus thought for a moment and nodded. It was a sensible enough plan. Granted, the recent violence and head trauma may have affected her, but more weapons did sound prudent, at least until they knew what was going on.

"We shall go the Luka's chamber," she told Korbinian. "He'll doubtless have several."

"And after that?"

Varanus cracked her neck and replied, "After that, we are going to find Ekaterine, give her something to shoot with, and sort all this out."

* * * *

Varanus hurried toward the upper levels, Korbinian following a few paces behind her and remarking on what he called the "manifold similarities" between Varanus's circumstances and the story of William Tell. Varanus was inclined to disagree, but as Korbinian was bleeding profusely all over the brocade carpets, she felt inclined not to mention it.

She had hoped that after escaping the dungeons she might have some better sense of what was going on, that there might be someone from whom she could demand an explanation. But there was not. The corridors of the castle seemed largely empty, though here and there she came across marks of blood and violence that led her to believe that the recent attempt upon her life was not altogether unique.

Most troubling, she thought, as she passed through one of the empty kitchens and helped herself to some roasted lamb, which was still sitting on a spit over one of the hearths. The kitchen staff, however, was nowhere to be seen. Varanus had no idea what to make of it.

Her concern only grew as she came upon a trio of bodies—two scholars and a soldier whom she recognized as Yevgeni of Pskov, one of Magnus's many fencing partners. They were all hideously brutalized with the blows of swords and axes, and strangely they had also been shot through with arrows.

"Archery at close quarters?" Varanus mused, studying the scene.

"Perhaps the arrows were meant to drive them in here," Korbinian noted, pointing to the room, which stood adjacent to the corridor, "where they could be massacred at leisure."

Varanus shook her head. "How monstrous. Who would do this?"

"Who can say?" Korbinian answered. "But it is certainly violence. Something is amiss. If you'll forgive my saying so, something is rotten in the House of Shashava."

"I think that Shakespeare is hardly appropriate at such a time," Varanus told him.

Korbinian looked at the bodies upon the floor.

"I would consider him more than usually appropriate under the circumstances," he remarked.

"We *must* find Ekaterine before something happens to her," Varanus said, suddenly very worried for her friend's safety. "I only wish that Lord Iosef were here."

"For protection?" Korbinian asked, sounding astonished at the very suggestion that Varanus might need it.

"Don't be silly," Varanus replied. "I want to explain to him what's happened, so I don't get in trouble for killing people." She took a deep breath and sighed. "I rather suspect there's going to be more of that before the day is out. I'd prefer for there to be someone who takes my plea of self defense seriously."

"More killing, *liebchen?* Surely not—"

Korbinian was interrupted as a young woman dressed in dark robes ran into the room and pressed herself up against the wall. Her eyes were wide with fear, and she looked on the verge of panic. It took Varanus a few moments, but she recognized the woman as Judith ben Loew, who in her mortality had disguised herself as a man in order to study under the great Rabbi Loew of Prague.

"Doctor Varanus?" Judith exclaimed, startled at the sight of her.

"Rabbi," Varanus replied, nodding in greeting. Though Judith's title of teacher had been obtained while in her guise as a man—Judah ben Loew—by the laws of the Shashavani, it was hers to claim. "Hello?"

Varanus did not know what else to say.

"Doctor, what are you doing here?" Judith asked.

"I...um..." Varanus stammered.

"Did he see you come in here?"

"No, of course not. I—" Varanus suddenly stopped and looked back toward the door, realizing something. It had been almost half an hour since she had killed Teimuraz. He could not be the one that Judith was fleeing. "Rabbi...who is chasing you?"

Judith was breathless with fear as she replied, "Brother Thoros—"

She was interrupted as a voice called from the corridor, "Where are you?" It was a man's voice speaking in a mirthful, singsong manner. "Come out, come out, wherever you are...."

"He's found us!" Judith hissed, her face pale with fear—or possibly blood loss.

Varanus ran to the door and looked out into the corridor. She saw a huge man dressed in silken robes walking in their direction, though he was still some distance away. He was a member of Sophio's Council, though which one she could not clearly place. She was cross with all of them for having placed her in confinement, and that anger made them all more or less run together into a collective mass. The man was covered in blood, and Varanus recognized his expression as one of delight at the very prospect of violence. He carried a composite bow of Shashavani make, a weapon so powerful that only the Living had the strength to draw it.

"That explains that," Korbinian noted, nodding toward the corpses and the arrows in them.

Varanus looked around the room. It was a simple antechamber for reading and discourse. If Thoros cornered them in there, there would be no escape.

"We must run," she said, nodding toward the corridor.

"Agreed," said Judith. She glanced through the doorway. "He's not looking. Go now!"

Varanus glanced into the corridor and saw that Judith was right: Thoros had turned to look behind himself, his whole attitude leisurely and disinterested. The thought of such a casual regard for impending slaughter made Varanus sick, though at the same time she felt some strange appreciation for it.

With Judith close behind her, Varanus dashed into the corridor and ran along it as quickly as she could manage. Judith's stride threatened to outpace her, but the woman grabbed Varanus by the hand and tried to keep pace, despite the danger. Varanus appreciated the gesture, though as she ran, sword in hand, she felt that it was somewhat unnecessary. She had half a mind to turn and face Thoros, to vent upon him the totality of her anger; but she realized that, old as he was, he would probably kill her in the struggle, so she restrained the urge.

The corridor turned sharply to the right, and Varanus bolted in that direction. She felt pain blossom in the area of her shoulder, but she ignored it. As Judith turned into the adjacent passage with her, the woman gasped in horror.

"Doctor Varanus!" she exclaimed.

Varanus paused and looked over her shoulder to see that an arrow had been shot into it and now sat lodged just below her shoulder blade. It hurt horribly, and the pain only increased as she looked at it and allowed herself to realize the extent of the damage.

What a damned nuisance, she thought.

"Rabbi, forgive my asking," she said, "but would you kindly...?"

Judith grimaced at the idea, her expression filled with sympathy for Varanus's pain.

"Doctor...?"

"Now, please," Varanus said. "We have no time."

Judith gritted her teeth and, with a few short, painful tugs, pulled the arrow from Varanus's flesh.

"Are you well, Doctor?" she asked when it had been done.

"I am in pain and hungry," Varanus answered, shuddering as she spoke. "I think that 'well' is no longer an option."

She took Judith by the hand, and they kept on running toward a gallery that overlooked one of the dining halls. Glancing back, Varanus saw Thoros meander into the passage behind them, stringing another arrow to his bow. Again, his movements were utterly relaxed, like a gentleman out hunting grouse.

Varanus and Judith ran on, but Varanus knew that it would only be a matter of moments before they were shot again. She glanced to the side and saw Korbinian running with them.

"What you require, *liebchen*," he said, "is a friend of considerably more years than you."

Before Varanus could reply, she saw a figure step out into the corridor in front of them. Varanus stumbled and very nearly collided with the newcomer, a woman of small stature, only slightly taller than she. Judith skidded to a halt as well and froze in place.

"Sister Marie!" she exclaimed.

It was another one of Sophio's advisors, Marie of Toulouse. Varanus halted at this realization. Was Marie going to try to murder her as well? It seemed a bit excessive, considering that she had only stolen some water.

Marie looked at them, startled, and then turned her gaze toward Thoros as he rounded the corner, bow in hand.

"Run," she said. "Get to the countryside. Now!"

Thoros raised his bow and took aim. Varanus grabbed Judith and bolted toward a set of stairs that led down into the dining hall below them. She expected Thoros's arrow to strike one of them at any moment. When it did not, she paused a moment and looked back.

She saw Marie shudder violently as Thoros's arrow struck her in the head. Varanus winced, anticipating the pain of such an injury. She expected Marie to fall, but the woman did not. Instead, she turned toward them, the arrow protruding from where it had lodged in her right eye.

"I told you to *run!*" Marie shouted at them as she pulled the arrow free. Having given her command again, she turned back toward Thoros and charged him.

Varanus knew better than to linger. She grabbed Judith again and ran to the stairs. Behind them, she heard the sounds of battle and the pained cries of both Marie and Thoros. Varanus felt a twinge of guilt at fleeing. She still had Teimuraz's sword. Perhaps she should turn and join the fight?

Korbinian appeared in the doorway ahead of her.

"*Liebchen*, be reasonable," he said. "Sister Marie is six hundred years old. Sister Judith is three hundred, and you are not even one! One suspects that there is little you can do that Marie cannot. And besides, you must find your friend. God knows what may have happened to her."

He was right about that. Varanus gritted her teeth and kept on running. She hiked up her skirts and hurried down the stairs alongside Judith. On the floor below, they broke out into the dinning hall with its long tables and rows of candelabra, their candles unlit. For the first time since fleeing her cell, Varanus realized that it was daytime. That was a problem. The old could escape into the countryside without fear, but the young would burn in the light.

Varanus would burn in the light.

These musings were suddenly interrupted as a body fell from above and crashed onto one of the candelabra. Varanus jumped in surprise, a motion mimicked by Judith. Turning, she saw Marie lying face-up atop the iron candleholder, its points driven into her back from the force of the fall.

Judith cried out, covering her mouth with her hands. Varanus cringed at the sight, having some idea of how it must have felt; for she knew, however damaging, such injury had not killed Marie.

A few moments later, Marie's eye opened, and she looked around in confusion. Presently, she turned her gaze toward Varanus and Judith.

"I am upside-down," she said, rather matter-of-factly.

"That would not be inaccurate, My Lady," Varanus said.

Marie looked around for a moment, struggling to get her bearings. She also struggled to move, which proved far less effective.

"What have I fallen onto?" she finally asked.

"A candelabrum," Judith said, her expression still horrified by the sight.

"Could you...help me off it?" Marie asked, her tone so detached that it was almost as horrible as the sight of injury.

Varanus and Judith each did their best to lift Marie from the spikes of the candelabrum, but they had twisted into Marie's flesh and would not let her go. Varanus looked up and saw Thoros standing on the balcony above them, grinning cruelly. He reached for a fresh arrow but found his quiver empty. Laughing, he lowered his bow, drew his sword, and began walking toward the stairs.

The sheer nonchalance with which Thoros carried himself infuriated Varanus. He was so confident in his ability to slaughter them all with ease that he did not even feel the need to hurry after them. Arrogance was a vice that Varanus had little patience for, especially when it was directed against her.

"I have an idea," she said to Judith. "Help me."

"Whatever it is, hurry," Marie told them. "If I am to die today, I will do it fighting, not stuck atop a decorative candleholder."

"Or course," Varanus said. After all, it was an attitude with which she personally agreed.

At Varanus's direction, she and Judith tipped the candelabrum onto its side. Marie sighed in irritation at the ignominy of it, but she did not complain. Bracing her foot against Marie's shoulder, Varanus gave the candelabrum a heave, and together she and Judith tore it from Marie's back.

Throughout the ordeal, Marie did not make a sound, which unnerved Varanus considerably.

When it was done, Judith helped Marie to stand. Marie rolled her shoulder and winced ever so slightly.

"That was uncomfortable," she remarked.

"So I would imagine," Varanus said.

The three of them turned and saw Thoros emerge from the stairway, sword in hand.

"I think we are in for a fight," Judith said, her voice quivering ever so slightly. As one of the scholars, she was unaccustomed to violence.

"No," Marie corrected, "*I* am in for a fight. Neither of you is old enough to face him." She glanced at Varanus and held out her hand. "Sword."

Varanus made a displeased noise and hesitated. She had no wish to be disarmed, not at such a time. But finally, she acquiesced and handed her sword to Marie.

"You can always get another one, *liebchen*," Korbinian reminded her, as he reclined on one of the tables. "If the world has gone mad and everyone is killing one another, there shall be no shortage of swords to be had, surely."

"Now," Marie said to them, as she stepped into Thoros's path, "I think it would be best if you left. Get out of the castle if you can. If you cannot, then hide. And may God be with you."

With that, Marie raised her sword and charged forward to meet Thoros as he ran at them, grinning gleefully, his own sword upraised. Varanus hesitated a moment more before good sense took her, and she fled with Judith into the depths of the castle.

CHAPTER SIXTEEN

At Zawditu's instruction, Luka led the Council members along a meandering path through the castle, bypassing any areas that could be used to stage an ambush. There was no way of knowing whom Margaret had recruited, and they could not afford to be reckless. Along they way they ran across groups of soldiers and scholars. At first none of them seemed any the wiser as to what was happening, but soon the Shashavani they encountered were panicked, fleeing from violence that had begun to break out all across the castle. It seemed that the conspirators had arranged for their coup to take place everywhere at once.

Anyone who proved peaceful was absorbed into the band; any who attempted violence or were in the midst of violently subduing others were immediately subdued themselves. Luka felt misgivings about being surrounded by men and women who might be in league with Margaret, but Zawditu was adamant: while their first duty was the safety of the Council, they were also responsible for the protection of the Order's civilians. Zawditu would not allow the one duty to undermine the other.

Along the way, their numbers had fluctuated. They had been separated from Marie of Toulouse in fighting near the armory and from Reza of Samarkand as they passed close to the Great Hall, which the conspirators seemed determined to occupy. Both were presumed dead. In addition, some two-dozen survivors had either been killed or lost in the confusion.

Luka marched at the head of the column with Zawditu, who refused every one of Luka's suggestions that she travel in the middle of the group with the Council members. Luka had not expected anything else, but he would have failed in his duty had he not suggested it. Still, the general of the Shashavani would not, it seemed, stand anywhere but at the head of her troops.

As they approached the gate leading to the western courtyard, Luka saw five guardsmen in armor and bearing muskets who barred their way. The guards quickly raised their weapons and took aim at the company bearing down upon them, but they hesitated at the sight of Zawditu.

"Hold!" Zawditu shouted. With Luka and Seteney beside her, she approached with a hand raised. "To whom are you loyal?"

The guards seemed surprised at the question, and their sergeant took a step forward in reply, bowing his head.

"To you, Strategos," he replied, "and to the Eristavi." He looked at the crowd again, his expression one of astonishment. "My Lady, what is happening?"

"A matter that shall be explained in time," Zawditu told him. "If you are loyal, throw down your arms and surrender to me. Now."

The sergeant hesitated a moment but quickly nodded and motioned to his troops. "Do as the Strategos says."

Still confused, the guards nevertheless began to disarm, placing their muskets on the ground and unbuckling their sword belts. All save one, who, after a moment of uncertainty, shouldered his weapon and leveled it at Zawditu.

"For the Winter King!" he cried just before he fired.

It was Seteney who reacted the fastest. As the guardsman raised his weapon, she drew her revolver and fired it twice, shooting the man in the chest. He jerked from the force of the bullets as they burst through his mail, and his shot went off-target, slicing past Zawditu's temple and leaving a shallow graze in its wake.

A moment later, Luka charged forward and grabbed the guardsman, slamming him into the wall. He gave the traitor a few solid blows to be sure the man was down and left him to bleed out on the floor.

"How are you, Strategos?" Luka asked, returning to Zawditu.

Blood was trickling down the side of Zawditu's face from her wound, but she seemed more irritated than pained. Though the sight of the injury worried Luka, it was probably one of the least serious wounds Zawditu had ever suffered.

"Well enough that you should not bother me with such questions," Zawditu replied, though the corner of her mouth showed the hint of a smile at Luka's concern.

The sergeant of the guards took a step toward them, his face pale at what had just happened. At his movement, both Luka and Seteney turned on him and readied their weapons.

"Strategos," the sergeant said, "I swear to you I had no knowledge of this. We are loyal, I promise you!"

"Of course you are," Zawditu said. "Were you traitors, you all would have shot at me as well, and I suspect one at least would have inconvenienced me with a proper wound." She took a moment to study each of the soldiers and nodded. "Pick up your arms and your new prisoner. We are departing and you are coming with us."

"Yes, Strategos!" the sergeant answered, relieved at her reply. He and one of the other guards grabbed the traitor and hauled him up from the ground. "On your feet, dog!" he shouted at the man.

Zawditu raised her hand and motioned for the group to follow her.

"Onward!" she shouted. "And my soldiers: keep a wary eye."

"Yes, Strategos!" they all shouted.

Zawditu led them out into the courtyard, flanked by Luka and Seteney. In the distance they heard the sound of gunfire, but Luka could not clearly place where it came from. The air was cold and dry, and it was almost painful to breathe. Snow covered the ground, but it was pale and bloodless. The fighting had not yet reached that part of the castle, and Luka was thankful for it.

Many of the Living hesitated at the doorway, fearful of the sunlight. Those young enough to be hurt by it concealed themselves as best they could beneath their clothes. In a show of kindness, those in the Shadow and the Living who no longer feared the sun, stripped off their coats and outer robes and gave them to their comrades.

Suddenly, a party of Shashavani came through the passage from an adjoining court, all armed and many armored. At their head was a member of the Living dressed in scholar's clothes but carrying one of Luka's Maxim guns, which she quickly turned toward them. They were all covered in blood, and several were wounded as well. Again, many of the Living were huddled together, shrouded against the touch of the sun.

"Identify yourselves!" the scholar shouted as her warrior companions took aim.

"Fools!" Luka answered. "Do you not recognize your own Strategos?"

Several of the soldiers began to lower their weapons in realization, while others seemed unsure. But the scholars—the woman armed with the Maxim gun and the robed academics behind her—still seemed doubtful, even fearful.

"The Master-At-Arms sought our blood! Why should it be different with the General?"

This caused a commotion among the crowd, and someone began shoving her way forward through the scholars, shouting:

"Because she is the Strategos!"

It was Mata Kaur, armed for war and drenched in blood. As she pushed past the Living scholar, she placed a hand on the Maxim gun's barrel and forced the weapon down.

"If anyone is loyal, *she* is loyal," Mata Kaur said firmly. "And I would rather die than suspect her of treason."

Zawditu smiled and motioned for Luka and the others to lower their weapons. She walked toward Mata Kaur, who met her midway across the courtyard and saluted with her sword. Zawditu nodded in reply, visibly pleased by the reunion with her aide-de-camp, and the two of them motioned for their parties to converge in the courtyard.

"Come along," Luka told the soldiers around him. "Let's be quick about it."

The two groups slowly approached one another, suspicious at first, but soon the tension dwindled as friends and comrades began to recognize each other and embraced one another with relief. Luka quickly joined Zawditu and Mata Kaur, followed by Seteney and the surviving members of the Council.

"Are you well, Strategos?" Mata Kaur asked as Luka arrived alongside them.

Zawditu wiped blood from her temple and replied, "Nothing I cannot manage. Though we have many wounded. It has been a bad day." There was a pause and she asked, "And you? Any injured?"

"Several," Mata Kaur answered. Indeed, from the way she carried her left arm—and from the blood tricking from beneath her sleeve—Luka saw that she was among them. "We must find healers, and quickly."

"We will go to the town across the river," Zawditu said. "We can fortify our position, tend the wounded, feed the hungry, and plan what is to be done next. Spread the word."

This had been addressed to Luka as well as to Mata Kaur, and they both nodded.

"Yes, Strategos," came the mutual reply.

There was a pause as Mata Kaur relayed the new plan to the soldiers beside her before she turned back to Zawditu and asked:

"What if there are other loyalists still inside?"

"I am certain that there are," Zawditu replied. She kept her expression calm and her tone matter-of-fact, but Luka could sense her anger at the prospect of abandoning them. "But we have with us a great mob already. Let us get them to safety and see what can be done."

As the command was spread throughout the crowd, Zawditu, Luka, and Mata Kaur began marching toward the outer gate, flanked by soldiers who stood ready in case the conspiracy had turned the outer guards as well.

"What of the Council?" Mata Kaur asked as they walked, blood from her wounded arm trickling onto the snow. "I see only four."

Zawditu grimaced and answered, "Sister Marie and Brother Reza were lost in the escape. I do not know their fate."

"And the others, Strategos?" Mata Kaur's tone was dark, as if she already suspected the truth but found it too horrible to assume.

"Margaret of the Hebrides, Thoros of Yerevan, Caroline of Burgundy, and Iese of Kartli are all traitors to the House of Shashava," Zawditu said grimly. "It was they who engineered this madness, who directed our brethren to slaughter their own. And they shall be punished for it."

Mata Kaur nodded, her own expression as grim as Zawditu's. "Fairfax has turned against us," she said. "We skirmished near the conservatory and I saw her directing the troops sent against us."

"Boris of Moskva as well," said Luka. The betrayal of his old friend still made him hot with rage. "I suspect it was through him that Fairfax and her soldiers were turned."

"No doubt," agreed Zawditu.

"Strategos," said Mata Kaur, "I was twice attacked by assassins among those I sought to rescue. One of them...." She tried to move her left arm to signify the injury, and the difficulty of it made her point just as clearly.

"Myself as well," Zawditu replied. "Only once, thankfully, to no effect."

Luka coughed a little as Zawditu continued to dismiss her own injuries.

"How are we...." Mata Kaur quickly lowered her voice to a whisper, though it was a whisper loud of enough to include Luka. "How are we to trust our own people?"

"Leave that to me," Zawditu said.

* * * *

They made for the town directly across the river from the castle, arriving with such haste and in such condition that the townsfolk rushed from their houses to see what was happening. It was not common for groups of Shashavani to walk among mortals except in grave circumstances. One or two visiting the elders or scholars of the village was one thing, but a veritable army of soldiers and refugees was cause for astonishment, or even fear.

The town was well chosen. Aside from its closeness, it was also the largest settlement in the valley, arguably a small city, with stone walls and fortifications and many towers. During warmer months, traders from the other villages would converge there to sell their wares, and it was from here that the valley's merchants would venture down from the mountains to trade with the outside world. This was also the seat of the mortal government where the elders of the valley would meet to discuss matters of importance, which were then sent as petitions to the castle.

Zawditu left Luka in charge of overseeing things while she and Mata Kaur went to explain their situation to the town elders. Though he disliked being dismissed from Zawditu's company, Luka attended to his task with all diligence, directing the soldiers to assemble in the town square to take stock of their arms and condition. The wounded were sent to be seen by the town healers, aided by the twelve doctors counted among the ranks of the rescued scholars. By the time Zawditu and Mata Kaur returned, the chaotic mob had been set into some sort of order. Zawditu was pleased enough to give Luka a smile of approval, which he rather enjoyed receiving.

Once the wounded had been tended, Zawditu ordered every able-bodied Shashavani to join her in the square in the shadow of an overhanging roof that shielded the Living from daylight. She reported that the town elders had upheld their oath of loyalty to the Shashavani and would stand firm behind the Council until the matter of insurrection had been dealt with. But though this news was pleasing, Luka noticed uncertainty in the eyes of the townsfolk. It was only a small step from insurrection to civil war. While none of the valley people had seen the great war of Basileios's rebellion, they knew the stories. Violence within the House of Shashava might easily fall upon them as well.

But Zawditu reported only the good news, wisely keeping the spirits of the survivors high for the present time. Then, after confirming that she and the Army stood fully behind Philippa and the other loyalist Council members, her expression became grimmer and she said:

"And now, let us address the matter all of us are thinking about, but none of us wishes to say. The House of Shashava has been disrupted by rebellion not by chance but through willful conspiracy to overthrow the Eristavi, her advisors, and the very Laws of Shashava."

There were a few gasps of horror at this suggestion, but most of the Shashavani were silent. They already knew as much or had guessed it.

"There is," Zawditu continued, "the possibility that some among us have entered into this conspiracy and may be waiting to carry out some other act of treachery. We all know this, and many of you may already suspect your neighbors of plots and schemes." She paused. "But it will do us no good to panic in this manner nor to let our imaginations run wild with the suspicion that our neighbors and friends may be plotting against us. I expect every one of you to remain calm and rational during this time of trial."

Luka glanced at the Council members who sat behind Zawditu, watching both her and the crowd. The snow had begun falling again, though only lightly. A dusting of it now covered their heads and their clothes, but as was often the case with the Living, they showed no sign of noticing. They had all recovered from the injuries with the typical speed of the Shashavani, even Philippa, once Margaret's sword had been removed from her heart.

In the square, Zawditu continued:

"If there are any among you who have joined this conspiracy, who have pledged their loyalty to Margaret the Hebridean, the so-called 'Winter King', mark me now. The Laws of Shashava speak to us of mercy, and I intend to show that mercy now. If you have committed no crime save to join in this plot, I hereby absolve you of your treason. You shall not be punished for it."

This statement brought murmurs of shock from the assembled Shashavani, and the Council members began to exchange looks and mutter to one another. Rusudan and Xasan both began to stand and exclaim in protest, interrupting Zawditu. But just as quickly, and with some unspoken accord, Lakshmi placed her hands on their shoulders and forced them to sit while Philippa stood instead. Zawditu turned to look at them.

"Does the Council wish to comment on the matter?" Zawditu asked.

"The Council agrees with and confirms your judgment, Strategos," Philippa said, smiling slightly and bowing her head. "Mercy is just, and division will do us more harm than good."

"Thank you, Sister Philippa," Zawditu said. She turned back to the crowd and explained her decision. "We have already suffered much at the hands of this conspiracy. I will not see this Winter King sow chaos and discord among us as well. So I say again, if there are any among you whose crime of treason is no greater than to plot and scheme, I absolve you of it now. Rejoin your sisters and brothers, and do not stray from the path of wisdom again.

"But mark me: if any of you continues to aid this conspiracy, if any of you raises a hand against your brethren, or betrays this trust to our enemies...." Zawditu paused and her gaze traveled across the crowd, giving the impression that she was looking at each and every one of them individually. "Then I will execute you personally."

The crowd was silent at Zawditu's words, perhaps struck dumb with fear. Certainly, it was a promise that she could easily carry out if she chose. But presently Luka noticed a sense of relief creeping throughout the assembled Shashavani. In one stroke, Zawditu had both relieved them of their urge for paranoia and assured them that they would be protected against further betrayal. And she had granted a means of escape to any conspirators who might now doubt their allegiance but would otherwise feel they had no choice but to continue or face death.

Suddenly, Luka caught sight of a dark shape moving against the snow-covered riverbank. Turning, he strained his eyes until he realized that it was a crowd of people pulling themselves out of the frozen river.

Was it an attack? But surely not. No sensible enemy would seek to invade a fortified town in daylight after swimming through icy water.

More survivors! he realized.

"Seteney!" he exclaimed, his tone urgent but still quiet enough not to interrupt the Strategos. "With me." He pointed to a group of soldiers. "You, you, you, follow."

Without another word, he ran for the riverside gate and down the stone steps that led to the embankment. Some of the town guards noticed him run past and joined him. As he drew near, he saw dozens of sodden, freezing scholars helping one another out of the river. There were some Living among them, but most still walked in the Shadow of Death, and they would soon be in its darkness if they were not brought someplace warm.

Their leader was a woman who stood on the riverside pulling the stragglers out of the water. She was bleeding from a wound in her side, and she seemed on the verge of collapse. As she turned, Luka realized it was Ekaterine.

"Cousin!" he shouted, running toward her.

"Luka!" Ekaterine exclaimed, her voice as excited as it was weak. She waved to him in greeting. "Oh, I think I'm going to—"

Luka reached Ekaterine just in time to catch her as she collapsed.

"Seteney, get everyone indoors!" he shouted.

"Sir," Seteney answered, before barking orders to the guardsmen and to whichever scholars seemed well enough to help the others.

Luka lifted Ekaterine into his arms. Ekaterine blinked a few times and smiled at him.

"You're carrying me," she said, "like you did when I was a little girl."

"Not so little anymore," Luka noted, carrying her back toward the town. "You have been eating too many English scones."

"Hush," Ekaterine replied, weakly poking him with her finger. "There's no such thing."

Luka frowned. "You've been shot."

"Not badly."

"Who are all these people with you?" Luka asked.

"Archivists," Ekaterine said. "And some others I met on the way."

"You got all these people out?"

"Mother always said I was clever," Ekaterine told him, smirking as best she could.

"You need a doctor," Luka said.

"Nonsense," Ekaterine protested. "What I need is a warm glass of…." Suddenly she opened her eyes wide. "Doctor! Varanus is still in there! We must help her!"

"Cousin—" Luka began, trying to calm her.

"*I* must help her!" Ekaterine cried, her voice weak from blood loss and exhaustion. Slowly her eyes began to flutter. "But I'm so sleepy."

"Stay awake, Cousin," Luka urged her as he ran through the snow. "Stay awake. We'll attend to the Doctor as soon as you're well. But you must stay awake!"

Ekaterine slowly nodded and forced her eyes open. She seemed strengthened by the notion that she had to remain awake to save Varanus. At least that was something, though it pained Luka to lie to his cousin.

After all, he thought, if Varanus still lived, she was trapped in her cell unable to escape. If she was not already dead, she soon would be.

CHAPTER SEVENTEEN

Varanus had no knowledge of what Luka thought about her chances for survival, which was just as well: had she known, she would have been very angry with him. Instead, she ran through the corridors of the castle alongside Judith, pausing at intersections and ducking into side rooms to avoid detection. She could not know for certain who else might be in league with Thoros and Teimuraz; lacking that knowledge, she resolved not to be seen by anyone she did not trust implicitly, and that was a very short list.

Above all, she had to find Ekaterine.

And of course, there was the looming threat of Thoros following some uncertain distance behind them. Varanus's ears twitched at every creak of a floorboard or a door, fearing that it might be the madman who had finally run them to ground.

As they continued along, Varanus found further signs of violence: bloodstains on the carpet, arrows and sword-marks in the woodwork, and corpses upon the floor. But for all the bodies, Varanus knew that they were too few for the violence inflicted. The dead may have been heavily outmatched yet still managed to do severe damage to their assailants, or it could have been that many of the victims survived and were taken elsewhere. But that latter possibility did not give Varanus any relief.

"Perhaps this was a kidnapping, *liebchen*," Korbinian suggested, as he ran along beside her. "The dead may have resisted. Perhaps that is why they were killed."

That made a degree of sense, Varanus thought, but it did not answer everything. Why take so many people prisoner? The halls were all but deserted. *Something* had happened to the Shashavani.

"Thoros tried to murder us," she said aloud, forgetting herself. "As did Teimuraz. This is not only about taking prisoners."

"Teimuraz tried to kill you?" Judith asked. "I thought it was only Thoros!"

Varanus silently scolded herself for addressing Korbinian aloud.

"Yes," she said. "In my cell."

"Horrible," Judith replied, scowling. "I wonder how deeply this goes." She paused as another thought came to her. "You were in a cell? You never seemed the meditative sort to me, Doctor Varanus, if you will pardon my saying so."

Varanus was silent, surprised by the question. How could Judith not have known of her confinement?

"*Liebchen*," Korbinian said to her, sounding only slightly disappointed, "surely few among the Shashavani have any care for the dealings of the Council, save for when they themselves are affected by it. I doubt that even half the Order knew of your crime, and most will have forgotten it by now. And certainly, those that do recall it will have far more with which to concern themselves at the moment."

No doubt he was right.

"Yes," Varanus told Judith, "Lord Iosef thought it would be constructive for me to spend some time isolated from the world."

Judith merely nodded and said nothing.

They continued on toward the upper floors. Varanus remained set on her plan to arm herself from Luka's private arsenal and then find Ekaterine. Judith seemed intent merely on keeping ahead of Thoros, and she made little comment on what direction they went.

After a time they passed along one of the upper galleries overlooking the Great Hall. Looking down, Varanus saw a tremendous crowd of people all clustered in the center of the room, surrounded by soldiers who kept them trapped in place with a wall of spears. There were both Living Shashavani and those of the Shadow in the crowd and among the soldiers. And, Varanus realized, the division was not purely soldier-scholar. There were robed academics among the guards and disarmed warriors among the prisoners.

At the sight, Judith gasped and asked softly, "What is this?"

"We've found where everyone is," Varanus said, also keeping her tone low. "They've been taken captive."

"But by whom?"

"That is the question," Varanus agreed. She peered out from behind the wall that concealed her. They were mostly hidden from the view from below, but if someone came through the gallery behind them, they would be seen for certain. "We're too exposed here. We should get inside somewhere."

Judith nodded in agreement and said, "There is a room further along." She pointed down the gallery to a room that stood overlooking the hall. "If it is empty, we can hide in there and still see what is happening."

"If it is empty," Varanus said.

But it was a reasonable point. In the gallery they would be seen eventually. If there were guards in the room, they could always run again, but otherwise it might give them a chance to rest.

Hurrying along, Varanus paused at the entrance, exchanged a look with Judith, and opened the door. The room was dark, lit by oil lamps that had been turned down to keep it in shadows. It seemed deserted, and Varanus, eager to be out of the gallery, hurried in without pausing. It only took her a moment more to realize that she had been mistaken as her eyes focused on the point of a long-bladed spear that appeared from the darkness inches from her nose.

Varanus froze, her eyes slowly taking in the weapon and then the figure holding it. She could not make out details, but she gauged it to be a woman with long black hair and a simple chokha-dress. Behind her, Judith hurried into the room and stopped short, also seeing that they had been ambushed. Varanus glanced at the nearest corner and saw the bodies of a man and a woman clad in mail. They had been killed and left piled up in the shadows.

"Oh no..." Judith murmured.

The woman holding the spear advanced into the light to get a better look at Varanus. It was Joan the Breton, once a noblewoman of Brittany who had turned pirate after the death of her husband during the Hundred Years' War.

"Doctor Varanus?" Joan asked, surprised. She glanced at Judith. "Rabbi ben Loew?"

Another figure appeared from the darkness, sword in hand. It was Magnus the Dane, his clothes bloodstained and tattered from extensive violence, just like Joan's garments. He reached behind Judith and quickly closed the door.

"What are they doing here?" he demanded, keeping his voice low.

"Better to ask them," Joan said.

"Are they armed?"

"No," Varanus interjected, unable to conceal her displeasure at the fact. She was still in desperate need of a weapon.

"Are they with us?" Magnus asked Joan.

"An important question." Joan turned her eyes back to Varanus and Judith and raised her spear. "Whom do you serve?" she demanded. "Answer me!"

"What?" Varanus asked. It was an absurd question. "I *serve* no one, and nor does she."

The idea! Claiming that she would ever serve another!

Joan relaxed slightly and lowered the spear.

"I believe them," she said to Magnus, who nodded and sheathed his sword.

"As do I," murmured a voice from the shadows across the room.

Varanus recognized the voice, and the relief she took from hearing it made her rush past Joan to be sure. She saw Vaclav the Moravian crouching in the darkness near the balcony that overlooked the Great Hall. He smiled in greeting at Varanus and Judith and motioned for them to join him.

"Doctor," he said, "I am pleased to see you released from your confinement."

"I am rather happy about it myself," Varanus agreed. She glanced at the crowd below them. "What is happening? Has everyone gone mad?"

"A *coup d'état*, it seems," Joan said, kneeling beside them while Magnus guarded the door. "We are still trying to make sense of it, but in Lady Sophio's absence, some portion of the army has taken up arms against us."

"That was why you asked who we served?" inquired Judith.

"In part," replied Vaclav. "The enemy has a sort of pass phrase. They say that they serve the 'Winter King' so that they might know one another. I have seen it happen twice already. It is not merely coincidence; it is a code."

"Ah," Varanus said. "And that is how you know who to kill: the ones that respond correctly."

Joan nodded. "Precisely."

"And who is this 'Winter King'?" Varanus asked.

"That I do not know," Vaclav told her. He leaned out a little and studied the crowd, which had begun to move, being turned toward the throne and the dais by their guards. "But I think we may soon find out."

Varanus looked into the hall and saw three figures step onto the dais, two women and one man. She recognized them as members of Sophio's Council—Margaret, Iese, and Caroline. They were all dressed richly, in robes and coats threaded with gold and adorned with gemstones. And they were armed, a point that Varanus did not fail to note. However much they might trust their soldiers, they trusted their own sword-arms above all.

The one called Margaret stepped forward from the other two and raised her hands in greeting to the crowd of prisoners. She spoke to them like a Roman Emperor addressing the plebs:

"Brothers and Sisters, welcome. Thank you all for accepting my... invitation."

She spoke with more sincerity and warmth than ought to have been possible in such circumstances, and ripples of suspicion, confusion, and fear began to spread through the prisoners. It seemed they knew not what to make of this. Being assembled for slaughter was as easy to comprehend as it was terrifying, but to be addressed in tones of kindness by one's captor was unnerving.

"I apologize for the rough methods of my compatriots," Margaret continued, "but I fear with such momentous events, we could not risk otherwise. But you are here now, and that is all that matters."

"Arrogant creature, isn't she?" mused Joan.

"Quite," Varanus agreed. "A coup is a coup. She acts like it were the French Revolution."

Joan looked at her in astonishment and asked, "Oh? Have the French had a revolution?"

"Yes, we did," Varanus replied. "A century ago."

Joan shook her head. "I must keep better track of current events."

Below them, Margaret continued:

"No doubt I am known to you. I am Margaret of the Hebrides, formerly of the Council advising our now-departed Eristavi, Lady Sophio. I have held my post for almost as long as Lady Sophio has held hers, and I have guided her as she has guided us.

"But I fear, Brothers and Sisters, that the time of Sophio's reign has passed. Like those who came before her, she has abandoned us for the world, never to return."

This seemed to surprise many of the prisoners who apparently had no knowledge of Sophio's departure.

"We are left, it seems, on the verge of chaos." Margaret turned her gaze toward each of the prisoners, locking eyes with each of them for the smallest of moments as she spoke. "I know that there are some among us who still remember the dark time when Shashava left us as well, so long ago. We trusted that our founder would watch over us always, and our founder abandoned us. We trusted that the Companions would watch over us always, and the Companions abandoned us as well. And now Sophio, the last of those who came before us, has betrayed us too, casting aside her responsibilities and leaving us to whatever may befall us."

This brought cries of protest and angry accusations from many of the prisoners, especially from the old. But among the young Shashavani, there was a hint of uncertainty, and they looked at one another, murmuring softly. It was obvious what troubled them: Was Margaret right? Had they been abandoned by the queen they hardly knew? And if so, what would befall them next?

Margaret held out a hand as if to stop such whispers of fear.

"But be at peace, Brothers and Sisters," she said, her tone both gentle and commanding. "Though Sophio has abandoned you, though Shashava and the Companions have abandoned you, know that *I* never will."

There was a pause. Margaret raised her head and placed one fist over her heart in a show of conviction even in the face of great personal sacrifice.

"In their absence and with the approval of my fellow councilors—" She motioned toward Caroline and Iese. "I proclaim myself Eristavi, your Prince, your Queen, from this moment onward until such time as one whose authority is greater than mine returns from the wilderness to relieve me of my burden."

Varanus almost laughed aloud at this, for surely Margaret meant the return of Shashava or the Companions, neither of which was likely. Then a dark thought fell across Varanus's mind. *Shashava, the Companions, or Sophio.* Certainly Margaret would not have usurped the throne if there were any real chance of Sophio returning. How could she be so confident of that? Had she engineered some plot to deal with Sophio as well? Or was it really so certain that Sophio would never return from her sojourn?

And if not, what did that mean regarding Lord Iosef?

"Shh, *liebchen,*" Korbinian murmured in her ear, perhaps sensing her unease at the thought of losing her mentor. "Your Russian will return. I do not doubt it and nor should you."

Korbinian was right, of course. Iosef was far too responsible to abandon his duties in such a way. He at least would return. The reassurance calmed Varanus somewhat, but it did not change the greater danger still at hand.

In the hall, Margaret's announcement was met with a mixture of outrage, disinterest, and acceptance. Though many of the Shashavani recoiled at Margaret's usurpation, there were those who seemed to care little for such a question of politics, and many others who showed relief at the idea of a quick and orderly succession.

Quick and orderly and bloody, Varanus thought.

"Brothers and Sisters," Margaret said, suddenly the benevolent monarch, the matriarch reassuring her children through her own authority, "I have no wish to confine you any more than has been necessary. I want to return all of you to your studies as quickly as possible, for the work we do here is both significant and glorious. You are, each of you, greater and more worthy than all the Nations of the world. Ours is eternity or some greater part at least." This statement was made, it seemed, for the benefit of those who still walked in the Shadow. "In each of you rest the knowledge of a thousand Libraries of Alexandria, the wisdom of a thousand Solomons, and a glory that the emperors of neither Rome nor China shall ever match.

"For too long have we been shackled to archaic laws and customs incompatible with our greatness. We have all been taught that the Law of Shashava is wisdom and justice. But tell me this: Is it wisdom for the greatest of minds to suffer a world governed by the foolish? Is it justice for the great to be confined by the whim of the small? We cloister ourselves in this hallowed place of knowledge, while beyond our borders all the world is dark with ignorance, ruled by corruption, and guided by malice. We have been told that we must keep ourselves secret, for else the world will fear us and destroy us."

Her face hardened and her tone fell into a sinister growl. "Why would they fear us, unless they were truly unworthy of us?" She let this thought linger for a moment before she continued, "Ours is the glory, my brethren. We should stride this world as giants, seeking knowledge where we wish it, unafraid of what the meek will think of us. For we are *lions*...and they are *rats*."

"This is heresy!" someone shouted from the crowd. "Lies! These are the words of a Basilisk!"

"A Basilisk, you call me?" Margaret asked, laughing. "You call me *that* like it were some unclean word? Like it still has some meaning for us now?" She extended her hand and pointed in the direction of her accuser. "Why should we be Shashavani when Shashava has kept us confined in darkness, without even the courage to remain with us and guide us into the light! We have languished in Plato's cave for too long. Those who came before us lied to us and promised us the light of wisdom, but they have denied it to us, shackling us with rules and tenets that have hindered our work and kept us barred from Truth!"

Again, while many of the prisoners reacted with outrage at her words, others, especially the young, seemed to offer a tacit agreement with her. Varanus knew how they felt: many of the protocols binding the Shashavani to secrecy and harmony had a tendency of obstructing or at least slowing the progress of research.

Especially when it came to the matter of sharing books, she thought.

Having made her point, Margaret offered her enemies a kind smile again, perhaps demonstrating to them—or more likely, to the undecided—that she was magnanimous even toward her detractors. Then, catching sight of something at the far end of the hall, her expression hardened.

"Brothers and Sisters, I would like nothing more than for this succession to have been easy and quiet," she said, "rather than this unfortunate inconvenience and show of arms. But know this: the steps I have taken today have been for your own protection, for we are all in danger."

The crowd parted amid gasps of shock as a figure began to walk the length of the Great Hall toward the dais. It was Thoros, and he was dragging something along the floor behind him.

"Earlier today, just as the Council had agreed upon my appointment," Margaret continued, raising her voice to reclaim the attention of her prisoners, "Philippa the Nicaean attempted the usurpation of the throne with the collusion of certain disloyal elements within our House and our Army. It was only through foresight and certain necessary precautions that the Council and I managed to stop them. They had with them a list of names of those who were to be killed to ease Philippa's ascent and to destroy any who might question whether we should be shackled to codes and conduct that have no further place in our world. My name was on the list, as were my supporters on the Council." She paused before adding, "And so were the names of many I see among you here, for it seems that anyone who has held disagreement with Philippa's philosophy has been deemed too radical to live."

She let this statement sink in for a moment.

"Now these *traitors* hide across the river, gathering their strength and plotting our deaths!"

By then, Thoros had reached the dais and joined Margaret. He held up the limp body of Marie of Toulouse for all to see. Marie's body was still marred with the marks of her recent battle with Thoros, for it seemed that severe blood loss had prevented them all from closing quickly. Thoros's sword had been thrust through her heart, leaving her exsanguinated and lifeless.

Varanus scowled at the sight, and she heard her companions murmuring in anger.

"Here is one of them!" Margaret announced, pointing to Marie's body. "Marie the Cathar, Philippa's spy! She and others have been left behind in our midst, like serpents hiding in the grass, waiting for our moment of weakness! Already Marie has committed countless murders throughout the castle, and she would have done more had Brother Thoros not brought her to heel." She pointed her finger toward the crowd. "And had my soldiers not brought you here for your protection, it might be any one of you lying dead in the halls!"

Varanus doubted that the prisoners really believed such a fiction, certainly not all of them; but she saw in their faces a slow, resigned acceptance, an eagerness to justify an accord with their captors so that they might return to their work. That was the great weakness of the Shashavani she realized: their scholarship. Only a few cared for politics and power, while the rest had their own studies and philosophizing, which counted more to them than the question of who ruled. If Margaret allowed them to go free, if she allowed them to carry on as usual, they might even start to believe her lies for the mere sake of convenience.

"Even among the wise, *liebchen*, convenience speaks louder than truth," Korbinian murmured sadly. "These fine scholars might debate the question of Caractacus's uniform *ad infinitum*, but the question of who has the right to rule? A matter both boring and trite, no doubt."

Below, Margaret drew the sword from Marie's chest and lowered the woman into a kneeling position, kneeling as well and holding Marie's shoulders to keep her upright. Presently, the wound in Marie's chest had closed enough for circulation to resume, and she began to sway of her own accord, struggling to move her limbs.

"But I am not without mercy!" Margaret declared, as much to Marie as to the crowd. "Despite her crimes, despite her betrayal, Marie is still our sister! And I would be loath to execute any of my brethren." She looked into Marie's eyes and said, "My dear Sister Marie, I would still gladly welcome you to our cause. If you would only swear your loyalty, renounce Philippa and the archaic Law of Shashava, confess your crimes, and accept just penance, then I shall embrace you once again as my sister." She motioned toward the crowd. "*We all shall*," she said, once again emphasizing to the crowd that she and they were together arrayed on one side, against Philippa and any other who opposed Margaret's will.

"All you need do is say these words," Margaret said to Marie, placing one hand on Marie's cheek and the other upon her bloody chest, "with your lips and with your heart. Then you shall be free."

Marie struggled to speak against the dizziness of bloodlessness, but she managed to reply with a clear, "No."

Margaret pulled her hand away from Marie's chest, her palm and fingers covered with blood.

"You must be starving from your ordeal, Sister," she said. "You need only convert to our cause and swear obedience, and I shall grant you a feast that would shame Croesus for a pauper. Swear yourself to me, and this will all be over."

Marie leaned forward and glared into Margaret's eyes. As loudly as she could manage, she announced to all the room:

"I will never renounce Shashava nor ever pledge myself to one such as you. I would rather die than betray the most sacred of oaths, one made to Wisdom and Truth and Justice."

Margaret seemed almost to smile at this for the briefest of moments, but perhaps long enough for Marie to notice. Then she stood, her countenance twisted with regret and resignation.

"So be it," she said. She motioned to one of the soldiers who stood nearby. "Master-At-Arms!"

The Master-At-Arms—Jane Fairfax, if Varanus recognized her correctly—passed her halberd to another soldier and drew an executioner's sword from a scabbard presented to her by a third. Fairfax walked onto the dais and stood behind Marie, lifting the sword and silently gauging the proper angle for the strike. Still almost bloodless, weak from trauma, and scarcely able to sit up, much less move, Marie simply folded her hands in her lap and murmured a small prayer. Her face was serene, somehow coming to terms with her impending demise, perhaps strengthened in her resolve by the knowledge that even after six hundred years of life, she had never once recanted her beliefs.

Margaret turned and addressed the crowd, now suddenly the unflinching lawgiver burdened with neither doubt nor remorse.

"Brothers and Sisters, see now how I will protect the faithful against their enemies. Our time of trial is almost done, but our enemies still lurk in the shadows, pretending friendship while plotting our demise. We cannot afford half-measures. We cannot hesitate. Only through unity and obedience will we be safe."

She raised one hand like Raphael's Plato imparting wisdom to Aristotle.

"Swear yourselves to me and to our cause," she said, "and I shall grant you feasts of plenty and return you to your studies, stronger and unbound by archaic falsehoods. Refuse and I shall have no choice but to deal with you as traitors...for who but a traitor would hesitate to swear so noble an oath?"

She paused a moment before she summarized in three simple words: "Convert—"

Fairfax's sword flashed in the light as it swung through the air. Though still of the Shadow, Fairfax's arm was strong and her aim true. There were gasps from the crowd, but most of the prisoners were silent as Marie's body collapsed onto the ground. Her head tumbled onto the dais and lay there, eyes closed, still basking in the serenity of moral certainty.

"Or die," Margaret finished.

CHAPTER EIGHTEEN

There was silence in the room. Varanus stared down at Marie's lifeless body, unable to speak. She had witnessed much violence in her lifetime, but this was cold-blooded execution and committed by Shashavani against Shashavani. She looked at her companions. None of them knew what to say.

"God preserve us," Vaclav finally whispered.

"She...she killed Sister Marie..." murmured Judith, her face pale at the sight.

Joan frowned and stood, motioning to the others.

"Come, we should leave," she said. "We have waited here too long. They may send more guards to check on the two that we killed."

Vaclav nodded. "You're right. Come."

"Wait a moment," Varanus said, holding up her hand even as she stood. She studied the crowd of prisoners, searching for the one face she hoped both would and would not be there. "Have any of you seen Ekaterine?"

"Not for some days," Vaclav told her, placing a hand on Varanus's shoulder. "She was sent to work in the archives after...." He quickly stopped and avoided addressing Varanus's crime. "God willing she is alive, but we cannot know that now."

"I do not see her below," Joan added, "whatever comfort that may give you." She nodded toward the door. "But we must leave before we are discovered."

Varanus took another look at the prisoners in the hall, but she did not see Ekaterine, whose face she felt certain she could have picked out of a crowd of thousands. And besides, Ekaterine was not the sort to allow herself to be captured. She was not among the captives. She couldn't be.

"We will find her, *liebchen*," Korbinian murmured. "Do not fear it. But first, you must not die."

"Yes, of course," Varanus said, nodding to Vaclav and the others. "Let us find someplace safer where we may plan our next move."

She followed the others into the gallery and away from the Great Hall. No doubt Margaret would be busy for some time, receiving the supplication of the faithful and beheading anyone who refused; but it was likely that her soldiers would be out patrolling before long, hunting for any stragglers. Varanus needed to be armed and ready before then.

She would find Ekaterine, and then the two of them were going to sort things out.

"How many do you think will convert?" asked Magnus.

"All of them, God willing," replied Vaclav.

"What?" Magnus exclaimed. "Why?"

"Convert by word, not in thought or deed," Joan explained. "If they do so, they will live long enough for Sophio to return and set things right. If they refuse...." She scowled at the thought of the fate that had befallen Marie. "It is a hard task to betray one's philosophy in word while holding true in one's own heart, but I hope that they can do it for all their sakes."

"What if they convert in their hearts as well?" asked Judith.

"Then they will die when Sophio returns," Vaclav said.

"Do you suppose she will return?" Varanus asked.

"She must," Judith said. "She would not abandon us."

"No, she would not," agreed Joan. "Sophio will return in time. She is too bound by duty to abandon us. But I do not know what Margaret believes will happen then."

"Perhaps she hopes her loyal converts will fall upon Lady Sophio and slaughter her with their numbers," Varanus suggested.

Vaclav scoffed. "I think that Margaret is mad, that is what I think."

They turned a corner and almost collided with a man and a woman dressed in soldiers' chokhas who were hurrying along in the opposite direction. The woman carried a double-barreled shotgun, the man a sword and a revolver. Varanus had seen them before in Luka's company, members of the cohort he had been training. But she knew nothing else about them.

"Anuka? Koba?" Vaclav exclaimed, recognizing them as well. But though he knew them, he did not lower his blade, and neither did Joan nor Magnus. "What are you doing here?"

Koba relaxed as he realized to whom they were speaking. "Father Vaclav—" He began to lower his weapons, but Anuka clicked her tongue at him and shook her head.

"We are going someplace, My Lord," Anuka said to Vaclav, her tone respectful but cautious. "And you?"

"The same." It was Joan who replied.

"My Lady," Anuka acknowledged, nodding. She did not lower her shotgun.

"Are you loyal?" asked Magnus advancing a step, his rapier leveled for a killing strike at Anuka.

Anuka took a step back and shifted her barrel to cover Magnus's face.

"Of course," she said. "But are *you* loyal?"

Realizing that the matter was likely to devolve into either violence or a pointless back-and-forth of whose loyalty was more loyal, Varanus sighed and pushed her way past Magnus. Planting herself directly in front of Anuka and Koba, she asked them:

"Whom do you serve?"

Anuka and Koba seemed to recognize the question, and they quickly exchanged looks. Varanus sensed Joan shift position behind her so that she might slay them all the faster when they responded with the correct pass phrase.

"Uh..." Koba stammered.

"We serve...the..." Anuka said, sounding no more confident than Koba.

They exchanged looks again.

"The King," Koba said.

"The King," Anuka agreed, with a nod. "The...the Winter King."

"Yes!" Koba exclaimed. "That one!"

If their hesitation hadn't given their allegiance away, Koba's final words certainly did. Anuka gave a resigned sigh and made ready to attack.

"They're not with Margaret," Joan said, lowering her spear. She reached out and pushed Magnus's sword away as Vaclav sheathed his own. "And nor are we," she told Anuka.

Anuka relaxed and pointed her shotgun away from them.

"Marvelous," Varanus said, clapping her hands together. "So we're all finished with trying to kill one another?"

"More or less," Magnus replied.

Varanus looked at Anuka and asked, "Have you seen Ekaterine?"

"Not for some days, no."

"What about Luka?" Varanus asked.

If anyone could help her find Ekaterine, it would be her cousin.

"We've no idea," Koba said. "We went searching for him, but there's no sign of him anywhere."

"He accompanied the Strategos to a Council meeting several hours ago," Anuka explained. "He took Seteney and Movses with him, and that is the last we've seen of any of them."

She sounded worried, which was to be expected.

Vaclav raised a hand to gather their attention and said, "We should keep moving. Eventually someone will come along who does serve the Winter King."

"We still have not decided where to go," Joan said.

"To the armory, of course," Magnus replied.

Koba shook his head. "Guarded."

"Which one?" Varanus asked. After all, there were several throughout the castle.

"All of them," Anuka said. "The enemy has secured the main complement of arms in the castle, and they are guarding the gates as well. I overheard talk of loyalists escaping earlier. I think they mean to prevent that from happening again."

"If we cannot escape, where are we to go?" Magnus asked. "Surely, they will hunt us down and kill us like dogs." He patted his sword. "Better to attack them head-on and attempt a breakout. If we die, it will be gloriously."

"They have set up the Maxim guns to defend the exits," Koba said, shaking his head. "And the volley guns from the armory. Few as their numbers are, even the Living would not make it past them."

Varanus folded her arms and addressed Magnus:

"Let us avoid any moments of 'death or glory' for the time being, Doctor Eriksen. We should find a secure location and make plans."

She liked the idea of having allies on hand to help her, but she was not about to leave without first finding Ekaterine. She meant to do a proper search of the castle before she would entertain thoughts of fleeing into the countryside.

And besides, there was her laboratory to consider. She did not intend to leave decades of work and notes behind where they could be rifled through, damaged, or plagiarized by anyone. Moving her materials to a place of safety would require a great deal of work, and she had not quite yet worked out how she was going to manage it.

"*Liebchen*, surely your life is more important than your work!" protested Korbinian, as he leaned past Magnus and gave her a kiss on the cheek.

"Nonsense," Varanus murmured back to him. More loudly, she asked her companions, "Where are we to go?"

"Not our rooms," said Judith. "They'll be searched once Margaret knows who is against her."

"Perhaps the archives?" suggested Varanus. Hopefully, she could induce the others to help her search for Ekaterine.

"Too dangerous," replied Joan. "Too far away. We need a hiding place on this floor, in this wing...or very near to it. And then we can plan where we are to go next."

Vaclav frowned and started to offer a suggestion, but he quickly reconsidered it with a shake of his head.

"I...I know a place," Koba said, a little hesitantly. After all, he was still very young and perhaps felt uncertain about speaking over his elders.

"Where?" Vaclav asked.

* * * *

Koba led them to one of the inner sections of the wing where it adjoined the original stronghold that formed one of the earliest parts of the castle. Joan and Magnus went ahead with him, while Vaclav and Anuka trailed behind to cover the rear. Varanus was still annoyed at having no weapon, and she considered demanding that Koba relinquish one of his, but she thought better of it.

They came to a dark reading room with wood-paneled walls and hanging tapestries. There were a few shelves of books, but their contents were mostly inconsequential. The purpose of the room was simply quiet study. Koba looked around to be sure that they were alone before he went to one of the tapestries and began searching behind it. A few moments later, he motioned for them to follow and then ducked behind the tapestry, vanishing from sight. When the tapestry fell back into place, there was no sign of the young man lurking behind it.

"A secret passage! How exciting!" Korbinian exclaimed in delight.

Varanus raised an eyebrow at him, but she followed all the same. Slipping behind the tapestry, she saw that Koba had opened a concealed door in the paneling that led into a short stone passageway. The others followed her in, and Koba quickly closed the door behind them.

"I knew of our secret passages," said Judith, "but I did not know about this one."

"I discovered it a year ago," Koba explained, lighting a lamp that had been left by the door and leading them into the darkness. "I am surely not the only person who knows of it, but I've never seen anyone else enter here."

They came to a room of moderate size, contained entirely within the old walls of the castle, with no windows to betray its presence. The lamplight revealed mosaics upon the walls and intricate, decorative brickwork. Even in shadow, even at such an age, the vibrancy of the colors had not been diminished. There were also countless chests of drawers that, upon investigation, were revealed to contain ancient rolls of parchment.

Joan and Vaclav began examining the room with astonishment that soon grew into excitement. Varanus glanced at the others and saw that they were as ignorant to the room's significance as she.

"Do you know what this place is?" asked Joan.

"It cannot be," said Vaclav. "But here it is."

"I have no idea," Koba told them, as he began to light the host of candles that filled the corners of the room, casting away the darkness. "I just thought it was a nice, quiet place to read."

"It is the private chapel of Nino of Imereti," Vaclav exclaimed. "I didn't think it truly existed."

"I had always assumed it to be in the catacombs," Joan told him, gazing at the images on the walls. "Imagine: this is where she meditated on the very nature of faith and where she held dialogues on the question of how and why we believe."

"Astounding," Vaclav agreed.

So that was it, Varanus thought. The room meant little to her, but it had been used by one of the Companions during the early days of the Shashavani Order. That indeed gave it significance, though she had little interest in the studies of even a great philosopher. Surely, the private laboratory of Konstantine would make for a much more interesting discovery.

"How could you not have revealed this place, Koba?" demanded Judith. "The history in this place!"

"It has only been a year," Koba protested, a little sheepishly. "I meant to get around to it eventually."

Vaclav gave Koba a stern look like an admonishing father and said, "You are far too young for a year to have so little significance to you, my boy. After a century, then that is a valid excuse."

"Surely other people must know of this place, My Lord," said Anuka, coming to Koba's defense. "Out of all the Shashavani, *Koba* is the one to discover so important a place?"

Koba shot her a look.

"*Thank you,*" he said, though his tone was one of protest.

"I find it unlikely as well," agreed Magnus. "I suspect that there are others, but few enough. We might not be discovered here."

He almost sounded disappointed.

"It will do for now," said Joan. She motioned for the others to join her in the center of the room. "For now, let us rest and plan. We have much work ahead of us. We must determine if there is anyone else who is loyal and still free, and if so, we must rescue them before they are lost to us."

"Agreed," said Vaclav. "And we must get food. We may not need it now, but in the coming days, we will feel hunger. And if we are injured in fighting, that hunger will become all the worse. Food stores of some sort may mean the difference between life and death."

Varanus raised a finger to draw attention to herself.

"If you will pardon the interruption," she said, "there is something we need even more than food at this moment."

"And what is that, Doctor?" Vaclav asked.

"Weapons," Varanus replied, "and lots of them."

CHAPTER NINETEEN

"And how do you propose we arm ourselves, Doctor Varanus, when the armories are under guard?" demanded Magnus. "Or have you changed your mind about a head-on attack?"

"Nonsense," Varanus said. "We will go to Luka's chambers. I doubt very much that our enemies would bother to place them under guard, and I know that Luka has his own supply of weapons there."

"This is true," Koba added. "I have seen them. He has a significant arsenal."

Joan frowned and folded her arms. "This I do not doubt, but we must be cautious. If you know of his private...supply of arms, surely others do as well, perhaps even those among our enemies. And what if he is disloyal? What if he has already distributed those weapons among Margaret's soldiers?"

"No!" Koba exclaimed, so furious at the very suggestion that he forgot himself before his elders. "That is impossible!"

Anuka laid a hand on Koba's shoulder to calm him, but she answered in agreement:

"Lord Luka would never betray us. I would trust that with my life."

Varanus was not inclined to offer up her very life on the matter, but she did have faith in Luka's loyalty. After all, he had been Lord Iosef's sworn brother and comrade for almost two hundred years. Iosef was too good a judge of character to associate so closely with a traitor. After all, he had seen the wisdom in making Varanus one of the Shashavani: such foresight could not be easily fooled by deceit.

"I have always admired your modesty, *liebchen*," Korbinian murmured in her ear, his sarcasm light and teasing.

"Hush," Varanus murmured back.

"I agree that Luka would be an unlikely traitor," said Joan, "but as I say, we must be cautious. And perhaps we should more fully explore these passages before venturing outside. Who knows where else they may lead?"

Vaclav nodded. "There is wisdom in that, Sister, but still, now is the time when they are most disorganized. Once they have finished with the prisoners, Margaret's soldiers will no doubt begin to patrol in search of stragglers. We may not have this chance again."

"So which do we choose?" asked Magnus.

"That is the question," agreed Vaclav.

Judith coughed softly to get their attention.

"We should do both," she said. "Some of us should remain and search the passages; some of us should acquire the weapons. A smaller group is less likely to be noticed in the corridors, surely."

"She's right," Varanus said quickly. "I will go to Luka's chambers and find the weapons. Who will accompany me?"

"I will," replied Vaclav. He looked at Varanus and gave her a confident smile, which pleased Varanus. She had hoped for his support, just in case something unfortunate happened along the way.

"And I!" added Magnus, putting a hand on the hilt of his sword.

Varanus sighed. That was not quite what she'd had in mind.

"And so shall I," said Koba.

"No, you will not," Joan told him. She looked at Anuka. "Nor you. You are both far too young for such a risk, and you still walk in the Shadow. If we are injured in this mad venture, we will heal. Either of you may die. Besides, Koba, you discovered this place—"

"And failed to mention it to anyone," noted Vaclav.

"You should be the one to map it," Joan finished, smiling slightly.

Koba was about to protest, but Anuka shushed him and bowed her head to Joan.

"Of course, My Lady," she said.

Impatient with the delay, Varanus cleared her throat and headed for the door.

"Excellent, it's decided. Come along, Father Vaclav...and whomever else."

* * * *

To Varanus's relief, Luka's chambers had been left as yet untouched. Perhaps Margaret's soldiers had been too busy taking the scholars prisoner to worry about ransacking. But they would, no doubt, return to loot the place before long.

As an officer and as Iosef's bodyguard, Luka enjoyed private quarters rather than occupying a place in the communal barracks with the other young soldiers. Normally the privilege of such privacy would not be given to a Shashavani of the Shadow less than three hundred years of age, but close association to Iosef—and by extension to Lady Sophio—carried with it certain advantages. Varanus herself enjoyed far larger quarters than she normally would have at her age.

But in keeping with Luka's tastes, the place was still small and spare, combining military stoicism with simple, homely comforts. The walls were bare stone, the floors bare wood, the furniture was not upholstered, and the fabrics were all rough wool rather than fine silk. Of course, there was a tremendous amount of wine, bottled and housed on a rack in one corner.

And there were weapons, shelf upon shelf of them: rifles and muskets displayed on the walls, swords and daggers in cases, and countless other curiosities of a martial nature scattered about the room. It was the most cluttered yet tidy room that Varanus had ever seen, and that was entirely the fault of the armaments.

The smell of tobacco hung in the air, and Varanus coughed several times to clear her nose and throat. Vaclav and Magnus were similarly affected. Those in the Shadow might enjoy the habit of smoking, but the senses of the Living were far too powerful to tolerate such a coarse odor.

"Ah, empty," Magnus said. He sounded disappointed.

"Indeed," said Varanus. "Let's not waste our good fortune."

She went to the nearest wall and began emptying it of its weapons, placing them lengthwise in the center of Luka's bed. Carrying them all would be a nuisance, so she decided it would be best to wrap them up in Luka's blankets and transport them like a bundle of sticks.

Vaclav and Magnus quickly joined her, selecting the largest calibre firearms and the sturdiest blades. If it came to fighting the Living, the weapons would either need to inflict great trauma or be tremendously sharp and precise.

"Ammunition," Korbinian reminded Varanus, as he reclined at the head of the bed.

"Ammunition," Varanus echoed aloud, for the benefit of Magnus and Vaclav. "Check the chests and drawers."

"I will find it," Vaclav said.

And find it, he did. It took a few minutes of searching, but presently Vaclav opened a large, iron-bound chest and found it filled with boxes of cartridges, both paper and metallic, of varying sizes, all neatly arranged for convenience. While a number of Shashavani soldiers still preferred musket balls and loose powder, Luka had taken to modern armaments quite easily, as witnessed by his insistence on buying the "latest thing" in warfare to have been invented each time he went abroad.

"We have little time," Vaclav said, as he closed the chest again and lifted it onto one shoulder. "We should return as quickly as we are able."

"Agreed," Varanus said.

She placed atop her pile of weapons the crowning piece of the collection—a tremendous elephant gun of great beauty and decoration, which had probably seen more use killing people than elephants. Having taken everything she considered to be useful, she wrapped the blankets around the guns and hefted her bundle. Magnus did the same with his collection of swords and axes.

Varanus checked to see that the passage was empty and led the way out of the room. They hurried back toward the hidden chapel, which was another floor up and halfway across the house. By now it seemed Margaret had made some progress with her prisoners, for they began to see small groups of soldiers patrolling the halls, though still in numbers too small to be of any great threat. Varanus and her companions merely hid in adjoining rooms or behind especially large pieces of furniture, preferring to avoid armed conflict wherever possible. While arms were more important than food, starvation would soon begin to gnaw at even the Living, and with starvation, their bodies would become slow to heal. Better not to tax themselves with hunger so early into their ordeal.

But as they ascended a set of servants' stairs—to better avoid detection—they heard the sounds of violence close at hand, coming from an academic hall adjoining the corridor. Varanus hurried to the doorway and glanced inside, while Vaclav and Magnus took up a position across from her.

Inside, Varanus saw a small group of Shashavani huddled behind a makeshift barricade of tables, chairs, and benches. They were mostly scholars, but she did see two warriors—the Armenia noblewoman Zabel of Ani and her student, Amadeus of Savoy—both of them hard pressed to safeguard the others against the onslaught of armored soldiers, who dove in around them from all sides. The scholars did their best to aid Zabel and Amadeus, but three had already been cut down in the fighting, and the rest were gravely injured. Varanus recognized their leader as the Persian philosopher Reza of Samarkand, a member of the Council that had condemned her to confinement. She had the momentary thought of leaving him to his fate for confining her, but such a thing seemed uncharitable.

"What are we to do?" asked Magnus, his sword already in his hand.

"Intervene, obviously," Varanus replied, her tone almost scolding. "Now we need a plan—"

At that moment, the soldiers, momentarily repulsed, regrouped at the center of the room. Their leader raised his sword above his head and shouted "For the Winter King!" And with that, the whole company charged the makeshift fortifications. Zabel, Amadeus, Reza, and the others braced themselves for the attack, but from the expressions on their faces, it seemed none of them held much hope for victory. They were all gravely wounded; had they not been among the Living, they would already be dead.

Vaclav set down the case of ammunition and drew his sword. Magnus quickly dropped his bundle of weapons, making ready for battle.

"A plan," Varanus reminded. "I'll intervene on the right flank. Father Vaclav, if you would—"

"For Shashava and the Eristavi!" Magnus bellowed and charged headlong into the fray.

Varanus sighed. "So much for a plan," she said, and set her bundle of firearms on the floor. Searching through Magnus's collection of melee weapons, she selected a pair of rather brutal-looking hand axes. "Once more unto the breach?" she asked Vaclav.

"You go to the right, I shall go left," Vaclav answered.

Varanus hefted one of the axes to test the balance. It was very good.

"Meet in the center," she said.

In a shared silence, she and Vaclav rushed into the room and charged the soldiers. Magnus was already in the midst of the fighting, but though his exuberance and skill at arms had already scored him three kills, it had cost him several nasty wounds that now bled freely. He would soon be hungry.

After this, they would definitely need to find food.

Varanus cut around the fighting to the right and dove into the enemy flank. Her small size and the silence of her arrival took the soldiers by surprise, and she brought down one man in two blows as she came upon him from behind.

On the barricade, Amadeus suddenly fell as one of the soldiers drove the point-end of a glaive into his side. Amadeus cried out in pain, and his wound boiled fiercely. The soldier's glaive was covered in freshly spilt Living blood, and it burned what it touched.

As Amadeus fell, the trauma overwhelming his strength of will, the soldier made sure of his incapability with a blow to the throat. She then raised the glaive high into the air and prepared to cleave Amadeus's head in two.

Varanus dove in and struck the soldier in the back of her leg where it was unprotected by armor. The woman cried out and fell to the side, using the glaive's pole to catch herself. Varanus leapt upon the soldier, bringing both axes down at her. The soldier threw her weapon up and blocked the attack. Frustrated, Varanus forced the glaive down and drove one axe into the side of the soldier's neck.

Another soldier appeared from the fray and thrust a sword at her. Varanus jerked away just in time. As the man made another attempt,

Zabel intervened and knocked his blade away. Varanus lunged forward and brought the man down in a flurry of blows with her axes.

There was something monstrously exhilarating about the fighting, and Varanus almost felt herself drifting away into a muddled haze as she hacked and swung, ducked and withdrew. It was almost like being intoxicated, though being drunk on bloodshed was a horrible thing to imagine.

"Come now, *liebchen*," Korbinian said to her, standing in the midst of the enemy, his face and clothes drenched in blood. "Surely our vices are only evil if they bring more harm than good. And what deed could be better than to save the lives of the innocent?"

"Perhaps," Varanus murmured. She paused just long enough to strike down another soldier as he passed her while exchanging blows with Magnus. This interruption seemed to offend Magnus greatly, but Varanus paid it no mind.

"Behind you, *liebchen*," Korbinian said.

At his warning, Varanus turned just in time to see a bardiche axe being swung at her head. She threw up her weapons to block the attack and fell backward. Her assailant adjusted his position and tried again, but before the attack could land, Vaclav stepped in from the side and drove his sword into the soldier's chest.

Breathing heavily, Varanus looked around the room. The fighting had suddenly ebbed. The attacking soldiers had fallen back in retreat, having lost almost half their numbers. Reza and the others were too exhausted to pursue.

"Glorious victory!" cried Magnus, even as he clutched his bleeding side.

"Near enough to it," agreed Zabel, though she looked skeptical. She quickly turned to help Amadeus as he struggled to rise despite his bleeding throat.

Vaclav quickly rushed to Reza, and Varanus followed him. Extending his hand, Vaclav helped Reza to stand.

"Are you well, My Lord?" he asked.

"Well enough," said Reza. He looked at Varanus and frowned. "Sister Varanus.... How fortunate you are here to assist us."

"Isn't it?" Varanus agreed.

She was concerned that Reza might elaborate and mention her confinement in front of the others, but to her relief, nothing was said about it.

"I take it you are not loyal to Margaret," Reza said to Vaclav.

"No, My Lord," Vaclav replied. "We are loyal to Sophio and to the Law of Shashava, which it seems Margaret has publicly abandoned."

"Indeed?" Reza asked, looking deeply troubled.

"I fear she seeks to make Basilisks of us all," said Vaclav.

Reza stroked his beard, greatly ill at ease. "Margaret demanded that we submit to her authority at the Council meeting. When we refused, she and her allies attempted to kill us. Without the intervention of Lady Zawditu and her forces, we would surely have perished."

"Where are the others now, My Lord?" asked Vaclav.

"Safely outside the castle, I hope. We were attempting to escape when we were ambushed, and I was separated from them, as were several others. Marie of Toulouse...." Reza paused, uncertain what to ask.

"Dead," Varanus said.

"Dead?" Reza's face fell at the thought. "How?"

"She was captured by Margaret and executed," Varanus explained. "Margaret demanded that she convert to her Basilisk ways, and when Marie refused, she was killed as an example."

Reza was silent for a time as the others helped each other up and tended to their wounds. Presently, he spoke:

"Darkness has fallen again upon the House of Shashava. We must take care if we are to bear through into the light."

"Indeed, My Lord," Vaclav said. "In the meantime, I am pleased to report that we have secured a place of safety, and we are in the midst of obtaining supplies."

Reza nodded. "Well done, Vaclav. Let us get the wounded there that they may have some time to rest."

"Yourself included, I hope, My Lord."

"I am perfectly fine, Vaclav," Reza replied.

"If I may..." Varanus said. "We ought to tend to the wounded first, so that their blood does not leave a trail for the enemy to follow. And perhaps we should rub down our boots as well."

Vaclav and Reza both looked at her, surprised at the suggestion. Presently, Reza smiled.

"Young Varanus," he said, "despite past...difficulties...I am at this moment very pleased to have you here with us and not in a cell somewhere."

"Nonsense, My Lord," Varanus answered politely. "Why ever would I be in a cell? I'm not really the meditative type, you know."

* * * *

They led the survivors—hastily cleaned to avoid leaving a trail—to the safety of the hidden chapel and appraised Joan and the others of the situation. The Living had already been healed of their wounds, but there were a few Shashavani of the Shadow as well, and they would need longer to recuperate.

"Are you well, Brother Amadeus?" Varanus asked, crossing to the man where he sat against the wall. Amadeus's wounds had closed and he was back on his feet, but he still touched his throat from time to time, as if remembering the pain of the fight.

Amadeus looked up and nodded. "Well enough, thank you Doctor Varanus."

"Does your wound still hurt you?"

Varanus knew that the blood of the Living was toxic, that it burned inside the body and could even poison a man to death. But she had never experienced it herself, and she was very curious about it.

"No," Amadeus said quickly. "No, there is no more pain. I simply... recall it. It was like...." He frowned at the memory. "It was like the touch of the sun. I never wish to experience it again."

"Curious," Varanus said. She smiled and patted Amadeus on the shoulder.

She crossed the room to where Koba and Anuka were busy sorting the weapons and ammunition, pairing the firearms with the corresponding shot. They glanced at her when she approached, but they did not stop her as she selected the elephant gun, a pistol, and a sword to go along with her axes.

"Doctor," said Vaclav, joining her by the weapons, "we are assembling parties to find food and supplies. Would you care to join one of them?"

"I cannot," Varanus answered. "I have a more pressing concern."

"More pressing than food?"

"Father Vaclav, I *must* find Ekaterine before something happens to her," Varanus explained. "I spoke to Lord Reza, and he says that she was not among the company that escaped the castle. So I can only assume that she is still here somewhere."

Vaclav nodded. "True enough, I suppose. Where will you look?"

"My rooms first," Varanus said. "She may have gone there looking for me." It would also give her the opportunity to get a change of clothes. "Failing that, I will search the archives."

"It will be dangerous to go alone," Vaclav said. "What happens if you are found?"

"Then I will kill everyone who gets in my way." It seemed such an obvious answer; Varanus couldn't imagine why Vaclav needed her to explain it.

Vaclav laughed and shook his head.

"You are a determined one, Doctor," he said. "And it is well for us that you are."

"Thank you, Father. Compliments are always appreciated."

"May I accompany you on your search?" Vaclav asked.

"Why...yes," Varanus replied, surprised at the offer. "I would certainly welcome your help. But don't you have more important things to search for, such as food?"

Vaclav gave another one of his smiles.

"Well, Doctor, you shall look for your friend, and I shall look for food. God willing, we shall find both."

CHAPTER TWENTY

Varanus found her rooms quiet and untouched when she arrived. A part of her had feared that they might have been ransacked, her tools looted, and her notes destroyed. Instead, she found everything neat and organized. Of course, more than half of her books were gone, appropriated by the librarians and returned to their "rightful place" in the archives, and her notes on the water experiments had been taken as well, used as evidence against her. But the rest of her belongings were still where she had left them.

For a few moments, the tidiness of the place gave her hope that Ekaterine might be there, keeping everything orderly in anticipation of her arrival. But it was not so. As Varanus searched her rooms, she found no sign of anyone. Still refusing to give up hope, Varanus called softly for Ekaterine as she searched under the bed, in the cupboards and the wardrobe, and anyplace else she could imagine a person hiding. But each place was empty.

"I do not think she is here," Vaclav said, as Varanus walked from her laboratory back into the main room.

"I fear you are right," Varanus agreed. "I had hoped...." She shook her head. "But no, it would not be that simple. She must still be in the archives."

"Hopefully." Vaclav tried to smile reassuringly, but he could not conceal his doubts about Ekaterine's fate. He glanced toward the door and said, "We ought to depart. It is not safe to remain in one place."

Varanus frowned and glanced at her laboratory. What was she to do about her things? Her notes, her journals, the fruits of two decades of research...what would happen to them when Margaret's soldiers eventually came to search the place? What might be destroyed? But then again, where could she hide it?

She saw Korbinian reclining on the sofa with his feet up.

"Be logical, *liebchen*," he said. "Margaret's followers may be mad and murderous, but they remain Shashavani. Surely they value knowledge far too much to vandalize your research."

Varanus considered this. Was it possible? Might even the mad Shashavani have respect for the sanctity of knowledge? Of course, it was such an uncertain thing on which to gamble.

"Then again, *liebchen*, twenty years of research is only twenty years. You have untold lifetimes in which to replace what is lost. But you only have one dearest friend."

Varanus nodded. Korbinian was certainly right about that. Shame on her for thinking of her work before thinking of her friend. After all, without Ekaterine, she might never get anything done.

She took a step toward Vaclav and the door when Korbinian added:

"Oh, but *liebchen*, you may wish to attend to your attire. I doubt you will have much opportunity to change your clothing again. You may as well take advantage of it."

Varanus looked down at her clothes, which were bloodstained and tattered. There was an unpleasant gash in the center of her blouse where she had trapped Teimuraz's sword. She certainly looked a sight, and the holes in her clothing would offer no protection against either weapons or spilled blood, which would burn her if it was allowed to enter her wounds. Nor would her current clothing safeguard her against the sunlight. It would be all too easy for an older Shashavani or one in the Shadow to kill her simply by opening a few windows during the daytime, and that was not something she could risk, not until she knew how long she would be trapped inside.

"Just a moment, Father Vaclav," she said, hurrying to her bedroom.

"But...I..." Vaclav called after her, motioning toward the door.

In the bedroom, Varanus stripped off her clothes and began pulling fresh garments from her wardrobe. She glanced toward the bathing chamber, silently wishing she had the time to wash, but that would be an impossible extravagance under the circumstances. Still, she found some water that had been left unattended in a basin by the bed and scrubbed the worst of the dried blood from her exposed skin and hair.

She knew that heavy skirts would be a liability in the event of fighting, but almost all her clothes were dresses—even among the Shashavani, where there was no restriction on one's clothing, the habits of youth were very hard to break. But she did have a new bicycle suit packed away in a cedar chest, which Ekaterine had given to her for her birthday. Apparently Ekaterine had taken quite a fancy to the fashion, though she had been forbidden from owning an actual bicycle due to an unfortunate incident in the library two years earlier.

For added protection, Varanus selected a leather coat and smock that she used in the lab, along with heavy leather gloves. She hid her hair beneath a thick hood, and in the end only her face was exposed to the elements. It would have to do.

"Doctor, what are you doing?" Vaclav called to her. "We have no time!"

"I am just coming, Father," Varanus answered, tucking her axes into her sword belt and returning to the parlor. As she went, she passed an old plague doctor's mask that sat on the edge of her desk. She had found it in the castle some time ago and had taken a liking to it. On a whim, she took the mask and tied it to her belt. Perhaps it would prove useful for protecting her face from the sun.

Vaclav looked at her as she returned and nodded.

"Ah, I see," he said. "You certainly look better prepared. I am suddenly envious."

"Our enemies wear trousers," Varanus replied. "It was an unfair advantage."

"Of course."

"Now, let us go to the archives," Varanus said. "I must find Ekaterine."

* * * *

"Varanus!" Ekaterine cried, waking with a start.

She found herself in a strange bed in a strange room with no idea of how she had come to be there. There was a warm fire on the hearth and the room was cozy, but it was completely unfamiliar.

Had she been kidnapped?

Ekaterine struggled to sit up, but she felt weak and quite possibly feverish. Was she ill?

Suddenly a dark figure loomed above her, reaching for her.

"No!" Ekaterine shouted, lashing out, pushing the figure away with one hand while searching for a weapon with the other.

"Cousin!" the figure shouted, in a voice that made Ekaterine pause.

It was Luka.

Ekaterine pulled her arms away and sat up a little more, though it made her a dizzy.

"Where am I?" she asked.

"You are safe," Luka said, sitting in a chair beside the bed. "You're in the town across the river." He took her hand and gently squeezed it. "Do you remember how you came here?"

Ekaterine put her hand to her head as she tried to remember. Everything was there, but she was having trouble putting it all together.

"I was shot," she said, touching her side. There was a fresh bandage there. In fact, her clothes had been removed entirely, replaced by a warm woolen shift. "And the water was very cold."

Luka nodded. "You were indeed shot. Do you recall by whom?"

Ekaterine thought for a moment while her attacker's face came into focus in her mind. She scowled at the memory.

"Jan of Holland."

Luka's moustache twitched. He knew that Ekaterine had regarded Jan as a friend.

"Well," he finally said, "the important thing is that you are here and you are alive. You suffered a very severe chill."

"I swam across the river, didn't I?" Ekaterine asked.

That would explain the fever.

"You did," Luka answered. His moustache twitched again. He was not happy about that.

How close to dying did I come? Ekaterine wondered.

"I had thought the river would be frozen over by now," she explained.

"Alas, not yet," Luka said. "But you will be pleased to learn that the people you led out of the castle have survived, though there are several other cases of fever. We shall have to watch them until it breaks." He smiled at her. "You saved dozens of lives, cousin. You should be proud of yourself."

Ekaterine returned the smile for a moment, but then she frowned.

"Where is Varanus?"

"Cousin..." Luka said hesitantly.

"Where is she?" Ekaterine demanded, leaning forward angrily.

"I do not know," Luka replied. "I have looked for her, cousin, but she is not among the survivors here. I fear that she is...." He frowned. "I fear that she is dead."

"No," Ekaterine said, shaking her head sharply. "No, she is not dead."

"Cousin—"

"I meant to go back for her once I had gotten the archivists out of the castle," Ekaterine said, her face twisting with worry. "I was going to look for her, but then I was shot, and there was the river, and I was dizzy.... I don't know what happened."

Luka laid a hand on Ekaterine's arm and looked into her eyes.

"Cousin, you have saved a great many people," he said. "You have done a good thing. I too mourn for the Doctor's loss, but there was nothing you could do for her. She was locked in a cell. How could you have hoped to rescue her?"

"Varanus is alive," Ekaterine replied, speaking very firmly, "and I need to go back into the castle and find her."

"She is *dead*," Luka insisted, "or soon will be. She is a scholar and not even past her century. She *cannot* survive, not even if she tries to throw her lot in with the enemy. She is Iosef's student and through him tied to Lady Sophio. For that alone, they will kill her. I am sorry, but there is nothing we can do for her."

"No, she is alive!" Ekaterine insisted. She tried to rise from the bed, but her head swam from exhaustion, blood loss, and fever, and she fell back against the pillows. "She is alive, and once I can leave this wretched bed, I will find her!"

Luka sighed and looked at her sadly. He started to speak, to repeat his insistence of the falsehood that Varanus might be dead—for surely, Ekaterine knew, Varanus *must not* be dead! But suddenly, Luka stopped as another thought came to him.

"Cousin," he said, "how *did* you escape the castle? You would surely have been ambushed and massacred going through one of the gates."

"I led them out through the cisterns," Ekaterine answered. "The spring...it empties out into the river through a tunnel."

"That tunnel is barred and sealed."

"We had Living among us," Ekaterine explained to him. "It took effort, but we broke through the bars." She frowned, suddenly concerned that she might get into trouble for the damage, not that she was normally so concerned about such things. Perhaps it was the fever confusing her. "I suppose it will need to be repaired once the castle is retaken. But it was the only way, I promise!"

Luka looked astonished for a moment, but he slowly rose to his feet. He brushed Ekaterine's hair gently and smiled at her.

"This is very important news," he said. "Cousin, I beg you, remain abed and rest. You both need it and deserve it. In the meantime, I must go."

"Where?" Ekaterine asked, confused at his sudden wish to depart.

"I must report to the Strategos and the Council," Luka explained. "You have just given me some very welcome news."

* * * *

Luka ran across the frozen town square to the fortified house being used as Zawditu's headquarters. He was stopped by the guards at the door on matter of principle, but they recognized him and allowed him to pass. He found Zawditu, Mata Kaur, and the Council seated around a table, discussing their next steps.

"...incidents of fever among those still living in the Shadow," said Rusudan of Tbilisi. "If we are not careful, it may spread. Steps must be taken."

"It will pass swiftly," reminded Lakshmi of Bengal. "Though in the Shadow, the infected remain Shashavani. They will not be ill for more than a day or two."

"It is not the Shashavani of the Shadow we need worry about," said Zawditu. "Lady Rusudan is correct. A fever among our own will spread to the townspeople, and they may not weather it so well."

"I think we are all agreed that there must be a strict quarantine of the sick," said Philippa. "Not only among the Shashavani, but also among the valley people, if disease strikes them. It is already their policy, but we must take extra precautions with so many people crowding their homes and streets."

"Let the Living tend to the sick in the towns and villages," suggested Xasan of Mogadishu. "There are many scholars among us, few of whom will be of any use in fighting. We have nothing to fear from cold or disease. Without our libraries, let us make ourselves useful in other ways."

"A sensible policy," Philippa replied. "Some of our number already perform such charitable works among our neighbors. This should not be any different. Are we all agreed?" She waited while the others nodded their assent. "Good. Next, the matter of food supplies. Sister Lakshmi, have you received the report of the mayor and the town elders?"

"I have." Though Lakshmi's face retained the near inscrutability of the Living, a hint of displeasure in her tone and a tension at the corners of her eyes told the news before she spoke. "Though the townsfolk have enough food for their own needs, our contingent has nearly doubled their population, and that will stretch them to the breaking point. Lacking sufficient winter stores, it seems to me that we have no choice but to impose a system of rationing."

"Both for them as well as for us?" asked Philippa.

Lakshmi nodded. "For both. And it must be a strict one as well."

"All the more reason for quarantine," Rusudan said. "Starvation will increase the risk of disease."

"And let us not forget that this is a hard winter," added Xasan. "The supplies of the townsfolk are already sorely taxed. Will they survive if we take their food as well?"

Philippa frowned and said, "We must take from further afield. We must pool the resources of the whole valley. That way we may spread the hardship thin enough for all to survive. All, or at least most."

"They have already given their yearly tithe!" Rusudan protested.

"Yes, and that tithe is locked in the storerooms of the castle," said Xasan, "where it will feed Margaret's forces through the winter."

"I simply mean that they will not be pleased at being asked to give more."

"This is true," said Philippa, "but they will understand the reason for it. If Margaret has truly turned Basilisk, violence against the innocent is only a matter of time. She *will* continue the tithe, and she will demand blood as well, whether it is given willingly or not. The villagers will understand this."

"I assume that we are giving up the partaking of blood for the duration as well," said Lakshmi.

"I see no choice," Philippa replied. "With the fever and the rationing, the villagers will not be able to give blood and remain healthy. No offers of blood can be accepted until this ordeal has passed."

"Agreed," said Rusudan, and the others nodded along with her.

Zawditu held up a hand and said, "Your pardon, My Lady...." She motioned to Luka. "Luka, come forward. What news?"

Having been summoned, Luka approached the table as the Council members turned their eyes toward him.

"Strategos," he said, "I do not wish to disturb, but my cousin Ekaterine has awakened."

"These are wonderful tidings, Luka," Zawditu said, sounding pleased. Then she paused and asked, "And...?"

Of course, Luka thought, good news about a survivor did not justify interrupting the meeting. But that was not why he had come.

"And she recalls the path she took to lead the archivists out of the castle," Luka explained. "She will be able to relate it to us quite clearly once she has rested a little."

"This is good news," Zawditu said. "Some of the others have given us accounts, but they have not been very conclusive. All they recall is something about a tunnel from the crypts."

"No one remembers where it empties out," added Rusudan, "and we are in no position to send parties to search for it within firing range of the castle."

"It is an old tunnel where the underground spring runs into the river," Luka said. "The way she took passes through the cisterns. The enemy may have placed a guard there, but it will not be substantial. They have no cause to venture so deep."

The members of the Council looked at one another, pleased with the news.

"Then let us gather our soldiers and retake the castle at once!" exclaimed Xasan.

"Yes, I agree," said Rusudan. "If we strike now, Margaret's forces may not have time to ready their defenses."

"No," Zawditu told them.

The members of the Council looked at her in astonishment.

"What?" demanded Xasan.

"Our forces are cold, tired, and hungry," Zawditu explained. "They must rest before venturing into battle against what is likely to be a superior enemy."

"Superior?" Lakshmi asked.

"We have among our number only a third of the Army and just over one quarter of the scholars," said Zawditu. "The rest we can assume are either in league with Margaret or are her prisoners."

"Or dead," said Rusudan.

"Likely some, yes," Zawditu replied. "I suspect that Margaret's goal is power, but there may be those among her company who are motivated by bloodthirst."

"Margaret may be a Basilisk, but she is no fool," noted Philippa, her tone distant and reflective. "She must know that she cannot administrate the House of Shashava without at least a large portion of its members, especially if she begins feasting upon the mortal servants. Nor can she hope to hold its defenses against rebellion with her numbers too severely reduced."

"Precisely," said Zawditu. "Boris of Moskva seemed confident that Margaret's coup would bring about positive change. He is a traitor and he must die for it, but even his treason was motivated by what he thought was best for the House. I suspect that the majority of Margaret's followers believe the same. If Margaret were to slaughter half her prisoners outright, it would cause unrest, and unrest is not something she can risk at so tenuous a time. No, she will attempt to induce the majority of her prisoners to accept her rule, allow them to become complacent and pliable, and then over time she will weed out anyone she cannot trust."

"It is what I would do," Philippa agreed, rather candidly.

"I acknowledge that we have time," Lakshmi said, "but still their stores of food are greater than ours. Waiting will only weaken us and strengthen them."

"Still, it may weaken their morale," suggested Rusudan. "If Margaret allows life to return to normal, the waiting will gnaw upon her soldiers."

Zawditu nodded. "Just so. They must be constantly in a state of readiness awaiting our inevitable attack. Margaret will not risk sending them against us until she is certain that hunger has weakened us to the breaking point, whereas we in our desperation may be mad enough to attack her. So her troops must stay alert, and alertness will bring fatigue."

"Then when do you propose to attack, Strategos?" asked Xasan.

Zawditu considered the question and quietly conferred with Mata Kaur. Finally, she replied:

"Within two weeks, I expect. Much longer and we will begin to feel the bite of hunger, and I do need my troops to be fighting fit. But the intervening time will allow the enemy's morale to erode, and that is of value to us. And of course, there is another reason." She looked toward Luka and asked, "Do you know what it is, Luka?"

"I..." Luka began, surprised at being addressed. He quickly cleared his throat and raised his chin, determined to look and sound impressive when he replied. "The new moon, Strategos."

"The new moon," Zawditu echoed, rewarding him with a slight smile.

"Why should the phase of the moon carry any importance?" asked Philippa.

"Consider this," Zawditu said. "When I attack the castle, through whatever road I choose, I must march my army across an open plain. Not only does Margaret control virtually all the stores of firearms, she controls all the artillery as well. If we move against the castle in daylight or by the light of the moon, we will be seen, and we will shortly be cut to pieces by Maxim guns and mitrailleuses. But if we wait for the new moon or for an appropriately dense storm, they will not see us coming."

"And there is the hope that the river may have frozen fully by then," added Mata Kaur.

"And the river may have frozen," agreed Zawditu.

"What difference would that make?" asked Xasan. "There is a perfectly good bridge, large and sound enough to march an army across."

"There is such a bridge," Zawditu replied, "and I would wager money that there is a soldier with a telescope whose sole duty is to watch that bridge for the first sign of an army crossing it."

"It is a sensible plan," Philippa interjected, folding her hands on the table. "I think we are all agreed on this. Strategos, this Council bows to your experience with the art of war, and we place our fate entirely in your hands."

"I thank the Council for its faith in me," Zawditu said. "But in truth, I think we are all putting our fate entirely in the hands of Luka's cousin and this secret tunnel of hers."

* * * *

Reaching the archives proved more challenging than Varanus had imagined. Hours had already gone by since Margaret's speech in the Great Hall, and whatever had been the result, the rooms and corridors were now filling with activity once again. The patrols from earlier had nearly doubled, and there were even a few scholars suddenly going about their business, though they appeared shaken by what they had seen. Varanus and Vaclav were repeatedly forced to backtrack and to take side routes in order to avoid detection.

"I do hope that your new friends find something useful in those passages," Korbinian said to Varanus as they ducked into the concealment of a side room for the fifth time that day. "Walking about in the corridors is becoming rather tiresome with all of these obstructions...."

Varanus gave Korbinian a look to silence him, but in fact she quite agreed. Anything that came from searching for secret passages would be quite welcome.

"This is becoming rather tedious," said Vaclav.

"Agreed," Varanus replied, "though I rather like the curtains in this room.

"Very pleasant," Vaclav agreed. "It reminds one of home. I feel inclined to put my feet up beside the fire."

"Alas...no fire," Varanus said.

"Alas."

Varanus checked the hall again and saw that the trio of soldiers from whom they were hiding had departed into the distance.

"They've gone," she said.

Vaclav nodded and they hurried to the next room. They were on the ground floor near one of the historical reading rooms, which had its own entrance to the archives. They had tried the main library first, but it was under guard, and there were even a few scholars setting the place in order. But the reading room was empty, and from there they descended into the maze of books and scrolls.

The archives were silent as Varanus entered. Either Margaret's forces had not yet reached them, or they did not consider them worthy of examination. The latter was the most likely: the archives were a chaotic maze, understood by no one but the archivists themselves. There was no reason to waste time and manpower holding them when the occasional search party would be sufficient to root out anyone who remained. But that at least gave the possibility that Ekaterine was still hiding there.

Varanus took a lantern from the wall and began hurrying through the rows of bookshelves, looking in every direction and softly calling Ekaterine's name. She was torn between shouting to alert her friend and keeping silent to avoid alerting anyone else.

"Silence would seem prudent, *liebchen*," Korbinian noted.

Upon reflection, Varanus agreed with him.

"I do not think that anyone is here," whispered Vaclav, as they searched through the dark chamber. He paused as they turned a corner and stopped before a pile of corpses. "Dear God."

"No!"

Varanus ran to the pile and began pulling bodies aside frantically, searching for Ekaterine. But to her relief, she saw that Ekaterine was not one of the half dozen dead. She collapsed to her knees, her gloves and smock covered with blood.

"Thank God," she gasped.

"Sister Ekaterine?" asked Vaclav.

"Not here," Varanus said. "Not here."

Vaclav nodded, but still he frowned at the corpses.

"Such barbarism," he said. "Who could visit violence on the innocent like this? Shashavani killing Shashavani.... It is unnatural."

Varanus saw a glint of metal. Looking more closely, she realized that all of the bodies held weapons—mostly daggers but also one sword.

"I think they died trying to protect the books," she said. "That is why they were killed: they fought back."

"What horrid irony that the books were never in danger." Vaclav scowled at the thought of such unnecessary slaughter.

"And yet, no Ekaterine," Varanus said. "Where can she be?"

Before Vaclav could reply, they heard the sounds of voices approaching them, accompanied by ironshod footsteps. Varanus and Vaclav looked at one another and ducked into hiding places on opposite sides of the bookshelves.

Three soldiers in armor came into view, dragging bodies behind them. Varanus shuddered for a moment and did her best to see if one of them was Ekaterine. Against her better judgment, she leaned out just enough to get a proper look. Again, Ekaterine was not one of the dead.

"Did you...?" one of the soldiers began, just as Varanus ducked back into her hiding place.

"There's someone down here," said another.

The soldiers dropped the bodies and drew their swords. They began to approach cautiously but quickly. Varanus looked at Vaclav with an apologetic frown. Vaclav merely smiled and tapped his own sword.

"How true," mused Korbinian. "These soldiers have committed violence against the innocent. How fitting that we should commit violence against them in return."

Varanus nodded at Vaclav and readied her axes. The first soldier came around the corner with his weapon at the ready, and Varanus rushed in to meet him, holding up one axe to deflect his blow while she swung for her attacker's ribs with the other. The next two soldiers charged at her to protect their comrade, and Vaclav grabbed one and stabbed him in the leg, the sword slicing nearly to the bone. The third attacker turned in place, now unsure of which one to attack.

Varanus's own enemy hacked at her savagely, but while the force of the blows was painful, the thick leather Varanus wore blunted the attacks and left her largely unharmed. She swept her enemy's leg out from under him and drove her axe into his throat.

The third soldier, now recognizing the threat Varanus posed, turned and attacked, forcing her back with a series of heavy blows that she was obliged to block and deflect. Seeing an opening, Varanus drove one axe into her attacker's arm, but the soldier's mail stopped the attack and the axe skidded off. The soldier kicked Varanus in the knee hard enough to break it, and then knocked her to the ground.

Stunned but not disabled, Varanus caught the next attack between both axes and forced the sword away. She threw one into the soldier's chest, and though the mail made the weapon halt and fall to the floor, it had been thrown with sufficient force to crack bones. The soldier grabbed at his chest and gasped for air. A moment later, Vaclav stepped forward and stabbed the soldier from behind.

Varanus accepted Vaclav's hand up and leaned against him while her knee began to pull itself together again.

"My thanks for that," Varanus said, kicking her leg a few times to be sure that the joint worked.

"Hardly a call for thanks," Vaclav replied. "It would seem that we are an effective pair."

Varanus looked down at the bodies and grinned slightly.

"I noticed that as well."

"Are you able to walk?" Vaclav asked.

Varanus tested her weight on the leg and nodded. "Well enough."

"Then we should hurry before they are missed," said Vaclav.

"Agreed." Varanus frowned and asked, "Father Vaclav, do you believe that Ekaterine is still alive?"

Vaclav was silent for a few moments before he answered, "I do not believe that a just God would permit two such fast friends to be parted for long."

"But would a just God permit this?" Varanus asked, motioning to the corpses on the floor.

Vaclav sighed sadly. "That is the question we ask ourselves."

CHAPTER TWENTY-ONE

Ten Days Later

It was morning and all the windows in the house had been left open, flooding the exterior passages with sunlight. It had been this way from dawn until dusk every day for the past week, evidently Margaret's attempt to trap the young and the weak who might still be hiding. The guard had been doubled yet again, which Varanus hoped would eventually tax the enemy to the breaking point. There were only so many people Margaret could trust with weapons, and as their numbers dwindled, they might be forced to leave one of the gates unguarded, making an attempt at escape possible.

Varanus paused at the entrance to a window-lined hall that looked out onto one of the courtyards. Ahead of her, two of Margaret's soldiers walked through the sunlight as they went on patrol. Midway across, one of the soldiers glanced back to see that they were not being followed, but the shadows were enough to keep Varanus hidden. When the soldier resumed her walk, Varanus glanced at Vaclav and nodded.

Keeping low, Varanus dashed across the hall, her arms outstretched, an axe in either hand. She had the plague doctor's mask down over her face to protect herself from the sun. Through the tinted lenses of the mask's eyes, she watched the two soldiers grow nearer and nearer. She ran silently, a trick she had learned over the preceding days made possible by the soft leather soles of her boots.

She had measured her pace well. The hall could be observed from the gatehouse outside and also from a balcony that ran above it. She could not risk killing in so brightly lit a place, but still the soldiers would have to die all the same. She waited until they had passed from the sunlight into the shadows of the corridor beyond, and then she quickened her pace to meet them.

A short distance from the soldiers where her footfalls might be heard, Varanus dropped to her knees and slid between them, striking each in the back of the leg with her axes. Taken by surprise, they cried out and fell to the ground, grabbing for their weapons. Varanus spun around and stood as Vaclav ran across the hall to join her, his larger build making it impossible for him to move silently. Varanus knocked one soldier aside with a sweeping blow and then brought one axe down upon the collar of the second. Vaclav reached her just as she finished killing the second soldier, and he drove his sword into the first.

They stood there for a few moments and looked at one another. Vaclav wiped blood from his face with his sleeve. Varanus reached up and touched her own face, hidden by the mask. Her hand came away with blood as well.

"It seems the mask was a good idea, *liebchen*," Korbinian said, lounging against the wall. He turned and pointed down the corridor. "I say, who is that?"

Varanus turned and looked where Korbinian indicated. She saw a scholar in robes standing a dozen feet away where the corridor intersected with another. The young man held a bundle of scrolls in his arms, and he stared at Varanus and Vaclav in wide-eyed silence. Vaclav slowly stood and stretched his empty hand out toward the scholar.

"Wait..." he said.

"He's going to run," Varanus said.

"Wait..." Vaclav repeated, taking a step toward the scholar.

The scholar turned and fled, his precious scrolls tumbling to the floor around him in his haste to escape.

Vaclav sighed loudly and lowered his head. "That was unnecessary."

"Unsurprising," Varanus corrected, lifting her mask. "You are rather tall and intimidating, Father Vaclav."

" 'Intimidating'?" Vaclav asked. "This said to me by the Plague Doctor?"

Varanus chuckled at this. She looked back the way they had come to see if anyone else had seen them. The sunlit hall was still empty.

"We should hurry," she said. "The poor fellow will bring more soldiers."

"We are late to meet Djata and Joan," Vaclav added. "God willing, they have reached the kitchens already."

"At this rate, they will have taken the food and left without us," Varanus replied, her tone dry.

Vaclav simply grinned.

They continued on quickly, rushing from room to room, ducking into and out of antechambers and corridors as necessary to avoid detection. It was a practice that they refined over the course of their ordeal, and it served them well.

"Soldiers," Korbinian said, moments before Varanus saw them: four men and women in armor and bearing rifles, who had just entered the corridor ahead of them.

"Quick!" Varanus hissed.

She grabbed Vaclav's arm and pulled him through the nearest doorway and into a small music room. She and Vaclav crouched behind a painted baroque harpsichord that some Shashavani must have had imported two centuries ago. They waited there as the soldiers marched past. It would not be long before the bodies were spotted or the hapless scholar alerted someone to their presence, so as soon as the soldiers had gone, Varanus and Vaclav hurried back into the corridor and down the nearest flight of stairs.

Varanus could already smell the scents of cooking meat and bread wafting up from the kitchens three floors below them. She descended quickly, tucking her axes away and drawing her sword to leave one hand free. Like Vaclav, she also carried a firearm—in her case, the elephant gun taken from Luka's chambers—but they both knew better than to use a loud weapon until there was no other choice.

On the landing above the kitchens, they saw Joan the Breton waiting for them with Djata of Mali—the great mathematician from Timbuktu. Joan carried a pair of swords, and Djata had a heavy bow similar to the one that had been used by Thoros. The sight of it made Varanus shudder slightly from the memory.

"All quiet below?" Vaclav asked softly.

Djata nodded and replied, "There were some soldiers but we...."

"In the closet," Joan explained, nodding toward a small room that stood nearby. The door was closed, but blood was already beginning to seep out from beneath it.

"Then let us be to business," Varanus said.

"To business," Djata agreed.

Varanus led the way down the final set of stairs and into the kitchen below. It was not the main kitchen, which sat near the Great Hall, but a smaller one intended to feed the scholars and servants of the east wing as they went about their business. It was a narrow room made entirely of stone, with a single great hearth over which sat a pot of boiling stew. A dozen cooks and their attendants were there in the midst of their work, and they froze at the sight of the blood-covered group that had just entered.

"Is anyone armed?" Vaclav asked.

"I see none," Joan replied.

"Nor I," said Djata.

"Then they live," Varanus said, advancing into the room. She opened the sack she carried. "Let us get some food."

The threat of hunger had plagued them ever since the start of the coup, but as the days passed and injuries were suffered and healed, that hunger had grown. Varanus herself was famished, though she suspected that the others, being older, were less severely affected. Still, she pushed up her mask and quickly devoured a freshly baked loaf of bread while the others began shoving foodstuffs into their sacks.

"P-please..." stammered the head cook, falling to his knees and holding up his hands. "Please don't harm us. We have done nothing!"

"Be at peace," said Vaclav, showing his empty hand. "Unlike your new master, we mean you no harm. But we must take your food."

"But we will be punished for it!" the cook protested.

"Not severely," said Joan, tasting some of the stew. "Mmm, this is very good." She held out the spoon to Djata. "Try it."

Djata took a sip and nodded with approval. "Very good. A pity we have nothing to carry it in."

Varanus, busy shoving bread and dried fruits into her bag, almost did not see Korbinian sitting upon the table until she reached for another loaf and found him in its place.

"*Liebchen*," Korbinian said, "I wonder something."

"And what is that?" Varanus asked absently.

"There was a boy, was there not? Tending the fire?" Korbinian tapped his chin. "What ever has become of him?"

Varanus looked over her shoulder and saw that Korbinian was right: the little boy who had, indeed, been tending the fire when they first arrived was suddenly gone. But where had he gone? He must have slipped out of the kitchen by one of the staircases.

"Where is the boy?" she asked the cook.

At this question, the cook's face became pale and he drew back.

"Please, you must understand," he said. "We had no choice."

"The boy?" Djata echoed, looming over him.

"The last time you took food from a kitchen, the cooks were made to repay in kind! Three of them, to death!" The cook backed away until he ran against a wall and could retreat no further. "They said it would only be a matter of time before you tried it again...."

Varanus closed her eyes and swore "*Merde*."

"Check the stairs! Quickly!" Joan shouted.

She ran for the main stairs while Djata checked the back staircase they had just used. He ducked around the corner and there was a gunshot. He turned back with a bullet hole in his chest and a frown upon his lips.

"Soldiers," he said. "More than a dozen." And with that, he turned into the stairway again and began shooting at their attackers.

"This way is clear!" Joan announced from the main staircase, before charging up the steps.

Varanus hurried to follow Joan. Glancing back, she spotted Vaclav and Djata making a fighting retreat toward them.

The main stairs emptied into a passage leading to the dining hall that served that wing of the house. At first the area seemed empty, but as Varanus turned, she saw a group of soldiers rushing at her and Joan from further along the passage. A moment later, two more came at them from the hall itself. Varanus stabbed one in the gut and threw up her hand to ward off another's attack. His sword cut deeply into her palm, but it did not succeed in severing anything important.

Roaring in pain and suddenly heady at the smell of blood, Varanus stabbed at her next attacker. Most of her blows were deflected by the soldier's chainmail, but two hit home, forcing him back. Behind her, Joan threw one of her opponents to the ground with a heavy shoulder blow and killed him with the sword in her left hand, meanwhile deflecting the strikes of the other with her right. Varanus quickly turned back and stabbed Joan's remaining opponent in the upper thigh before leaving Joan to finish him off.

At that moment, Vaclav and Djata burst out of the staircase and into the passage. Vaclav threw himself at the nearest press of attackers, hacking at them with heavy overhand blows, while Djata drove away any who sought to flank him. Varanus and Joan quickly rushed forward to help them.

As Djata reached for a new arrow, another soldier appeared at the top of the stairs. The ambush party on the other side had found them. Djata reversed the arrow in his hand and stabbed the new attacker through the throat before shooting his intended target.

"We must withdraw!" Joan shouted, blood gushing from a deep gash that had been torn into her side. Vaclav and Djata were similarly injured from the sword blows and gunfire of the enemy. "Into the dinning hall!"

Varanus joined them in a fighting withdrawal, only then realizing that she too was sorely injured. Despite the protection offered by her coat and smock, she had been cut to the flesh along her arms and ribs. In the hall, Varanus, Djata, and Joan held the doorway while Vaclav dragged one of the tables to them. Together, they upended the heavy object—designed to withstand the might of the Shashavani—and barricaded the doorway.

Varanus quickly unslung her elephant gun and joined Djata in firing upon their attackers, who quickly withdrew. As the enemy fell back, Varanus felt herself shiver at the realization that only a few of them were dead. Even the gravely wounded were able to drag themselves to safety. This revelation chilled Varanus as much as it fascinated her. Unless they made certain of a kill, one of the enemy might be up again and hunting for them a few days later—or a few minutes later, if the enemy was among the Living. She had always appreciated the resilience of the Shashavani. What she had not appreciated was just what that meant for their situation. Their guerilla attacks had certainly cost Margaret some soldiers, but perhaps the death toll was not nearly as high as Varanus had hoped.

"Focus on the now, *liebchen*," Korbinian murmured. "Whether *they* live or die, *you* must live."

Varanus nodded quietly to herself. She glanced at Djata, who stood behind the table with an arrow strung, waiting for an enemy to appear again. Varanus quickly stood and shouldered her firearm.

Behind them, Vaclav and Joan were busy checking the doors of the hall. Each one, it seemed, was locked and barred from the other side, which Varanus ascertained from their conversation.

"A trap!" Joan exclaimed, before swearing several times in a variety of languages. "What ignominy!"

"It could be worse," Vaclav said, as he slammed his shoulder into the next door, testing how securely it stood.

"Quite so," Joan agreed. "They could have marksmen on the balcony above us." She pointed upward.

Vaclav looked up and frowned. "Kindly don't invite the Devil with good ideas." He slammed his shoulder into the door again. "I think this one is weakest."

"How can you not break down a simple door?" Joan chided, even as she threw her own shoulder into it.

"This whole castle was built with the Shashavani in mind," said Vaclav. "I suspect even the Eristavi would require a few minutes' work to get this open."

Varanus was about to listen further, but she suddenly saw a fresh group of soldiers rush into the passage and advance in their direction. They carried rifles, muskets, and bows in addition to their swords, and their fire quickly drove Varanus and Djata into hiding again.

"There's no need to rush, Father Vaclav!" Varanus called. "They're merely attacking again!"

She felt slightly wicked saying it, but it was what she thought.

In between volleys, she and Djata popped above the barrier to shoot again. This time, Varanus did her damnedest to inflict fatal wounds to the head or the heart. Let Margaret's troops try to stand again after she was finished with them!

Suddenly, the crowd of enemy soldiers parted, and a large man dressed in plate armor stepped into view. Varanus vaguely recognized him as Alexios of...well, of someplace. Anatolia perhaps. They had passed a few words over the years, but their interests had never really converged. And now it seemed their interests were quite different. She wished to be alive, and Alexios clearly did not agree. He carried one of the new Maxim guns, which was supported by a leather cord looped over one shoulder.

Varanus felt very displeased at the thought that a weapon she had purchased was going to be fired at her.

A moment later, Alexios began shooting, raking the barricade with bullets, a number of which even punched through the heavy reinforced wood. Varanus felt a sting in her belly where two rounds had struck her and passed through. She tasted blood in her mouth, but it was nothing she could not handle. She sprang to her feet and fired both barrels of the elephant gun at Alexios, but one shot was intercepted—likely an accident—by two of the soldiers, who fell to the ground in a bloody heap. The other bullet tore a chunk out of Alexios's arm, but he simply switched hands and kept shooting.

That pause was long enough to give Djata an opening. He rose up and shot three arrows in rapid succession. Each hit Alexios in the chest. Two were deflected by the heavy armor, but one penetrated deeply—all the way through the flesh if Alexios's sudden expression of pain was any indication. But again, it did little good. Alexios was Living. He kept coming, and his next burst of fire tore more holes in the table and ripped Djata's left side to pieces.

Djata fell to the ground beside Varanus, who dropped flat to avoid being torn asunder as well. She still felt one bullet graze her head, cutting a path through her flesh and even biting into the side of her skull. She quickly felt the wound, but realized with relief that it had not penetrated her brain. She was not yet old enough to take a bullet in the brain without some repercussions. Thankfully the blood that covered her gloves was only from those still in the Shadow, and touching the wound did not hurt. But she realized how foolish she had been all the same.

Beside her, Djata sat up, grunting with pain. His arm and part of his leg had been torn apart even to the bone, and he would not be using his limbs for some time to come—not without fresh blood or plenty of food to stimulate healing. But he was still in the fight, and he held out his hand to Varanus.

"Your pistol, if you please," he said.

Varanus was momentarily surprised, but she realized that without both arms, Djata's bow was now no longer of use to him. She quickly drew the revolver from her belt and passed it to him. The two of them kept low to the ground as the next burst of machine gun fire erupted above them, and then they quickly rose and resumed firing.

Varanus had expected the enemy to advance on them in the time that they had been hiding, but it was not so. Instead, Alexios and the riflemen were still a few dozen feet back, although the distance did nothing to diminish the threat of their weapons.

Why had they not stormed the barricade when given the chance, Varanus wondered.

Behind her, Vaclav and Joan finally smashed the door open.

"Quickly!" Vaclav shouted.

"Hold the door," Joan told him, rushing back toward the barricade. "I'll fetch them."

Varanus started to rise, but another burst from the machine gun forced her down again. Pistols and rifles she might face with near impunity, but the volume of fire from the Maxim gun was something even a Living Shashavani had to respect.

There was a pause and she started to rise again. A moment later, she heard the sound of metal bouncing against stone and then two small thuds upon the wood of the table. As she helped Djata up, Varanus glanced into the passage and saw two iron balls that had come to rest beside the table. It took only a second for Varanus to see and recognize the smoke of a slow-burning match.

"Grenades!" she shouted.

Joan, still approaching them, looked puzzled.

"What is a grena—" she asked.

A moment later, the explosion threw Varanus off her feet and into bloody unconsciousness.

CHAPTER TWENTY-TWO

Varanus woke to the scents of cinnamon, clove, and evergreen. Startled for a reason she could no longer remember, she opened her eyes and looked about her to make sense of things. Instead, what she saw only confused her further. She lay on a comfortable sofa placed at one side of an elegantly furnished sitting room. The gas lamps were pleasantly low, but the room was not too dark, and there was a fire burning in the fireplace that made the shadows feel cozy rather than sinister. Everything was calm, and suddenly Varanus could not remember why this seemed strange to her.

It was the red parlor in Fuchsburg Castle, she realized, appropriately named for everything was in shades of red, accented in gold and brass. Across from her, Varanus saw large windows that looked out onto a snowy courtyard that held a tree of incredible size—taller even than the castle that surrounded it. The tree had been decorated with baubles and silver, and countless candles burned in its branches, illuminating the evergreen against the darkness. It was the great tree of Fuchsburg, decorated every winter in celebration of Christmas. How could Varanus have forgotten it?

Just beyond the windows, Varanus saw two figures standing together on the outside balcony, admiring the tree. One was a tall man of about thirty, lean but strong, with Varanus's own fiery auburn hair. It took Varanus no time at all to recognize him: her son Friedrich. He had his arms around a young woman of similar age, whose face—framed with dark brown hair—seemed so familiar, yet Varanus could not quite place it.

"And that is the story of the Fuchsburger tree," she heard a nearby voice say softly.

Varanus sat up slightly and looked around. She saw Korbinian seated in a chair a short distance away, leaning over with his arms resting on his knees as he recited some tale to a half dozen small children. The children—three redheads, two blonds, and one with Korbinian's own black hair—were all dressed for bed in nightshirts, and none of them seemed in the least bit intent on sleeping, which was only to be expected. After all, it was Christmas Eve....

"Another!" cried one of the children—a redheaded girl of about eight, who, as the oldest, seemed to be the leader of the group. Her demand was echoed by the others, who all grinned hopefully and tried to look as cherub like as possible.

"*Another story?*" asked Korbinian, stroking his chin. Even at about fifty, he had lost none of the youthful playfulness that Varanus so adored. "I don't know, Greta, I think that it is time for bed."

"We *must* have another story," insisted one of the boys. "We simply *must*, Grandpa!"

"Someone's very insistent," Korbinian replied, raising his shoulders to subtly change his stance from doting to looming. "Especially, young Theodor, as I know that you, and *you* Greta and Karoline and Jesse and Alexander and Ilse—" He looked at each one of the grandchildren as he named them. "—tried to steal some spiced pies this afternoon from Aunt Sophie and Uncle Josef."

The children quickly looked down, upset at having been found out. The youngest two even hid their faces behind their hands, as if hoping such action might conceal their guilt.

"That was very naughty, you know," Korbinian said, his voice just scolding enough to get the point across without becoming so harsh as to spoil the holiday fun. "And you wouldn't want Father Christmas to learn that you were naughty, would you? Not after all the nice presents he brought you."

"No..." the grandchildren admitted reluctantly.

One little boy clutched the toy he held and looked around as if afraid the Christmas spirit might swoop in and take it away as punishment.

"So in that case," Korbinian said with a smile, again the doting grandfather, "why don't you all run along to the kitchens with Auntie Johanna for a nip of warm cider, and then it's off to bed with you!"

The grandchildren giggled excitedly at this and bounded to their feet, lest Korbinian suddenly change his mind. Korbinian turned to the young woman who sat in the chair beside him and asked:

"You don't mind, do you?"

The woman—in her mid twenties and clearly Korbinian's daughter if her raven-black hair was an indication—smiled and patted him on the hand.

"Of course, Father," she said, before rising to her feet and shooing the children toward the door. "Come along, hurry, hurry." She glanced at Varanus, who quickly closed her eyes so that it might appear she was still asleep. "Do give my love to Mother," Johanna said to Korbinian. "I think I shall retire after I have put the little ones to bed."

"Do not sleep too late," Korbinian said to Johanna. "Christmas is a time for wine and song, not lying abed."

Johanna chuckled softly and gave Korbinian a kiss on the cheek.

"Of course, Father," she said. "Good night."

Still smiling, Johanna gathered up the children and guided them out the door and in search of the promised cider.

Varanus sat up, still muddled from sleep. Korbinian turned toward her, and he smiled in delight to see that she was awake. He rushed to her side and sat beside her, cradling her in his arms.

"Oh, *liebchen*," he said, kissing her hair, "I did not mean to wake you."

"I think I have slept long enough," Varanus replied. She rested her head against Korbinian's shoulder. "I didn't realize I had fallen asleep. Do forgive me."

"Of course, of course, my love," Korbinian said. He held her tightly and gave her a gentle squeeze. "It is late. Well after midnight. Wenzel, Erich, and Gertrude have all gone to bed."

"Very sensible of them, no doubt," Varanus replied. Her thoughts remained confused. Something remained amiss, though she could not discern what it was. Still, there was no reason to upset Korbinian with her muddled thoughts. She reached up with one hand and stroked Korbinian's hair. It was flecked here and there with silver—only to be expected at their age—but it was still as beautiful as she remembered. Indeed, he was still as beautiful as she remembered, despite the passage of thirty years.

Korbinian took her hand in his and pressed it to his lips.

"I love you, my dearest Babette," he said, "more than all the world. Every day we are together is a blessing, now and forever."

Varanus smiled at him and said, "In my dreams I feared I had lost you."

"Nonsense," Korbinian replied. "You shall never lose me. Ours is a love that can never die. Not even God Himself can stand between us. You and I are one, from now until the end of time."

"I know," Varanus told him, nestling her head against his shoulder, "but dreams are dreams. One may...forget oneself in them."

"May your dreams be as they are, *liebchen*," Korbinian said, "but I promise you will never lose me in them, for I will never leave you in this world or the next."

"I know," Varanus replied. She looked at her son, Friedrich, where he stood on the outside balcony. Her *first son*, she reminded herself: she had several, didn't she? "I do fear Friedrich will catch a cold if he remains out there for long."

"We have both warned him," Korbinian answered, laughing softly. "But he is a grown man, prone to foolishness as all men are. It is Yekaterina I worry about."

"Yekaterina?" Varanus asked, before she remembered the name of Friedrich's wife.

Korbinian shook his head, though he seemed amused rather than angry. "I have cautioned them both many times about taking care...well, Yekaterina being with child, you know. And their fifth child no less! She should know better! But she is stubborn, and I suppose I cannot imagine Friedrich married to anyone less willful than he is."

"It is a good son who chooses a willful wife," Varanus said, as her memories slowly returned to her alongside wakefulness. "A true man desires an equal. Only a little boy is afraid of a woman who knows her own mind."

Korbinian grinned at this and nuzzled Varanus's temple before kissing her upon the cheek.

"I know this to be true," he said, brimming with delight. After a few moments, he looked toward the fire and sighed. "Ah, but poor Leopold."

Varanus looked at where Korbinian indicated and saw a blond man in his late twenties dozing in a chair beside the fire. He had short hair and an elegant moustache, both of which suited him, but as Varanus studied him, she felt certain that dark hair would have suited him better. Dark hair...like his father.

"Poor Leopold," she agreed. Leopold was their second son. She knew that. She had always known that. But then, why did seeing him seem at once familiar and also so alien?

"Maria was the perfect wife for him," Korbinian continued. "Perhaps not an Yekaterina, but...well, she knew her own mind. And they were very happy for it."

"We raised a good son," Varanus agreed, "and he chose a good wife. But...." She thought for a few moments, trying to draw up the memory of what misfortune had robbed her second son of his wife. "But tragedy happens even to those most deserving of happiness. Theodor took her from us."

It had been a death in childbirth, hadn't it?

"It was hardly Theodor's fault," Korbinian said. "It is simply God's will. For God causes us sorrow for reasons beyond our understanding. If we could know the mind of God—"

"We could tell him why he shouldn't do such stupid things," Varanus finished. "But we cannot, so we must simply accept."

"Doctor," said a voice, softly, but clearly.

"Quite so, *liebchen*," Korbinian agreed.

"Doctor."

Varanus sat up, suddenly confused. The voice was not Korbinian's, nor did he seem to hear it, but still it was there.

"Doctor."

"Has everyone else gone to bed?" Varanus asked, trying to keep her thoughts coherent despite the distraction.

"Wenzel, yes," Korbinian said. "And Erich. Apparently our dear boys have a 'duel' in the morning. You know, they insist upon reenacting that time that I beat Alfonse des Louveteaux at swords every Christmas. Perhaps they will grow out of it one day."

Varanus frowned. "With our luck, they will pass the tradition on to their children."

"No doubt," Korbinian answered, chuckling.

"Doctor."

Varanus quickly stood, alarmed by the voice that echoed over and over again, but which no one else seemed to notice.

"My love..." she said, "will you pardon me a moment?"

"Of course," Korbinian replied, also standing. "Are you well?"

"Yes," Varanus said, "I just need a moment to myself...."

Her voice trailed off as she walked to the door, following the sound of the voice. She moved quickly but with uncertain steps. The fog had returned to her mind for some reason, though she could not understand why.

"Doctor."

She hurried into the hallway outside, the unceasing repetition of the voice driving her almost to madness. It was so strange and yet so familiar.

Varanus picked up her skirts and ran down the hall, past doors that seemed to close as she reached them, though she thought they were already shut. She turned a corner and came to a halt. Before her stood a tall, broad-shouldered man dressed in a fine frock coat and a suit that would have been fashionable twenty years ago. His hair was silver and his back was to her, but as Varanus slowly approached, one hand outstretched, the man abruptly turned toward her.

It was her grandfather, William Varanus, alive and well, hale and healthy. A nagging thought in the back of her mind told her that he was dead, that he had died six years earlier, in 1887. But that could not be, for here he stood, alive and well.

Grandfather smiled at her and took her hands in his.

"Grandfather...?" Varanus asked, her words catching in her throat. She had so much that she wanted to ask him. But all she could do was repeat, "Grandfather...."

Grandfather smiled at her. With one hand, he stroked her cheek and looked upon her like he had done when she was a little girl.

"Doctor?" he repeated.

* * * *

"Doctor? Doctor, can you hear me?"

Varanus smelled blood and gunpowder. She opened her eyes and saw Vaclav's face hovering just above her as he patted her cheek in an effort to wake her. Varanus sat up violently, her forehead nearly colliding with Vaclav's chin as she was seized with a momentary panic. Varanus grabbed for the knife on her belt and held it up defensively as two more faces floated behind Vaclav's, their features blurred and indistinct.

"Calm, Doctor, calm," Vaclav said, drawing back and showing his empty hands. "You are safe, though I feared you would not wake."

Varanus looked from side to side, still holding up the knife until the blurriness in her eyes faded and she recognized Vaclav's companions as Djata and Joan. They were both bloody and singed. Djata's arm was still ragged from the machine gun fire, its healing slowed by starvation. Joan was much the same, and both of them had been struck with splinters of wood and metal fragments from the grenades.

"What happened?" Varanus asked.

She looked at herself and saw that she was little better. Her clothes had protected her from some of the damage, but a few pieces of shrapnel had cut through the leather and into her flesh. One fragment in particular jutted from her chest just below her collarbone. She reached up and yanked it free. The wound hurt, and it did not bleed as freely as it should have bled.

"Starvation, *liebchen*," Korbinian said to her. He stood behind the others, young and beautiful as ever, and covered in blood. "You are hungry and your body has little blood to spare."

Varanus sheathed her knife and accepted Vaclav's hand as she stood. "What happened?" she repeated. "I remember...a machine gun...an explosion...."

"I learned what a grenade is," Joan said. "I cannot say that I wish to repeat the experience."

"Nor I," agreed Djata. His leg seemed to have healed enough for him to carry weight upon it, but he still treated it gingerly. He ate a mouthful of bread, perhaps in the hopes that it might grant some acceleration to an already strained healing process. "The enemy is well armed and apparently anticipating us. They knew that we would need food eventually. The more injuries we suffer, the more hunger wears us down."

Vaclav handed Varanus her elephant gun and said, "They laid a trap, and we were caught in it. It is by God's mercy that Joan was able to drag you to safety when you lost consciousness." He pressed two finger-tips against Varanus's temple until Varanus became annoyed and gently pushed his hand away. "The fracture in your skull appears to have healed, which is some good fortune."

A fractured skull would certainly explain a lot. Varanus could not clearly remember the things she had dreamed, but she was troubled by them all the same. With her eyes working properly again, she took a moment to get her bearings. They were hidden in a small closet of some sort, paneled in wood but built directly into the stone of the keep. It was likely another one of the hidden passages they had discovered through-out the course of their week's ordeal. Like most of them, it looked to have been deserted for a century at least.

"How did we escape?" Varanus asked.

"In the smoke and confusion, we were able to flee the hall and bar the door behind us," Joan explained.

"It held long enough for us to reach here undetected," Vaclav added, motioning to their hiding place.

"Barely long enough," Joan said dryly.

Varanus frowned. "There is a problem. Unless there is a traitor, they cannot have known where or when we would go to take more food."

"Agreed," said Joan. "And there cannot be a traitor, or else they would simply have come for us in the chapel."

"So they must have set the ambush for us knowing that we would *eventually* visit one of the kitchens for food," Djata finished, scowling. "And not knowing where we would strike, they have surely laid such traps at *every* kitchen and storeroom."

Vaclav's mouth tightened with worry as he said, "Zabel, Magnus, and Amadeus also went to find stores. The lower pantry in the north wing...."

Joan exchanged a look with Djata and grabbed her sword.

"We must go to warn them," she said. "Or to relieve them, if it is too late."

"The gallery with the Frankish antiquities is empty this time of day," Djata said. "It is nearby and also away from where we were ambushed. It should be a safe route."

"It is the best we can hope for," Joan agreed. She nodded at Djata's arm. "Can you use your bow?"

Djata flexed his wounded arm and grimaced, less with pain than with annoyance—for at his age, pain was an afterthought to the Living.

Though the bone showed in places, enough flesh had regrown that it could move, though only poorly.

"Not for a few hours more," he said, "barring a hearty meal before then."

"Exchange with me," Joan told him, offering her sword and taking the bow and arrows.

"We should separate," Vaclav said. "Four are easier to spot than two."

Djata nodded in agreement. He pointed toward the corner of the closet and said, "There is a passage behind that paneling. It should lead you a few hundred feet to the north."

"I remember it," Vaclav answered. "The Doctor and I will meet you at the storeroom. God willing, there is no trap and we have all worried for naught."

"God willing," Joan agreed, "though He has been so *unwilling* these past days, I cannot imagine that it will change just for our convenience."

* * * *

Varanus followed Vaclav into the passage, which descended several uncomfortably steep steps before continuing on. The passage was dark, as was to be expected, but here and there a fragment of light shone in through cracks in the masonry. It was enough to navigate by; besides, there was no way to go but forward.

They were inside part of the keep's walls, and the way was narrow. Varanus had only a little difficulty slipping through, but Vaclav was forced to shuffle along sideways. Every few dozen feet, they passed adjoining rooms, sometimes sealed up with stone or brick and sometimes simply with wood. Had they cared to break out of the passage, it would have been a simple enough thing, but the tunnel's anonymity was far more important. With it, they could bypass much of the castle.

As they continued along, Varanus suddenly heard voices speaking from the other side of a wooden wall. She would have thought little of it, but she recognized the principle speaker as Margaret the Hebridean. Vaclav recognized the voice as well, and he stopped to listen. Varanus found a narrow gap in the boards, and she peered into the room to get a look.

She saw Margaret, Thoros, Iese, and Caroline standing together in a moth-eaten parlor. The room had clearly seen little use, though Varanus could not say whether the conspirators had simply come upon it for their most recent conversation or had appropriated it as a meeting place in the wake of the coup.

"There is no cause for concern, Iese," Margaret said, her tone calm and authoritative.

"No cause for concern?" replied Iese. "This is a *shambles!* Our forces are being slaughtered in our own fortress! Almost two weeks and we have yet to run these mongrels to ground!"

"All in due time—"

"And worse," Caroline interjected, "Zawditu's army sits comfortably encamped across the river, and we do nothing to stop them! We should ride out against them now while we still have the chance!"

Thoros, who seemed only half interested in the argument, merely said, "We cannot attack our enemies in a fortified position while they still have agents here ready to strike at our back."

Having spoken his piece, Thoros returned to his business, which seemed to be a nonchalant walk around the circumference of the room, idly examining the furniture and dusty objects that filled it.

"As Thoros says, we can do nothing until Reza and his followers are rooted out!" Iese snapped. "And every day they pass alive is another list of casualties and stolen supplies!"

"If we were not forced to keep the gates and walls fortified against Zawditu and Philippa, we would have enough soldiers to hunt down anyone still hiding in the castle!" Caroline replied. "Our only option is to move against the town and slaughter Zawditu's forces!" She pointed an accusing finger at Iese. "With the outside threat destroyed, Reza's followers will fall to despair and surrender."

"That is nonsense—" Iese began.

"*Silence*," Margaret said.

She did not raise her voice, but she spoke forcefully enough to be heard. Iese and Caroline suddenly fell silent and looked at her, their expressions now tinged with fear.

"Good," Margaret continued. She smiled and placed a hand on Caroline's shoulder. "Caroline, they are correct: until we have hunted down the enemies lurking among us, we cannot risk sending our army against Zawditu's position." She looked at Iese and took him by the arm, mirroring her hold on Caroline. "But do not fret so. It is...*unbecoming*." Margaret bared her teeth as she said the word. "The ones who stalk us from the shadows are dying, if only slowly. They have little food and are poorly armed. And now that we have properly secured the supplies, they will starve and succumb. We have laid our traps, we are learning their movements, and soon enough we will find their hiding places. They will not last the month, I assure you."

Behind the wall, Varanus frowned. She glanced up at Vaclav and saw that his expression was the same. Margaret was correct. No matter how hard they fought, without outside relief, it was only a matter of time before they were either lost to starvation or their hiding place was discovered.

"And do not forget, dear Caroline," Margaret continued, suddenly clenching her hand around Caroline's arm, "it was your cult that failed me."

Caroline gasped in pain and struggled to pull away from Margaret, but Margaret would not allow it. She continued to squeeze until it seemed the bone might break, and Caroline slowly contorted as even her Living flesh could not ignore the pain.

"It was not my fault!" Caroline protested. "I did all that I was meant to do!"

"Yes," Margaret agreed, leaning over her, "you identified those who were susceptible to fanaticism and revealed yourself as the Virgin Mary. You stoked the fires of madness in their hearts and made them ready to make war upon the Shashavani. *What a pity they did not wait as they had been instructed!*"

Margaret released Caroline and threw her to the ground, now shouting, "If your cultists had been properly commanded, they would now be massing in town, in the very midst of Zawditu's camp, ready to destroy their supplies and shelter and to commit wild acts of violence. And had they done that, we would not now be waiting here, relying on the cold and on hunger to sap the strength of Zawditu's army. Instead, I am left to wait for the winter to carry out that task. Oh, we shall move against them, Caroline; but thanks to your failure, I shall have to wait a month or more before weakness has set in."

"We do not have that much time," Iese protested. "The Winter King expects—"

"I know what the Winter King expects!" Margaret snapped, taking Iese by the throat. "I mean for everything to be perfect and in order when our master arrives to assume the throne. And to that end, Iese, I have given you the task of pacifying the House, and as yet you have failed!"

Thoros laughed at this and returned to the conversation, placing his back to Varanus and Vaclav.

"Consider that, Iese," Thoros said. "Your task was pacification, and yet I thought of lying in ambush." He looked at Margaret and added, "Perhaps, Eristavi, the task of pacification should be mine instead."

Margaret sneered and released Iese, who fell into a heap beside Caroline. Turning, Margaret advanced on Thoros and replied:

"Pacification, Thoros? Do not forget that I must have a living, functioning House of Shashava to hand over to our master. I know what you did that first day, Thoros. I know that when you were supposed to be rounding up prisoners so they might swear their allegiance, you were *slaughtering them!* My subjects! That sort of thing causes unrest, you know."

Thoros did not react with the same fear as Iese and Caroline, but he did quickly temper his tone and drew back a pace.

"It was concealed," he said. "It was blamed on our enemies."

"It was contrary to my orders, Thoros," Margaret answered. "I do not tolerate disobedience and neither does the Winter King!" She turned her gaze toward Iese and Caroline. "Nor do either of us tolerate failure! So pick yourselves up and start making yourselves useful!"

In the darkness behind the wall, Varanus frowned. She looked up at Vaclav and whispered, "Margaret is not the Winter King."

"No," agreed Vaclav. "I had assumed she was, but now.... Clearly she serves some greater power, one that has not yet arrived from the wilderness."

CHAPTER TWENTY-THREE

Varanus pressed her face against the boards of the wall and watched Margaret and her conspirators as they continued to speak, now in calmer tones. Thoros remained at the back of the room, polishing his sword as he only halfheartedly listened to the conversation.

"It seems he becomes bored when not engaged in needless slaughter," Korbinian observed.

"So it seems," Varanus agreed softly.

A moment later, she cringed at having spoken. She did not fear Thoros hearing her, despite how close he stood: she spoke softly, and the noise of Margaret ranting surely drowned her out. But what if...?

"What was that?" Vaclav whispered, looking at her.

"I...nothing," Varanus quickly replied. "It seems Thoros becomes bored when not engaged in needless slaughter."

"You make a habit of talking to yourself, Doctor," Vaclav said, looking back through the slits in the wall. "I hope it is nothing serious."

"One time hardly makes a habit, Father Vaclav."

"No," Vaclav agreed, "but a dozen...?"

Varanus felt the blood drain from her face. A dozen times? Had Vaclav heard her speaking to Korbinian a dozen times? He must think her mad!

"I—"

Vaclav quickly laid a hand on Varanus's shoulder and whispered, "Do not think that an accusation, Doctor. It is not. I trust you and your sanity more than any other, certainly right now. But when we return to the chapel...." He smiled in a fatherly manner. "If there is something that weighs upon you, something you might find relief in discussing.... Well, I *was* a priest. I consider myself very good at listening."

Varanus thought about the offer and smiled, nodding slightly. "Thank you, Father Vaclav," she said ambiguously. "I will consider it."

She might accept the offer to unburden herself, or she might not. She would have to ask Korbinian about it first; to do otherwise would be extremely rude. But the offer certainly was kind.

"Now then," Margaret said, folding her hands in front of her, "if we have all regained our senses, there is a matter of festivities to discuss."

Iese drew back slightly, eyeing Caroline, who still sat on the floor, clutching her broken arm.

"Festivities?" he asked.

"Festivities," Margaret repeated. She paused a moment and said, "Oh, Caroline, do get up. You are embarrassing yourself whimpering like that."

Caroline's mouth twitched and she quickly stood. "Forgive me," she said, holding her head up and setting her mouth against the pain. "A momentary lapse."

"Good," Margaret said, gently patting Caroline's cheek. "Yes, festivities. As you know, while Sophio reigned, she held a regular feast for the whole of the Shashavani Order to remind us that we were all part of one community...a *family*, if you will. And now that she is gone, never to return, I believe it would be wise to revive the practice. It will give our loyal followers a sense of continuity and order. And as it will be Christmas in two days, I can think of no better occasion for such merriment."

"I still question whether your subjects are as loyal as you believe," Thoros said. He paused for a moment and sniffed the air. Perhaps the musty room troubled him. "They obey because of our strength, not because of their goodwill."

"True," Margaret said, "and that is all the more reason to reassure them that I am the rightful Eristavi. The rank and file of the Order desire calm and normalcy. I will give that to them." She folded her arms and locked eyes with Thoros. "Or are you questioning my judgment?"

Thoros quickly looked down and replied, "No, Eristavi."

"Good." Margaret clapped her hands. "So, in two days we will bring the whole of the House to the Great Hall and grant them a feast." She looked at Iese and added, "And if *someone* carries out the task appointed him and roots out the vermin plaguing us, then perhaps we shall have some public beheadings as well! Won't that be a pleasant Christmas entertainment?"

"Yes, My Lady," Iese replied, looking away nervously.

Margaret turned as the door opened to reveal a young woman—the executioner who had murdered Marie of Toulouse—in the company of several more soldiers.

"Ah, Fairfax, what is it?" Margaret asked, her tone beginning as a question and ending as an irritated demand.

Fairfax bowed to Margaret and replied, "News, My Lady. The trap has sprung."

"And?"

"Our forces encountered two groups, My Lady," Fairfax said. "One was ambushed by Alexios of Anatolia and, after sustaining injuries, was able to escape."

"Damnation," Margaret swore.

"The second was met by forces under Jan of Holland," Fairfax continued, "who has cornered them near the Moravian Hall in the north wing. They are putting up a hard fight, but there are only three. They will fall soon enough."

"Splendid!" Margaret exclaimed. "Go with all speed, Fairfax, and bring these dogs to heel. I want them captured and questioned." She turned to Caroline and smiled at her. "Caroline will accompany you and carry out the interrogations. She is eager to regain my approval, aren't you Caroline?"

"Yes, Eristavi," Caroline said quickly.

"Do whatever you must," Margaret instructed. "I want to know where our enemies are hiding. Executions, Caroline!" She reminded. "Executions in time for Christmas!"

Caroline nodded, looking as cheerful as she could manage. But she was afraid and could not hide it completely.

"Well?" she snapped at Fairfax. "Don't stand there gawking! Take me to the prisoners!"

"They are not prisoners yet, My Lady," Fairfax answered, her tone dull and annoyed.

"They had better be so when I arrive," Caroline warned.

"Of course," Fairfax said. She motioned toward the door. "This way, My Lady."

When they had gone, Margaret turned to Iese and said, "It seems you may have just received a reprieve, Iese. Though if Caroline learns the whereabouts of these mongrels before you do, I shall be sorely disappointed."

Iese stiffened. "Whether she discovers their location, I will be the one to hunt them down, Eristavi. I swear to you."

"Good," Margaret said.

"We must hurry," Vaclav murmured. "We have to rescue Magnus and his comrades before they are killed or captured. Djata and Joan will need our help. It sounds as if they will be facing an army."

Varanus nodded. "Agreed."

She and Vaclav began to shuffle further down the passage, but suddenly Thoros sniffed the air again and glanced over his shoulder in their direction. Both of them froze in place, afraid that he might have heard them.

"Do you smell...*gunpowder?*" Thoros asked.

Margaret hurried to his side and sniffed the air.

"No," she said, "but I do smell...." She smiled. "Blood." She advanced toward the wall with a hand outstretched. "There is someone in the wall...."

"We should run," Vaclav said.

"Very sensible," Varanus agreed.

Varanus bolted down the passage behind Vaclav, moving toward the north wing. A few moments later, the wooden paneling of the wall smashed apart as Thoros forced his way into the passage. He grinned at the sight of them.

"Well, well, well," he called after them as he gave chase, all but clawing his way between the narrow walls. "We have rats in the walls.... Run, run, run little rats! I will catch you all the same!"

* * * *

The passage continued on in darkness for several hundred feet. Varanus and Vaclav fled as quickly as the tight confines would allow. Varanus could hear Thoros following some distance behind, struggling even more than Vaclav, his armor catching on every obstruction it brushed against.

More than once, Varanus felt an urge to turn back and meet Thoros head-on, but she knew better than to risk it. Even restricted by the close quarters, Thoros had the advantage of strength and age. Attacking him directly was likely suicidal.

Finally, they reached the door at the end of the passage. It opened into a small storeroom in the north wing, which had, of course, been looted by Margaret's forces early during the coup. At first the door did not open, but Vaclav struck it again and again with his shoulder until it finally gave way. Forcing an opening, Vaclav pushed his way out and helped Varanus through the opening.

"Where do we go?" Varanus asked as they ran into a nearby hall. "To find Magnus?"

"Not until we have escaped," Vaclav replied. "I pray that Djata and Joan will be able to manage whomever has been sent to take them, but I would not tempt fate by bringing an old warrior like Thoros to the battle."

"Perhaps we can divert their forces," Varanus suggested, "if they join Thoros in chasing us."

"That is my hope."

But though they had a good lead on Thoros, they could not escape him entirely. Only a few moments later, he entered the hall behind them, shouting loudly for soldiers to raise the alarm.

"I think you will get your wish," Varanus said.

Vaclav chuckled as they turned a corner and made for some stairs. "Let us hope I am not given cause to regret it."

They reached the top of the stairs and ran across a stone balcony that overlooked one of the castle's many reading rooms. The windows to the room were open, and Varanus made sure her mask was secure over her face before plunging headlong into the sunlight.

An archway at the far end of the balcony beckoned to them. The shadows promised Varanus some relief from the danger of sunlight—which was already causing her skin to prickle beneath the sword slashes and bullet holes that had perforated her clothing. But as they reached the midpoint of the balcony, Varanus saw a group of soldiers coming into view from the adjoining corridor, blocking their path with spears and swords.

Vaclav halted and turned back, as did Varanus. But it was too late to try a retreat: Thoros had reached the top of the stairs, accompanied by two more soldiers who had been summoned by his shouting.

Thoros extended his sword toward Vaclav and Varanus and shouted, "Subdue the infidels!"

Varanus sighed and exchanged a look with Vaclav. Vaclav nodded without speaking, and the two of them stood back-to-back...or as near to it as they could manage with the difference in height. Varanus drew her elephant gun and aimed it at the cluster of soldiers blocking their escape. Vaclav readied his sword and faced Thoros.

"This is going to be unpleasant," he remarked.

"Nonsense," Varanus said. "Nothing like a little slaughter to relieve the monotony."

Vaclav laughed loudly at this, but he was cut off as Thoros gave the order to "attack!" and charged at them. The soldiers followed his lead and rushed in, though they seemed more reluctant, especially the four attacking Varanus. Perhaps the elephant gun was something of a deterrent: as Shashavani of the Shadow, they stood a good chance of dying if they were hit by the large calibre bullets.

Varanus decided to put it to the test. She braced her feet and fired both barrels at her adversaries, making sure to aim for the chest. Her first target was shot dead and fell to the ground. The second was hit in her shoulder, which the bullet all but obliterated. The wounded soldier stumbled and collapsed to her knees from the pain, but it did not escape Varanus that she remained alive and a threat.

There was no time to reload, so Varanus dropped the elephant gun and drew her axes. She knocked aside the first spear that was thrust at her and bounded forward inside her enemy's reach. As she came in close, she struck the nearest target in the leg with both axes to force him down.

The length of the spears made it impossible for her to stay with Vaclav, but she trusted that he would manage without her.

The soldier she had just wounded toppled over as his thigh was torn to pieces from Varanus's vicious hacking. As he fell, Varanus got a proper look at his face. To her great displeasure, she recognized him as one of the men she had brought down over a week ago. She had assumed him dead, like all the other soldiers she had fought, but it seemed that was not the case.

"I suppose, *liebchen*, the solution is to make sure they are dead when you leave them," Korbinian called to her. He sat on the balcony, watching the fighting with a smile upon his bloody lips.

"You're not helping," she told him, without even bothering to conceal her statement.

"I *am* doing my best," Vaclav replied as he parried Thoros's blade and then stabbed another man through the belly.

"Carry on, Father Vaclav," Varanus said. "Don't mind me."

She brought one axe down onto the throat of the man at her feet, making damn sure that he was dead this time. The next soldier on her side of the balcony lunged at her with his sword, and Varanus quickly retreated, battering his attacks away with the axe in her left hand. She moved to the side and allowed him to come at her. He was quicker and more forceful than she had anticipated, and after a few parries, the soldier managed to get a blow through that tore the sleeve of Varanus's coat and cut flesh.

Swearing in French, Varanus drove her shoulder into the man's stomach and pushed him backward until he stumbled over the body of his dead comrade and fell onto the floor. Varanus leapt upon him and struck him again and again in the chest and face with her axes, roaring aloud, until it seemed certain he could not live.

Varanus started to get up but suddenly a spear was driven into her shoulder, forcing her onto the ground and pinning her. Startled, Varanus looked and saw the remaining soldier—the woman who had lost her arm—gripping the spear with her remaining hand and holding Varanus down as well as she could manage. The woman swayed a little from blood loss, but her face was set with the same inhuman determination that Varanus had seen Luka display after similar trauma. Even in the Shadow, Shashavani were Shashavani: they did not easily succumb even when a mortal would give in to death.

Varanus tried to struggle, but the soldier only held her more firmly. The blow had probably been aimed for her heart, but it had thankfully missed. She was restrained but not immobile.

Behind her, Varanus heard another body hit the floor. She looked toward Vaclav, about to call to him for help, but Vaclav was in no position to assist. Both of the soldiers he had faced were down, possibly dead if their wounds were any indication—though perhaps not, Varanus reminded herself. Now Vaclav faced Thoros, and the duel between them was an affair of great brutality.

Both men hacked at one another with their swords, blocking one another's blows with attacks of their own. Soon their arms and chests bled freely from the wounds that were inflicted. Vaclav's mouth was set in a grimace, focusing hard on the fight; Thoros, in contrast, grinned in delight at the bloodshed and laughed aloud.

"Give in, Hussite!" Thoros shouted. "You are too young to best me!"

"By a hundred years?" Vaclav asked. "Little enough time at our age."

He twisted at the waist and broke through Thoros's defense, knocking Thoros's sword away and cutting into the armor along his ribs. Thoros made a noise of pain and withdrew a pace, but before Vaclav could take advantage of this breathing space, Thoros advanced again with an overhead blow, forcing Vaclav to throw his blade up to parry.

"Do not let your arrogance deceive you, Thoros," Vaclav chided him, forcing Thoros's sword away. "I am as strong as you. I am as skilled as you. I will not be an easy victory."

"Perhaps," Thoros replied.

He made a low cut toward Vaclav's legs, which Vaclav quickly blocked. Thoros drew his sword up as if to recover for another blow and then smacked the pommel of his weapon against Vaclav's chin.

"But you are not as ruthless," Thoros added.

As Vaclav staggered backward, drawing up his sword defensively while he recovered from the disorienting strike, Thoros hefted his blade and brought it down upon Vaclav's sword hand, severing it cleanly at the wrist. Vaclav cried out and fell back again, staring at the stump of his arm. He quickly grabbed for a knife at his belt, but before he could draw it, Thoros hacked through Vaclav's leg and then plunged his sword into Vaclav's stomach. Vaclav collapsed to his knees, struggling to stay upright as blood spilled from him.

"No!" Varanus shouted, fighting to stand, to reach Vaclav. She could already see what was about to happen, and she had to stop it! But the soldier who kept her pinned had strength enough to overpower Varanus's famished muscles.

Thoros ignored Varanus and drew his sword from Vaclav's body. He laughed and pointed the tip of the bloody weapon at Vaclav's face, his attitude triumphant and dismissive.

"I have been told that I am not allowed to kill without extending the offer to join us in service to the Winter King," he said. "I find it a pointless effort, but orders are orders. So, Hussite, I give you a choice: you may renounce Shashava and the false laws, join our ranks, and reveal to me the location of Lord Reza and his followers. Or I will kill you now and mount your head above the chair in the Great Hall as a lesson to any who would oppose us. It really is a very simple choice: convert or die."

Vaclav laughed weakly. Despite the weight of fatigue, injury, and starvation, he raised his head in defiance and replied:

"The King of Hungary could not force me to convert when he threatened to have me burned as a heretic. What chance could you have?"

Thoros sneered and raised his sword. "Good," he said, and clove his weapon through Vaclav's neck.

"No!" Varanus screamed, as Vaclav's head fell to the floor and rolled against Thoros's feet. "No! No! No!"

"Be quiet!" snapped the remaining soldier, already swaying on her feet from blood loss and trauma.

Varanus felt her head pounding as she stared at Vaclav's lifeless eyes. She had so little blood left, but that which remained boiled inside her. A strength she had not known in days suddenly returned to her, flooding her with its fire. She grabbed the spear that pinned her and tore it from the soldier's hand. With the support of the spear gone, the soldier tumbled to the floor, her injuries preventing her from standing. Varanus pulled the spear free from her shoulder and drove it into the soldier's chest.

Quiet yourself, she thought, though when she tried to speak, all she managed were a few guttural snarls.

"Well, well..." Thoros said, turning toward her. "The masked fiend that has been terrorizing my soldiers these past days. You and your comrades have been quite the nuisance to me." He raised his sword. "I shall enjoy this."

Varanus tried to offer some retort, but again all she managed were snarls. She snatched up her axes and charged at Thoros, roaring like a beast even as she heaped insults upon him in her mind. Thoros seemed surprised by Varanus's ferocity, and her first attack managed to break through his defense and draw blood.

But Thoros did not remain unprepared for long. He kicked Varanus savagely to force her away and began hammering at her with his sword, driving her backward and to the ground beneath the might and savagery of his attacks. Each time Varanus tried to seize an opening, Thoros intercepted her and forced her away. It was all that Varanus could do to deflect Thoros's blade.

Growing frustrated, Varanus waited until Thoros stood mid-swing and threw an axe at his face. Started, Thoros interrupted his attack and jerked away as the axe clipped his ear.

"Damn you!" Thoros shouted, renewing his attack. "Die you gnat!"

Varanus withdrew to the railing of the balcony and evaluated her situation. Thoros had the advantage of strength and speed, but most of all he enjoyed height, which made it all too easy for him to deflect Varanus's attacks and keep her pinned in place.

Climbing onto the railing, Varanus turned to face Thoros. As he came at her again, Varanus raised her remaining axe high above her and leapt at him, bringing her weapon down two-handed, aiming to cleave his head open.

It was a good plan, Varanus concluded, and it would have worked too, had Thoros been mortal. But he was Shashavani and centuries her senior. With inhuman speed, he intercepted her with a blow to the chest, shattering her ribs and almost rending flesh beneath the leather of her coat.

Varanus was lifted into the air, and she fell backward, tumbling over the railing and down toward the stone floor below. Though dazed from the blow, she remained conscious until she hit the marble with a painful crack, saw a flash of white, and then saw nothing but darkness.

CHAPTER TWENTY-FOUR

It was the burning touch of the sun that snapped Varanus back to consciousness. The vacant nothingness that had filled her when her head struck the stone floor was suddenly boiled away by the telltale stinging of daylight where it touched skin exposed by the holes in her coat. Varanus jerked her head up and rolled onto her side, giving her exposed back a moment's reprieve while the sun began to burn her chest and abdomen. Her head still swam from the impact, and she felt blood trickle down her cheek, but she was alive and awake.

And it was well that she was, for looking upward she saw Thoros on the balcony, leaning over the railing. At first he looked amused, but as Varanus stood—aided by the nearby wall—his expression became one of shock and anger. Perhaps he expected she had been knocked out so soundly that she would simply burn to death before ever waking again. Still, Varanus was not about to tempt either the sun or Thoros. Tucking her head down to relieve the pounding in her temples, she bolted for the nearest doorway.

Glancing back, Varanus saw Thoros drop from above and land firmly on both feet. His snarled at her, shouting obscenities in at least three languages as he charged at her. Varanus waited no longer but kept on running as Thoros gave chase. She ducked and dove down each passage that presented itself to her, working hard to place some distance between herself and Thoros, whose stride outpaced hers. She was suddenly thankful for his age, for in his day even big men had been much shorter, and the difference between them was not so great as with a younger Shashavani.

Here and there, groups of scholars crossed Varanus's path, though they all quickly drew away in fright at the masked creature running past them. But Varanus took advantage of the newcomers, darting behind them or shoving them into Thoros's path. Thoros shoved them away just as quickly, and with little regard for their safety, but it was enough to slow his chase. A few minutes later, Varanus was able to duck behind the pillar of an indoor cloister before Thoros rounded the corner. Not seeing her, Thoros swore again and continued on into the next room, a trio of soldiers following behind him.

Varanus gasped with relief when they had gone. Thoros was like a dog bent upon nothing but running his prey to ground, and Varanus was grateful for it. Had he taken a moment to search the cloister, he might have smelled the blood that hung about her. Thankfully, Thoros's single-minded obsession with the chase would not allow him to pause long enough to detect his prey.

"Best not to be complacent, *liebchen*," Korbinian observed, as he leaned around the pillar from the other side. "They will be back eventually, when the lout realizes that he has lost your trail."

Varanus nodded. "I should find the others," she said. "To tell them about...."

She stopped, unable to speak of Vaclav's death. She gritted her teeth and fought back tears. They would not help, not now.

"There will be time to mourn fallen friends later," Korbinian said. "And to exact revenge. But now, you must find your allies and see what has become of them."

"The Moravian Hall," whispered Varanus.

She checked to see that the hallway was empty before she left her hiding place. She was in the north wing and not too far from the Moravian Hall. With her axes gone, Varanus drew her sword and darted back the way she had come, carefully pausing at ever corner and intersection to be sure she was not seen. She had no wish to find Thoros on her trail again before she rejoined Joan and Djata.

But as she approached the Moravian Hall, she realized that her allies had encountered the enemy and that it had not gone well for anyone involved. She smelled blood before she came across the first corpses—two soldiers who lay where they had fallen, pierced by arrows. Shortly after were three more bodies, torn apart by both arrows and sword wounds. The floor was slick with blood, and Varanus walked carefully, in part to avoid slipping but mostly to reduce the noise of her footsteps.

At the doorway to the hall, she found even more bodies strewn about the corridor. The corpses had been dealt with violently, but they had all died fighting. Their own weapons were drawn and caked with the blood of their enemies. At least one of the soldiers appeared to have died not from outright injury but from exposure to the blood of the Living, which had seeped into his wounds as he lay upon the floor. Fortunately, the blood had lain for long enough that it was probably no longer a danger, but the smell of it made Varanus hungry. She could not drink—because that would be cannibalism and because it might still be toxic—and that made her hunger all the worse.

"Water, water, every where," Korbinian whispered in her ear, "and all the boards did shrink."

"Water, water, every where," Varanus agreed softly, "nor any drop to drink."

Varanus looked past the open double doors and saw another cluster of bodies on the floor, again having died in battle. But their deaths had still achieved results. Varanus saw Djata and Joan lying near the door, where they must have fallen while trying to fight their way inside. Another look revealed where they had been trying to go: the bodies of Magnus, Zabel, and Amadeus were slumped over a makeshift barricade of benches placed near the door. All of them were alive, but likely not for long.

Two more soldiers stood by the bodies, their weapons raised in case one of the Living recovered enough to pose a threat. They were led by Jan of Holland, who stood beside Caroline of Burgundy, covered in blood and looking deeply worried by the losses among his forces. Caroline did not seem to share his concern: she held a military hammer in one hand and gleefully brought it down upon Amadeus's head. From the state of Amadeus's body, Varanus gauged that Caroline had already beaten him with it several times before.

"Well?" Caroline shouted at the body. "Will you talk now? Or must I continue?"

Amadeus did not answer.

"You fiend!" snarled Zabel, rising as best as she was able despite being almost eviscerated. "He is dead!"

"Restrain her," Caroline instructed Jan, before poking at Amadeus's body with her hammer. "Hmm...perhaps she is right, though."

Jan pressed the tip of his sword against Zabel's chest and pushed her back down. To Caroline, he replied, "I believe it is so, My Lady. Perhaps you would prefer to interrogate the prisoners more gently...while we still have some."

"Do not question me, Hollander," Caroline replied. "Four still remain. And they will recover in time. Won't you, sodomite?" she asked Magnus, kicking him in the ribs.

"Is that you, Caroline?" Magnus asked, his breath rasping from a collapsed lung—courtesy of a spear wound that had torn open one side of his chest. "I would know your shrill, jealous voice anywhere...."

Caroline kicked him again and raised the hammer to strike him, but she was interrupted as Zabel, struggling to push away Jan's sword, shouted:

"I will kill you, you traitorous Frank!"

In a fury, Caroline turned toward Zabel, drew a pistol from her belt, and shot the woman in the head.

"I am *Burgundian!*" she shouted.

Jan sighed and withdrew his sword. "Again, My Lady, perhaps some restraint is in order."

"She will recover," Caroline replied. "One bullet through the brain will not kill someone of her age." She looked at Amadeus. "What a difference a few hundred years makes."

"Indeed, My Lady," Jan said. He glanced toward the door, forcing Varanus to duck back into hiding. "Where are my reinforcements? You!" He pointed at one of his soldiers. "Get to the nearest guard post. Find out what is taking the others so long. I require hands to carry bodies."

"Yessir," the soldier replied, hurrying for the door.

"And have someone ready the cells!" Jan called after him, before turning back to Caroline and Magnus.

Varanus pressed herself against the wall to avoid detection as the soldier ran past her. Glancing into the hall to be sure that no one was looking, she scampered after him and drew her knife. The soldier paused and started to turn at the sound of her footsteps, and Varanus jumped upon him and drove the knife into his throat before he could scream. Varanus glanced back in case someone had heard, but to her relief, she remained undetected.

Creeping into the Moravian Hall, Varanus weighed her options. She was in no condition for outright fighting, certainly not against someone of Caroline's age. She approached the remaining soldier and readied her knife for a throw. If she could kill him and catch him before he fell, it was possible no one would notice. Of course, if the soldier's metal armor or sword hit the floor....

"Allow me, *liebchen*," Korbinian said, gently taking the knife from Varanus's hand.

He gave her a tender kiss upon the lips and crept up beside the soldier. There was a pause, and then as the soldier began to turn, Korbinian drove the knife into his throat.

The blow was a good one. The spray of blood went against the wall, and though the soldier gurgled as he fell, his noises were soft enough that it did not draw the attention of either Jan or Caroline. Varanus hurried forward and caught the man's body as it collapsed. She grabbed for his sword, but it slipped through her fingers.

Merde, merde, merde!

Varanus cringed, waiting for the inevitable clatter of steel on stone, but it did not come. Surprised, she looked down and saw the sword hanging just above the floor, clutched in the hand of Djata of Mali. Though too injured to rise, Djata met Varanus's eyes and gave her an understanding nod. Varanus nodded back and carefully lowered the dead soldier to the ground. Retrieving her knife, she approached Jan and Caroline.

Ignorant of Varanus, Caroline knelt over Magnus and prodded him with her hammer. Dried blood had caked over Magnus's face, sealing his eyes shut, but the sneer he gave Caroline was as good as any defiant look.

"I can make things very pleasant for you, Magnus," Caroline said, "or I can make them very painful. All you need to do is tell me where your friends are hiding."

"Every conversation with you is painful, Caroline," Magnus replied. "No amount of treason will alter that."

Caroline snarled and struck Magnus in the ribs on his injured side. Magnus shuddered and made a noise, but his expression remained the same.

"You *will* tell me what I want to know," Caroline said. "Or I will pry it from one of your companions. But know that it will go easier on you the sooner *one of you* tells me."

Magnus sighed wistfully and said, "Oh, Caroline, Caroline...." He coughed violently before he continued in a weak if jovial tone, "Have I ever told you of my illicit tryst with the Duke of Buckingham? Oh Lord, poor King James was most distressed. He had me banished from England for fear that I would steal his favourite away from him."

Caroline growled in frustration and struck Magnus again.

"Sodomite," she repeated.

"Frank," Magnus replied, laughing.

"*I am Burgundian!*" Caroline shouted, drawing back her hammer and preparing to bash in Magnus's head.

Varanus darted forward and drove her knife to the hilt into Caroline's throat. Taken by surprise, Caroline lashed out blindly with her hammer. Before Caroline could properly recover from the shock, Varanus twisted her knife to increase the wound and pulled the weapon free, giving Caroline a solid kick for good measure. Blood sprayed into the air, and Caroline fell backward onto the floor.

Jan had also been taken by surprise, but it was not enough. He turned on Varanus and lunged at her, cutting her across the back. As Caroline's blood sprayed everywhere, some of it fell upon Varanus's wound, which stung angrily and boiled. But thankfully there was not enough blood to cause any more harm than the pain.

Varanus lashed out with her knife, trying to keep Jan back. She had taken her opportunity, but it would do her no good if she could not bring Jan down before Caroline recovered. But as Jan came at her again, she saw one of Zabel's eyes open and blink a few times. The hole in the woman's head had not yet healed, but she seemed to retain enough co- herence to realize what was happening. As Jan withdrew and made ready for another attack, Zabel kicked him in the knee, unsettling his balance and making him stumble.

It was the opening Varanus needed. She leapt upon Jan and drove her knife into his throat again and again until he fell to the ground. She kept stabbing until he stopped moving.

There was a breathless pause, and then Varanus heard the sound of Caroline struggling to rise. She turned and saw the woman crawl onto her knees, clutching at the deep gash across her throat.

"You...die..." Caroline gurgled, struggling both to speak and to maintain consciousness from the sudden loss of blood.

Varanus was in no mood to mince words with her, not after Vaclav's death. Caroline was not Thoros, but she would do for now.

Snarling in guttural tones that she had meant to be words, Varanus charged into Caroline and knocked her to the ground again. Caroline struggled, and for a moment she held Varanus back, using her superior strength to level painful blows with her hand against Varanus's chest and neck. But each time Caroline moved to strike Varanus more blood spurted free, and it was soon a fight she could not win.

Howling with fury, Varanus brought her knife down upon Caroline in jagged cuts that tore and tore until it looked like the Burgundian had been set upon by a wild beast. Only when Caroline stopped struggling and collapsed did Varanus finally stop. She slowly rose to her feet, drenched in Caroline's blood. It was some mercy that the fresh wound across her back had not been exposed to the fruits of her violence, or else Caroline's blood might have done her grave harm in such quantity.

It took Varanus a short time to regain her senses, heady as she was with the thrill of slaughter. But presently, she realized that the others were slowly picking themselves up off the ground. Djata and Joan supported one another, while Zabel sat up with the aid of the barricade. Magnus clawed at his face to clear the blood from his eyes, and he slowly sat up as well.

"Doctor Varanus?" he asked, sounding surprised.

"Hello, Doctor Eriksen," Varanus replied, offering him a hand up.

Magnus stood with difficulty, being careful not to let his open wounds touch the blood that drenched Varanus's clothes.

"From the sound of things, I took you for a tiger," he said.

"I shall take that to be a compliment," Varanus told him.

"Good," Magnus replied. "It is one."

Varanus smiled at this.

Magnus looked around the hall, searching for someone who was missing. "Where is Vaclav?"

"Yes, where is he?" asked Joan as she and Djata reached them. "Did he not come with you?"

"He...I..." Varanus stammered. She could not bring herself to say the words.

But Magnus understood all the same. His face became pale—even for a Shashavani—and his hands quivered.

"No...."

"Yes," Varanus said. "I tried to save him."

"Of course you did," Djata told her, his mouth twisted with anger but his eyes sympathetic. "You are so young, Varanus. If Vaclav could not have withstood it, there was nothing you could have done."

Magnus shook with anger as he asked in a low tone, "Who did it?"

"Thoros," Varanus replied. Speaking the name made her clench her fingers around the hilt of her knife.

"Then there truly was nothing you could have done," Joan said. She sighed and shook her head. "We should have gone with them," she told Djata. "I had thought our route would be the more dangerous."

"As did I," Djata said. He turned to Varanus and Magnus. "I am sorry. Vaclav was a friend, and I know that he was dear to both of you."

"I will kill him!" Magnus roared, the anger making him forget the severity of his wounds. "I will kill Thoros with my bare hands for this!"

"If I do not reach him first," Varanus said.

"No one will be killing Thoros today," interrupted Zabel, who had recovered enough to sit up. She clutched at her stomach to keep it intact, but the bullet hole in her head had almost closed. "None of us are in any condition for more fighting." There was a pause. "Could someone fetch me a clean cloth to tie around myself? I would like to keep my insides... inside."

"Allow me," said Joan. She released Djata and hobbled over to the nearest wall, returning with a set of curtains that she began to tear into large bandages.

As Joan bandaged her abdomen, Zabel sat up and her eyes fell upon Amadeus's body. Her face remained emotionless, as was common among the Living, but her anger was palpable. Magnus knelt by the body and searched for any signs of life, though it was an unlikely hope, and in the end it proved to be unfounded.

"I am sorry, Sister," Magnus said.

"He was too young to survive it," Zabel said, her voice cold but shaking with anger. "I knew it when she struck his head." She looked away, her mouth twisted in a frown. "He was a good man and my finest student. Such waste."

"At least Caroline was punished for it," Djata noted. "Vengeance is something, if only a little."

Zabel nodded, but said, "Cut off her head."

"Surely there is no need," Djata replied. "She has been...well slaughtered by the hand of young Varanus."

"It was well done, truly," Zabel said, giving Varanus an approving look. "But Caroline is our age. She may survive this. I was shot in the head and I am well enough."

"Ah, that is true," Djata agreed.

"I will handle it," Varanus said, before anyone else could volunteer. She had set out to kill Caroline and saw no reason not to finish the job. She drew her sword and hacked at Caroline's neck until she finally severed the spine at the joint—the vertebrae themselves were far too strong to cut. Kicking the head away, she said, "Done. Now we should go."

"Agreed," said Zabel. She looked at her student's corpse. "What about Amadeus?"

"We must leave him," Joan answered, tying off the bandages and helping Zabel to stand. "I am sorry, Sister, but we must move quickly to avoid capture, and none of us is in a fit state to carry his body."

Varanus cleared her throat. "Speaking of capture, Jan the Hollander seemed to be expecting reinforcements. As I said...." She pointed toward the door.

"Yes, of course," Djata said. "Leave it to the child to remind us of our predicament."

"I—" Varanus began to protest, but she thought better of it and held her tongue. *The child?* she thought. *What nonsense!*

Zabel leaned on Joan and clutched her bandaged stomach with her other arm. "Magnus, fetch the food. We will eat on the way."

"Eat?" Magnus asked, surprised. "What about the others."

"We are wounded, they are not," Zabel replied. "Though if anyone complains, I will amend the situation."

Magnus nodded and grabbed two large sacks from behind the barricade. The arm on his injured side did not rise properly, and Varanus crossed to him and took one of the sacks to relieve the burden. She opened it and took a moment to savor the scents of baked bread and roasted meat: it seemed that before the ambush, Zabel's party had enjoyed better luck in their kitchen. Varanus took a piece of cooked lamb and held it out to Magnus.

"Eat," she said.

Though momentarily surprised, Magnus cracked a smile at her and took the meat with his teeth.

"Thank you, Doctor," he said out of the corner of his mouth before he began chewing.

Varanus nodded and ate a piece herself. The flavor of meat was very pleasant after a week of deprivation, and the rush of energy that followed was remarkable. Within moments of swallowing, Varanus actually imagined that she could feel the wound across her back closing. She quickly distributed more morsels among the others and led the way to the door.

"We should hurry," she said. She held up one bloody arm. "We must clean ourselves before we venture back to the chapel, and we will be hard pressed to do it without discovery."

Covered in blood as they were, the stench would follow them and lead the enemy to their hiding place unless something was done about it.

"She is right," said Djata. "And with reinforcements coming, we must hurry indeed."

CHAPTER TWENTY-FIVE

That night, Varanus joined Reza and the others in the chapel to discuss what was to be done. Even with the foodstuffs provided by Zabel's party, there was little to go around and certainly nothing to last until rescue. And, as the day's events had shown, obtaining food from then onward would be a difficult task, one met with ambush and bloodshed at every turn.

"We must strike, My Lord," Joan said to Reza. "Whether we attack and seek escape or simply endeavor to die in glorious combat, there is no choice."

"No choice save starvation and inevitable surrender," Reza agreed, "which is no choice at all."

There were murmurs of agreement from the others.

"We must attack soon," said Djata, "while we still have some strength in us. The longer we remain, the more it will dwindle."

"You will find no dispute with that, Brother Djata," Reza said. "Let us attack before the week is out. The only question is when and where such an attack will strike the enemy most harshly."

There was silence as the others looked at one another. It was both wise and necessary to make such an attack, but in truth it would be an act of suicide. The question that remained was how best to make their deaths count; how best to make the enemy suffer in trade for their own lives. It was a grim realization and one that was not easily answered.

"If I may, Lord Reza..." Varanus said, stepping forward. As the youngest member of the survivors, she had kept out of the discussion until now.

"Sister Varanus," Reza answered, nodding. "Come forward and speak. What do you have to say?"

Varanus approached Reza and bowed her head.

"My Lord, before Father Vaclav was killed...." Varanus flinched at the words, remembering her friend's death too clearly. "He and I overheard Margaret speaking to her fellow conspirators. She spoke of holding a feast in the Great Hall to celebrate Christmas. She intended it to...

to confirm her authority, to make her the new Sophio in the eyes of the House."

Reza considered this quietly for a little while. At length, he nodded.

"That does seem like her," he said. "And truly, it would help grant her some illusion of legitimacy, mimicking the protocols of the rightful Eristavi. Christmas, you say?"

"It will be late Christmas Eve or early Christmas morning," Zabel said. "The occasion will be nothing but a justification. With so much recent unrest and bloodshed, the sooner she reaffirms her control, the sooner she strengthens her hold."

Reza thought for a little while and nodded. "Christmas Eve, then. We will arm ourselves, eat our fill from what stores we have, and assault the traitors in the Great Hall." He looked at the others and said, "I will not order any of you to join me in this. I will go, and I will give my life if it means seeing Margaret and her cohorts slain. But any of you who choose to remain here, to carry on as best you can in the hope of Lady Sophio's return, you have my blessing."

The others looked at one another, and there were murmurs of uncertainty from those scholars who were unfamiliar with war. But Judith of Prague stepped forward and spoke:

"We may not be warriors, My Lord, but we are Shashavani. We will all gladly give our lives if it means the destruction of these Basilisks and the liberation of our House."

"What a day it is when scholars speak the words of soldiers," said Magnus, laughing. "And what better cause for which to die than one that will drive the peaceful to wrath and the treacherous into Hell!"

* * * *

Turkestan

Iosef sat with Sophio at the edge of the Aral Sea, watching the waves break upon the frozen shore as the sun set behind them. Iosef's bones ached. The agonizing fatigue he had felt midway through their journey had increased tenfold, and his very body cried out with pangs of hunger. It was a remarkable experience, as intriguing as it was painful. In his mortality, he had only known hunger with his stomach; now it revealed itself to him with every part of his being.

He held Sophio in his arms, gently running his fingers through her hair, sometimes fighting against the wind as it whipped Sophio's braids into a sort of halo around her head. The stranger, Olga, sat a few feet away, also watching the water. After weeks of traveling together, she still seemed just as friendly as when they had met upon the road and just as secretive. She eagerly spoke of anything and everything, save her identity and purpose.

"Do you trust her?" Iosef asked softly. It was likely that Olga could hear them even at such a distance, but it was possible that the wind and the waves would drown them out.

Sophio thought about the question before she smiled and said, "I *feel* that I ought to...and I *know* that I should not. Does that answer your question?"

Her smile became playful for she knew that her answer said little.

"No, it does not," Iosef replied, kissing her ear.

"When I remember who she is," Sophio murmured, "I will tell you whether she can be trusted. Until then, she is our...mysterious sojourner, our companion on the road whom we can neither trust nor distrust."

Iosef sighed. "Sometimes I think you delight in tormenting me."

Sophio looked into his eyes, trying almost with success to appear aloof and serious as she replied:

"My love, I delight in everything about you, including your torment."

Iosef could not help but laugh at this, and he nuzzled Sophio's cheek. "You are a cruel mistress, beloved."

"Not cruel!" Sophio protested. "I could never be cruel." There was a pause, and her eyes flashed with distress, perhaps at some memory almost forgotten. "To you. I could never be cruel to you."

Iosef quickly kissed her hand.

"What troubles you, my love?" he asked.

"I nearly had a man bled to death for my pleasure," Sophio murmured. Though it was subtle, her tone was horrified.

Iosef remembered the incident: two decades ago, Sophio had demanded more blood than the donor could safely give simply because she enjoyed the taste. That night she had forgotten herself and her nature.

"It was only the once," Iosef reassured her.

"Twice," Sophio corrected. "It happened twice."

"No lasting harm was done, and now it has been forgotten," Iosef said. "You must not torment yourself with what might have happened. It was simply the weight of the world bearing down upon you."

Sophio shook her head and replied, "Do you not understand, husband? Those were the actions of a Basilisk. For a moment I became a Basilisk. I forgot reason and dignity and obligation. I discarded the sanctity of mortal life. I abandoned myself and my nature at the behest of pleasure and excess. I became like Basileios and his followers."

She looked into Iosef's eyes, for the moment terrified at her own power.

"I became like those that I most despised, Iosef," she whispered. "And who can say that I will not do it again?"

"I say," Iosef replied softly, stroking Sophio's cheek. "You are the wisest and the strongest of us. Faced with your centuries of guarding the House of Shashava against corruption, any of us might have lost ourselves to temptation as well. Surely we would have! And unlike you, we would not have pulled ourselves back from the abyss."

Sophio looked at him silently for a little while, perhaps considering his words. Presently, she smiled and raised Iosef's hand to her lips.

"You are correct, beloved," she said. She sighed. "I have needed to be in the world for so long; I have allowed myself to wonder too much. It is a lesson I shall not forget. Perhaps you and I should sojourn together more often." She smiled slightly. "Once every hundred years, perhaps. Often, but not irresponsible."

"I would like that, my love," Iosef replied, chuckling at Sophio's joke. "Often indeed."

Sophio smiled, pleased at his reply, and leaned back in Iosef's arms. They watched the sea in silence for a little while as the sun receded and the darkness began to draw across the water. Iosef glanced at Olga once or twice, keeping an eye on her. Sophio did not seem to find her threatening, but Iosef was young enough to still feel the lure of caution.

Presently, Sophio drew his attention again as she pointed toward the sea and said:

"How beautifully she dances. Don't you think so?"

Iosef turned back, surprised by the question. He looked out onto the water, but the place that Sophio indicated was, of course, empty. Even in the growing darkness of the moonless night, Iosef could see that there was nothing there but the waves.

"I see no one, my love," Iosef murmured, uncertain if Sophio was playing a game at his expense. It was unlike her, but what other explanation could there be?

Sophio frowned and pointed again, her finger outstretched toward the empty black horizon.

"There," she said. "The girl in sable." When Iosef did not respond, Sophio held one hand up above her head. "The girl with the horns in black dancing upon the water. Tell me you see her, Iosef. She is looking at us now."

Iosef shook his head slowly and wrapped his arms tightly around Sophio to reassure her, even as he was forced to reply, "There is *no one* there, my love. Nothing but the sea and the sky. Not even moonlight."

Sophio looked bewildered by the statement, and she began to protest. A moment later, she seemed to remember herself and closed her eyes, gently shaking her head. Opening them, she studied the sea again and sighed.

"You are right, of course," she said. "There is nothing. No one." Her mouth twisted with displeasure. "I lost myself again. I thought that my madness had passed, and yet it haunts me still."

"No, no, my love," Iosef insisted, murmuring in her ear. "It was a momentary lapse. A vision brought on by fatigue. Perhaps a memory from long ago."

"Perhaps," Sophio whispered. It did not sound like an affirmative.

Iosef placed a hand on Sophio's cheek and looked into her eyes, smiling at her.

"We are both exhausted beyond measure, my love," he said. "Starved, frozen, tired from the road. Surely this is to be expected now and again." He laughed softly. "I count it a miracle I did not begin seeing visions while we were still in Persia, I am so exhausted."

Sophio smiled at this and caressed the back of Iosef's hand with her fingertips.

"If you are so tired, my dear Iosef, I could carry you. We are only a day or two away."

"And what sort of anchorites would we be, carrying one another?" Iosef asked. "No, I shall walk beside you, hand-in-hand, until we reach the tomb of Arslan Khan, and then I fear I shall collapse and be of no further use to anyone."

This made Sophio smile, and she kissed Iosef on the cheek.

"You shall always be of use to me, husband. From now until the end of time."

"What a wonder it is to have eternity," Iosef agreed.

They were interrupted as a figure loomed over them. Iosef looked up and saw Olga approaching, leaning on her staff. The wind pulled at her hair as it streamed around her face, dancing as if alive.

"Come along, my turtle doves," Olga said, tapping her staff against the ground impatiently. "We ought to be away from here. We are so very near our goal, we should not delay."

"You do not wish to rest?" Sophio asked.

Olga looked out upon the water and replied, "We have rested long enough for tonight. I do not like this place. The stars are strange."

The statement was an odd one, and Iosef looked up to see what Olga meant. The sky was black, no doubt obscured by clouds. There were no stars to be seen, strange or otherwise.

"There would seem to be no stars at all," he said.

"Precisely why I find them strange," Olga answered. She tapped her staff again. "Come, come, I shall lead the way."

Olga lit a torch and held it out against the darkness—for truly, the growing night was very dark, even for the keen eyes of the Living. Iosef took Sophio's hand, and together they followed their strange companion along the shore, past dancing waves beneath a starless sky.

CHAPTER TWENTY-SIX

Svaneti
Christmas Eve (Julian Calendar)

As night descended upon the Shashavani valley, the loyalist army broke camp and advanced across the field under the cover of a moonless sky. They went in small companies of a dozen or so, crossing the frozen river with great care lest the ice crack beneath their weight. It was hard going without lamps or torches. The snow had begun to fall again, and the wind was bitter. But the conditions were all the more ideal: with the darkness, the clouds, and the snow, there was little chance of the army being observed as it approached the castle.

Ekaterine was in the advance party, along with Luka, Seteney, and some others, their armor muffled with cloth and their weapons blackened with pitch. Ekaterine herself wore no armor, but she carried a dagger borrowed from one of the soldiers. Luka stuck close to her side as she led the way toward the hidden passage she had used to escape.

It was a tunnel in the lower wall, little more than a drain used as an outflow for the castle's springs. Most of the water was captured and stored in the cisterns for use, and so there was little but a trickle left, but during times of heavy rain or when the spring overflowed, it was useful to prevent flooding.

There were supposed to be three sets of bars that blocked the tunnel at regular intervals, preventing anyone from entering from outside. But these had been crudely torn out of the walls and lay discarded in the icy, toe-deep water. Luka looked at them and then turned toward Ekaterine as if expecting an explanation.

"We had to escape," Ekaterine said, shrugging. "So we chipped away the mortar and broke out the bars."

"*How?*" Luka demanded. "This is meant to be impenetrable!"

"We had Living with us," Ekaterine explained. "It took some effort from them, truly, but I rather suspect that the bars were meant to keep out mortals, not Shashavani."

"Likely enough, I suppose."

Safely inside the tunnel, they were permitted to light lanterns for guidance, but these were still kept shuttered except for a sliver of light in case soldiers were posted inside. It was a reasonable precaution, for as they crept into the cistern chamber, Ekaterine saw firelight coming from above them.

She held up a hand for the others to stop and went ahead into the chamber. It was a tall vertical pit of stone through which all of the unwanted cistern water was flushed. The cisterns themselves—tremendous water-filled tanks—rose above them on three sides, each fed partly from the springs and partly from rainwater captured on the rooftops, filtered, and deposited into the tanks by way of pipes.

Ekaterine listened carefully and heard voices speaking on the platform above them. It seemed that soldiers had been placed on guard to protect the water supplies, though they did not appear to have noticed that anything was amiss in the pit below. Ekaterine looked at Luka and motioned with her head. Then she pointed from the staircase to the platform and mimed a walking motion with her fingers. Luka nodded his understanding, though he seemed a little exasperated with her pantomime.

Luka signaled for Seteney to join them and then directed the others to wait. He led the way up the stairs, drawing his sword as he did so. Ekaterine drew her dagger and followed him, trying not to be too annoyed by Luka's insistence upon leading. After all, *she* was the one who had escaped from there, not he. She doubted Luka had so much as visited the cisterns in the past hundred years.

At the top of the stairs, they saw five men and women in armor standing around a small fire, warming their hands against the chill. They wore armor and carried weapons, but they all faced toward the doorway into the main castle, as if they were more afraid of attack from within. It was peculiar, but it was agreeable all the same.

Luka began to whisper some instructions to Seteney, but Ekaterine was in no mood for delays. She crept around to the back of the guards, her dagger at the ready. Luka looked at her and spread his arms in frustration. Ekaterine pointed at the five guards with her weapon and gave Luka a look that demanded to know what was causing the delay. Finally, throwing up his empty hand, Luka nodded at Seteney, and the two of them approached the group with swift but quiet steps.

Finally! Ekaterine thought.

Once Luka and Seteney were nearly in range, Ekaterine charged the nearest soldier. The man was taken quite by surprise, only hearing her footsteps at the last moment, and by then he could do little but turn to face his killer. Ekaterine covered his mouth with her hand as she drove the dagger into him.

Luka and Seteney each had swords and put them to good use, hacking the soldiers to death viciously. One soldier tried to run for the door instead of fighting, and Ekaterine bolted after him, managing to catch and leap upon him just before he escaped. The two of them struggled for a few moments as Ekaterine tried to stab him and he tried to grab her weapon to turn it against her. Ekaterine gritted her teeth and finally, unable to overpower her enemy, struck her forehead against his face. The impact of the blow made her head swim, and she rolled onto the floor, momentarily dazed.

When she regained her senses, she saw Seteney standing over her, pulling her bloody sword out of the soldier's body. Seteney turned and smiled at her slightly, offering her a hand up. Ekaterine took the hand and stood, brushing herself off and doing her best to look presentable.

"An effective if unexpected improvisation," Seteney said.

"I have a hard head," Ekaterine replied. There was a pause, and then she could not help but add, "Like my cousin."

Seteney looked like she wanted to agree, but she merely grinned and replied, "As you say."

They returned to Luka, who was busy killing the last of the soldiers. Blood now stained the platform, but the cisterns were protected by sealed covers, so there was little concern of contamination.

"Seteney," Luka said, "go and inform the Strategos that the way has been cleared. The gate is ours."

"Sir," Seteney replied with a nod.

Luka turned to Ekaterine and looked at her. He seemed annoyed but at the same time relieved. After a while he smiled and placed his hand on her cheek.

"One of these days, Cousin," he said, "your rashness will be the death of you."

Ekaterine frowned. "And to think I imagined you might compliment me on my quick thinking."

"Quick running," Luka corrected.

"Tush," Ekaterine said. She knelt by the fire and rubbed her hands together. "It is bitter cold, even in here."

Luka knelt beside her and said, "It is winter. Christmas, even. Or it will be soon." He shook his head. "To think that there will be so much blood shed on Christmas."

"Yes," Ekaterine agreed sadly. "Still.... At least it isn't Easter."

Luka stared at her silently for a time before he simply shook his head.

"You so often know how to find the positive side of everything," he said.

"I know," Ekaterine said, grinning.

"It is *infuriating*."

"I know that as well," Ekaterine replied. In the pit behind them, she heard the muffled sounds of Zawditu's soldiers creeping their way in and up the stairs. "I know that there's a war to be fought," she told Luka, "but when we get upstairs, we must try to find Varanus. She will be worried sick about me." Ekaterine frowned and bit her lip at the thought. Varanus would be just as worried about her as *she* was about Varanus. "And she'll be cross with me for not coming to find her."

"You were half frozen from the river," Luka said softly. "She would understand."

Ekaterine did not particularly like the way Luka said "would" instead of "will", but she kept it to herself.

"Promise me you will help me find her."

"Cousin..." Luka began, his expression falling.

"*What?*" Ekaterine demanded.

"The Doctor...is dead," Luka said. "How many times must I say it?"

It had been the ludicrous refrain Luka had repeated to Ekaterine any time she made mention of Varanus, and Ekaterine was growing tired of it.

"Don't be absurd, Luka," she chided. "Of course the Doctor is alive. She's very clever and not at all the sort of person who would up and die without telling me."

"Cousin," Luka replied, "the Doctor has been trapped in the castle for almost two weeks. She is not past her century; she cannot survive on her own."

"Now see here—"

"We do not know what has been happening here, but as she is Lord Iosef's student, I am certain Margaret will have killed her as a member of Lady Sophio's household."

"She's not dead," Ekaterine repeated.

"She *is* dead."

"She isn't."

"She—" Luka began, but he stopped as the first of the soldiers reached them. He leaned down and whispered to Ekaterine, "Believe what you wish, Cousin, but denying the plain truth will not prevent it. You shall only be all the more hurt by it when you can deny it no longer."

"We shall see," Ekaterine said. "We shall see and I shall be right."

Luka exhaled with annoyance and turned away to greet the soldiers who joined them. After the first dozen arrived to secure the position, Lady Zawditu appeared in the company of several bodyguards. Ekaterine gasped at the sight of her, for surely it must have caused no small consternation for the Strategos to venture on so dangerous a mission. But of course, no general of the Shashavani would be inclined to lead from the rear unless it was necessary. How better to direct her forces in the field than with them in clear view?

Ekaterine quickly bowed to Zawditu and withdrew so as not to interfere, but she did listen as Zawditu approached Luka and addressed him:

"Neatly done, Luka. Little resistance, it seems."

"Little enough, Strategos," Luka agreed. "And it may interest you to know that they stood guard over the cisterns rather than the drain. Perhaps they expected a greater threat from within than from the outside."

Zawditu nodded. "An intriguing possibility." She glanced back down into the pit. "I must confess, I feel much less secure now that I know the tunnel can be breached, even if it is only by the Living. It will have to be attended to once the Council is back in control."

"Of course, Strategos," Luka said.

Zawditu rested one hand on the pommel of her sword and drummed her fingertips against the hilt.

"Once we have arrived in force, we will advance into the castle and make for the nearest armory. As memory serves, there is a small one several floors above us."

"There is," Ekaterine said. "Four floors up. And we can go the entire way by a single staircase, if you're willing to risk confined quarters." Then, realizing that she had interrupted, she quickly covered her mouth with her hands. "Uh...I mean...forgive me."

Zawditu laughed and said, "We are advancing blindly, my girl. Any intelligence is of use. You are Ekaterine, are you not? Luka's cousin?"

"Yes, My Lady," Ekaterine replied, bowing her head.

"It is thanks to you we know of this route," Zawditu said, "and for that I am grateful to you. It was brave of you to accompany us."

"Oh, thank you, My Lady, but I couldn't not come," Ekaterine explained. "My friend, Doctor Varanus, was trapped inside during the... misfortune. I must find her before something happens to her."

Luka cleared his throat. "I have already explained to my cousin that the Doctor is surely dead. Explained *repeatedly*," he added.

"Indeed?" Zawditu asked. She looked at Luka and placed a hand on Ekaterine's shoulder. "But she has hope, Luka. And we must all have hope."

"As you say, Strategos," Luka said, though he did not seem happy about it.

"I for one hold the hope that there may yet be people still alive in the House of Shashava," Zawditu said, "and your friend the Doctor among them."

* * * *

They reached the armory in short order, moving in a series of large packs that kept a few dozen feet of distance between one another but still held enough cohesion for mutual reinforcement. Ekaterine had the good sense to keep back from most of the fighting, though she did pull her weight once upon the stairs when a party of Margaret's soldiers ambushed them on one of the landings, and she was the closest person to the doorway.

As expected, the armory was guarded but only by five soldiers. They put up a token fight but surrendered almost immediately once Zawditu presented herself. Zawditu left a party of her own troops to safeguard the room and to watch the prisoners, while the rest of her forces equipped themselves with a better selection of arms and armor. Luka seemed greatly relieved at being able to take one of the rifles, even joking that they should have stopped by his own chambers, which were even better supplied. Ekaterine shook her head at him.

"Aim the volley gun at the door," Zawditu told one of the guards she had assigned to the armory, directing the placement of the weapon while the others made ready to depart. "If the enemy comes to displace you before you can be relieved, you must hold as long as you are able."

"As you command, Strategos," the guard replied.

"Where do we go now, Strategos?" Luka asked, as Zawditu rejoined him and Ekaterine.

"To the next armory," Zawditu replied. She paused a moment to check the fit of the armor one of her soldiers had appropriated from the stores. She turned back and said, "And the next one after that and so on. Our first step must be to deprive the enemy of their weaponry. Once that is done, we shall have to move through the castle floor by floor and bring Margaret's forces to heel."

"Shall we make to capture the gates as well?" asked one of the soldiers.

"No, there is no need for it," Zawditu said. "We control the only entrance that we require, and so long as the enemy holds the gates, their numbers will be spread thin." Zawditu took a look around the armory to see that her soldiers had finished arming themselves. "Enough. Let us continue. I would have this castle in hand before the traitors realize we are here."

"As you command, Strategos," Luka said.

It certainly sounded sensible enough to Ekaterine. She had a rifle and a sword that had been taken from the armory, and she kept them at the ready as she followed Zawditu and Luka into the hallway. They advanced onward, making a circuit of the house on their way to the next store of arms. Again they met some resistance in the corridor, though it was light. Most of the place seemed deserted. But Ekaterine did not fail to notice the periodic stains of blood that here and there covered the floor and walls along their path. The House of Shashava had seen even more violence since the coup, and some of it was very recent indeed.

As they passed through a quiet gallery, Ekaterine suddenly heard footsteps approaching from an adjoining passage. So did the others, and Zawditu quickly motioned for her troops to take up positions securing the area. Ekaterine shouldered her rifle and took aim. A moment later, a party of some dozen Shashavani rushed into view before them, their own weapons—swords and firearms—outstretched. Then two more groups rushed into the gallery from opposite ends. The newcomers had been stalking them, despite their many precautions.

Not that a small army can really be all that stealthy, Ekaterine reminded herself.

"Halt! Drop your weapons!" shouted one of the strangers, a woman with dark hair who carried a spear. Ekaterine recognized her as Joan the Breton. Joan stood beside a Persian man who appeared to be the group's leader. At her other side was a tiny figure in tattered leather clothes, whose face was concealed behind a plague doctor's mask.

"You drop yours!" snapped Luka.

There was a short pause and suddenly the masked figure cried, "Ekaterine?"

That voice!

"Doctor?" Ekaterine asked, pushing her way forward.

The figure tore off its mask to reveal Varanus, her face haggard from starvation. Ekaterine handed her rifle to Luka—who gave an exclamation of surprise—and she ran to embrace Varanus, holding her friend tightly for what seemed to be ages and was still not nearly long enough.

Ekaterine had to confess that some part of her had actually wondered if Varanus was still alive. It was such a relief to see Luka proven wrong about that.

"My God, Ekaterine," Varanus said, "I was worried sick about you! Where did you disappear to? I needed you, you know."

"I am so sorry, Doctor," Ekaterine answered. She took the opportunity to embrace Varanus again, which took Varanus by surprise, having foolishly assumed that the hugging was over. "I had to rescue a bunch of archivists, and then I fell in the river and caught a chill, and after that it was two days past, and they said I couldn't go looking for you."

"How beastly of them," Varanus agreed. "But from now on, whenever there is an unprovoked attempt on my life, you are forbidden from being more than twenty feet away from me. It's just not the same killing people without a friend."

"Killing people?" Ekaterine asked.

Zawditu cleared her throat and stepped forward. At the sight of her, several of the strangers who had kept their weapons raised now lowered them.

"My Lord Reza," she said to the leader of the group.

"Strategos," Reza replied, stepping forward and exchanging nods with Zawditu.

"We feared that we had lost you," Zawditu said.

"For a time, I feared that I had lost myself." Reza frowned slightly and studied Zawditu's forces. "What are you doing here?"

"We are retaking the castle, My Lord," Zawditu answered. "And if you will pardon my asking, what are you—any of you—doing here?"

"Well may you ask," said Reza. "Having escaped slaughter and conversion, we have been in hiding these past two weeks. Now we go to make war upon Margaret."

Zawditu frowned and asked, "Conversion?"

"Margaret demanded pledges of loyalty from the members of the House in exchange for their lives," explained Joan. "It seems she wishes to convert the whole House of Shashava into Basilisks. Those who refuse die."

Zawditu nodded and asked, "Marie of Toulouse?"

"Among the first to be executed," Reza said grimly.

"Margaret shall be punished for this," Zawditu said.

"Indeed she shall, Strategos, and you and your army are welcome to join us in the endeavor," Reza told her. "Indeed, your numbers and skill at arms will be most welcome. For our part, we assumed...we assumed that we would not return from this effort."

"Thankfully that no longer need be the case," Zawditu replied. "Where is Margaret hiding herself tonight?"

"In the Great Hall." It was Varanus who answered, joining the conversation without much concern for matters of seniority. To Ekaterine's surprise, neither Reza nor Joan seemed to mind it, while Zawditu smiled slightly at Varanus's candor. "She is holding a Christmas feast to prove that she is the new Sophio."

"That's...peculiar," Ekaterine said.

"Margaret is a madwoman," Varanus replied, "and I for one am growing impatient with the time we are spending not killing her."

CHAPTER TWENTY-SEVEN

Bolstered by Reza's survivors, Zawditu's forces went in search of Margaret. Several smaller contingents were dispatched to capture the remaining armories, but if the conspirators could be taken all in one place, it would make for a much easier recapture of the castle. Luka again was at Zawditu's side, and he was himself flanked by Seteney. He was relieved to see Koba and Anuka both alive and well, and they followed close behind him. Both were saddened by the loss of Movses, but it only made their little band all the more determined to exact vengeance.

As they neared the Great Hall, Zawditu motioned for the wings of her force to spread out and encircle. Some went on the ground floor, others to the balconies above. There were guards aplenty in the surrounding halls, and they could not be allowed to maintain their positions. Luka and his force remained with Zawditu as she went directly to the main doors of the hall, which stood open to them. There were guards posted at the door, but as Zawditu's company advanced against them, they went pale and fled back into the main chamber, shouting with alarm.

Luka started to rush after them, knowing that it was too late to avoid attention. Zawditu held up a hand to stop him.

"Orders, Strategos?" Luka asked.

"We are still outnumbered, especially by the Living," Zawditu said, approaching the doors. "It would be desirable to avoid a pitched battle with the whole population. I intend to induce their surrender through words, if possible. Then I will behead Margaret and her fellow conspirators as traitors, and afterward I shall have a cup of my favorite coffee, which I have sorely missed these past days."

"And if words prove ineffective, Strategos?"

"Then I shall induce their surrender through other means," Zawditu answered.

They stepped across the threshold and into the Great Hall. The chamber was lit with great fires upon the hearths, with torches, and with candles upon candelabra and chandeliers. The household of the Shashavani had all turned out for the feast, it seemed, and the many tables were filled with people, most of whom hunched over their plates with sullen and fearful expressions. The Great Hall was also filled with Margaret's soldiers, all bearing arms in case the crowd of scholars became unruly. They were already on their way to meet Zawditu's forces at the door.

At the far end of the hall, Luka saw Margaret seated in Shashava's chair, a goblet raised high into the air. Iese of Kartli and Thoros of Yerevan sat on either side of her, and none of them seemed quite aware of the alarm being raised. Directly behind Margaret's chair stood Fairfax, the former Master-At-Arms, a halberd resting against her shoulder.

Decorations decked the walls and tables, and colored glass lamps cast shades of crimson and blue across the hall, but Luka felt his stomach turn when he saw that there were other adornments as well. Severed heads had been placed on spikes throughout the Great Hall, with their headless bodies left to hang from the upstairs railings. Their stench filled the room, and it was as sickening as the sight of the desiccated faces gazing upon the diners like watchmen. Luka recognized the countenance of Marie of Toulouse, which held a position of prominence just behind Margaret. Luka saw others as well: Vaclav the Moravian, Amadeus of Savoy, and a dozen more that he had last seen passing in the corridors of the House, alive and well.

"Dear God..." he whispered.

"God is no longer in this place," Zawditu said. "And I mean to correct that."

She advanced to the main table. A Shashavani seated nearby bolted from his chair at the approach of armed men and women, and Zawditu used his seat to step up onto the table without breaking stride. Luka advanced parallel to her on the ground, holding his sword out toward the soldiers who came to meet them. Seteney, Anuka, Koba, and the others crowded around him, and they met the approaching enemy halfway across the room. Boris the Muscovite pushed his way to the front, holding a bardiche axe.

"Luka?" Boris exclaimed. "What are you doing here?"

"We have come for your head, Boris," Luka answered.

Across the chamber, Margaret dropped her goblet. It fell onto the table and spilled its contents: blood rather than wine, and likely not given willingly by whatever mortal had contributed it.

"What is the meaning of this?" she demanded, climbing onto her chair for a better look.

"Margaret of the Hebrides," Zawditu announced as she advanced along the table, "Thoros of Yerevan, Iese of Kartli...justice has come for you."

Margaret gasped at the sight of Zawditu and shouted, "Guards! Seize the traitors! And bring me the head of the False Strategos! She serves the usurper Philippa!"

Margaret's soldiers stood off against Zawditu's, their weapons held high and ready. Many were firm in their conviction, but Luka saw that several appeared hesitant. They looked exhausted and haggard, and doubt had set in. The scholars at the tables began to rise, exchanging words with one another. None of them seemed eager to attack Zawditu, but neither did they seem eager to disobey Margaret.

Zawditu reached the middle of the table and stood, one hand upon the hilt of her sword.

"Hear me now," she announced to the assembled company. "I am Zawditu, daughter of the House of Solomon, Lioness of Judah, Marshal and Strategos of the Shashavani. I come before you in the name of Sophio and the Council. Those of you who serve under arms know me well. Those of you who serve with letters are, I trust, familiar with my reputation, whatever attempt the traitor Margaret has made to sully it. She is the usurper, and I have come for her head."

"Kill her!" Margaret repeated, climbing onto the table in a rage. Behind her, Thoros and Iese drew their swords, and Fairfax raised her halberd, though she seemed more intent upon watching the situation of the common soldiers than attending to Zawditu.

"The punishment for treason and usurpation is death," Zawditu said. "It has already been administered to Caroline of Burgundy, and it will be levied against any who tonight stand with Margaret." She held up a hand to silence the fearful cries of the scholars, who began to push against each other in panic. "Hear me! The fate of the usurpers is sealed, but your fates are not. I have been authorized to give clemency to any who surrender to me now. If your only crime has been the unwitting support of these traitors, then throw down your arms and beg mercy and you shall be spared."

Silence descended upon the room, broken only by the shuffling of feet, the creak of leather, and the clinking of mail. Then, with cries of "Mercy! Mercy!" the scholars ran from their seats, some crowding around Zawditu, throwing their hands toward her and professing their innocence, while others pushed their way against Margaret's soldiers in an effort to escape the chamber. Suddenly the room was in chaos, knocking apart the cohesion of the defending ranks.

Boris began shouting for his troops to hold their positions and attack, and this seemed to settle things for the soldiers. In scattered pockets, but with growing numbers, some of the soldiers threw down their weapons and began to shove their way past their comrades, professing their loyalty to the House of Shashava.

"Hold your positions!" Boris demanded. "Do not throw down your arms! Any who throw down their arms are to be slain at once!"

He grabbed for the nearest deserter and threw the man to the ground. He brought his bardiche down to cleave the man's head in half, and Luka lunged forward, driving his sword into Boris's arm. The bardiche struck the stone floor, cutting the deserter's shoulder but not killing him.

The order to kill their comrades further galvanized the soldiers, and several began fighting their way through the others, shouting their loyalty to Shashava and to Sophio without bothering to disarm.

Luka grinned at Boris and said, "I think you have lost your war, Brother. Perhaps you should surrender as well."

"I have not lost!" Boris roared. "I have not even begun!"

Boris and what remained of his force rushed at Luka, screaming blood and death. Luka smiled grimly, suddenly remembering Movses in the moment the boy had died.

"For Shashava and the Eristavi!" Luka cried, and he met Boris's charge with steel and with hatred.

* * * *

Varanus watched the chaos below from one of the upstairs balconies. Ekaterine was with her, as were the soldiers who had secured the position and who were now watching the fighting with muskets raised, patiently waiting for an opening to fire upon the enemy without risking either their comrades or the ones who had already surrendered.

"We should be down there," Varanus said.

There was a bang as Ekaterine shot one of the enemy soldiers in the crowd with her rifle. She glanced at Varanus and nodded, though she did not necessarily agree with the statement.

"Mmm hmm," she said.

Varanus gripped her sword and exhaled. She wanted to be down there in the thick of the fighting. But while the past week had reacquainted her with combat, it was a kind of short, vicious fighting for which she was best prepared, with few people and no bystanders.

"Oh, look at Margaret," Korbinian said. He was leaning over the railing and pointed across the room. "Can she be fleeing? What a curious thing."

Alarmed, Varanus looked away from the melee and toward Margaret and the other conspirators. She saw Margaret's executioner, Fairfax, pull Margaret down from the table, all but dragging her master to the door—though surely Margaret could not be resisting too hard, or Fairfax would not have had the strength to pull her along. Iese backed away alongside them, and Thoros went last of all, shielding their escape. Varanus looked at Zawditu, but the general was too heavily engaged in fighting to give chase, though she clearly saw the traitors escaping and redoubled her efforts to reach them.

"I'm going after them," Varanus announced.

Ekaterine looked at her, startled. "You're doing what?"

Without bothering to reply, Varanus bounded onto the railing, pulled her mask down over her face, and jumped.

"This may not be a good idea," Korbinian noted, as he fell toward the floor beside her.

"I know," Varanus told him with a smile.

She landed on the table a little ways from the end, collapsing to one knee with a painful smack while keeping her sword raised high above her. She was bruised from the impact, but nothing was broken. Rising, she ran for the far end of the table, her eyes locked on Margaret as Fairfax pulled the woman toward the door, shouting something indistinct about needing to withdraw to a safer position.

Ahead, Zawditu fought against Alexios of Anatolia and two Shashavani of the Shadow, trading blows back and forth and striking at any others who tried to intervene. Though their situation was desperate, those soldiers who had not yet given up seemed to have regained much of their courage. Perhaps they had convinced themselves that, if they fought well and hard, they would still win the day and break the loyalist forces once and for all.

And, Varanus realized, it might actually be true. Both sides were almost evenly matched, even after the mass defections. And the traitors who remained were very well armed.

Zawditu struggled to advance, tilting her head with each thrust to see past Alexios. Her mouth was set in a scowl as she cut and thrust at Alexios and the others like a woman possessed, desperate to get past them and put an end to Margaret's treachery. Fighting was the only option, for she was too tall to slip under Alexios's reach, and the way was too narrow to go around him.

Lady Zawditu is too tall, Varanus realized, *but I am not.*

As she reached the fighting at the middle of the table, Varanus ducked under a spear as it was thrust at Zawditu, ducked again beneath Zawditu's blade that swept down to parry the spear, and jumped to a nearby chair. She bounded to the next chair and leapt back onto the table. Alexios saw her, of course, and he stabbed at her with his sword, but Varanus rolled beneath the strike. A moment later, Zawditu seized the opening and thrust her sword into Alexios's chest, forcing him to face her again and leaving Varanus free to continue on. In gratitude, Varanus drew her knife and threw it into the back of Alexios's leg. Alexios stumbled from the injury, and Zawditu took the opening and drove her sword into his throat.

Varanus picked herself up again, ran to the end of the table, and leapt for the door. A soldier loomed to the side of her as she landed, and Varanus slashed him across the face before running into the corridor.

* * * *

Margaret and her cohorts made no attempt at stealth in their retreat, and Varanus followed them at a distance as they made their way to one of the side gates. There they stopped, and Varanus concealed herself in the shadows to observe them and wait for an opportunity to strike. Having finally run them to ground, Varanus was suddenly faced with the question of just how she expected to kill three Living Shashavani at once, not to mention their bodyguards.

"It is a puzzle, isn't it, *liebchen?*" Korbinian mused as he knelt beside her, resting his chin on his hand.

"Hush," Varanus murmured.

At the gate, Thoros turned back and shouted at Fairfax, "We should not have fled! It will be disastrous to our soldiers' morale!"

"I merely suggested what I thought to be prudent, My Lord," Fairfax answered, her tone cold and professional. "Forgive me if I overstepped my authority, but I saw little hesitation from you at the time." She looked at Margaret. "My Prince, I trust you have seen the wisdom in my actions. I could not allow you to be taken."

"More likely killed," Margaret mused. Though she tried to appear calm, it was obvious that she was seething with anger. "No, you were right, Master-At-Arms. We will wait here until the day is won to make our return to the hall all the more triumphant."

"Assuming all is not lost," said Iese, his voice sullen.

"Why should we be lost?" asked Thoros, idly testing the weight of his sword, the same sword that had killed Father Vaclav. "We have the advantage of numbers, even without the scholars."

Fairfax hesitated for a moment and then contradicted him: "Forgive me, My Lord, but we do not. Perhaps in total, but our soldiers are scattered throughout the house while theirs came in force. And there were many among our ranks who surrendered. If we were not outnumbered before, we surely are now."

Thoros turned on Fairfax and raised his sword. "I should cut out your tongue for your impudence, child of shadows! Know your place. You do not contradict the Living, and you do not contradict me!"

"Pardon, My Lord," Fairfax said, lowering her eyes. But Varanus could tell that she did not mean it, and perhaps Thoros realized it as well.

"Enough, Thoros," Margaret snapped. "Though she speaks out of turn, the Master-At-Arms is correct. We are outnumbered. We must trust Boris to hold his ground and break the enemy." She scowled. "Though I am again given to question his abilities. He assured me that all entrances had been sealed. Clearly they were not. Just as he assured me that the Army would gladly join our side, even Zawditu and her officers, given a sufficient show of strength."

"And they did not," Iese said. He ran his fingers through his beard. "If only Caroline's cult had done its duty and murdered them all when they fled into the countryside."

Margaret frowned. "Indeed, there are a great many 'if onlys', and I am displeased by them." She began pacing back and forth upon the threshold as the bitter wind of winter blew in from the frozen night. "I promised my king a victory, and it would have been delivered had it not been for the failure of those under me. But it is upon my head that the blame for this shall fall. You realize that, do you not? I was the architect of our victory, but instead I shall be remembered as the architect of our defeat, simply because those who served me could not carry out the tasks I gave to them!"

Iese and Fairfax drew back from Margaret, perhaps sensing danger as her tone grew shrill and frantic. Thoros kept his distance as well, but his attitude seemed more dismissive than cautious.

"The Winter King was to arrive in springtime, and I was to present an orderly house. Instead, I have been undone by chaos and incompetence!"

"I am beginning to question whether there truly is a 'Winter King' at all," Thoros grumbled. "I believed it at first, but I grow skeptical."

"Do you?" Margaret demanded. "You question my word, Thoros?"

"I do," Thoros answered coldly. "I think that perhaps you invented this mysterious lord and master, this faceless conqueror from the wilderness, to give us all greater confidence in your fractured plan. 'Only a few months, and then a godling shall descend upon the valley and rule us with might and majesty.' Either you are lying, Sister, or you are quite insane."

In a rage, Margaret took a few steps toward Thoros, her face contorted. Thoros drew back and raised his sword defensively. Fairfax rushed toward them—though not between them, Varanus noted.

"My Lady, My Lord," she said to them, "infighting will do us no good, not at such a time."

Margaret paused and folded her arms.

"This is true," she said. "But you will watch your tongue, Thoros. The Winter King is real. I have seen our master with my own eyes, as did Teimuraz."

"Teimuraz is dead," Thoros remarked. "He cannot vouch for it, can he?"

There came the sound of hurried footsteps from down the corridor, and the others turned toward them. Varanus pulled herself further back into the shadows and tucked herself into a ball to avoid being seen. Presently, she spotted Boris the Muscovite running toward them as swiftly as he could manage with a mangled leg. He had been grievously injured. One eye was missing, one arm was hacked almost cleanly off below the elbow, and his good hand clutched at his chest, where it bled from numerous wounds. He shuffled to a stop before Margaret and fell to his knees.

"Boris, what is the meaning of this?" Margaret demanded.

"My Prince, forgive me," Boris gasped, "but we are lost."

"*What?*"

"It is true!" Boris coughed a few times and spat blood onto the floor. "My troops have been broken, scattered, to be hunted down by Zawditu's forces. It is like the first day again, only now the positions are reversed!"

Margaret turned away, making noises of anger and disbelief. "Not possible!" she snarled. "Not possible!" Then she turned back and looked at him. "You fled?" she asked.

"What?"

"You fled," Margaret repeated. This time it was not a question. "I made you my general, Boris, and I instructed you to lead my soldiers and defeat my enemies."

"My Prince, I swear—"

"Instead, you failed to deliver me the whole of the Army," Margaret continued. "You failed to destroy Reza's band of outlaws. You failed to find and seal whatever gate Zawditu's forces have used to enter. You have failed even to hold your position in battle!" She took Boris's chin in her hand and scowled at him. "You are failing me quite a lot, Boris. Perhaps you were a poor choice. And now you have abandoned your men and fled when I required you to stand firm against my enemies."

"I did everything I could!" Boris protested. "Everything within my power! I came to warn you that we had lost the day!"

"You should have held the line," Margaret said, "and sent a common soldier to warn me."

In a panic, Boris motioned to his mangled body. "I did my best! I would have died had I remained!"

Margaret looked into Boris's eyes and said softly, "You *should* have died. And I will correct that error."

"No! Please—"

Margaret took Boris's head in her hands and twisted it around until it had nearly reversed. Boris let out a dying gasp, and his body fell onto the ground.

"Master-At-Arms," Margaret said, gazing down the corridor.

"My Prince?" Fairfax asked, stepping forward.

"You are my new general," Margaret answered. "For whatever that is worth at such a time."

"It is worth the world, My Prince, I assure you," Fairfax replied. "We have suffered a grave defeat, it is true, but that cannot be helped. You gambled and you lost." When this made Margaret glance toward her angrily, Fairfax took a step back and added, "If you escape now, there will be time and opportunity to plan revenge. But if we remain, you will die and your work will come to nothing."

Margaret snarled for a moment, and then she threw back her head and laughed. It was a bitter, desperate noise.

"How right you are, Fairfax," she said. "There is nothing for it. We will escape by the southern pass. Come...." She paused and turned her eyes in Varanus's direction, peering into the shadows. "What is that?"

The others turned toward the shadows and slowly approached. Varanus felt her breath catch in her throat, and she knew that she had been discovered. Better to get in the open where she could fight or flee as necessary.

She stepped from the corner and walked to the center of the hallway. Thoros gasped at the sight of her, and his eyes flashed with anger.

"You!" he shouted.

"The masked bogeyman," Fairfax said softly. "The Plague Doctor that haunts my soldiers. I have heard of this one."

"The one that escaped me," Thoros said. He lifted his sword and pointed it at Varanus. "But you will not escape me now, little rat."

Margaret sighed. "Thoros, we have no time for this. Fairfax, kill it."

"No!" Thoros barked, holding up his hand. "No, this one had the gall to escape me. I will deal with it. Go on ahead. I will meet you shortly."

Iese shook his head and said, "You are a fool, Thoros. There is no time!"

"Go!" Thoros repeated as he slowly advanced on Varanus. "I will meet you at the southern pass."

"As you wish," said Margaret, walking toward the gate. "But be quick about it. We will not wait for you."

"This will be *very* quick," Thoros answered with a chuckle.

Varanus considered running. It was probably the most sensible thing to do. But she simply could not bring herself to flee from the fiend that had murdered Vaclav. She would surely die facing Thoros, but what sort of friend would she be if she did not attempt revenge?

In fact, Thoros made the matter very easy for her. Shouting violently, he charged her the moment his comrades had departed through the gate, bringing his sword down at Varanus from above. Varanus dove sideways and avoided the blow, but Thoros quickly recovered and thrust at her with tremendous speed and precision, stabbing her through the side. He drew out his sword and swung at her again, aiming for her head. Varanus ducked under the blow and dove forward. She hit the ground, rolled, and as she came up on her feet, cut a slash across Thoros's exposed arm.

Thoros did not seem to care, nor did he pay any mind to the next dozen cuts and slashes that Varanus managed to inflict. But Varanus certainly felt each and every blow that Thoros heaped upon her, until her bones cracked from the strain, and her flesh bled freely.

"You should give up and die," Thoros remarked. "Simply kneel and show your throat. I will cut off your head, and all of this will go away. You'll be free."

"Free?" Varanus asked, scoffing at the word. "Like you 'freed' Father Vaclav?"

Thoros frowned, having heard her speak for the first time.

"I know that voice..." he said.

Without hesitation, he bounded forward again and struck Varanus upon the side of the head, sending her to the ground and knocking the mask from her face. Varanus's head ached from the blow, but she fought through the dizziness that threatened to take her and stood again, brushing away the hair that fell across her eyes.

"You!" Thoros cried, sounding astonished and perhaps even ashamed. "The child! Iosef's student?" He suddenly laughed. "I assumed you were dead."

"Brother Teimuraz tried and failed," Varanus said. "*You* tried and failed. Twice."

"I will not fail this time," Thoros snarled, and he lunged at her again.

Varanus scampered backward to avoid the attack and dove in past Thoros's range. Thoros tried to disengage, to bring his sword to bear again, but Varanus stabbed him in the belly, driving her sword in to the hilt.

At first she felt a sudden rush of triumph as Thoros's face contorted with pain and astonishment. But before she could congratulate herself on having felled the bloodthirsty Goliath, Thoros grabbed her by the throat and threw her into the nearest wall. Varanus hit the stones with a crack and slid to the floor, momentarily stunned. She struggled to rise as Thoros approached her, pulling her sword from him and casting it aside as he came. But Varanus had scarcely risen to her feet when Thoros grabbed her again and threw her across the hall.

Varanus landed on the ground, gasping for air. Her starved and battered body cried out for nourishment, preferably mortal blood, and there was nothing she could do to sate it. But the pain and the hunger and the fear of the moment flooded into Varanus like heat, pooling with her anger until she shook with energy, suddenly more alive than she had been for ages.

Grabbing her sword and snarling like a beast, Varanus ran at Thoros. She ducked under his next swing and sliced him across the belly, making him howl. Turning back, Varanus thrust her sword upward, preparing to drive it beneath Thoros's ribs. But there was a flash of steel, a burst of pain, and the blow did not land. Instead, Varanus's sword clattered onto the ground, still gripped by her now severed hand.

Shaking violently, Varanus collapsed to her knees as her blood flowed from the stump at the end of her forearm. There was little blood left in her, but what remained now spurted upon the floor, leaving her dizzy and weak. Varanus struggled to get up, to attack again, but she simply could not.

Thoros laughed and crouched before her.

"Not so confident now are we, little rat?" he asked. "I told you it would be easier if you gave up and died. Instead, you have wasted my time, and I will make you suffer for it."

"Go to Hell," Varanus said. "Perhaps the Devil can teach you some manners."

Thoros snarled and replied slowly, "I will enjoy killing y—"

As he spoke, Varanus summoned up her last reserves of strength—what little remained after two weeks of starvation—and punched Thoros in the face, forcing her severed stump of an arm into his mouth and spraying her blood down his throat.

Shocked and horrified, Thoros grabbed Varanus and, with some struggle, forced her away. He retched and gagged, trying to spit out the offending poison, but it was too late. A few moments later, he clutched at his stomach and fell back onto the floor, writhing in pain. His body convulsed, and he screamed as his flesh began to boil from the inside. Soon the burning poison had forced its way to the surface, and it began to tear holes in Thoros's flesh up and down his body. It was like the touch of the sun, only worse. Soon Thoros's writhing slowed as his own strength gave out. He lay there unmoving, possibly dead or at least close to it, as what remained of his flesh corroded away, leaving behind little but ash and bone.

Varanus smiled at the sight. She had killed Thoros of Yerevan, one of the Living many times her senior. Vaclav's death was avenged. That was something to be proud of.

And so, it was with great satisfaction that Varanus allowed herself to slip away into the darkness as her body gave out, finally succumbing to its injuries. The last thing she heard before oblivion was Ekaterine screaming her name.

And then there was silence.

CHAPTER TWENTY-EIGHT

Christmas Day (Julian Calendar)
Turkestan

Iosef's party reached the tomb in the small hours of Christmas morning, in the stifling darkness before dawn. There were no stars in the sky to supplement the new moon, and the darkness left even the Living almost blind. Iosef could sense to some degree the lay of the land just before each footfall, and both Sophio and Olga walked with what seemed to be no difficulty at all, never stumbling once; but all the same, Olga had made torches for them during the daylight hours so that they might see the tomb when they reached it.

While dark nights were not a rarity in winter, Iosef could not help but feel unnerved by the utter blackness that shrouded the land. It seemed somehow unnatural, like a cloud of ink suspended somewhere just above his head. The stars were there, but he was not allowed to see them.

By the flickering torchlight, Iosef saw the tomb of Arslan Khan as he came over a small rise in the land. It sat upon the shore, only a short distance from the cresting waves. It was a great pile of stones and earth that formed a dome perhaps two-dozen feet in every direction. It was certainly not the anonymous gravesite that Iosef had imagined. Something so large could not have been missed by passers by, and yet its location had somehow been lost to history. It seemed a miraculous thing.

"Here it is," Sophio said, approaching the tomb. "For centuries I have dreamed of finding it."

"The lost tomb of the failed conqueror," Iosef agreed, joining her. He felt a hint of unease as he neared the tumble of stones, and he scolded himself for harboring such superstition. The dead were the dead, and that was all. "And yet, Arslan Khan's very failure makes it all the more enticing. A man who by his very death caused one of the greatest armies in history to crumble...."

"Imagine how the world would be shaped if the Kara Keçi had won the day," Sophio said softly. "The Mongols were horrifying in their brutality, but they granted liberty of faith, and they allowed commerce to flourish. In the wake of their bloodshed, there was a time of peace."

"And it would not have been so with the Kara Keçi," Olga said, approaching the two of them. "The horsemen of the Black Goat knew nothing but violence and death. Had Arslan Khan won the day, his empire would have stretched as far, if not further, and it would have witnessed nothing but the horrors of Kiev and Baghdad repeated again and again across the world. For the Black Goat desires nothing but blood, and so do its children."

The way that Olga spoke unnerved Iosef, and he turned to look at her. The woman's expression was serious, but her eyes flitted about, looking everywhere and never fixing upon one thing. Iosef knew that the very old were often peculiar in their habits, easily given to distraction, but distraction was not far from madness.

"Thank God such a thing does not exist," he said, and waited to measure Olga's reply.

Olga looked back at him with a "Hmm?" She seemed distracted as if she had only half heard him. But after a moment she smiled and said:

"Whether the demon exists or not is irrelevant. The history of the world is one endless litany of crimes committed by men who believe that something is true without any proof that it is. I do not fear the Black Goat, for I do not believe in it. But I think it is right to fear men who do believe in it, for when men believe in a thing, there is little they are not capable of doing in its name."

She knelt down and picked up the skull of some horned animal that had been left upon the ground. The birds had picked it clean of flesh sometime in the past, though it must have been ages ago, for now the place was quiet and empty, shunned by all living things.

"We are in a place of death," Olga mused, gazing at the skull. "We speak of mortals walking in the Shadow of Death, but this...this place is surely in its darkness."

"Indeed," Iosef said.

"Come," Sophio said to them, taking them each by the arm, "let us find the door and open it. After seven hundred years, the Khan will no doubt enjoy a private audience again."

There was a brief silence, and suddenly Olga began to laugh, though the sound was muffled by the heavy salt air.

"I have missed your company, Sophio," she said, dropping the skull and walking with them around the tomb. "You are refreshing after so long in the world."

"And yet, you do not tell me who you are," Sophio replied.

"I am Olga," Olga said. "And I shall tell you more presently." She paused and looked over her shoulder into the darkness. "Once our business is concluded and we are on our way again."

"And what if we are to remain for some time?" Iosef asked.

Olga glanced toward the dark sky and said, "I think that is unlikely."

They found the entrance on the eastern side of the tomb, facing the sea. An archway of stones framed the doorway, but this was blocked by a single massive boulder that had been rolled into place in front of it.

"I see now why the Mongols were never able to open it," Sophio said. "Twenty strong men could not manage it, I think."

"Twenty men would not be able to push it at once," Iosef noted. "However, I daresay the three of us can manage it well enough."

Olga looked at him and said, "I like you, Young Iosef. Your boundless optimism is most inspiring."

* * * *

It took them almost an hour, but working together, the three of them managed to pry the boulder loose from the doorway and push it onto its side a short distance away. As the tomb was opened, the air inside rushed out with a hiss. It held a foul odor, which made Iosef shudder. There was something unwholesome about it, a kind of corruption made stale by ages of abandonment.

The sea wind suddenly picked up again, blowing hard across the shore and making the torch flames flicker violently. Thankfully, it also cleared the air and dissipated the stench of the tomb. Iosef took a deep breath and exhaled.

"Shall we venture inside?" he asked.

"I think we shall," Sophio told him. "One does not often have an opportunity such as this. We must take proper advantage of it."

In the flickering torchlight, Olga sniffed the air and looked into the darkness, her eyes darting about again.

"Go ahead without me," she said. "I must...see to something. I shall return before long."

Sophio tilted her head and gazed off into the darkness. After a moment, she nodded and said, "Of course."

Olga set her torch down on the ground and walked off into the darkness, staff in hand, sniffing the air and looking in all directions with a peering gaze.

"What was that about?" Iosef asked, when Olga had finally vanished.

"There is someone else here," Sophio said. "Another one of the Living. And very old. Our new friend Olga has gone to find whoever it may be."

Iosef shuddered at Sophio's words. He had known that there was another Shashavani lurking near the tomb—both Sophio and Olga had agreed on that point weeks ago—but to hear it said with so little concern unnerved him more than he had anticipated. And again he wondered at Olga's true identity.

Was she Edith? Or was Edith the one waiting for them?

"Ah, but is she going to catch it or to join it against us?" he asked aloud.

"That remains to be seen," Sophio answered. She looked at Iosef and smiled. "But whatever occurs, I will protect you. Have no fear."

"I am only ever fearful for you, beloved," Iosef told her. "Though I know there is no cause for it."

Sophio touched her forehead to Iosef's and murmured, "Truly, my love. Certainly less cause than for me to worry about you." She kissed him tenderly and then said, "Come, let us see how Arslan Khan was put to rest."

They laid their walking sticks against the doorway and went inside, holding their torches out for illumination. The burial chamber was a sort of long oval with an arched ceiling high enough that Iosef could stand without striking his head. It was a tremendous piece of engineering for a nomadic civilization, and Iosef wondered how long Arslan Khan's subjects had labored to build it.

The tomb held a veritable treasure hoard; it was filled with chests of gold and precious stones, statues and silks, and other things looted from the trade caravans of the Silk Road. There were helmets and shields, shirts of armor, swords, bows, and spears propped against the walls, all proclaiming the Khan's glory in life by their presence in death. Iosef examined one of the spears and found, to his great amazement, that it showed no signs of rust or decay. The other weapons and the armor pieces were the same, each perfectly preserved in defiance of time. But surely that was impossible.

At the far end of the tomb sat a long sarcophagus carved from stone and decorated with intricate images. Behind it, pressed against the wall, was the statue of some profane creature with the body of a man and the head of a four-horned goat. The workmanship was excellent and the statue almost lifelike, which made Iosef momentarily hesitant to approach.

But approach he did, with Sophio at his side. After all, carved stone and dead things could do no harm. Iosef knelt at the sarcophagus and lifted the lid. Inside, wrapped in fine silks, lay a desiccated body, a corpse so withered that it was little more than bones wrapped in its own leather. This was surely Arslan Khan, for the body was dressed in expensive armor, and its hands clutched a finely made sword.

"Incredible," Sophio whispered. "No attempts at mummification and yet flesh remains. Truly, we should be observing an ossuary, not this."

"Given the state of the other relics, I am surprised not to find him wholly preserved," Iosef said, only half joking. "I wonder what the secret of this can be."

Sophio looked at him, smiled softly, and pulled Iosef's hood up over his head.

"You will wonder longer if you remember to conceal yourself before the coming of sunlight," she said. "It is almost dawn, and the doorway faces the rising sun. Be kind to me, and do not burn yourself to death in your excitement."

Iosef chuckled and said, "As you wish, my love."

He turned his eyes back toward the body and noticed a glint of metal that came from neither sword nor armor. Reaching down, he drew a small amulet made of a silvery metal from the folds of silk that wrapped the corpse.

"Now then, what do we have here...?" he mused. He tested the weight of the amulet and found it to be very light. "Aluminium?" He looked at Sophio. "I think that this is aluminium."

"Impossible," said Sophio. "How could a medieval people have obtained such a metal?"

Iosef pondered the question and raised the amulet into the light. On one side he saw a series of markings that may have been writing, though he did not recognize them as letters. On the reverse was a curious emblem: a lidless eye surrounded by the ouroboros, a serpent devouring its own tail. It had not been carved or forged, but rather cast and then stamped with such precision and cleanliness of detail that it could only have been done by machine. Even the lettering on the back was clearly marked like the work of a typewriter, not some artisan scratching at hot metal.

Iosef sighed and shook his head, disappointed by the realization that the amulet could only be a forgery.

"You are correct," he said to Sophio. "This was not made by a medieval people. It must have been placed here by someone in recent years."

"Then we are not the first to open the tomb," Sophio noted, her tone ever so slightly disappointed. "That is unfortunate."

"Still, everything else appears to be untouched," Iosef reminded her. "Whoever left this trinket for us to find seems not to have disturbed anything else."

That particular realization made him uncomfortable.

"It could only be one of the Living," Sophio said.

"Perhaps our new *friend*," Iosef suggested, his tone emphasizing that he remained skeptical regarding Olga's motives.

"Perhaps." Sophio frowned. "Or perhaps it was Teimuraz, playing some manner of trick upon us. He claims not to have entered, but we know that he was here."

Sophio might have said more, but she suddenly stopped and raised her head like a wolf scenting something.

"Teimuraz has indeed played a trick upon you," called a voice from behind them, "but it has nothing to do with that bauble. At my instruction, he has induced you to come to me, Little Sophio, that there might be a reckoning for past sins."

Alarmed, Sophio stood and turned toward the doorway. Iosef did likewise and saw the figure of a man standing there, clad in the dusty robes of a pilgrim, illuminated by the murky gray light of pre-dawn. The man stood some five and a half feet tall, and his body was broad and powerful, though he was clearly suffering from starvation and privation of the road. His hair was dark and curly, and he wore a thick, if neatly tended, beard.

"*You!*" Sophio gasped. "I killed you! I cut off your head myself! You are dead!"

"I am far from dead," replied Basileios the Accursed, "despite your best efforts. I learned that night so very long ago—the night that you betrayed me to my enemies—that by a certain age, we Living become quite...resilient. A beheading, which is so efficacious in the young, becomes a mere inconvenience to the old. There is but one way to kill us, Little Sophio, and it is a trick I intend to show you firsthand...."

Sophio stepped forward and held a hand out in front of Iosef.

"Stay behind me, Iosef," she said, as she slowly advanced toward Basileios.

"My love, no..." Iosef protested, advancing with her. "Let us face him together."

Sophio placed two fingertips against Iosef's chest and stopped him in place with but a little effort. Having made her point, she looked into Iosef's eyes and said, "*Stay behind me*, please. I cannot fight well if I must worry about you."

Iosef nodded reluctantly and stepped back. Sophio touched his cheek and smiled. Then she turned again and walked toward Basileios, her long braids writhing behind her like serpents.

Basileios smiled as she approached and said, "Come to me, child. Come to your death."

"I have already killed you once, Basileios," Sophio answered, flexing her fingers. "I will do so again. And this time, I will let the birds of the air and the fish of the sea feast upon your bones."

Sophio reached Basileios, and they fell upon each other, clawing and striking like wild animals, landing blows that bruised flesh and cracked bone. Iosef watched from the other side of the tomb, forcing himself not to join the fight. It was his instinct to rush to Sophio's protection, but that instinct was foolish. Sophio was so much stronger that Iosef would only be a distraction, and one that might prove fatal.

But how could Basileios be alive? For the past two hundred years, Iosef had known the stories of the traitor's death, and it was not a tale that Sophio would have lied about or embellished. Indeed, she was as shocked to see Basileios as Iosef.

It was difficult to keep track of the fighting, for Sophio and Basileios moved with unnatural speed and precision, striking, countering, advancing, retreating, all with thousands upon thousands of tiny calculated movements that together formed an attack. They seemed almost to flicker as they fought, their limbs moving and working independently but somehow achieving a greater purpose.

Then Basileios took an opening and grabbed Sophio by the throat. Before Sophio could break free, Basileios bounded toward the nearest wall and slammed her repeatedly into the stone, striking hard enough to stun her, if only for the moment.

In his mind, Iosef knew that it was not the end, that Sophio would break free and carry on fighting, but in his heart, he was overpowered by fear for her.

"No!" he shouted, and against Sophio's orders and his own better judgment, he rushed at Basileios, grabbing one of the swords in passing.

Basileios glanced toward Iosef in surprise, and Sophio took the moment to strike her arms against the joint of Basileios's elbow, forcing him to drop her. Snarling, Basileios kicked Sophio savagely in the stomach and then fell back, forcing the dislocated joint back into place so that it would heal.

"Iosef, no!" Sophio cried, looking toward him. "Stay back!"

"I think perhaps a distraction is in order," Basileios said.

He grabbed one of the spears that lay against the wall, turned, and threw it at Iosef in one fluid motion. In the blink of an eye, Iosef felt pain in his chest as he was hurtled backward. His back struck the statue that stood over the sarcophagus, and the spear drove deep into the stone, pinning him in place.

"No!" Sophio shouted, her tone the same desperate one that Iosef had used only moments before. "Iosef!"

Iosef shook his head to clear the cloud of pain. He looked down at the spear shaft as it protruded from his body. He looked back at his beloved Sophio, who now stood torn between fighting Basileios and rescuing her husband. And he looked at the sun as it began to rise over the sea with a creeping tide of light that would soon flood the tomb with pain and death.

With determination and desperation, Iosef grabbed the spear and tried to pull himself off it, but it had landed on a high diagonal, and his arms were weak from fatigue. The spear was soon slick with his blood, and every time Iosef pulled himself a little further forward, he slipped back again. He grabbed for his cowl to cover his face from the light, but it had fallen back out of reach.

Panic began to fill Iosef as he struggled, and he saw that same panic in Sophio as she looked at him. She tried to run to him, to save him, but Basileios leapt upon her and forced her to turn back to the fight.

"Leave him out of this, Basileios!" Sophio cried. "This quarrel is ours, not his!"

"He is of you!" Basileios replied. "And so he will die with you. Know that his last living memory will be the sight of your death."

Sophio ducked away from Basileios's next attack and struck him in the ribs with the heel of her palm. "You are mistaken, Basileios. He will see *you* die by my hand, and he shall have an eternity to delight in the memory of it!"

Basileios fell back a step and grabbed the nearest of the many swords. With it, he deflected Sophio's next blow, the blade cutting into her arm and making it bleed. Then he reversed the sword in his hand and drove it into Sophio's side. Sophio cried out and stumbled, and Basileios kicked her leg out from under her, knocking her to the ground.

"I have planned this for so long, little one," Basileios said, kneeling over Sophio. "I have savored the thought of my revenge for centuries. And I shall enjoy it. It is not by chance that you came to be here. I knew it would take something so tantalizing as this place to prick your curiosity and draw you out, so I sent my spies to plant a whisper of it and lure you to your doom."

"And Edith?" Sophio asked, lying limply beneath him. Iosef could not imagine why she did not struggle, why she did not free herself from Basileios's grasp, and he cried out to her, begging her to fight.

Both Sophio and Basileios ignored him.

"Edith?" Basileios asked, sounding genuinely surprised. "Edith the Saxon? Why should you ask of her? She is in Rome, doing great works."

"Not here?"

"Why would she be here?" Basileios replied. "My revenge is for me alone. I would not sully the delight with accomplices."

"That is all I wished to know," Sophio said.

As Basileios leaned over her, his triumph now measured by confusion at Sophio's words, Sophio grabbed him by the hair and drove her forehead into his face. Basileios reeled away, spitting blood, and Sophio punched him in the throat and threw him off her. She stood, swaying dizzily, and drew the sword from her side. She looked at it and dropped it to the ground.

"I am not so easily taken, Basileios," Sophio said. "And now that I know that you did not send Olga to find us, I need simply wait until she returns, and together we shall kill you. Time is against you now, not against me."

Basileios wiped the blood from his mouth and smiled. He pointed toward Iosef, who remained trapped by the spear, as the first rays of sunlight began to creep into the mouth of the tomb.

"Oh?" he asked. "Are you so sure of that? Will you stop the sun, like Joshua?"

A look of distress crossed Sophio's face. She turned to rescue Iosef, but Basileios would not allow her to withdraw. He advanced on her with a torrent of blows and forced Sophio to face him again. And so the fight resumed, with each of them punching and kicking with the force of hammers against stone.

Iosef continued working his way up the spear, but it was an agonizing struggle. Time and again, Sophio glanced back toward him, her eyes pleading for him to try harder, to free himself, to hide from the sun; and each time Sophio looked at Iosef, Basileios seized the opening and landed a heavy blow, forcing Sophio's attention back to him.

Finally, as the sunlight reached the midpoint of the tomb, Basileios let out a sigh and shouted, "Enough!"

"Tiring, Basileios?" Sophio asked, lunging at him again.

Basileios laughed and grabbed Sophio's wrists, holding her back. She struggled to free herself, but he did not relent.

"You surprise me, Sophio," he said. "You put up a better fight than I believed. You are not the child I once knew."

Sophio's eyes flashed as she said, "I was not the child you once knew the *first* time I killed you."

The corner of Basileios's mouth twisted in a snarl.

"Let me tell you a secret," he said. "I said that there is only one way to kill our kind. Do you wish to know what it is?"

"What?" Sophio asked.

Basileios's snarl became a smile as he said:

"The only way to truly kill us...is with fire."

He released Sophio's arms and spread his fingers. A haze appeared about his hands like mist upon water. Something blue-colored sparked upon his fingertips, and suddenly his hands were wrapped in flame, in a burning halo that seemed not to touch his flesh.

"What?" Sophio gasped, drawing back in shock. "How is this possible? What sorcery—"

Basileios lunged at her and grabbed her by the shoulders, laughing with delight.

"There is much you do not know about us," Basileios said, digging his burning hands into the folds of Sophio's robe, "and much that you will never know." He pulled Sophio in close. "But I want you to die knowing that your pet will soon follow you and that you cannot save him."

"No!" Sophio shouted, fighting against Basileios.

But she could not fight the flames, which coiled around her and threaded themselves into her clothes. Basileios thrust Sophio away, and she stumbled backward, trying frantically to brush away the fire. The flames caught hold of her hair, and in a few moments her flesh too had begun to burn.

Sophio fell to her knees, screaming in anger and pain and fury, struggling to grab Basileios and make him burn with her. But Basileios backed away, holding his fire-wreathed hands high in triumph.

"Burn, child!" he cried. "Burn!"

Sophio collapsed in a heap and rolled toward Iosef. Now the strength had left her, and she did not even fight as the fire boiled her flesh and charred her bones. She looked at Iosef as the fire closed in around her face and mouthed the words:

"I am sorry, my love. Forgive me."

"No! No! No!" Iosef screamed, struggling to pull himself free from the spear and dragging himself hand-over-hand toward her. But it was not enough.

The flames burned with an unnatural heat, devouring Sophio's flesh and bones until nothing remained but ashes. Then there was silence as the fire died away, its work done.

"That was...very pleasant," Basileios mused, gazing into the fire that still flickered around his fingertips.

"You fiend!" Iosef shouted. "I will kill you! I will kill you!"

"Mmm, I think not," Basileios replied. He stepped over the ashes, which began to dance about in a sort of haze from the wind of his passing. "No, I think I will kill *you* before you can annoy me with any more empty threats."

Basileios held one hand out toward Iosef as he approached, but within a few paces, the flames began to flicker and burn low like a candle almost out of wick. Basileios frowned and looked at his other hand, where the flames were dying as well. Within moments, the fire had died altogether.

Basileios shook one hand in the air as if trying to induce another conflagration, but it did not come.

"Well," he said with a sigh, "that is an inconvenience. I suppose I could simply tear your head from your body, but...." He smiled at Iosef. "But you are *her* whelp, so I think burning is the only proper death for you. Still," he added, looking down at the floor and the creeping light of the sun, "only a few minutes more, and the dawn will do it for me."

"Mark me!" Iosef said, gasping as he pulled himself further along the spear, only to slide back again on his own blood. "I will not rest until you are dead and your soul burns in Hell for what you have done!"

Basileios chuckled almost wistfully. "Ah, I remember what it was to be young and to make idle threats. But now I am old, and I make only real ones." He folded his arms and looked at Iosef. "Much as I would like to watch your death, I fear I must be on my way. My agent Margaret is busy preparing the way for me in the valley."

"Margaret...the Hebridean?" Iosef gasped. Surely not! How could a member of the Council be party to such treason?

"Indeed," said Basileios. "She expects me by the spring, and it would be rudeness to arrive late." He paused and held up a finger. "There is one thing I would like to ask you before I leave and you die. Who is Olga?"

"I am," called a voice from the doorway.

Basileios turned to face the new arrival, and in doing so he cleared Iosef's view. Iosef saw Olga standing at the entrance of the tomb, wreathed by the dawn, which shone about her hair in a golden halo. Her eyes fell upon Basileios, and a flicker of astonishment crossed her face, but it was soon replaced by anger.

"You!" she growled. "You live!"

"I do," Basileios said.

"That will soon be corrected."

Olga advanced into the tomb to where Basileios could see her face more clearly. Now it was Basileios's turn to look surprised.

"Well, well," he said. "Little Valdemar."

Olga drew herself up until she stood at her full height, half a foot taller than Basileios. She grinned at him with utter hatred and replied:

"Oh Basileios.... That a Greek should ever call a Rus 'little'."

CHAPTER TWENTY-NINE

As Olga moved further into the tomb, she looked around in the dim light. A frown crossed her lips.

"Where is Sophio?" she asked.

As she spoke, the wind began blowing hard from behind her, tearing at her robes and hair, and causing the ashes upon the ground to whip up and writhe about her feet. Coincidence, surely, but an unnerving one. And as Olga looked down and saw the quantity of ashes, her eyes widened with understanding.

"No..." she gasped.

"I fear that Sophio is no longer among the Living," Basileios replied, chuckling.

"How could you do this, Basileios?" Olga demanded. "She came to us as a child! She was a daughter to all of us!"

Basileios sneered and said, "She was no child when she cut off my head. She thought she had murdered me. I repaid her in kind."

"You are a fiend, Basileios," Olga snapped, pointing an accusing finger at him.

"And you are more sentimental than I recall, Northling." Basileios picked up the bloodied sword from the ground and pointed with it as he spoke. "I killed Sophio; now I will kill her apprentice, and then I will kill you."

Olga looked at Iosef for a moment, pondering something. Then she dropped her staff and took a spear from the wall.

"Come, Basileios," she said. "Leave the boy. Face me."

She beckoned with one finger and slowly backed toward the entrance. Basileios tilted his head and hesitated as if sensing a trap. He glanced at Iosef and said:

"By the time I kill her, boy, you will already be burning. I wish that I could stay and watch as the sun takes you, but.... Dear Valdemar and I have a long history that I am eager to cut short."

He patted Iosef on the cheek dismissively. Iosef grabbed for the hand, but Basileios swatted him away as easily as if Iosef had been a child. Basileios turned and departed the tomb, shouting for Olga to make ready for her death.

As Basileios walked away, Iosef grabbed at the spear impaling him and struggled all the harder to pull himself free. His hands slipped against the blood-slick wood of the spear, and his own weight pulled him back, but he did not relent. As the sunlight crept ever closer, his vigor intensified with the strength of desperation. As Iosef struggled, the wind continued to howl, flooding the tomb and blowing hard against him as if it wished to hold him back to allow the sun to take him.

Finally, amid agony and terror, Iosef reached the far end of the spear. Beneath his weight, the spear finally tipped downward, breaking free of the statue. Iosef fell onto the ground and pulled what remained of the weapon from his back. He gasped and coughed, blood spilling over his lips and onto the sunlit floor. The blood boiled in the light, hissing and withering into vapor.

Iosef pulled his cowl over his face and wrapped his cloak around himself to shield against the sun. He lay there in silence for a few moments to regain his strength. Then, with renewed resolve, he rolled onto his hands and knees and crawled to the place where Sophio had died. Much of the ash had already blown away, but some remained, woven across the stone floor by the wind. Iosef reached out and touched the ashes with his fingertips, feeling his body shudder with anguish.

Sophio was dead. Sophio, who had been the cornerstone of his life for almost two hundred years, was dead. She was dead, and she would never return. A part of Iosef had been torn from him, and it lay now in those ashes, forever lost.

Something tumbled from the folds of Iosef's clothes and landed upon the floor, scattering the ashes and sending them away on the wind. It was the amulet. In a daze, Iosef reached down and picked it up again, clutching it in his hand as if it were Sophio herself.

Iosef stood and slowly walked to the entrance, holding his cowl down to protect his face from the sun. Outside, he saw Olga and Basileios upon the shore, trading blows back and forth by the light of morning. Olga's spear had been broken in half, and now she wielded it like a rapier, thrusting it one-handed. She deflected most of Basileios's blows and repaid him with deep wounds of her own.

As Basileios came in for another attack, Olga caught his sword and forced it downward until the point struck the ground. Pinning it there, Olga brought her foot down against the sword's blade, snapping it in half with a single stomp. Basileios snarled and drove his shoulder into her, pushing her back. Then, looking at the shattered sword in his hand, he threw it away into the sea. Having disarmed her enemy, Olga took what remained of her spear and did the same.

Unarmed, they came at each other again, kicking and punching, rending and tearing, inflicting wounds as grievous as if they had been made with weapons. Each tear of the flesh and each broken bone soon healed, but as the minutes wore on, the healing process began to slow. Injuries that ought to have vanished quickly now remained, only gradually closing. Their blood was everywhere, boiling where it flowed together and burning their wounds. Had either of them been much younger, the blood alone would have done them serious injury. Only the resilience of age protected them from each other's poison, and even age could not prevent the pain.

"You are looking tired, Basileios," Olga said, throwing him to the ground and withdrawing a pace. Given some breathing room, she pulled hard on her arm to reset a shoulder that had been dislocated in the fighting. "I expect you're hungry, aren't you?"

Basileios stood, staggering a little as he tried to support himself on a broken leg that stubbornly refused to mend. He laughed away Olga's comment, but he did indeed sound tired, and there was a half-starved look in his eyes.

"How long have you waited here, in this place of desolation?" Olga mused. "Weeks? Months? A year? Long enough for hunger to set in, even at our age. The flesh does not mend so easily when we have not fed, does it?"

"The same is true for you, Little Valdemar," Basileios said. "You look as starved as I."

Olga stretched and slowly approached Basileios, who tensed and readied himself to meet her.

"It is not the same," Olga said. "I have made myself accustomed to fatigue and starvation. I hear they are good for the soul."

Basileios laughed at this.

"I expect you indulge yourself at every turn, don't you, Basileios?" Olga asked him. "There is strength in gluttony, I will grant you, but it comes at a cost. Even now, your body cries out for blood, and it does not know how to respond when its lusts are not indulged. You have fattened yourself on luxury and corruption, Basileios, and look at how your excess is repaid."

"My excess has made me powerful," Basileios snapped. He shifted his weight and hobbled toward Olga, but his broken leg still could only half support him, and he stumbled as he moved.

"Leg giving you trouble?" Olga asked in a mocking tone.

"It is well enough for my purposes."

"If you had fresh blood in you, it would already be mended," Olga said. "But in starvation, your body has used its stores of vitality greedily, while mine has done so sparingly." She rolled the shoulder of the arm that she had just put back into place, and she stretched her neck to ease the tension in the muscles. "I need not even defeat you, Basileios. If I force you to keep fighting for an hour, you will collapse of your own accord. And then I will kill you."

"I think not."

Basileios tensed as Olga drew near. At first he seemed to shy away, crouching to keep his distance as he held his weight upon his good leg. But it was a ruse and one that Olga seemed to expect. Metal flashed in the sunlight as Basileios drew a dagger from inside his sleeve and lunged at Olga. She met him with outstretched arms, and again they collapsed into a chaotic mess of blows and bloodshed.

Unable to gain the upper hand, Basileios drove the dagger into his own flesh, coating it with his blood. Then, as Olga struck him in the chest, Basileios turned the dagger and stabbed Olga viciously with it. The wound sizzled with the poison, and Olga slouched over, crying out. But however painful, even the poisoning would not stop her for long, and Basileios knew it. Instead, he struck Olga in the face to stun her and then lifted her into the air and threw her toward the tomb. Olga's lower back struck the edge of one of the great rocks, and Iosef heard the crack of bone.

Olga tumbled to the ground and was still for a moment. Then, as Basileios came toward her, she lifted her head and tried to get up. While her arms and upper body still obeyed her, her legs responded only poorly to her attempts to stand, and she fell back into the dirt.

Iosef expected Basileios to come at her then, to finish the fight while he had what appeared to be the clear advantage, but it seemed that the very sight of Olga struggling to rise again was enough to give Basileios pause. He tested the weight on his leg again and found that, though stronger, it was still not healed. He looked at Iosef and then at Olga, and finally he glanced away further along the shore, perhaps contemplating escape before Olga's shattered back could mend.

"What is the matter, Basileios?" Olga demanded, slowly crawling toward him. "You're not afraid of me, are you?"

Basileios looked at her and laughed, dismissing such a suggestion, but he withdrew a pace all the same.

"I grow tired of this," he said. "You have been a diversion, Valdemar, but I must attend to my business."

"You *are* afraid," said Olga, her tone mocking. Then suddenly it took on the tone of helplessness, an affectation that still could not fully conceal the fury hidden behind it. "But surely there is no cause for fear, Basileios. I am crippled! What has a whole man to fear from one who is crippled?"

At this, Basileios hesitated again, weighed Olga's words, and then withdrew another pace to keep his distance.

Olga tried again: "I am a barbarian, Basileios. What has a Greek to fear from a barbarian?"

Again the statement resonated with some prejudice in Basileios's mind, and again he hesitated before withdrawing, his face contorted with anger and uncertainty, ashamed to flee but unwilling to continue the fight.

Olga tried a third time, her tone reaching such a fevered pitch that she could no longer hide the rage and disgust in her tone:

"I am a woman, Basileios! What has a man to fear from a woman? Now face me!"

Basileios drew away again and stroked his beard with his fingertips.

"No, Valdemar, I think not," he said. "I am tired, and while killing you and the boy would please me, my loyal followers await me."

"You will never reach the valley, Basileios," Olga said, still crawling toward him. "I sensed your corruption from as far away as the Indus. And if I did, the others will as well. They might ignore you in the world, but if you approach the valley, we shall converge on you and tear you apart. And besides, old as you are, you cannot hope to take the castle on your own. Even without Sophio, the Living there would in time wear you down and break you."

"The way has been prepared for me!" Basileios shouted, still backing away. "They will welcome me with open arms as their true lord!"

Olga spat at him and said, "Come to me, Basileios. I will welcome you with open arms as well!"

Basileios laughed bitterly and continued his retreat.

"When we meet again, Valdemar, I will be whole and fed. And then you shall die by my hand."

Olga roared in frustration as Basileios continued to retreat, gaining greater and greater distance until it became clear that there was no chance of her catching him until her back had healed.

"You know you cannot beat me, Basileios!" she shouted after him. "Not in the days before and certainly not now! I will find you, and I will destroy you!"

But Basileios had hobbled away, and he paid her no mind, focused only on the thought of escape. Roaring again, Olga collapsed onto the ground and lay there in silence. Iosef pulled his robes around himself and slowly approached her as she rolled onto her side and sat up slightly.

"Ah, young Iosef," she said. "Come, sit by me. Sit with an old woman as she contemplates the birds."

"Yes, My Lady," Iosef replied hesitantly. He slowly sat beside her, trying to come to terms with what he had just seen and heard. Sophio was dead. Basileios was alive. Valdemar was a woman. The last point was of no great concern, but it stood contrary to what Iosef had assumed for two centuries, and this lesser confusion somehow compounded itself with the greater horror of loss and revelation.

Olga sighed and stared out at the sea, and silence descended upon them while they waited—Olga for healing, Iosef for instruction. Presently, Iosef spoke.

"You are Valdemar?" he asked.

"I was called by that name once, yes," Olga replied.

There was a long silence and then Iosef said, "I always thought that you were a man."

He expected Olga to take offense at this mistake, but instead she laughed.

"When I first came among the Slavs seeking fortune and glory, they thought me a man as well," Olga said. "They called me Vladimir, and the name pleased me."

"And when they learned that you were a woman?" Iosef asked.

Olga smiled. "Then they called me the 'She Wolf', and I liked that even better." She paused and her smile fell. "But not now, I think. Now I am simply Olga, a wanderer."

Iosef stared at the sea, his shoulders hunched over and his face downcast. In each cresting wave, he fancied that he saw Sophio's face looking back at him. The wind that blew hard against him carried whispers of her name.

"I cannot believe she is gone," he said.

Olga nodded and said, "I know."

"I wish to weep," Iosef confessed, "but I have forgotten how."

"That is...common among us," Olga assured him.

"It is torment."

"Tears may come in time," Olga said, "or in time you will learn to do without them. To weep is a luxury that the Living must eventually do without."

Iosef hugged himself, remembering the power and the softness of Sophio's touch, the scent of her hair, the delight in her eyes each time she saw him.

"How are we to go on without her?" he asked.

How am I to go on without her? he wondered silently, but did not say.

"Find the next eldest who may be trusted," Olga said, though she sighed in understanding of the quandary. "Make him or her Vicar of Shashava until Shashava's return."

"I sometimes wonder if Shashava ever will return," Iosef confessed. It felt strange saying such things to someone he barely knew, but at the same time, it was liberating. There was no preconception of judgment to hold back his words.

"Over that we have no power," Olga replied. "Merely faith and hope."

"My hope is stretched thin," Iosef said, frowning.

"Hope is not hope if it is not tested," Olga said. She sat up fully and flexed her feet as her legs began to respond to her again.

"What are we to do when Basileios reaches the valley?" Iosef asked. He could not imagine standing against him, and even the elders of the Order would be hard pressed to manage it. And if what Basileios said was true.... "Do you believe that he has spies? That his agents now control the House?"

Olga considered the questions for a little while, gazing into the sea as the wind blew through her hair. Presently she answered:

"I believe that he has spies. I do not believe that they are in control. The Shashavani are too strong to fall to such treachery."

"Sophio was lured out here to die," Iosef said, his voice quivering with the realization. "I brought her to her death."

"She brought herself here," Olga told him, her tone admonishing for the guilt she sensed in him. "And Basileios killed her. You were the cause of neither." She looked down at her hands as they slowly closed into fists. "But I cannot believe that he would murder her so willingly. She was a child when she came to us. She was *our* child, with five mothers and five fathers and Shashava. Her death was filicide just as surely as if Basileios had sired her himself."

"She joined the Order when she was a child?" Iosef asked, startled by the revelation. He had always assumed that Sophio had been a grown woman, as was customary.

"We waited until she had grown before giving her the cup," Olga explained, "but yes, she arrived as a little girl, alone and of her own accord. She had come following the stories of Shashava the miracle worker. I never knew who her people were or why she had left them." Olga sighed sadly. "And I suppose now I never shall."

"Nor shall I," said Iosef. "I do not know how I shall go on without her. Better perhaps to give myself to the sun, here in this place, that she and I might be together in eternity."

Olga turned and looked at him, her eyes alight with anger at his words. She grabbed Iosef's shoulder and held it hard enough to be painful.

"I know that you are yet young," she said, "but that talk is foolish, and I will not hear of it. Life is precious, and in a world that seeks to take it at every turn, you must not surrender it willingly. Sophio died to save you, and I daresay she would have done so again and again until the end of time were it in her power. Do not cast aside her sacrifice so eagerly. You must live, if only for her memory."

Iosef shuddered and looked away, but he nodded and said, "You are right. Basileios did not kill me. I will not do his work for him."

"Good," Olga said. She studied Iosef a few moments more to be sure of his sincerity and then released him. "Besides," she added, "you must return to the valley and warn them that Basileios lives. They must root out his spies and make ready in case he does attempt an attack."

"I...?" Iosef asked. "Surely...we...."

"I will not be going with you," Olga replied. She flexed her legs, and finding them whole and responsive again, she stood and stretched her newly mended back.

"Why not?" Iosef asked, also standing. "Surely you must return to us to bring order. If one of the Companions were to become Vicar—"

"It would be disaster," Olga replied. She looked at Iosef and saw the confusion in his eyes. Taking him by the arm, she led the way back to the tomb where she had left her staff. "Do you know why Konstantine, Mordechai, and I remained so long after Shashava and the other Companions had departed?"

"No, I do not," Iosef confessed.

"In our folly, we allowed Basileios to reign as vicar," Olga said, "but even had he been trustworthy at his post, it would have been a mistake to leave one Companion within the House while all the others departed. For surely you know, young Iosef, that each of us, each Companion to Shashava, favored certain principles and philosophies over all others. Medicine or war or theology. Our students and our students' students, and all those who have come after us, each descend from one such school of thought, every new member adding his or her own insights and research to an ever-expanding philosophy. All except Sophio, of course. She was her own, belonging to all of us and none of us save Shashava, and so she existed outside our traditions and our schools, as do you."

Reaching the tomb, Olga took her walking stick and leaned upon it, the signs of fatigue, starvation, and injury showing upon her face.

"If I were to return on my own," she said, "without any other of the Companions, it would signal to the Shashavani that my school of thought was greater and more worthy than the others, for I had returned when the others had not. And though I would try to rule wisely and impartially, my own prejudices would find a way to seep through. I would favor matters of governance and war, questions of politics, the nature of society, and other practical concerns. I would not mean to do it, but it would happen. And in so doing, it would signal to the others that those subjects were more worthy than matters of faith or thought or natural philosophy. At first it would be harmless, merely an inclination, but eventually it would become academic dogma. And dogma is death to the intellect.

"So you see, I cannot return home until I have either found the other Companions and convinced them to join me or until Shashava returns to guide us all."

Iosef exhaled and looked away. "I suppose I see the wisdom in that," he said, "though things would be easier were it not so."

"All things would be easier were the world not the world," Olga told him. "Besides, I must hunt Basileios for a time. He will sense me following him, and through that, I may force him to avoid the valley long enough for you to bring warning that he lives."

"And what am I to tell them?" Iosef asked.

Olga considered the question and replied, "Tell them the truth. Basileios is alive, he has spies among the House of Shashava who lured Sophio to this place, Sophio fought Basileios and was slain, and you were left to die in the sun. Only you did not die. You escaped and returned to bring them warning."

"And you?"

"No," Olga said. "No, you must not tell them about me. Let all the Companions remain a distant memory for now. Otherwise, they might select the next Vicar of Shashava with me in mind, whether favoring or disfavoring those of my tradition. Such an appointment must be unbiased or else it is no good."

"What if they think I was somehow complicit with Basileios?" Iosef asked. "When word came of the tomb's discovery, I was the one who suggested that we examine it. Sophio wished to but she hesitated."

He fell silent as another twinge of guilt struck him. It was his fault. If not for him, Sophio would never have come there....

"Basileios knew that the mystery of Arslan Khan would be enough to tempt Sophio to this place," Olga said. "You may have suggested it, but she wished it, and she decided to do it. If it had not been you, she would still have been induced by one of Basileios's agents. Basileios is no fool. He would not have waited here for so long unless he was confident that Sophio would eventually arrive."

"But if they think that I helped kill her..." Iosef began.

Olga laid a hand on his arm and said, "Foolish boy. I traveled with the two of you for only a few weeks, and it was plain enough for me to see the sincerity of your affections. No one who has lived alongside you for decades could possibly imagine that you would do her harm, and only a fool would think that you even could."

"That is true enough," Iosef said softly.

Olga touched his cheek and smiled sadly at him.

"I must go," she said. "Basileios flees, and I must run him to ground before he can make further mischief."

"Will you be able to...to manage him unaided?" Iosef asked hesitantly. He certainly did not want to offend Olga with the question, but he did not relish the thought of anyone facing Basileios the Accursed alone. The tales of Basileios's violence and malice had so elevated the very thought of him that Iosef instinctively assumed he would be the most dangerous of all the Companions: he the general and they merely scholars.

Valdemar laughed aloud at the question, but she did not seem insulted.

"Oh, do not fear for me, young one," she said. "Of us two, I was always the stronger fighter." She smiled slightly. "And the better king. I think he hated me for that. Though sometimes he seemed to harbor other sentiments as well." She shrugged, dismissing the question, and placed a hand on Iosef's shoulder. "Now then, my boy, return home with all speed, and do not let thoughts of destruction misguide you. Sophio lives on in you, and for that you must live as well."

And with that, Olga turned and began walking along the shore in the direction of the steppe, following the route that Basileios had taken. When she had gone, Iosef gazed at the sea for a time, still hearing Sophio in the whispers of the wind and the waves. Then, forcing his resolve, he cast one last look into the tomb that had become his beloved's final resting place and took his walking stick from the door. Despairing at the thought of leaving Sophio's remains exposed to wind and weather, Iosef set his shoulder against the boulder and, with much effort, rolled it back into place, sealing the tomb.

"Sleep, my love," he whispered to the wind. "Sleep, and may we be together again in our dreams."

Iosef set his back against the sun and began the long, forlorn walk home with the wind his only companion, softly whispering in his ear:

"Sophio, Sophio, Sophio."

CHAPTER THIRTY

Two months later
Svaneti, Georgia

The day found Varanus and Ekaterine out on the snow-covered plain beyond the river, riding through the frozen pasture on horseback. They both wore warm fur coats with high collars over their dresses, though only Ekaterine had reason to fear the cold. Varanus was covered similarly to her friend to ward off the sun, and her fur hat was wide-brimmed and supplemented with dark glasses and a veil.

In the time that followed the retaking of the castle, Varanus often found it necessary to escape out-of-doors, to be away from the stifling confines of a place that had witnessed so much bloodshed and such betrayal. It was all but impossible to go a day without passing at least one person who had sworn allegiance to Margaret, and while Varanus supposed it was just as well that so many had been pardoned, the sight of them made her think of Vaclav's death, and that made her hate them.

They had outnumbered Margaret's followers, and yet they had accepted her rule out of fear. It had simply been easier for them to go along with it all, and Varanus had no patience for such a thing. So, whenever she could no longer bear the voices whispering in her thoughts that this person or that person was secretly plotting against them, she took Ekaterine for a ride to calm her nerves. And in truth, it was getting to be almost a daily habit.

They went armed, of course, with sword, pistol, and rifle. "To hunt rabbits", Varanus always claimed, but really it was to be ready for when the next great betrayal came. Indeed, she simply could not shake the feeling that there was still treachery afoot in the House of Shashava, and she did not intend to be caught unprepared.

Upon a small hill overlooking the river, Varanus turned and saw a group of villagers watching them. After a moment's panic at the thought that they might be servants of Margaret fomenting revolution, Varanus calmed herself and realized that they were simply travelers on their way into town: likely farmers going to buy some needed goods to finish out the winter or perhaps to sell an overabundant surplus now that the worst of the season had passed.

"Do you think they will ever trust us again?" Varanus asked Ekaterine.

Ekaterine looked toward the villagers and waved. The villagers, perhaps not expecting this response, turned away quickly and continued on their way. Ekaterine's face fell a little.

"I suppose they have little reason to," she said. "I don't know how many of the servants Margaret bled and feasted upon, but the number is not insubstantial. That is clear enough from the empty kitchens and servant's hall. Not one of them remembers the dark times under Basileios, when such slaughter was commonplace, but surely stories have been passed down to them."

"I fear they believe we are the same," Varanus said. "That we have become monsters in their eyes."

"To some, perhaps," Ekaterine agreed. "But most will understand what was done, and they will know that those who now rule fought to protect them against the tyrant. And that is something."

"Mmm," Varanus answered, not entirely convinced.

"Besides," Ekaterine said, "of course they will trust us again in time. We are their sole protection, the guardians of their way of life. They have no choice."

Varanus nodded, agreeing with Ekaterine's assessment, though at the same time it saddened her to contemplate it. Trust was not trust when it came born of necessity.

"Do you think it was right," Varanus asked, "to pardon so many?"

Almost all the scholars who had sworn allegiance to Margaret had been pardoned and so had far too many of the surviving soldiers. Varanus would have hanged them all for what they did, but there were few enough Shashavani as it was. Perhaps the Council balked at the thought of losing any more of their brethren.

"I think it was necessary," Ekaterine replied. "Fratricide is such a horrid thing. It is the sort of thing done by Basilisks, not by Shashavani."

"I suppose so," Varanus said, not quite agreeing. There was a pause, and then she asked, "How is Luka, by the way? Still cross with me?"

"Indeed he is, and you know why," Ekaterine answered, though she sounded amused at it.

Luka had not taken well to the news that Varanus had entered his rooms and pillaged his private armory, and he still refused to speak to her until she apologized for it—which, of course, Varanus had no intention of doing.

"Still," Ekaterine added, "he is rather proud of what you accomplished during the siege. I heard him just the other day bragging to some of the soldiers that he was the one who trained you."

"Hmph," Varanus replied, but she smiled all the same. It was true: Luka had been the one who had trained her in the arts of war when she had first been inducted into the House of Shashava, and she now understood the reason for it. She had allowed her lessons to slip a bit in recent years; she would not make that mistake again.

She flexed her hand, feeling a little stiffness lingering in her fingers and wrist. It had regrown, of course, though it had taken a few days. But while it was effectively the same hand she had lost, it still felt odd. Perhaps she would get used to it in time: it was only the first time she had lost a limb.

"How is the hand?" Ekaterine asked.

"Well enough," Varanus replied. "A little stiff, but I suppose that is to be expected."

"Well, you have only been using it for a couple of months," Ekaterine said, her tone joking. "The last one you'd used for fifty years. One doesn't become accustomed to a new pair of shoes overnight."

"This is my hand," Varanus protested, "not a pair of shoes!"

"Would a glove analogy be more appropriate?"

Varanus chuckled softly and shook her head at Ekaterine. Then she frowned and gazed off toward the mountains.

"I almost died that night, didn't I?" she mused aloud.

Ekaterine's expression fell at the question, and she said, "Yes, very nearly. When I found you...." She looked away, troubled by the thought.

"Starvation is a cruel mistress," Varanus said. "In fact, I am amazed that I survived at all. I don't remember being given any blood until I awoke a few days later. And lacking fresh blood, I should not have survived."

Ekaterine shifted in the saddle, suddenly uncomfortable. Varanus looked at her, an idea beginning to form in her mind.

"You know," Varanus added softly, "if I were to guess, I would say that someone gave me blood around the time I collapsed. It seems the only way I could have recovered."

"Yes, but who could possibly have given you blood?" Ekaterine asked cautiously. "I was the first person to find you, and I never left your side until you woke. It's simply...impossible."

Varanus smiled and took her friend's hand.

"If...hypothetically...someone had given me her blood when she found me, she would surely have saved my life, and I am...*would be* eternally grateful to her."

Ekaterine returned the smile and said, "I am certain that such a person would be relieved beyond describing simply because you are alive." Then she quickly added, "But it's simply not possible. I found you, and you were always among Shashavani. And Shashavani do not drink the blood of Shashavani. It is forbidden."

"Of course," Varanus agreed. "Such a silly thought. Still, only the blood of the Living is poisonous. One still in the Shadow *could have* given me blood, and that *could have* been the thing that saved my life. And I would be so thankful for it, beyond measure. But, as you say, Shashavani do not drink of other Shashavani, so of course it didn't happen."

"It certainly did not," Ekaterine agreed, giving Varanus's hand a squeeze.

A flicker of movement at the edge of Varanus's vision distracted her, and she looked toward it. She saw a dark shape approaching them from across the snow-filled valley. It was a figure dressed in worn and dirty robes, hunched over from pain or exhaustion and leaning on a staff as it came. For a moment Varanus thought it might be Iosef and Sophio, but there was only the one figure. Then she realized what that meant, and she kicked her horse into a run and rode to meet the wanderer, desperately praying that it was not Sophio bringing news of Iosef's misfortune.

Reaching the figure, Varanus swung down from her horse and rushed forward to look beneath the cowl.

Let it not be Sophio, she pleaded silently. *Let it not be Sophio.*

And indeed it was not. At the sight of Varanus, the figure fell to its knees, unable to go on. Beneath the cowl, Varanus saw the face of death, withered and desiccated. It was man, but he was barely recognizable as such. He was gaunt, and the skin was pulled tight around his bones. His eyes were hollow. But for all that, Varanus recognized him almost immediately, and her heart clenched at the sight.

It was Iosef, so worn from starvation, cold, and the road that he was all but a walking corpse.

"My Lord?" Varanus asked, holding him by his shoulders to keep him from falling. "My Lord, what has happened to you?"

Iosef opened his mouth and through parched lips whispered:

"Basileios lives."

* * * *

Some hours later, Iosef lay half conscious in a warm bath, devouring a plate full of roast meat in those scattered moments when he found himself awake enough to do it. He had also been given a chalice of fresh blood, but he had consumed that immediately. It was probably the only reason he was conscious at all. And now with fresh water, blood, and meat in him, Iosef began to feel more like himself, more alive. At least, he felt alive in body. His soul was another matter.

He had been left to rest and recover in his own rooms, which had likely been intended as a mercy, but in fact it was not. Everything he saw there, from the walls, to the curtains, to the painted ceiling reminded him of Sophio.

Presently, he heard the door to the main chamber open. It was unusual to have someone intrude upon the private rooms of the Eristavi, but he suspected that having arrived alone and incoherent, he was now more or less in custody until the Council could sort out what had transpired during the sojourn. He was effectively a prisoner, though of course no one would speak of it as such.

Iosef sat up as Philippa of Nicaea entered the room, her hands folded in front of her. He bowed his head to her and began to rise, looking about for a cloth to dry himself.

"My Lady," he began, about to beg pardon for the state of his arrival.

"Please, remain as you are Brother Iosef," Philippa said, raising a hand to stop him. She took a chair from by the wall and placed it at the foot of the bath where she sat and smiled at him. "I hope that you feel recovered from your ordeal."

Iosef sank back into the water and nodded. "Indeed. Or rather, as recovered as I may be in such a state."

"Perhaps you were too young to walk such a hard road," Philippa said, "but you returned to us all the same." She paused. "However...."

"Sophio did not return with me," Iosef finished. It was the inevitable question. There was no point in avoiding it.

"Can you tell me why?" Philippa asked.

"Because she is dead," Iosef replied, his tone flat and emotionless. It was the only way he could say the words.

Philippa nodded. Clearly this answer did not surprise her, though it did seem to trouble her. Iosef was suddenly put in mind of Basileios's words regarding hidden spies. Then again, Philippa's distress at the news seemed real enough, if subdued by her great age. And, Iosef recalled, she had spoken against Sophio venturing out, while others had encouraged it.

How easy the temptation of paranoia, Iosef thought.

"How did she come to die, Iosef?" Philippa asked softly.

"She was lured there to be ambushed and killed," Iosef said. He sat up again and reached for Philippa's arm. "Sister Philippa, you must arrest Brother Teimuraz at once!"

"Brother Teimuraz?" Philippa raised an eyebrow.

"There was a Basilisk lurking there, at the tomb of Arslan Khan," Iosef explained. "He claimed to have sent agents here to draw Sophio out and bring her to him. Teimuraz was the one who brought word of the tomb. He must be one of the ones in league with our enemy!"

"Who was the Basilisk, Iosef?" Philippa asked.

Iosef hesitated. He knew that the true answer would be met with astonishment and disbelief. It would sound more fanciful than a lie, and it might further turn suspicion against him. But then again, it was his duty to warn them.

"It was Basileios," he said. "The Basileios. I do not know how he survived, but I swear to you it was he. Sophio recognized him before...."

He fell silent again and looked away.

"Well..." Philippa mused. "Ordinarily, I doubt I would believe you. But we have ourselves suffered certain peculiarities."

"Peculiarities?" Iosef asked.

"A conspiracy of Basilisks lurking in our midst attempted to usurp the throne in Sophio's absence," Philippa said. "They demanded mass conversions, rejection of Shashava's laws, and allegiance to a 'Winter King'. Teimuraz was one of them." She paused a moment. "They were led by Margaret of the Hebrides, who you may recall—"

"Encouraged Sophio to go," Iosef said.

Philippa nodded. She folded her hands in her lap and said, "Recount to me your travels, Brother Iosef. Tell me what happened. Tell me how you come to be alive."

Iosef relayed the story as clearly as he could remember, passing rapidly over matters of no importance without omitting them. He hesitated a moment when he came to Olga, trying to judge whether he should break her confidence or lie to Philippa. It was only a moment of hesitation, but it was a moment too long. As he resumed his tale without mention of Olga, he saw a glint of suspicion in Philippa's eyes. But Philippa said nothing, and Iosef continued on as if nothing had happened.

"When we opened the tomb and ventured in," Iosef concluded, "Basileios was there waiting for us. He followed us inside, and Sophio confronted him. I was...injured—" He touched his chest where the spear had penetrated him, the memory returning to him clearly despite the absence of a wound. "—and in the end Basileios overpowered Sophio and burned her to ashes."

"He burned her?" Philippa asked.

"He..." Iosef stammered. He could think of no way to explain it that did not sound far-fetched. "He burned her with fire from his hands. I do know how to describe it other than that. His hands took flame, and when he touched her with them, she burned as well. I realize that it sounds impossible, but—"

Philippa closed her eyes in thought and held up a hand.

"No," she said softly, "I have heard of this. It is said that Jelena of Raska knew this technique. I have not seen it myself, but I accept that it may be true." Then Philippa looked intently at Iosef and asked, "And what of you, Iosef? How did you survive?"

And there it was, Iosef thought. The fundamental danger in his position, for truly there was no way the he could have lived without the intervention of one far older than he was. But to mention a rescuer would prove all the more problematic.

"As I said, My Lady, I was gravely injured. Seeing that I was no threat to him, Basileios left me to be taken by the sun."

"No, he did not," Philippa said.

"My Lady?" Iosef asked, for a brief instant entertaining thoughts of fear.

"Basileios did not leave you to die," Philippa said matter-of-factly. "You are Sophio's only student, the continuation of her intellectual lineage. Basileios would want to obliterate you along with her, as punishment for her beheading him and overthrowing his tyrant kingdom. He would not have left your death to chance."

Iosef took a breath and exhaled. He did not know what to say.

"However," Philippa continued, "I am confident that you are not in league with him. You would certainly not conspire to murder Sophio. I have seen how you look...looked at her when you thought you were not observed. I may have forgotten what it is to feel such devotion, but I have not forgotten how it looks in others."

"Indeed, My Lady," Iosef said.

"The only explanation I can fathom is that you were saved by the intervention of another," Philippa said. "Someone very old indeed. And that being the case, I wish to know who it was."

"She swore me not to divulge her name," Iosef replied.

"Oh..." Philippa sighed. "What a pity." Then she fixed Iosef with a hard look. "It seems that you will have to break a sworn oath. But under the circumstances, I am certain that both she and God will forgive you. Give me the name."

Iosef hesitated again and looked away.

"Valdemar the Rus," he said. "I do not expect you to believe it, but it was so."

Philippa thought about it for a few moments and replied, "I do not *disbelieve* it. All of the Companions sojourn. We might meet them upon the road and never know it. Though again, it may have been a student of Valdemar assuming the name. There are many in the world *nearly* as powerful as the Companions. But let us return to that later. Whoever your liberator was, why did he not return with you?"

"Because it was Valdemar," Iosef replied, "and she said that she had no wish to rejoin the House of Shashava without the other Companions, lest it sway the Order to reject other schools of thought in favor of her philosophies."

"I suppose that is...plausible," Philippa said, a little reluctantly.

Iosef leaned forward and added in Greek to emphasize the pronoun, "*She* said it. *She.*"

Philippa frowned for a moment and slowly closed her eyes as if trying to summon up a long forgotten memory. Presently, she opened them again and said, a little surprised, "I think I almost remember that.... She...." Then Philippa shook her head. "Ah, but it is gone. Still, that point is immaterial. Man or woman is irrelevant. What matters is that Basileios walks the world and that he sent his agents to work evil among us. Vigilance will be necessary. The Council knows that."

She meant that they would be suspicious of him.

"I understand," Iosef said.

"Good," Philippa replied. She stood and smiled. "Rest yourself, Brother Iosef. I need you well when I bring you before the Council next week."

"Before the Council?" Iosef asked. "Am I to be examined?"

"In a way," Philippa said. "In a way."

* * * *

Iosef's return had taken Varanus by surprise, and much as it relieved her to find him still alive, the state of his arrival equally alarmed her. She had never before seen Iosef so fragile. Her mentor's strength had always been a source of reassurance to her. Seeing him in a state of walking death was terrifying. Varanus always worried about Iosef's well-being, but for the first time she actually contemplated the possibility of him dying, and it was not a prospect she liked.

Once she heard that Iosef was on his feet again, Varanus went to see him immediately, bringing Ekaterine with her for good measure. There might still be spies about waiting for a moment of weakness to strike, and Varanus was not about to lose either her friend or her mentor to an assassin's blade. Ekaterine told her that she was being silly, that the conspiracy had been rooted out and there was no longer any need to fear, but Varanus could not bring herself to share Ekaterine's optimism.

There were soldiers on guard outside Iosef's door, which surprised Varanus. As a reflex, she placed her hand behind her back and reached for the pistol she had hidden beneath her coat. But she had no reason to believe the soldiers hostile, and she did not draw.

"You are becoming paranoid, *liebchen*," Korbinian said to her, leaning against the door between the two soldiers. "Surely, these men are friends. Only the most loyal would have been allowed to guard your Russian, whether it is done for his protection or his confinement."

That was true. Varanus released the weapon and stood as tall as she could before addressing the soldiers:

"Open the door, please. I would like to see Lord Iosef."

"My apologies, Sister Varanus," said one of the soldiers, "but I fear we cannot do that."

"*Cannot?*" Varanus asked, bristling at not being called by her proper title, though she reminded herself it was likely oversight rather than insult. "I find it unlikely that you cannot open a door."

"The Council has ordered that Lord Iosef see no visitors except on official business," said the second soldier. "I am sorry, Sister, but you are not authorized."

Ekaterine put her fists on her hips and said, "Well that is simply nonsense!"

"I wish to see my mentor," Varanus told the soldiers. "I am worried about his well-being and his safety."

"You are not authorized," the soldier repeated. "The Council—"

"The curious thing about the Council," Varanus interrupted, "is that we have just come from having tea with two of its members, Joan of Brittany and Djata of Mali. You may have heard of them."

The soldiers shifted position uncomfortably and glanced at one another, uncertain how to respond.

"They were really quite pleasant," Ekaterine added cheerfully. "And you told such wonderful war stories. I especially enjoyed the one about the grenade!"

"Yes, thank you, Ekaterine," Varanus said. She looked back at the soldiers. "In fact, gentlemen, half of the Council is now composed of people with whom I served during the recent unpleasantness. They were elevated precisely because their loyalty is beyond question, and I would think that mine is as well."

"It is not *your* loyalty that is in question, Sister—"

"You doubt Lord Iosef?" Varanus demanded. "What nonsense! Open the door at once!"

"Sister, you are not authorized—"

Varanus huffed angrily and said, "Very well, if you will not grant me entry, I will go speak to Lord Reza about the matter. I helped save his life, you know. I am certain he will grant me your 'authorization', but I suspect he will be angry at having to be bothered about it!"

The soldiers exchanged looks again, and one of them held up a hand as Varanus turned to go.

"Wait," he said. There was a pause, and then he opened the door. "Five minutes."

Varanus went to the doorway and looked at him with one eyebrow raised.

"Five minutes?" she asked. "No, I think not. I will speak to my mentor for as long as I deem necessary." She turned to Ekaterine. "Keep these gentlemen company, will you? I would prefer to remain undisturbed."

"Of course!" Ekaterine replied. As Varanus went into the room, she heard Ekaterine clap her hands with delight and say to the soldiers, "Now then, let me tell you all about *scones!*"

Varanus suspected she would get into trouble for doing this, but she did not have the patience to ask for permission. If she was summoned to account for her actions, she would simply explain the concern she felt for her mentor's well-being and ask her friends on the Council to intervene. She knew that Djata, Joan, and Zabel at least would speak in her defense, and she hoped that Reza would take her side as well.

The main room in Iosef's chambers was dark, lit only by a few candles and by the feeble moonlight from outside. It did not take her eyes long to adjust, however, and she saw Iosef seated midway into the room, reading a book by firelight. At the sound of her approach, he put the book down and stood.

"Good evening, Varanus," he said, turning to face her.

"Good evening, My Lord," Varanus replied.

She took a moment to study Iosef's face. She saw that he had recovered from his ordeal, at least physically. His body was whole and healthy again. The flesh no longer clung tightly to the bones of his narrow face, nor was his skin like tanned leather any longer. He was, mercifully, the same man who had left them four months ago. But in his eyes there lurked deep sorrow and anguish. It was a sentiment Varanus recognized and which she herself had felt in the time following Korbinian's murder.

"How are you?" she asked him.

"That is a question I have become accustomed to hearing," Iosef replied. He smiled slightly, but there was no humor in it.

"Truly," Varanus insisted. She had no interest in pleasantries and reassurances.

"I am...." Iosef paused and took a breath. "I am in pain. A part of me is gone, and I will never have it back. I feel empty, Varanus, like a hollow man."

Varanus took Iosef's hand and said softly, "I know. She made you complete. Now you have been broken in two, and you do not know whether you wish to be mended or simply to crumble into dust."

"Yes," Iosef said, after a short pause. "Yes, I would say that is correct. You know such loss yourself."

"Surely my loss cannot compare to what you are suffering, Sophio being torn from you after two hundred years," Varanus replied, "but yes, I know a portion of it."

"I will persevere," Iosef said, looking away. "It is not right that I should trouble you with it."

"It is no trouble," Varanus insisted. "I should like to ease your pain, if I may. No one should ever experience such a thing."

Iosef smiled, though with difficulty. "It is not fitting that a mentor should lean upon his student for support. Reassurance is the mentor's duty."

"Duty be damned," said Varanus, giving Iosef a genuine smile of her own. "It is a poor student who disregards the good of her teacher."

Iosef's smile became a little more certain, and he said, "You are the best of students, Varanus, and I am thankful for it."

"One does one's best, My Lord," Varanus answered.

Iosef glanced toward the windows and the dark sky, and his face fell again, no doubt with more thoughts of Sophio. Varanus would need to pull him away from such melancholy, and what better restorative than work? And besides, she had no wish to leave him alone if it could be helped. She did not fear that he would do anything foolish, but she still did not trust that all of Margaret's followers had been dealt with. She would not see Iosef returned to them alive, only to have him killed in the House of Shashava!

"My Lord," she said, touching his arm, "if you will indulge me."

"Of course," Iosef answered, looking back at her.

"I have some questions of a philosophical nature that I would like your advice on." She motioned to a chair. "It may take some time. May we sit?"

"Of course, Varanus," Iosef said, sounding relieved.

"I do have many questions," Varanus emphasized. "Perhaps Ekaterine and I should move into your rooms for a few days. And to keep you company."

"No, Varanus," Iosef answered, "I do not think that will be necessary. But...the sentiment is appreciated."

"Of course, My Lord," Varanus said. "Of course."

* * * *

Iosef went to the Council chamber the following week, as Philippa instructed. He had been questioned by her three more times and by certain other elders as well. He did not know if they were satisfied with his answers, but none of them were pleased by his news. When he arrived before the Council, the very air in the room felt grave.

He saw several councilors missing. The traitors who followed Margaret were gone, of course, and also Marie of Toulouse, who, he was told, had been murdered by them. In their place were new faces, elders he recognized to varying degrees: Joan of Brittany, Djata of Mali, Zabel of Ani, Nikoloz of Guria, and Hildegard of Bremen. All of the Council members looked at him curiously when he entered, but they said nothing.

The Council was just concluding some matters of administration, principally a question of supplies being addressed by Sister Hildegard, who as an abbess during her mortality had transformed her convent into one of the wealthiest religious institutions in northern Europe.

"So if we continue with the present system of rationing for the remainder of the month," Hildegard said, "we will not only enjoy sufficient stores to last until spring, but we will be able to repay the villages in kind for the sacrifices they made on our behalf during the recent misfortune."

"A sensible enough suggestion," said Reza of Samarkand. "All those in favor?"

There was general agreement from the Council, and Reza nodded to Hildegard.

"Now," he said, "for our next matter, I require your indulgence, Sister Philippa."

"Oh?" Philippa asked, sounding surprised. "What have I done now?"

"Our peers and I have spoken a great deal about a matter of importance these past few days," Reza said.

"Without consulting me," Philippa noted.

"For a reason that shall become clear to you," Reza assured her. "As we have been informed by Brother Iosef, our Eristavi will not be returning to us. She has fallen at the hands of an enemy working in league with the same traitors who attempted to usurp Shashava's throne and who drove our house into bloodshed and disorder. And while I am skeptical as to the alleged identity of Sophio's killer, I do believe Iosef's claim that she is dead."

Iosef bristled at the way Reza spoke the words "alleged identity". No doubt most of the Council questioned the validity of his words. It was only to be expected, but following the anguish of Sophio's death, such disbelief made him angry.

"The time has come to appoint a new Vicar of Shashava to reign over us and guide us until Shashava or the Companions return," Reza continued. "I have spoken to the rest of the Council, and we are unanimous."

"I see...." Philippa said cautiously, perhaps anticipating another coup like the one that had just been put down. Though could it be a coup if the majority of those governing accepted it?

"You are now the eldest among us," Reza said, "younger only than certain scholars who have already refused political authority. And moreover, you showed great foresight in anticipating the danger of unrest in Sophio's absence when the rest of us did not. You guided the loyalists who took shelter in the countryside, and you worked well with the Strategos to safeguard our people and made possible the retaking of the castle. And above all, you led the Council in exile when it would have been easier to fall to despair. In all, very admirable work. Precisely the work of the Vicar of Shashava."

Philippa looked surprised. "Do you mean to say...?"

"Sister Philippa, we are agreed that we wish you to assume the mantle of Vicar and to take the chair in Sophio's place. It is a hard task and a great responsibility, but we are agreed that you are capable of it."

Philippa was silent for a time, blinking on occasion as she pondered the offer. The other Council members waited patiently. At such an age, they were used to long periods of contemplation on such matters, when others of greater youth might have become restless by the lack of response.

Presently, Philippa bowed her head, stood, and said, "Brothers and Sisters, I fear that I must humbly refuse."

Reza began to speak but suddenly found that he had no words to use.

"What?" asked Joan the Breton. "Sister Philippa, this is a great honor! And you are the most capable for the task. Why should you refuse it?"

"Brothers and Sisters," Philippa said, "I have come to realize that the burden of rulership is simply too great a weight for any of us to bear alone. Let us not forget that Sophio, the oldest and wisest among us, who knew Shashava and the Companions centuries before we were born, was brought low by it. *Even she.* It was simply too much for any one person to withstand. And she was elder to all of us. If she could not manage it, I know that I cannot."

"Then what would you have us do?" asked Rusudan of Tbilisi. "Exchange the post every few decades like some trinket?"

"No," Philippa replied. "No, I say we abolish the post altogether."

"What?" asked Djata of Mali. "You suggest anarchy, Sister?"

"Nothing of the sort," Philippa said, holding up her hands for patience. "There must be a government for the House of Shashava, and that government must be just and ruled by wisdom. But save for the chaos of

Margaret's insurrection, this council both maintained order and properly administrated the needs of the House for months without the presence of a Vicar. Let us make the Council the supreme authority over the Shashavani Order until such time as Shashava or the Companions return."

"There *was* a council to govern after The Three departed," Reza said. "It fell to infighting and violence."

"It fell to infighting because the members all sought to be Vicar of Shashava," Philippa replied. "If we are all agreed that only a council will have the authority to rule the Shashavani, then any who seek to become a tyrant will be unable to claim the Vicarship to legitimize their rule. It is the best we can hope for in the absence of one of the truly old."

"And if there is a deadlock?" Joan asked. "There are ten of us. If we are divided evenly, what then?"

"I would trust that on matters of great importance, we would be capable of finding compromise," said Xasan of Mogadishu, "but it remains a valid question. Who is to cast a deciding vote?"

"Regarding that...." Philippa extended a hand toward Iosef and beckoned him forward. "As you know, despite his youth Iosef has served the Council well over the past century. He has kept us informed of developments in the outer world, and he has carried out such tasks in it as we have required of him."

"Because he was the Eristavi's student," Reza reminded her.

"Yes," Philippa said, "and so he remains. Iosef is young, but he is wise and loyal, and he is the only student taken by Sophio in her thousand years. He has proven that he is of value to the House of Shashava. I suggest that we make him our secretary to keep us apprised of matters both in the House and in the outer world. And if there proves to be an issue that we cannot resolve through compromise, let him cast an eleventh vote for it."

"Iosef has just returned from the wilderness where Sophio died!" exclaimed Xasan. "I do not say that he is in league with the enemy—"

"Though it could be so," added Zabel.

"Though it could be so," Xasan agreed. "But even if he is not tainted by contact with the one that killed our Prince, how are we to say that he is even capable of such a burden so soon after the death of his wife?"

They spoke as if Iosef was not there to hear them, which was not surprising. The very old often spoke of the young in such a way. It was not quite being dismissive and not quite forgetting.

"You would offer me the throne of Shashava," Philippa said with a laugh, "but you do not trust my judgment in this?"

"Let us ask Brother Iosef whether he even wishes such a post," said Nikoloz of Guria. He looked at Iosef. "Well? Do you feel yourself capable of this responsibility so soon after your lady's death?"

Iosef was silent for a moment and forced himself not to look away at the mention of Sophio.

"If the Council has such faith in me, I will do it," he said.

Let such service be a lasting penance for having brought Sophio to that place and for failing to protect her there. It was a foolish thought, but it would not leave him.

"Good, that is settled," said Reza. "The question then remains, do we trust him with the task? I think in this matter we must be in complete agreement before any such position is granted."

"Oh, I have no doubt that we shall reach consensus," Philippa replied. "Though I fear it may take us all night."

* * * *

In the end, it did. Daybreak had almost arrived when the Council had finally heard all points of view, addressed all concerns, and queried Iosef on more matters than he could clearly remember—most of them unrelated to anything at all, save in the mind of the questioner.

He returned to his rooms in silence. His new appointment was prestigious and very honorable, but he could not delight in it. Indeed, he could not delight in anything after what had happened.

He walked onto the balcony and stood there, watching the sky as it slowly lit with the fire of dawn. He would have to escape into the darkness eventually, but he had time before the sun arrived. The oblivion it offered was a temptation, but Olga had been right: he was all that remained of Sophio now. He had to continue no matter how heavy the burden.

The cold winter wind blew past him, stinging cheeks that could no longer feel it and whispering Sophio's name in his ear. The wind had always done that, every day since Sophio's death.

Perhaps it was madness.

Iosef reached into his pocket and felt the metal disk that he had taken from the tomb. He pulled the amulet out and looked at it, feeling the ache of sorrow. It was, in its own way, the last bit of Sophio left. They had found it together. Now, it was all that remained of her: a metal trinket of uncertain origin, taken from the place that had become her tomb.

Slowly, Iosef sank to his knees and bowed his head. For the first time in two months, he felt his will to release his anguish overpower his body's disinterest in such a mortal habit.

Iosef placed his head in his hands and, for the first time since Sophio's death, he wept.

www.ingramcontent.com/pod-product-compliance
Lightning Source LLC
Chambersburg PA
CBHW020229260626
47156CB00002B/599